DON'T
FORGET
THE
GIRL

PRAISE FOR *DON'T FORGET THE GIRL*

"Rebecca McKanna has made a thorough study of the true crime zeitgeist: she knows our hunger for gory details, our ghoulish speculation; she knows all the tropes of podcasts and Netflix shows. In her smart, layered debut, she takes all this and asks us: But what of the bereaved? What do they hold to when the world makes a spectacle of their loss, turning the flawed, complex, funny person they loved into a scary show to binge? The result is a page-turner that's also a fresh story of forgiveness, memory, and hope. McKanna shows us past the sensationalization of the brutal and untimely death of a pretty girl to something deeper: a love story between three friends."

—Kelsey Ronan, author of *Chevy in the Hole*, a *New York Times Book Review* Editors' Choice

"Rebecca McKanna masterfully draws us into the story of two women seeking answers years after their friend's death, before time runs out on the serial killer suspected of her murder. Beyond the mystery, *Don't Forget the Girl* is an exploration of grief, asking what we become in the wake of tragedy, what we need from those who leave, and how we move on. Be ready to be wowed by McKanna's deft hand, which holds a mirror up to a society that glamorizes the killer but too often forgets about the girl who was lost and the people who loved her. Fans of Gillian Flynn and Laura Lippman will love this haunting and heartbreaking literary thriller."

—Natalie Lund, author of *We Speak in Storms*

"McKanna punctuates the 'girl' thriller phenomenon and punctures our societal fascination with true crime with a page-turner that gives voice to the victim. A talented new voice in crime fiction."

—Lori Rader-Day, award-winning author of *The Lucky One*

"*Don't Forget the Girl* is a moving and suspenseful exploration of friendship, identity, and the reverberations of violence. An unforgettable debut."

—Beth Nguyen, author of *Owner of a Lonely Heart*

"*Don't Forget the Girl* has everything you'd want in a genuine literary thriller: clear and beautiful writing, complicated and nuanced characters, clever and unexpected turns in form and plot, and a ripped-from-the-headlines story at the core that makes you slow down and race ahead all at once, forward to a murderer's execution and backward to his unthinkable acts and their devastating shock waves. Rebecca McKanna has written a vivid, propulsive, sensational debut that's both an indictment of our violent and toxic culture and a celebration of women and survivors and the essential role of collective memory in bringing about change."

—Porter Shreve, author of *The End of the Book* and *The Obituary Writer*

"This is the kind of book I crave. It's an insightful, courageous exploration of friendship, sexuality, reputation, and self-deceit... AND it's a mystery novel I could not put down. Rebecca McKanna has written a nearly perfect subversion of the true crime genre. By exploring storytelling in all its shapeshifting forms—from private secrets to public 'official' narratives—she subverts the limitations of the dead girl trope, bringing to life a textured, complex story of three women finding their way through the constraints imposed by family and society and self. There are so many jaw-dropping twists and awe-inspiring scenes of beauty and grief. I cannot wait to press *Don't Forget the Girl* into the hands of all my friends."

—Kate Reed Petty, author of *True Story*

DON'T FORGET THE GIRL

A Novel

REBECCA McKANNA

sourcebooks
landmark

Published by Sourcebooks Landmark, an imprint of Sourcebooks
P.O. Box 4410, Naperville, Illinois 60567-4410
(630) 961-3900
sourcebooks.com

Library of Congress Cataloging-in-Publication Data

Names: McKanna, Rebecca, author.
Title: Don't forget the girl : a novel / Rebecca McKanna.
Description: Naperville, Illinois : Sourcebooks Landmark, [2023]
Identifiers: LCCN 2022050980 (print) | LCCN 2022050981
 (ebook) | (trade paperback) | (epub)
Subjects: LCGFT: Thrillers (Fiction). | Novels.
Classification: LCC PS3613.C5434 D66 2023 (print) | LCC PS3613.C5434
 (ebook) | DDC 813/.6--dc23/eng/20221122
LC record available at https://lccn.loc.gov/2022050980
LC ebook record available at https://lccn.loc.gov/2022050981

Printed and bound in Canada.
MBP 10 9 8 7 6 5 4 3 2 1

For the friends who were more than friends,
I know what it meant to me.

*Some girls have their entire lives
ahead of them.*

—Lynn Melnick, "Obviously, Foul Play"

BREE
OCTOBER 2015

In twenty-five days, he'll be dead.

The number beats a steady rhythm in Bree's mind as she leaves her office in the fine arts building and walks outside onto the campus lawn. *Twenty-five days. Twenty-five days.*

The students at the tiny college where she teaches take advantage of the unseasonably warm October afternoon, and she stares without really seeing them. Guys in track T-shirts toss a Frisbee to one another while a trio of girls in bikini tops lie on brightly colored beach towels, enjoying the sun.

Twenty-five days.

Do they have any hope he'll tell investigators anything helpful before then? She wants to get home so she can read more news articles.

It takes her a second to realize one of the boys playing Frisbee is staring at her. It's her student Zach, watching her with the intent expression he wears in her classroom after she asks a question about the use of light in a photograph or the balance between foreground and background. She makes a quick, almost involuntary gesture with her right hand like she's shooing away a fly.

Don't, she wills him. *Someone will notice.*

His gaze moves from her to the Frisbee cutting through the blue sky above him. Bree glances back at her phone's screen as she walks. It still shows the Associated Press article. She closes the tab so she doesn't have to look at the photo of Jon Allan Blue. It's one of the media's favorite pictures: him on the stand at his trial—eyes crinkling at the corners, long-fingered hands gesturing languidly like when she knew him.

The letters from him sit in her desk drawer. He must have found her campus address online. Three letters in two years. White envelopes addressed in neat Palmer script. In the bottom right corner, someone stamped in red: *Mailed from a state correctional institution.*

The familiar thoughts bubble up: *If I had just listened. If I had just paid more attention—No*, she tells herself. *Don't go there.*

One of the girls tanning waves at Bree. It's another of her students—Alayna—wearing a black bikini top and cutoffs. Her bleached-blond hair sits in a knot on top of her head, appearing almost white in the bright sun, as she sits up on her cherry-colored towel.

This is the trouble with such a small school. Bree can never move around anonymously.

"Hi, Hadley," Alayna calls, still waving.

They've taken to calling Bree this, her students. By her last name—like she's some beloved coach they'll follow unquestioningly.

Bree waves back but still feels dazed as she nears the faculty parking lot. *Twenty-five days.* This is what she waited for all these years—him to pay for what he did. And yet, with the date finally set, it doesn't feel anything like she thought it would.

Partly, it's that he's everywhere now. When she put the Republican Primary Debate on in the background while grading her students' photography portfolios the other night, a Republican senator talked about the importance of the death penalty for "heinous cases like Jon Allan Blue." When she checked out at the grocery store last week, loading whiskey and frozen tater tots onto the belt, she saw his face peering from a magazine cover under the headline "Blue Proclaims Innocence While Victims' Loved Ones Beg for Answers." There's even supposed to be a fucking television show about him premiering soon.

He's everywhere, and Abby is nowhere. A name buried deep in his Wikipedia page, under the heading "Other Possible Victims." And in twenty-five days, the only person who knows what happened to her will be gone, a corpse lying in the execution chamber at the Kentucky State Penitentiary.

———

Although it's only 3:00 p.m. when Bree arrives at the small ranch-style house she rents near campus, she pours herself some Fireball, the cinnamon-flavored whiskey popular with her students. It goes down easily while she reads through news articles. No one mentions investigators' plans for questioning him or speculates about the odds of him finally confessing.

The familiar anxiety tightens her chest as the sun sets, although it isn't like when she was in her late teens and early twenties, before a doctor prescribed an antidepressant. Back then, the slightest noise could provoke a panic attack. It was part of why she liked spending evenings with Detective Frye. He made her feel safe.

She doesn't want to think about Frye, so she checks her email.

It's a horror show of missed deadlines. The one from her friend from graduate school, Pia, especially weighs on her. Pia curates a photography exhibition for emerging female artists. The deadline is nearing, and she wants to know where Bree's submission is.

In grad school, Bree's photography started to get attention, winning some contests and grants. She mostly shot portraits of women. The woman working the counter of the adult video store, her expression bored while she scanned DVDs of young women dripping in cum. Bree's neighbor with the short, bleached hair shot in profile as she bent over the gas stove in her apartment to light her cigarette.

Bree clicks on a folder of some recent photos she's taken. She didn't feel anything when she shot them, and she doesn't feel anything looking at them now. Photography used to be a hunger. Now it seems like something hanging over her head—homework she's procrastinated on long enough that it looms too large to tackle.

By the time night falls, Bree's well and truly drunk, even though she has to teach tomorrow morning. She sees all the things she should do. The overflowing garbage can in the kitchen stinks, and she has no clean underwear. She's lost count of how many times she's told herself, *Tomorrow I'll do better. Tomorrow I'll take photos/eat something nutritious/go to bed on time/finally do laundry. Tomorrow, I'll treat myself like I'm someone worthy of care.*

Tonight, though, she stands over the kitchen sink and eats shredded cheese directly out of the bag for dinner. While she chews, she stares out the window overlooking her backyard. It butts against a small, wooded area, and in the light from a half moon, she sees fallen leaves that have blown onto her patchy, overgrown lawn. The previous renter installed a garden plot and chicken coop. Under Bree's expert care, weeds have overrun the garden, and the coop collapsed, leaving a jagged pile of rotted wood and chicken wire where yellow jackets make nests.

While she stands there, tongue searching her lower lip for a stray bit of cheddar, the motion-activated light switches on. The yard looks even worse in its brightness, illuminating the patches of dead grass. Because of the alcohol, it takes her a moment to realize what triggered the sensor. When she sees it, she drops the bag of cheese into the sink.

A man stands where the edge of her yard meets the woods. Because the light doesn't reach that far, she can only see his silhouette against the trees. He's tall and broad-shouldered and looks like he's dressed in all black—or is that just the lack of light? Her heart beats fast, and she feels dizzy. She wishes she weren't drunk right now because she's not sure what to do. Call the police? In moments like this, she can never tell how much her past might be making her overreact. Could it just be someone cutting through the woods on their way to a neighbor's house? Would a reasonable, non-traumatized, sober person call the police? Would she be this scared if she hadn't spent the past few hours thinking about Jon Allan Blue?

She steps away from the window to make sure the doors are locked and grabs her cell phone from the living room, keeping it in her hand. When she goes back to the window, the person is gone. She watches for a solid minute but doesn't see any movement. The motion-controlled light switches off, plunging her yard into darkness.

Just someone cutting through to get to a friend's house, she tells herself. *A college student on his way to a party.*

She's walking back to the sink to put the shredded cheese away when the knocking starts. At first, it's soft and tentative, and she can't figure out exactly where it's coming from. As it grows louder and more insistent, she realizes someone's at the back door. She's still got her phone in her hand, and, mouth dry, heart pounding, she's ready to dial 911 when a familiar voice calls her name.

She unlocks the door and opens it to find Zach standing on her doorstep, smiling, wearing a black hoodie and dark jeans.

"You scared the shit out of me," she says as he walks inside. "What are you doing skulking around my yard dressed in black?"

"The last time I came over you told me I should be more careful about people seeing me." He studies her for a moment. "Are you drunk?"

She's embarrassed—both that she overreacted to seeing someone in her yard and that he caught her drinking alone. Thankfully, an eighteen-year-old is easily distracted. She grabs the bottle of Fireball and gestures toward her bedroom.

"Come on. You've got some catching up to do."

He kicks off his sneakers and follows her like a puppy, padding down the hallway in his socks. She wonders if this is how she looked, all those years ago, when she followed Frye into his bedroom. Had he watched her teenage self with the same mix of arousal and shame she feels now?

She drinks straight from the bottle before handing it to Zach and perching on the edge of her unmade bed. He stands in front of her, bringing the bottle to his lips, his shirt rising to expose his lean stomach and the dark-blond hair leading to the top button of his jeans.

On the bed, her phone lights up with a text. It's another

reminder from Pia about the photography exhibition. *You need to put your work out there*, it reads. *We're not getting any younger.*

Bree's camera sits on her dresser, coated in a layer of dust. It's not that she can't see potential photos—Zach's head tilted as he swallows, his milky neck exposed, the liquor bottle catching the light from her bedroom lamp. It's a good shot, but she doesn't feel any pull to grab her camera. Instead, she stands, takes his head in her hands, and brings her lips to his.

———————

In the morning, she keeps her eyes closed, her breathing steady, listening as Zach zips his jeans before gently shutting the bedroom door. Only when the front door opens and closes does she roll over to lie on her back.

Her head pounds, her mouth cottony. She reaches for the ibuprofen. The nightstand is a disaster, a still-life of a thirty-year-old shit show: empty beer cans, wadded face wipes smeared orangey from her foundation and black from her heavy liquid liner, empty condom wrappers, an orange prescription bottle of Zoloft, the almost-empty bottle of Fireball, a metal one-hitter, and a baggie of shitty weed. Somehow more embarrassing are the attempts at self-care: two glass vials of facial serum and a pot of expensive moisturizer, the bottle of gummy vitamins, sheet mask wrappers, and the essential oil diffuser. Because, sure, she's spending nights smoking weed and drinking with her eighteen-year-old student and eating shredded cheese over the kitchen sink, but why not make sure her bedroom smells like peppermint and her skin is properly hydrated?

There isn't water, and she's not in any shape to walk to the kitchen yet, so she washes the ibuprofen down with some luke-warm beer either Zach or she left in the bottom of a dented can. She gags a little but manages to swallow.

Something occurs to her while she lies there waiting for the painkiller to take effect. The panic cuts through her hangover, and she grabs her laptop from the floor to check the calendar. After doing the math, she turns to the internet. She reads the results and feels sick. It's impossible to know if it's an early symptom or just her hangover. *You can't think about this right now,* she tells her-self. *This is a problem for Future Bree.*

It was something Abby said a lot—*That's for Abby in Two Hours to deal with. That's for Tomorrow Abby to handle.* She'd say it in a self-deprecating way, her eyes rolling at her own procras-tination. After she was gone, these moments would be erased in every vigil, in every newspaper article. They flattened her into a one-note character, the missing girl, perpetually beautiful and smiling, sweet and saint-like. Until, soon, more gruesome deaths overshadowed her, and she was forgotten entirely.

After her classes are finished, Bree drives to the only drugstore in her small town. The bored-looking girl working the checkout isn't one of Bree's current or former students, so Bree walks to the feminine care aisle in search of the pregnancy tests.

In front of the feminine washes—the ones that make vaginas smell like someone's grandmother's potpourri—a one-gallon bottle of Hawaiian Punch sits discarded. Bree sees why it was abandoned—the bottle leaks a puddle of red liquid onto the tile. If Bree stands back, she can get the puddle and the rows of tampons and pads into a shot. It could be a good composition, if a little on the nose. She sees the technical merits of it, but there's nothing pulling her toward shooting it.

She bends down to study the pregnancy tests behind the locked case but hears a familiar voice.

"Hadley!"

Alayna is standing next to the condoms.

It's wrong to have favorites, but Alayna is one of Bree's. She's short and round-faced and works long hours at Dollar General. She reminds Bree of herself at eighteen. It's a narcissistic reason to want to mentor someone, but Bree can't help it. Bree's careful to step away from the pregnancy tests and toward the menstrual products.

"I'm sorry I missed today's class," Alayna says. "But I had to cover someone's shift at the last minute."

Everything Alayna says sounds like a question even if it isn't. She has a great photographic eye, taking digital photos of the women in her life—her grandmother holding a Newport 100 between red acrylics while looking out at their backyard. A chained bulldog running on a circle of bare earth. Her best friend in a pink bra and black underwear, pinching the fat on her waist as she stares at her reflection in a toothpaste-spotted bathroom mirror.

Bree grabs a box of super absorbency tampons and tells Alayna it's fine.

"Can you send me your PowerPoint?" Alayna asks. "The guy whose notes I borrowed didn't do a great job."

Bree nods. She wishes, though, she could tell her: *Look, you're going to get an A in this class no matter what, so just calm the fuck down.*

Although Bree doesn't feel especially youthful lately, she's still the young, cool professor. She rarely enforces deadlines and listens when students vent about things. Some of them probably think she's a pushover, but life is hard, and Bree so rarely has her own shit together. The closest relationship she has right now is with a boy whose name is in her grade book and who's too young to remember 9/11. Who is she to judge anyone?

"I shouldn't have asked him for the notes," Alayna says. "I really only did it because I wanted him to ask me out."

"Oh?" Bree says. Before she started teaching, she wouldn't have believed the things students would confide. But in almost four years of teaching college students, she has heard about herpes outbreaks, mental breakdowns, students' porn addictions, and so many other deeply personal confessions.

"I just can't tell from social media if he has a girlfriend or not," Alayna says, peering at her phone, her neon yellow acrylic nails tapping against the screen. "There's a girl from his hometown he takes pictures with, but I haven't seen him with anyone here."

She shouldn't ask, her colleagues wouldn't ask, but Bree loves gossip. "Who was this whose notes you borrowed?"

"Zach," Alayna says.

Bree's head snaps up, and then she immediately looks down, as if she's carefully studying the sanitary pad offerings. *One-hundred percent leak-free comfort!* one box advertises.

"Well," she tells Alayna, staring at a box of overnight pads with wings. "It was good to see you. I'll make sure to send you the PowerPoint."

"Great," Alayna says, still not leaving.

"Have a good night."

"Thanks," Alayna says, still standing there. "Do you think it's bad to ask a guy out? Like, does it seem desperate?"

Alayna's expression is so earnest, her wide eyes watching Bree, her small mouth pursed. Bree has seen this with other female students. They'll come to office hours and ask things like: *Are you married? Do you have a boyfriend? Where did you go to school?*

She's a paper doll they're holding up, seeing if they, someday, might want her life. It's an achievement she's even tricked them into thinking it's worth considering.

She has to swallow a few times and clear her throat before she answers. "I think a woman should always ask for what she wants."

Alayna smiles so wide her dimples appear. "Thanks, Hadley."

Before Alayna leaves the aisle, she selects the exact type of tampons Bree grabbed and follows her to the checkout line.

When Bree gets home, she sits at her computer and types Jon Allan Blue's name into the internet search bar. That's how she thinks of him—by his full name, careful even in the privacy of her own mind not to slip up, not to think about the person he was to her before his name started appearing in newspapers.

She knows reading more about him right now is a bad decision, but she can't stop herself. It's the same impulse that makes her search Abby's name sometimes or scour cold-case forums about her. It will distract her from her late period and her guilt about sleeping with Zach the way pressing on a bruise might. Sure, it will hurt, but doesn't she deserve to hurt?

She scrolls past articles about the execution date and finds think piece atop think piece:

Jon Allan Blue typifies toxic masculinity, and we should all pay attention.

Jon Allan Blue's toxic masculinity isn't anything special, and it's wrong to give him attention.

It isn't Jon Allan Blue's toxic masculinity we should be concerned with—it's his white privilege.

Stop saying Jon Allan Blue is hot!

Further into the search results, she sees the TV show that's about to come out about him has been designated by *Entertainment Weekly* as "must watch."

She pulls up IMDb and scrolls through the cast list. Of course, Abby's name isn't in the credits as one of the characters, although there is "Screaming Girl" and "Terrified Girl Running" and "Crying Girl." Bree supposes Abby could have been any of those. She doesn't know. She wasn't there. She has no idea what her final hours were like.

Sometimes it seems like an answer—any answer—to what happened to Abby that night is what Bree needs to move on. To stop typing Blue's name into search bars and pick up her camera again. To stop screwing around with one of her students and date someone her own age. To get her shit together and let go of all the guilt and grief that has settled on her like a heavy coat.

She pictures what the University of Iowa's campus looked like twelve years ago. The real campus—not some Hollywood approximation. The lawn picturesque in the autumn sun. Orange, red, and yellow leaves glowing bright in front of the limestone buildings' arched windows and ornate stonework. Abby, Chelsea, and Bree drinking Red Bull and vodkas at a bar with beer-sticky floors, clutching the fake IDs Chelsea got them. Eating quesadillas the size of dinner plates at bar close, Abby's head on Bree's shoulder. The three of them sprawled on the grass in the Pentacrest on sunny days, the Beaux-Arts buildings looming over them as they napped or read for classes, ladybugs crawling across their bare legs. Early morning in sweatshirts, shotgunning cheap cans of beer in the parking lot of the football stadium, the air full of smoke from grilled burgers and brats, the thrum of the drumline reverberating in their bones as the hours collapsed toward kickoff.

Then, for one second, she sees *the* moment in exact detail: Abby crying under the statue of the Black Angel in her Hermione Halloween costume, snowflakes collecting on her coppery hair. Chelsea and Bree watching her, not putting their arms around her, letting her walk away. Her footprints in the snow leading down that blacktop path. The last trace of her they ever saw.

CHELSEA

OCTOBER 2015

Chelsea's driving, late for a dinner party, when a soft-voiced reporter for the local NPR station announces it: Jon Allan Blue's final appeal was denied this afternoon. His November 3 execution date will stand. Kentucky's governor has no plans to offer a stay.

The Chevy in front of her stops, brake lights casting a red glow over Chelsea's face. She's so distracted she doesn't slam on her brakes until it's too late. A sickening thud drowns out the radio for a moment.

The Chevy's driver flips his hazards on, throws his driver's side door open, and runs up to her Prius. He's a white man in his mid-forties in a canvas Carhartt coat. Through her closed door and window, she can make out some of what he's yelling: *Stupid… What the fuck? Just paid it off!*

Before opening the door to face him, she makes sure her coat is unbuttoned.

"Did you hear me?" he demands once she stands in front of him. "I asked what the fuck is your problem? You can't watch where you're going?"

She clocks the exact moment it happens. His eyes drop to her clerical collar, before jumping back to her face. She can almost see the wheels turning as he opens his mouth then shuts it again.

"Are you a reverend or something?" he asks, finally.

"An Episcopal priest," she says. "I'm sorry about your car. Is there any damage?"

He stares at her instead of his rear bumper. Chelsea keeps her expression neutral. It's a calculated gamble. Sometimes a woman in a position like hers just makes men even angrier.

He inspects the damage while cars drive around them. Although it was warm today, the temperature dropped as the sun set, and the chilly air smells like vehicle exhaust. In the glare of Chelsea's headlights, a red paint spot the size of a silver dollar mars his bumper. Otherwise, it doesn't look like there's been any damage.

"Should we exchange insurance information?" she asks.

He hesitates, staring at that spot of red. When he turns back to her, he doesn't meet her eyes. "Look, I'm sorry about swearing at you. It's just been a long day, and I really wanted to get home to my kids."

"I completely understand," Chelsea says. "I have my insurance card in my car, if you want to take a photo of it."

He rubs the back of his neck. "Look, I've got a buddy who owns a body shop. I'm sure he could buff the paint out no problem, and there's no other damage."

"You're sure?"

He smiles. "Yeah."

She shouldn't do it—she shouldn't play into it—but she can't help it. She gives him her most pious look and says, "You have a blessed evening."

———————

Chelsea's forty-five minutes late by the time she arrives at Melissa and Steve's two-story redbrick home. After parking on the street behind Daniel's truck, she walks up their driveway. Jack-o'-lanterns sit on the neighbor's front porch, and the air smells like burning leaves. Despite the warmth of the day, that familiar chill is in the air. In a few weeks, it will be exactly twelve years since she last saw Abby.

No one answers when Chelsea knocks. The front door is unlocked, creaking open as she says, "Hello?"

The entryway and living room are dark, but she hears someone talking toward the back of the house. Past the dining room, there's a faint greenish light coming from the kitchen. The voice, as Chelsea nears, becomes unmistakable.

"I won't lie to you," Jon Allan Blue says. "I don't want to die."

When Chelsea steps onto the laminate, she realizes the kitchen is empty, but someone left on the small green banker's lamp sitting by Melissa's cookbooks. The radio is on in the corner, and she immediately walks over and turns it off, silencing Blue.

She stands there for a moment, her back to the room, pressing the heels of her hands into her eyes. *You just have to get through a few more weeks*, she tells herself. *Then the worst of the media circus will be over.*

Is that true, though? Now he's part of the zeitgeist. Now he'll never die.

The awareness comes upon her suddenly. She's no longer

alone in the room. She whirls around, only to find Daniel stand-ing in the entryway to the kitchen holding a bottle of beer.

"We're all out back," he says, setting the bottle next to the kitchen sink. "Steve made a fire. There are hot dogs and s'mores."

He opens the fridge and grabs a beer. After he throws his bottle cap and empty beer into Steve and Melissa's recycling bin, he studies her.

"I heard the news. About Blue. You okay?"

"I'm fine," she says as the tension in her chest tightens a notch.

"Chelsea, you can talk to me."

"I said I'm fine."

He opens his mouth to press her, but Melissa opens the back door and Chelsea pastes on a bright smile as she greets her.

———————

Outside, everyone sits in camp chairs except for Steve, Melissa's husband, who's standing next to the firepit, dropping more wood onto the flames. He's a quiet guy with a blond man bun who works at the carpentry shop with Daniel and loves playing board games so complicated it takes twenty minutes to explain the rules.

As they all hold hot dogs over the fire on roasting sticks, the other couple Melissa and Steve invited eye Chelsea's clerical collar. Daniel does, too. He's told her before that she shouldn't wear it in social situations.

"It makes it hard for people to feel comfortable connecting with you," he's said in the past. "They feel like they have to keep you at a distance."

She's never known how to explain it to him—that's exactly the point.

The other couple, Gina and Jason, just moved in next door to Melissa and Steve. Jason has taken a job as industrial engineer at the 3M plant in Forest City, coming to Iowa from Idaho. Chelsea has had so many colleagues at conferences confuse the two states. She tells Gina and Jason this, how people would ask: *Is Iowa the one with the potatoes?* And she'd have to say, *No, you're thinking of Idaho. That's the one with the potatoes.*

"So, what does Iowa have?" Jason asks. The lenses of his dark-framed glasses reflect the firelight.

"We have corn," Melissa says.

"Hogs," Steve says.

"The World's Largest Truck Stop," Daniel says.

Gina, the wife, is one of those blonds who have almost white eyebrows. She turns to Daniel and Chelsea. "Are you from Iowa originally?"

"Chelsea is," Daniel says. "But she went to Sewanee for seminary. I was living in Chattanooga, but the school hired me to do some carpentry work in the chapel."

"And you fell in love," Melissa says, smiling. She looks exactly like what she is: a kindergarten teacher from Iowa. Chelsea can picture her sitting at the front of a classroom, reading the kids a story with her bright smile, makeup-free skin, glossy brown hair, and shapeless dress. She would do all the voices. There's a sensuality about her, though, that cuts the wholesomeness. As she finishes her s'more, she licks her fingertips in a way that's suggestive but doesn't seem to be purposely so. Chelsea both envies her lack of self-consciousness and pities her for it as a thread of saliva connecting Melissa's mouth to her index finger catches the firelight before breaking.

Steve nudges the logs with a fireplace poker, and Chelsea desperately tries not to think about Jon Allan Blue in that sorority house. When she was twenty-two, she went to a Halloween party where someone dressed up like Blue, complete with a fireplace poker dipped in red paint.

While they make s'mores, Gina prattles on about some MLM she works for, selling dietary supplements and nutritional shakes. Everything she says seems like it comes from the company's marketing department. Chelsea's face is warm from the fire. She licks melted chocolate off her fingertips and zones out. In the camp chair next to her, Melissa places a charred marshmallow onto her graham cracker. After Gina finishes talking about the vitamins and minerals in the company's trademark Blaze Powder, Melissa says, "Isn't that interesting?" which anyone from the Midwest knows is code for *Shut the fuck up.*

Gina, although not a native Midwesterner, appears to be a fast learner and changes the subject, asking Melissa about the kindergartners she teaches.

"Well," Melissa says, putting another marshmallow on her roasting stick. "You would be staggered by how many of them have iPhones."

Everyone starts decrying the phone-addicted state of their world, with Gina sharing that her twenty-year-old sister even takes her phone into the bathroom.

"Can you imagine?"

Chelsea laughs politely, although she always brings her phone into the bathroom. What's more soothing than taking a shit while scrolling through curated pictures of the best parts of people's lives?

"Chelsea's always on her phone, it feels like," Daniel says. "I'll leave the room for one second, and when I get back, she's like—" He mimes holding a phone and tapping on it, his eyes exaggeratedly wide, and everyone laughs.

"It's a good way to connect with some of my younger parishioners," Chelsea says. "They'll text or DM me on social media."

Although this is true, she knows it's not the only reason. Partly, she just likes the clean perfection social media gives you. The complete control over what people see and when.

"That's so sweet," Gina says. Her head's tilted, as she smiles at Chelsea. "If you want to get young people involved in church, that's the way to do it."

For a moment, Chelsea's baffled. Why is she being so nice? What's her angle? Then, as she smiles once more before popping another marshmallow in her mouth, Chelsea realizes: she's just a kind person who genuinely thinks what Chelsea's doing is nice. Chelsea feels a lump in her throat. What does it say that someone's genuine enthusiasm is so baffling and foreign to her?

They move from talking about social media to sharing what TV shows they're watching. Melissa and Steve have been binging *The Great British Bake Off.*

"I've been watching *Call the Midwife,*" Chelsea says.

"You already started it?" Daniel asks. "I thought we were going to watch that together."

"I'll rewatch it with you," Chelsea says, shrugging.

Gina gives a little laugh. "The show we've been obsessed with lately is a little less PBS than all of yours."

She and Jason tell them about a true crime show they've been watching. Chelsea zones out, like she does when anything true crime–related is discussed, but she's pulled back in when Gina mentions the trailer for a new show she just saw.

"It's that series about the murders that happened across the Midwest, maybe a decade ago?" she says. "The guy who killed the sorority girls?"

Everyone stills, and there's only the sound of the fire crackling and the wind moving through the tree limbs. Somewhere down the street, a car drives past, its bass throbbing.

Since Gina and Jason aren't from Iowa and don't realize how well known the murders are, Jason thinks their silence is from lack of recognition.

He clarifies: "The one they're going to execute soon. Jon Allan Blue."

Obviously Daniel knows, but judging by Melissa and Steve's expressions, they know, too. Chelsea wonders if Daniel told Steve. Although it's possible Melissa or Steve searched her name online and found the interviews she did a few years ago after she visited Blue in prison. Steve clears his throat, and Melissa bites her lower lip.

"Is something wrong?" Jason asks.

It's Daniel who explains, his palms resting on his jeans, as he stares at the fire. "Chelsea was friends with Abby Hartmann, one of the girls Blue killed."

Jason looks down while Gina leans forward, unable to hide her curiosity. "She was one of the girls in the sorority house?"

Go fuck yourself, Chelsea thinks.

Once again, it's Daniel who explains. "No, she disappeared before the sorority house murders, but they've always believed he was the one who killed her."

It's the same old wound sliced open here in this unfamiliar setting. Abby the afterthought. Abby the forgotten one.

"I think the way you handled it was admirable," Melissa says.
"Going to pray with the man who did that? Forgiving him? It's a
beautiful thing for a priest to do."

If Melissa only knew what her visit with Blue had actually been
like, she wouldn't be saying any of this, but Chelsea knows she's
only trying to be nice in an awkward situation, so she manages a
smile and thanks her.

Gina clears her throat. "I'm so sorry. I get why you'd find the
series upsetting."

No, Chelsea wants to tell her. *No, you will never get it.*

As the fire dies down, everyone goes inside. Daniel and Melissa
do the dishes and share cooking tips while Steve, Jason, and Gina
talk about people in their neighborhood. Chelsea excuses herself, stepping outside and sitting in one of the camp chairs. The
embers in the firepit glow in front of her.

She should go back inside, smile wide, and show everyone that
what happened didn't upset her, but instead she stares into space
and fidgets with her watch's band. When that doesn't satisfy her,
she picks at her cuticles, ignoring the sting when she's too rough
and a half moon of blood appears on her thumb's nail bed.

The execution will happen in less than a month, and she is
not the person she hoped she'd be by now. She thought she'd be
someone who could think about Abby with the tiniest amount of
equanimity. Someone who could listen to people talk about Blue
without needing to claw at her own skin.

As she's bringing her thumb to her mouth to clean up the blood, a voice startles her. "Pretty, isn't it?"

She cranes her neck to see Jason standing there, gesturing to the dying embers.

"It is," she says, affixing a smile to her face.

He clears his throat and sits in the chair next to hers. "I'm sorry about what happened."

"It's fine," Chelsea says, and she hopes she sounds like she means it.

She assumes he'll nod and they'll change the subject to something polite, and then he'll go back inside with his conscience cleared. Instead, he leans toward her. Once again, she can't see his eyes, only the embers reflecting in the lenses of his glasses.

"At least a TV show like that will get people talking. Remind people what those poor women endured. What your friend endured."

When Chelsea wears her clerical collar, she's usually able to push down her anger, to become still and quiet and "choose her priesthood," as someone in seminary phrased it. But tonight, she can't do it. When she speaks, her voice is low and rough.

"You have no fucking idea what you're talking about. That's not why people watch those shows. That's not what those shows do. They just make him bigger. People want to know what he did and why, but they don't give a shit about the women he hurt."

She has never sworn while wearing her clerical collar, but Jason doesn't appear fazed.

"It really upsets you."

She gives a surprised snort of laughter. "Of course it upsets me."

He holds something out to her—a napkin. Once it's in her hands, she realizes she's crying.

"I'm sorry," she says, dabbing her eyes the way Abby always used to—careful not to wipe and ruin her makeup.

"Don't apologize." She's surprised by the tenderness in his expression. She must look really fucking pitiful. He pats her shoulder, and they both get up and walk back toward the house.

As they reach the door, he hesitates. "This might be a long shot, but I know someone who might be able to help. Have you ever heard of the podcast *Infamous*?"

———

Once they're home in bed, Chelsea doesn't tell Daniel about Jason's idea. Daniel would say this is because she's "emotionally withholding," which is the reason he wants them to pay an ungodly amount of money to do a couples retreat next month to learn how to have "intimate conversations."

Maybe it's true. Maybe she is emotionally withholding. But also, she already knows what he'd say if she told him: *This is a bad idea. It'll be just like visiting Jon Allan Blue—something you think will help you heal but instead will make it even harder for you to move on. And that's what you should be focused on—moving on.*

Besides, *Infamous* is a huge podcast with a rabid following. There's no use upsetting Daniel about something that might not even come to fruition.

"I'm sorry that happened," he says, lying next to her, petting their cat, Pippa, who is between them. "The TV show coming up like that."

He's using his gentle voice, the one he adopts when he's talking about something to do with Abby. It used to soothe her. Now, sometimes, it feels like a performance he's putting on. Like he's playing the part of the Long-Suffering Nice Guy Husband in a play only he knows about. She pictures him studying his script, thinking, *I've got to be off-book by Thanksgiving.*

"It's fine," she says.

"Obviously it isn't."

She feels something damp on her cheeks and realizes, for the second time tonight, she has started crying without noticing. She hates that TV show and Detective Frye's book and fucking Jon Allan Blue for getting the attention he's always wanted. Most of all, she hates herself. She hates that she can still be brought to tears about this a dozen years later.

"I don't want to talk about it," she tells Daniel, wiping her eyes with the back of her hand, and then pressing her face into the yeasty smell of Pippa's fur.

"Don't shut me out," Daniel says, his voice low and pleading. But she can't give him what he wants. She can't go there with him or with anyone. He takes a breath, as if he's going to say something more, but then he lapses into silence. She's grateful. This is why she married him. He doesn't push.

Soon after, he's snoring. She knows she won't sleep unless she takes an Ambien, so she scrolls through social media while she waits for the sweet release of the pill.

Despite being a photographer, Bree rarely posts to social media, but she has tonight, uploading a photo with no caption. It's a picture someone took of Abby, Bree, and Chelsea when they were fifteen. They're sitting on the limestone steps at the back of the Old Capitol, Abby's head tilted back as she laughs, Chelsea's head resting on Bree's shoulder. The sun creates a soft lens flare in the top right of the photo.

Chelsea studies the picture for a long time, wondering what made Bree post it tonight of all nights. Is she hearing the constant chatter about Blue's upcoming execution, too? Does it feel as destabilizing to her as it does to Chelsea? Like all the hard work she's done to claw herself into a life in the present is going to be ripped away, and she'll be pulled back to those endless dark hours right after Abby first went missing?

Chelsea doesn't like or comment on the photo. She and Bree have not spoken in nearly a dozen years. She clicks on Bree's profile and scrolls through the photos. Bree hasn't posted any pictures of her art in a long time, but back several years, Chelsea sees them. Portraits of women, mostly. A woman working the counter at a gas station, rows of cigarette boxes behind her, blue eyeliner smeared around her brown eyes, neck angled down toward the lottery tickets. It reminds Chelsea of the paintings of saints. Bree has a way of making people in the humblest circumstances look almost holy.

In a picture of Bree from nearly four years ago, she wears overalls and holds a green bottle of beer. She's staring at something beyond the frame, and she looks happy. There's a lump in Chelsea's throat, and she blames Ambien for the wave of emotion. She tries to click off Bree's page but likes the picture by mistake instead.

Shit. She immediately unlikes it, but the damage is done. Bree will know Chelsea's been stalking her old photos. She's grateful the Ambien numbs her mortification. After setting her phone down, she picks it back up and searches: *Jon Allan Blue TV series.*

Ryan Worth, a former teen heartthrob best known for his work on a Disney show about a talking hedgehog, is playing Jon Allan Blue. He looks like Blue if Blue had been three times more handsome and ten times more charismatic.

She puts headphones in so she won't wake Daniel and hits Play on the trailer. A drumbeat accompanies shots of a handcuffed Worth walking down a hallway interspersed with flashes of dead girls—young women facedown on unmade beds, blood blooming from their heads, the naked flesh of their backs bruised and battered, femurs and tibia clustered in wooded areas with skulls smiling up from beds of pine needles. It goes so fast, Chelsea isn't sure if any of them are supposed to be Abby or if, once again, she has been ignored.

The drumbeat stops. The screen goes black.

"I'm just a normal guy," Ryan Worth says. It's what the real Jon Allan Blue said at trial.

She can't watch any more, but she isn't done tormenting herself, so she types Abby's name into the search engine. Autocomplete helpfully suggests *Abby Hartmann Disappearance, Did Jon Allan Blue Murder Abby Hartmann, Did They Find Abby Hartmann's Body?*

The image results are mostly her missing person photo, which was also her senior yearbook picture. Abby's round face and tanned, even skin. Hazel eyes that looked green if she wore certain colors. Skinny eyebrows she over-plucked while standing in underwear and a tank top, leaning over their dorm room mirror. White teeth with a right canine that stuck out a little too far. Hair she dyed a coppery color, although she got mad if anyone called it red.

"It's auburn," she'd say, rolling her eyes.

In the photo, she's wearing a black, strapless dress. Chelsea borrowed it once on a choir trip to New York City. She remembers how it felt against her skin. The little sections of dark glitter could rub your arms raw if you weren't careful. The photographer had Abby pose with her chin resting on her hand, showing off the silver bracelet she always wore with its heart-shaped charm engraved with her initials.

Under the collection of photos, Google says, *People also ask: When will Blue be executed? When was Jon Allan Blue Sorority House Murder? Who was Abby Hartmann?*

ABBY

Chelsea's tongue is in your ear when you hear Bree's key in the door. You're on the futon, bra off, right hand jammed down Chelsea's unbuttoned jeans, left palm pressing into her sharp hip bone, her hair a dark curtain over your face.

The two of you felt bad Bree's dad didn't have the money for her to live in the dorms with you and that she'd be stuck living at home, so you gave her a key to your room as a consolation gift. It hadn't occurred to either you or Chelsea how much Bree would use the key and how that might interrupt your own plans.

Bree wasn't supposed to be back from her art class until noon, but the knob is turning. Chelsea grabs the ugly afghan her mother knitted out of scratchy acrylic yarn and throws it over you both. The two of you sit rigidly next to one another, and you reach for the remote, turning up the volume on a rerun of *America's Next Top Model*.

When Bree opens the door, she gives you a funny look, tilting her head. "You guys look cozy."

"It's cold," Chelsea says. She sounds like a robot. She's doing what she always does when she's nervous, tugging her watch's band. While Bree drops her backpack on the dingy tile, you swat at Chelsea's hand, mouthing, *Stop*.

You try to focus on the show. Adrianne won some challenge and chooses Elyse to split the prize with her, a night in a fancy French hotel. As they prepare to sleep, lying together in a king-sized bed, Adrianne says, so tenderly, "Goodnight, slut ho."

Bree runs a hand through her long, blond hair. The tips are pink. You and Chelsea dipped them in Manic Panic this summer while the three of you fantasized about what your first year at college would be like. Bree's wide-set eyes narrow, her long face tilting down like a queen surveying a disloyal subject.

"I really need to know something," she says, and you're sure this is it. You're sure you're about to have a conversation you really, really don't want to have. But Bree plops down next to you on the futon.

"Do you think Tyra Banks is pretty even though she has a five-head?"

Chelsea looks at you, a smile spreading across her face, nose wrinkling, dark eyes warming with relief.

"I think she's hot," you say.

Bree nods thoughtfully, eyes glued to the screen. "My forehead is big, too. I hate it."

"You're beautiful," Chelsea tells her.

You watch the show. The photo-shoot challenge requires the girls, covered in oil and water, to pose naked on a bar.

After a while, Bree says, "I don't think it's cold in here. I think it's kind of warm, actually."

Chelsea looks at you, and you both smile.

You and Bree walk to your acting class on the west side of the river. You pass Brother Dave, a campus fixture. There are other preachers and demonstrators who pass through town, but they're just visitors and usually older: a man with a long, gray beard holding a sign saying, *Go and sin no more!* A man with white hair like the fuzz on a baby chick shouting, "Abortion is murder," his stoop-backed wife handing out fliers covered with gory pictures of dismembered fetuses.

But Brother Dave is a townie and not much older than you. He's not bad-looking. If he weren't wearing his canary-yellow "Hell Is Forever" T-shirt, he wouldn't look out of place in one of the bars downtown, with his sunglasses and strong jawline.

"Cover yourself or face eternal damnation," he yells to Bree.

Her jeans are so low-riding, you can see a four-inch strip of bare skin between the top of them and the hem of her pink tank top. It's cool for September, and goose bumps stud her bare arms.

Brother Dave has been yelling at you both since you were in high school—about the evils of masturbation, homosexuality, and exposed cleavage. Bree is deeply unfazed by today's comments. She smiles and waves.

"If you got it, flaunt it, Brother Dave," she calls, briefly flashing her crooked teeth, before becoming self-conscious and closing her mouth.

Bree's body is perfect, the kind you'd see in a music video, but she's so insecure, so desperate for male attention, it makes you cringe sometimes. You love her, you do, but you don't know how to say, *Stop trying so hard. You're embarrassing yourself.*

The crew team rows down the river, and you stop on the pedestrian bridge to watch. The leaves haven't turned yet, and everything is still green and lush. You breathe the river's mud and wet dog smell.

In the middle of the bridge a rusted sign says, "Last death from drowning:" and then a piece of metal is bolted onto it, reading "129 days."

Lately, you find yourself thinking about time passing. You're used to having everything ahead of you, but your high school years are finished. Will you blink and find college over just as fast? Will you end it as you began it—hiding this thing with Chelsea from everyone? As much of a coward at twenty-two as you are at eighteen and as you were at seventeen?

The summer you were twelve, you and Chelsea snuck into a house under construction in your neighborhood. Chelsea climbed in through the space where the basement window would be installed. Although you were taller, she was stronger, and she lifted you from the bare, reddish earth into the half-built house. Before she set you on the concrete, her hands under your armpits, she spun you around once.

You were dizzy when your flip-flops hit the ground, smelling the overpowering scent of new wood and freshly laid cement. You stared at the chipping lime-green polish on your toes and then back at Chelsea's face. It felt like you were falling headfirst into a well, except Chelsea was the well and there was no bottom to it.

A high-pitched, sharp sound startles you, and a guy runs past, blowing on a red, metal safety whistle. Almost every student has one now. The administration handed them out during orientation, at the Welcome Week events, and even before home football games. It's because of the girls who have gone missing.

Girls in Nebraska and Western Iowa. Girls near your age. One college student in Lincoln was walking back to her sorority house through an alley behind Greek Row. A friend saw her and talked to her through the window of his fraternity house. After they said goodbye, she was only sixty feet from her sorority. Her body was found a few weeks later in an abandoned barn. Another teenager was walking home in Sioux City. Police found CCTV footage of her and a man in a hoodie walking together near her house. She was never seen again.

Someone else blows another safety whistle behind you. Then a guy runs past to catch up with the first boy, the whistle between his teeth.

This isn't a rare scene on campus. The administration probably meant well, but they hadn't considered what would happen if you gave twenty thousand undergrads whistle key chains. Every weekend, that same shrill noise sounds downtown as students walk to and from bars, like birds calling to one another. Every tailgate. Every football game in the student section. Even just a normal afternoon when a few students are bored walking across the Pentacrest. That same metallic blare, making the safety whistles effectively useless, since everyone has learned to tune them out.

When you reach the theater building's huge glass lobby, the sun shines on the bright red carpet. Bree is just a step behind you.

In your high school plays, she was always stuck playing "Second Poor Woman" in *Robin Hood* or "Girl" in *Gramercy Ghost* while you were the lead roles. You assumed you deserved the parts you were awarded, but your junior year, the school put on *A Midsummer Night's Dream*. All Bree wanted was to play Helena. She carried around a battered paperback of the play she borrowed from the library, murmuring Helena's lines in the locker bay.

The more you beat me, I will fawn on you:
Use me but as your spaniel, spurn me, strike me,
Neglect me, lose me; only give me leave,
Unworthy as I am, to follow you.

The auditions were held in the small green room instead of onstage, all of you packed together, sweating in the stuffy room. When Bree read a scene, you saw something you had never noticed before. She was better than you.

But when the cast list was taped outside the theater's doors, it was your name next to Helena. Bree tried hard not to show her jealousy. She hugged you and said she was excited to wear a lot of glitter in her role as a fairy. Then, a few days later, 9/11 happened, and no one was thinking much about who was playing what part anymore.

Still, you never forgot Bree was more talented than you were but had been passed over anyway. You never forgot that your mom always donated money to the theater boosters and was friends with Mrs. Lindbergh, the theater teacher, while Bree's mom had been the town drunk who died in a car accident when Bree was only three.

As you walk through the theater building toward the little studio where your class is held, your stomach clenches. You always get nervous before Acting I. In high school acting classes, you did the same stale improv exercises and practiced boring monologues from *Antigone* ("...for, when you died, with mine own hands I washed and dressed you, and poured drink-offerings at your graves; and now, Polyneices, 'tis for tending thy corpse that I win such recompense...").

Your college acting instructor, Jay, is not interested in "that bullshit." He believes acting is a medium to "access the most authentic parts of ourselves." He's a grad student who looks like an extra in a movie about surfers. You might see him up on his board, riding a wave, his sun-bleached hair slicked back with seawater, his tan face scrunched in concentration, as the main characters have a heartfelt conversation on the beach in front of him.

Today, you all sit on the wood floor, facing the barre and full-length mirrors. Bree's reflection in the mirror nervously clicks her tongue ring against the bottom of her front teeth. Jay looms over you and the twelve other students. Clad in khaki shorts and a pale pink polo with a popped collar, he wears the same silver ring on his pinky that he always does. It shows the comedy and tragedy masks—the universal symbol for the theater. Part of you thinks this is sweet, but another part of you thinks it's cheesy as hell.

Your classmates' faces in the mirror watch him with unblinking eyes. Sometimes you try to remind yourself that he's just a twenty-seven-year-old grad student who has only been in a commercial for the local bowling alley. After getting a strike, he turned to the camera, flashing his white teeth, saying his one line, shrugging, "That's how I roll."

No matter how much you try to reason it away, you want his attention just as much as your classmates do.

"Today we're going to tap into primal emotions," Jay says.

He speaks so softly you have to lean forward to hear him. You think it's a technique he uses to keep you all on edge, hanging on every word. It works.

Jay bends his knees, sucks in a breath, and screams. His face reddens, and the cords of his neck protrude. In the mirror, you see

Bree startle. After a few seconds, he closes his mouth and straightens his knees.

"As artists, we have to be in touch with all our emotions," he says, his voice soft again, although now a little hoarse. "Even the ones society tells us to hide—anger, sadness, fear. I'm going to have all of you scream. It sounds simple enough, but you'll be surprised how hard it can be to really let go and, when you do, what emotions come up."

One by one, your classmates stand—a guy in an Ozzy Osbourne T-shirt screaming until he breaks off, raw-voiced and panting; a girl resting her French-manicured acrylics on her tanned, slim thighs as she wails like a banshee. Sometimes, though, they don't start out screaming with much gusto, the noise weak and halfhearted, as if they're self-conscious.

"Louder," Jay yells at these students, until they're leaning into the sound.

When it gets to Bree, she doesn't just bend her knees. Instead, she crouches her whole body, hands balled into fists, blond hair falling over her face. Her scream sounds like something from a horror movie, an anguished shriek that raises the hair on your arms. When she's done, her face is still red, her eyes watering.

"Goddamn," Jay says, surveying her.

She smiles, clearly pleased with herself, and wipes her eyes, smearing a little mascara under them.

"How did that feel?" Jay asks her.

"Really fucking good," Bree says, her eyes wide.

She sits down, and Jay gestures for you to stand. You're one of the last students to go, and you're surprised how self-conscious you feel standing in front of everyone. Your scream starts out weak. Although you want to let go like Bree did, for some reason you can't. You can't give yourself over to it. You're aware of everyone's eyes on you, and you feel tense and guarded.

"Louder," Jay says.

You try widening your stance and sucking in more air before letting out another scream, but you know you're still holding back.

"Really put your whole self into it," Jay says. When you break off, he scratches his head, surveying you as if you're a long-division problem he needs to solve.

"We'll keep working on it," he says.

When you return to the dorm, you sit with Chelsea on the futon and place your lips on the delicate skin right above her T-shirt's collar. It was one of the parts of her body you started to notice in middle school, along with the curve of her neck and heat of her skin when she leaned over you to look at a page of *Seventeen*.

Over the years, you let your eyes linger on her longer than you should have, but as time passed, you caught her doing the same thing. You'd turn your head from *The Real World* and see her eyes on you rather than the screen.

You lean against the futon and tell Chelsea about the acting class—how Bree could scream so freely, and you couldn't. It may be stupid—it's just some little exercise—but you feel wounded Bree was so much freer than you were. You want Chelsea to wrap her arms around you and tell you to forget about it.

Instead, worry lines appear between her full eyebrows. Taking your hand and squeezing it, she says, "Don't you think you'd have an easier time letting go if there wasn't so much we're hiding?"

As soon as she finishes the question, you stand. This is a conversation for Future Abby. "I should study for French."

Chelsea shakes her head. "You always want to talk about this later. This is later."

Her expression is patronizing. Like she's looking at a small, scared child she pities. It makes you snap at her. "Well, what do you want, then?"

Her eyes widen at your tone and then narrow. "I want you to stop being such a fucking coward. How about that? That's what I want."

You stare at each other. Then, sighing, she leans against the futon, staring at the water-stained ceiling tiles.

"I want what other people have," she says, shrugging. "I don't want to keep sneaking around and hiding from Bree. When my mom asks me if I want to go on a date with some dumb guy she's met, I want to be able to say, 'No, actually...'" she breaks off, swallowing. " 'Actually, I'm with someone, and you know her, and she's great.'"

Down the hall, someone slams their door. A group of girls' laughter rises then fades as the stairwell door creaks open. You think about last week when you talked to your mom on the phone while she was waiting at the nail salon. She had let out a sigh of displeasure.

"They have that Ellen DeGeneres talk show on in the waiting area."

"I didn't know she had a talk show," you said.

"It just started," your mother said. "And I doubt it will last. The way she rubbed people's noses in things, trying to normalize *that lifestyle*."

Chelsea's still staring at you. You let out a long sigh. "My parents aren't going to be happy for us. Your parents aren't going to be happy for us. We don't even know Bree is going to be happy for us."

"Let them be unhappy," Chelsea says.

You think about yourself in class—too self-conscious and guarded to let go. "Maybe I'm just not as brave as you."

"That's a cop-out," Chelsea says. "You're the one who gets on stage in front of people."

How can you explain it to her? That's the exact opposite of what she's asking you to do. To stand on stage, playing a part, is the most satisfying thing in the world. *Look at me,* you tell people. *Look at this illusion I've made. You can stare at me but you're really seeing someone else, someone I created just for you.* But invite people to look at who you really are?

"I'm not ready yet," you say.

That expression of pity is still on Chelsea's face as she steps toward you, kneeling next to where you sit at your desk, and takes your hand.

"A compromise?" she says. "We'll just tell Bree."

"Maybe."

Chelsea's face goes blank. You've known her since you were ten, but there are still so many times her expressions are inscrutable. She drops your hand and goes back to the futon, sitting down and picking up her book.

"Just give me a little more time, okay?"

"Okay," she says, but she doesn't look at you.

You really should study for French, but you watch her instead, her head bowed over her poli-sci textbook, dark hair shining under the dorm's harsh overhead lights. She's wearing her high school girls' soccer T-shirt. All through high school, her uniform was mostly shirts from the various sports teams she was on and cargo pants and baby tees, although, for school dances, she wore dresses and let Bree twist her hair into elaborate updos. It was strange to see her like that, the height from her hairdo bringing out her delicate bone structure, making her dark eyes appear even larger.

"What?" Chelsea asks, noticing you staring. She's marking her place in her book with her index finger.

There's a part of you who wants to say it. Even right here, in this shitty dorm room that smells like mildew and hairspray. *I love you*, you want to say.

"What?" Chelsea asks again, cocking her head.

"Nothing," you tell her and look away.

———

The next day you take your seat in the lecture hall for your intro psychology class. Discarded copies of the campus newspaper are ubiquitous, and a headline from the copy at your feet catches your eye. You pick it up even though its edges are ripped and someone's dirty shoe print adorns the front page. Your professor begins his lecture, but you don't really hear him. Instead, you study the school photo of a teenager near your age. A girl with auburn hair who looks like she's laughing at a joke the photographer cracked just before he snapped the picture.

The headline says, "Girl's Body Found: Third in Last Four Months."

EXCERPT FROM
THE MIDWEST MANGLER: MY HUNT FOR JON ALLAN BLUE

BY DOUG FRYE

Everything changed in the early hours of a freezing November morning when a sorority girl from Alpha Psi Theta called 911 in hysterics.

"Please come now," she said. "My friends—there's so much blood. I don't know what happened, but someone *hurt* them."

I've listened to the recording of that call a number of times over the years. What I can't get over is the way the girl emphasizes the word *hurt,* as if, until that moment, she never really knew how inadequate the word could be for certain types of brutality.

By the time I stepped into the sorority house, I had been a police officer for twenty-six years, a detective for fourteen. A good chunk of that time was spent patrolling Chicago's South Side. I thought I was familiar with all the ways a human body could be brutalized.

On the news, reporters would describe what Jon Allan Blue did to those women as a "bludgeoning." That word, like *hurt,* is simply inadequate for what I found when I walked into the upstairs bedrooms of the sorority house.

If you're holding a fireplace poker, as Blue was, and your victim is asleep, it wouldn't be hard to kill them. The crime scene made it clear, though, that he hadn't just wanted to kill these women. He wanted to obliterate them.

BREE
OCTOBER 2015

In the next town over, where she's less likely to run into her students, Bree walks down a drugstore aisle with all the tampons and lube and yeast infection treatments, and a sad, Muzak version of "Girls Just Wanna Have Fun" plays. She crouches in front of the pregnancy tests, but they're locked behind a glass case.

She interrupts the twentysomething guy stocking Pedialyte in the next aisle. He has dyed black hair and a lip ring. When he bends down to unlock the case, he asks, "Which one do you want?"

"The cheapest one?" It comes out like a question, even though she's worked for years to stop the uptick from creeping into her voice.

He turns to look at her. "My girlfriend didn't like that one. She uses this one."

He hands Bree one priced in the mid-range. She's seen commercials for the brand on TV. A pretty brunette emerges from her marble-topped bathroom to give her smiling husband the positive test before they embrace.

"The cheapest one," she says again, this time without the question mark at the end.

At the checkout counter, the older, female cashier doesn't say anything as she scans and bags the test. But when she hands Bree the receipt and the bag, she says, "I hope it's whatever result you want, honey."

Maybe it's her mommy issues, maybe it's hormones, but Bree has to blink back tears as she smiles and nods at this kind-eyed woman whose gray roots peak out from her dyed brown hair. *Deb*, her employee name tag says.

How would Bree's life be different if Deb had been her mom? Bree used to ask herself this question about all kinds of women when she was a kid. While eating a strawberry Pop-Tart, she would watch Paula Zahn and her perky blond bob anchoring *CBS Mornings* and wonder, *What would it be like if she were my mom?* She'd wonder about various female teachers. Mrs. Kiddle, with her sandy pixie cut and frumpy denim dresses. Ms. Schar, who wore wire-rimmed glasses and, when she pointed out the bones on the skeleton living in their classroom, held its limbs so gently. Mrs. Olds, with her honking laugh and the lilac perfume that wafted around Bree when she came over to help with a long-division problem.

Of course, the real question was: *What would it be like to have a mom—any mom?*

The drugstore is connected to an old, sad mall, and Bree walks past the closed food court and the empty stores with their metal security grilles. She can smell the Bath & Body Works from around the corner but passes it and walks to the bookstore.

There's a table at the front with all the autobiographies and books by the caucus candidates—Clinton in black and white with her fist thoughtfully to her chin on *Living History*, a much younger Trump leaning with a smirk on *The Art of the Deal*.

Every four years, people suddenly pay attention to Iowa. Presidential hopefuls show up in the state to eat pork tenderloins and look at the butter cow at the Iowa State Fair. They sit in diners in rural towns saying, if they get elected, they won't forget the people who live in flyover country. The candidates are always different but that's the same. As are the editorials from East Coast reporters who write think pieces about the state as if they're doing ethnography on an unfamiliar, primitive culture. They complain they can't find almond milk, even though Bree has some in her fridge right now. They talk about how flat and boring the landscape is, although any Iowan knows Nebraska's really the flat and boring state. They cherry-pick the most rural anecdotes, even though Bree, a lifelong Iowan, has never been on a farm other than during a kindergarten field trip.

Bree passes Ben Carson smiling in his pleased yet almost pharmaceutically sedated way on *Gifted Hands*, and, on the cover of *A Time for Truth*, Ted Cruz manages somehow to look creepier than the serial killers in the neighboring true crime section.

She's planning to skip the true crime section, but then she sees it. *The Midwest Mangler: My Hunt for Jon Allan Blue* by Doug Frye. The cover is another of the media's favorite photos of Jon Allan Blue—one where he's in a beige jail jumpsuit, sitting in the courtroom, face toward the cameras, lips upturned in a small smile, as if he's enjoying a private joke.

Bree picks it up and checks inside the book jacket. Frye's author photo shows an aged version of the man she knew—hair graying at the temples and receding even farther up his high forehead. There are more lines on his face, but he's still got that smile. The crooked one with his eyebrows raised that says, *Maybe you'll regret this, but won't it be fun for a while?*

She doesn't flip through the book's pages. She doesn't think she can stand his narrative of that time. Detective Doug Frye working tirelessly to find the murderer of the Alpha Psi Theta sorority house victims. Not Detective Doug Frye sleeping with the best friend of the missing girl while he strung her along, assuring Bree that Abby's case would be solved, that he wouldn't give up just because higher-profile murders had happened.

A bright red sticker saying "Now a TV Series" sits on the cover's bottom right corner, and she carefully peels it off with her fingernail and sticks it over Blue's face before leaving the store.

Twenty-three days. That's how long they have to get answers. How hard is Frye working right now to get Jon Allan Blue to talk when he's doing interview after interview and walking the red carpet for that stupid TV show's premiere?

She cuts through Von Maur to leave the mall, so she can start the forty-five-minute drive back to her town. As she passes the junior's section, she watches a mother and preteen fight about jeans.

"What's wrong with them?" asks the mother, who doesn't look much older than Bree.

"They're ugly," the daughter says, looking at her phone rather than her mom.

Bree thinks about her own mother. She has no memories of her, but she keeps a photo of her in her bedroom. It's always the first thing she unpacks in a new place—sort of a *fuck you* to all the people who considered her mother trash.

Someone, Bree's late father, probably, had taken the photo when Bree was about two. In it, Bree was playing with a Barbie in the grass, clearly absorbed in whatever fantasy she had created. Her mother stares down at her, her long blond hair shining in the sun. She looks like a prettier version of Bree—her face heart-shaped instead of long, her nose smaller and more feminine, her cheekbones higher.

Whenever Bree looks at the picture, all she sees is someone staring at her with complete awe, as if her very existence, her ability to hold a big-titted plastic doll, was a fucking miracle. She knows only a few people will look at you like that in your life, and she's already lost one.

As she nears the shoe section, she sees the back of a mother and teenage son as they look at sneakers. She wonders what it would be like to have a son, maybe one who's sweet and a little dumb. Like the golden retriever of sons. She sees boys like that in her classes—boys who smile a lot and carry milk jugs full of water and talk about what their coach said to them. They listen to what Bree says about their photographs, their brows furrowed, heads tilted. They turn in work on time, and their faces crack into relieved smiles when they receive Cs on assignments.

She does not want a daughter. Who would want a daughter? Sometimes Bree's female students scare her. They scare her most when they carry themselves with self-assurance, because these are the girls who don't even know enough to be afraid. Bree watches those girls in her classroom and wonders, *What will the world take from them?*

The mother bends low toward the pristine white leather of a pair of Nikes, gesturing to the son. It isn't until Bree gets closer that she clocks the resemblance, at least from behind, to Zach. The same almost six-foot frame with broad shoulders. The same sandy hair that's long on top and shorter on the sides.

It's when she notices the little raspberry-shaped birthmark on the back of his neck that she realizes this person doesn't just *look* like Zach, this person *is* Zach. Zach and his mother turn around, and he sees Bree, too. His first instinct, when seeing her, God bless him, is to smile. But then he clearly remembers his mother beside him, and his features cloud into something watchful and worried.

Bree says nothing. He says nothing. His mother doesn't even notice Bree and says, "I think the black wouldn't show dirt as quickly, honey."

Zach's mother looks like him. They have the same square jaw and low hairline. Her hair is flat with highlights that are growing out. She's one of those women whose foundation is a little too dark, contrasting against her pale neck. She's probably not even ten years older than Bree.

With horror, Bree realizes she and Zach's mother have the same purse, a slouchy, faux-leather shoulder bag Bree bought at Target a couple years ago. There's something painful in picturing them both looking at that purse and thinking the same thing. No one would ever confuse it for a fancy bag, but for a Midwestern woman on a budget, this was probably the best they were going to get.

So many times, Bree said to other professors over beers, "Who would ever sleep with a student? They're children." And she meant it. They were young and dumb, and did she mention *young*? She knew several professors, all male, who had married former students.

She *would never* cross that line, she told herself.

And then, one day, she had.

Who could this hurt? Bree asked herself the morning after she and Zach slept together for the first time.

Zach gives Bree one final smile over his shoulder, before

following his mother toward the clearance shoe racks. Bree watches him go, the plastic bag with the pregnancy test wrapped around her wrist.

———————

After Bree pees on the pregnancy test, she leaves it alone in the bathroom, shutting the door behind her as if she can keep it separate from the rest of her life. She sits on her couch and sets a timer for three minutes.

Bree's phone vibrates soon after, but it isn't the timer for the pregnancy test. It's a text from Zach.

That was crazy! Why were u in my hometown? i'll be back on campus tmrw. miss u

She stares at that "u." She pictures Zach's lean body, the swell of his bicep under her palm. She thinks about the first time she blew him. Afterward, he looked at her like she was an angel.

"Thank you," he said, like the polite Midwestern boy he was.

Where is he right now? Is he still at home, sitting next to his parents on the couch, watching football, a bowl of his mom's homemade chili on his lap?

She has another minute on the timer, so she opens a social media app on her phone. There's a notification that Chelsea liked one of her photos late last night. But when Bree goes to the picture, a photo of Bree in grad school wearing overalls and drinking a beer on her front porch, Chelsea isn't in the list of names who have liked it.

She pictures Chelsea doing a deep dive into her social media, going all the way back to Bree's grad school days. She can see it—maybe Chelsea still drinks too much like she used to, and a clumsy finger hit the heart by the photo before realizing what she had done and undoing it.

Bree has done many a messy, late-night, embarrassing deep dive, because she is—she thinks—messy and embarrassing. But Chelsea? Chelsea the wholesome, put-together priest? There's something oddly moving as Bree pictures Chelsea paging through her old posts.

Bree pulls up Chelsea's social media. She has done it so many times that these photos—pictures of events she didn't attend with people she doesn't know—seem familiar. She has analyzed them as intensely as the work of her favorite photographers.

Photos of Chelsea and her carpenter husband (not Jesus, an actual carpenter) sitting on an IKEA couch with a sleek black cat between them. Caption: *Look at this queen.* Photos of pages of the *Book of Common Prayer* with excerpts underlined in faint pencil or highlighted a bright lemon. Captions: *Such grace.* Or: *One of my favorite verses.* Or, just a heart-eyes emoji.

Nightly cups of herbal tea with her bright-eyed, smiling husband, screenshots of Chelsea's phone alarm set for 5:00 a.m. with prayer hands and cross emojis and the caption *Through Him all things are possible—even making me a morning person.*

Although they stopped speaking, Bree has not stopped living out parts of Chelsea's daily life with her: watching her in seminary in Sewanee, Tennessee, swimming under waterfalls and sitting at a kitchen table stacked high with books on Greek and Latin. A video of her walking across the University of the South's green lawn. When Chelsea was the seminarian at a church in Iowa, Bree watched her sermons on YouTube. It was jarring hearing that deep, rich voice from her teenage years talking about

Lazarus rising from the dead instead of reading the dirtiest parts of *Cosmopolitan* magazine aloud.

The Chelsea Bree knew was honest to a fault—so blunt that sometimes Abby would scold her. "Chelsea," she'd say, like she was admonishing a dog. And Chelsea would always reply the same way: a shrug of the shoulders and a muttered "What? It's the truth."

But everything Chelsea posts to social media has this fake tinge that irks Bree.

In their years apart, Chelsea still shaped Bree's life. She was the reason Bree applied for grad school and left her boring office job. She was the reason Bree read certain books or tried cooking certain foods. Chelsea seems okay despite everything that has happened, and Bree can't help but look at her as a map to that okayness—even though she's skeptical of it, even though she resents the fuck out it, even though she thinks, *I thought we agreed to be broken together.*

When the timer for the pregnancy test chimes, she's pulled back to the present. It seems right that she's still thinking about Chelsea. When she was a senior in high school and her period was three days late, Bree bought her first pregnancy test with Chelsea. She was too nervous to look at the results, so Chelsea did it for her, grimacing as she set the test down on the counter, her little nose scrunched. "Ew, I think I got your piss on my hand."

Bree silences the timer on her phone, walks to the bathroom, grabs the door handle, and wonders if her life is about to change.

———————

On Monday, she sits in her office with her head in her hands.

"Professor Hadley," a male voice says. "Are you okay?"

It's Zach, standing in her doorway. His expression is equal parts concerned and hopeful. No doubt he's hoping she'll lock her door and fuck him on her desk.

She just finished a meeting with her chair, Marianne, a ceramicist who says her vases are Marxist critiques of imperialism, although they just look squat and misshapen to Bree. Marianne talked with Bree about the best way she could position herself in her tenure dossier. It was generous of Marianne to even take the time to help, but while she encouraged Bree to get more exhibitions and publications, all Bree could think about was the pregnancy test's treacherous second line, the smug way it appeared so distinctly, as if it didn't want to leave her any hope of ambiguity.

Before they parted, Marianne commended Bree on her teaching, saying, "The students *love* you."

Oh, if you only knew, Marianne, Bree thinks. *Professor Hadley. Really living out the college's mission of engaging students through hands-on pedagogy.*

Fuck.

Zach is still staring at her. She can't stand to look at him right now. His eager face. His boyish smile.

Once, they were watching a Hawkeye game together. The quarterback made a long pass to the tight end, who ran it into the end zone. Bree looked over and saw Zach's expression—his lips parted, his face cracked open in a smile, eyes wide. He looked so innocent, so gleeful, so fucking *young.*

How has she messed up this badly?

Bree tells Zach she has to get on a conference call, smelling his cheap body spray and the tea tree oil he uses for the pimples on his chin. His face falls as she shoos him away.

When she tries to shut her door, he says, "Wait, are we okay?" He looks so concerned her heart pangs.

"We're fine," she tells him. "I've just got to take this call."

Once she's safely back in her office with the door shut, she starts searching abortion providers online.

Beside the paternity issue, there are innumerable reasons to get an abortion: her student loans and pitiful bank balance. Her selfish lifestyle. But even before she took the pregnancy test, sometimes when she drives forty-five minutes to the nearest Target, she'll walk through the baby aisles, touching the tiny white socks as soft as lamb's wool. The little bibs, the terry cloth rattles—everything soft and pastel.

She's surprised at the thought going through her mind right now: *I wish I deserved this.*

———

As Bree leaves the art building, her phone vibrates. It's an unfamiliar number from an Iowa City area code. She assumes it's a Hillary Clinton phone banker and hits Ignore, walking across the lawn in the fall sunlight, passing a group of girls who have gathered around another girl's phone, gesturing to the screen and laughing.

When her phone vibrates again a minute later, Bree plays the voicemail. The message starts, and she hears his voice for the first time in a decade.

"Hi, Bree," Frye says. He doesn't use any of his former endearments: *baby girl, kiddo, sweet one.*

"I know it's been a long time," he says. "I'm sorry to call out of the blue." At first, she mishears, thinks he's saying, *I'm sorry to call about Blue.* He goes on: "Could you call me when you have a chance?"

Frye pauses long enough Bree thinks the voicemail's over, but then he clears his throat, his words rising above the sound of the girls laughing on the lawn.

"Bree, it's about Abby."

CHELSEA

OCTOBER 2015

A few days after the bonfire, Chelsea sits in her office in the upper level of the parish hall. Outside her window, it's growing dark. She knows she should wrap up—Daniel often complains how late she arrives home on weeknights—but there's always another email to respond to, another parishioner who needs something, another committee meeting to attend, or question to answer. Today alone she counseled an elderly widow with a terminal cancer diagnosis, finished a fundraising plan for a new HVAC system, mediated a heated dispute about the types of creamers that should be provided at coffee hour, and met with the head of a women's shelter about how the church could help.

Normally, that would be a light day, but she's been tense. On her drive to the church, Terry Gross had Ryan Worth on NPR.

"What was it like to play Jon Allan Blue?" she asked him.

"It was important to me not to glamourize him," Worth said, before Chelsea changed the station. Not to glamorize him? She unwittingly caught part of the series' latest trailer, and they had Worth as Blue driving a Mustang as police cruisers chased him down a country road, gravel dust kicking up behind him, while he wore Wayfarer sunglasses and an indie rock cover of "Sympathy for the Devil" plays.

Would having someone tell Abby's story make this any easier to bear? Jason emailed her the podcast host's contact information, and it sits in her inbox between an ad from the vestment company where she last bought altar robes and a complaint from a parishioner that there weren't enough vegetarian dishes at the church potluck.

She turns off the lights and locks the parish hall before walking next door to the sanctuary. It smells like the incense from Sunday's service and the old wood of the pews. Crossing herself, she steps into a row and pulls down the velvet kneeler. She clasps her hands on the back of the pew in front of her.

Since she'd grown up Catholic, so many of the Episcopal Church's rituals were already familiar to her when she went to her first service in her early twenties. At first, she thought of it as Catholic without the hang-ups—all the beautiful ritual, none of the weird denouncing of gay people or not letting women be priests. Of course, over time, it became more to her than just a palatable form of her childhood religion.

She kneels with her eyes closed, hands still clasped. Since she was young, she has always felt a warm, crystalline connection with something larger than herself. Even in those messy, angry years immediately following Abby's disappearance, she at least had that. But lately, whenever she tries to pray, it feels like she's holding a telephone to her ear and no one is on the other end.

The sanctuary doors creak open and then slam shut. Chelsea's heart flutters—people who come into a church unannounced, especially at night, are often desperate. She has care packages in her office for just this purpose—with bus passes and phone cards, clean socks, and granola bars—but she's conscious that she's a five-foot-nothing woman alone in the building.

Before she stands, she makes sure her fingers can reach the pepper spray on her key chain. She knows she seems paranoid and overly fearful to some people, but they have no idea how terrifying it was in her early college years. Every girl had been scared shitless. The police put on free self-defense trainings. The teacher made them call him "Coach." He used Abby and the Alpha Psi Theta girls as examples.

"We're not going to let you end up like them," Coach said. "We're going to give you a fighting chance."

As if it were their fault. As if all Abby needed was Coach's training and she would still be alive.

Chelsea rises and turns around, heart still pounding, and finds herself facing a fourteen-year-old girl with dimples, pink hair, and a septum piercing. It's only Elly, one of her younger parishioners. Unlike parents of the other youth in the congregation, Elly's parents don't attend church. Chelsea isn't sure if they attend somewhere else or what they think of Elly attending.

As Chelsea walks closer to where Elly stands at the back of the sanctuary, she realizes the girl's face is slick and puffy from tears.

"What's wrong?" Chelsea asks.

"My mom isn't so happy with me right now."

Chelsea gestures for her to sit in the nearest pew. After Elly plops down, Chelsea sits next to her.

"I told her I had a girlfriend," Elly says, meeting Chelsea's eyes with something like defiance, almost as if she expects Chelsea to adopt the same attitude as her mother, even though there's a pride flag in the parish hall, and it's no secret the Episcopal Church is affirming of queer people.

Chelsea wants desperately to say the right things to her. She tells Elly that God loves her just as she is. She confirms she still feels safe at home. She tells her it was brave of her to do what she did.

"You could tell she just wished so much I'd take it back," Elly says, a fresh wave of tears brimming.

They sit together in silence for a while. Chelsea tries to pray, *Please help me say the right thing to this girl*, but no insight dawns on her. After a few minutes, she asks Elly how she's feeling now.

"It is what it is," she says, picking up her phone and tapping on its cracked screen. There is so much world-weariness to her, so much would-be-brave faux disinterest.

"I understand how hard it can be when people aren't accepting," Chelsea says.

Elly's head snaps up. Her expression reminds Chelsea that, although she's always been sweet and easygoing, Elly is still a teenager. She meets Chelsea's gaze, and her face is as cool and dismissive as only a fourteen-year-old girl's can be.

"Well, you can't *really* understand," she says. "I mean, you're straight."

In moments like this, Chelsea has thought about saying, *No, I'm bisexual*. But somehow, it never feels right. How can she share that when her only reference point with women is a secret she vowed never to tell? In some ways, it seems like an appropriate penance. Chelsea pushed Abby so hard to tell people all those years ago, and she shouldn't have. It wasn't her place.

Still, there's something lonely in nodding to Elly and saying, "You're right. I can't understand."

———————

After Elly goes home, Chelsea walks back to her office and opens the email from Jason again. *Rachel Morgan*, it says, and then there's a phone number with a New York City area code and an email address.

Chelsea doesn't listen to true crime for obvious reasons, but the podcast is big enough she's absorbed some details through osmosis. Each season, Rachel, *Infamous's* capable host, chooses one notorious crime to dig into and shares lesser-known but compelling stories related to it. The show's tagline is *The crimes you know, the stories you don't.*

The other seminarians talked about *Infamous* back when it started airing. The first season was about that young pregnant woman on the West Coast who was murdered by her husband in the early 2000s. Chelsea remembers watching the original news coverage of the crime in Abby's living room as they drank sweating cans of Mtn Dew they placed on coasters to avoid damaging Mrs. Hartmann's perfect Ethan Allen furniture set. Abby's house had high ceilings, white carpets that still had vacuum lines on them, and gleaming bathroom sinks the Hartmanns' cleaning woman kept free of toothpaste spots or coils of loose hair.

They had been seniors in high school, and the woman's disappearance seemed sad, of course, but it hadn't seemed real. She was married, pregnant, and twenty-seven years old. She felt too remote, too far from their lives as teenagers, to hit close to home. And as soon as a case was big enough to be on TV like that, with

Linda Joy's hamster face spouting half-baked theories on cable news, it became larger than itself, a caricature. Something too circusy for Chelsea to feel any real emotion about.

Of course, a few months later, when it was Abby who Linda Joy was hypothesizing about, when she was calling Bree and Chelsea "reckless girls and worse friends" on her show, it all felt different.

Googling Rachel Morgan, Chelsea sees photos of a woman near her age with thick, brown hair and hazel eyes behind cat-eye glasses. A scar snakes from her upper lip to her cheek. It's this scar that stops Chelsea. How did she get it? What does she know of violence?

She plays the first episode of the first season. Listening to Rachel's voice is like taking a Xanax, so rich and soothing, with that hint of a lisp. When Rachel interviews the murdered woman's mother, Chelsea pauses it. It's obvious from the woman's cracking voice that she's trying not to cry.

Maybe it's a bad idea to reach out to this person. Daniel would say it is. True crime never did anything but make things worse in the past. It tarnished Abby's memory further and severed Chelsea and Bree's friendship. But watching Blue become some weird celebrity in the weeks leading up to his execution is unbearable.

Chelsea pulls up Twitter and searches his name. Some of the tweets are about the soon-to-be-released TV show, but it doesn't take long before she finds them. The women who mail Blue love letters and lacy underwear. The women who tweet that he just needs someone who understands him. Girls—not even women, many of them—who tweet about how much they want to fuck him.

She teaches her confirmation students that prayer isn't meant to change God but to change the self, so she prays for guidance. Even though she doesn't feel anything, after a moment, she opens a new message and types in the podcast host's email address.

———————

When they moved into the run-down Victorian they're trying to renovate, Chelsea hung pictures of Mary everywhere—little wooden Greek icons on the windowsills, Mary wearing rich, jewel-toned cloaks, her sober face holding the infant Jesus, their cheeks touching. A painting of Our Lady of Montserrat that Chelsea inherited from her grandmother, Mary's and Jesus's skin dark, golden halos around their heads.

Chelsea always felt she could go to Mary even if God or Jesus felt too distant, too divine, or, honestly, too male. Despite her connection to Mary, though, it's Daniel who understands how to care for things, how to nurture.

It's Daniel who walks around with a small red watering can to tend to each of the plants, mixing eggshells and coffee grounds to fertilize the soil. It's Daniel who cooks their meals with such care and bakes the bread Chelsea's church uses for communion. It's Daniel who strips thick layers of white chipping paint off the antique wood doors. He's the one who makes sure Pippa's water is fresh. He's the one who repaired and refinished the stairs, taking something broken and making it new and sturdy.

While Chelsea sits at her desk in the corner of the living room, it's Daniel who putters around the kitchen making lentil soup as freezing rain hits the windowpanes. In moments like this, it's impossible for Chelsea to picture being without him. The sky outside is dark, she has an inbox full of parishioners' complaints and needs, and it's hard for her to imagine how bleak the world would feel if she were all alone without his comforting presence.

When he kisses her goodbye to go to the carpentry shop for the rest of the afternoon, she feels a pang of guilt for not telling him about the podcast. She tells herself that, once she knows if it's even a possibility, she'll talk to him about it.

When they first met, while Chelsea was in seminary, she was drawn to how safe Daniel felt. At their wedding, one of his vows was something like "I'll tend to your heart." And he always has. He's patient, and she has never worried about him hurting her. She knew from the moment Daniel first kissed her, he would never cheat on her, never make her doubt herself, never make her worry.

In her inbox, an email appears from an older, male parishioner. *Some Thoughts about Your Most Recent Sermon*, the subject line says. Chelsea will save that one until she's taken a Klonopin.

Her phone vibrates on her desk, a New York City number appearing on the screen. As she stands and answers, her heart beats fast. Rachel Morgan sounds different than she does on the podcast—her voice isn't as gentle, and she talks faster. Rachel asks about the weather in Iowa. They make polite small talk before Rachel clears her throat.

"I was interested in the articles I found about you visiting Jon Allan Blue."

Chelsea pictures her studying the article on *Jezebel*, Chelsea's teeth photoshopped as white as her priest's collar. She still remembers the opening line: *When Chelsea Navarro went to death row to visit the man she believed murdered her best friend, it wasn't to rage at him—it was to pray with him.*

Despite what the article said, Chelsea hadn't gone to pray with him or to forgive him. But afterward, when the reporter asked Chelsea why she wanted to pray with him, Chelsea hadn't corrected her. The actual experience had been such a letdown, and her real reason for going had been pitiful. She saw how the story of a young priest sitting across from the man who hurt her friend, praying with him, could help people.

Radical Forgiveness, the headlines read. There were interviews. A literary agent emailed to ask if Chelsea had thought about writing a memoir. And finally, a feature article in *Christianity Today*.

She met a lot of influential people in the church because of that article. She received invitations to retreats and conferences to speak about forgiveness. And one of the organizers at one of the conferences was on the search committee for the position Chelsea currently holds. What does it say that so much of her current life is thanks to a lie? Is that why that warm, crystalline connection she's always had with God feels so blocked and cold lately?

"That was a long time ago," Chelsea tells Rachel.

"A few years ago." There's silence for a moment. "Can I be honest with you, Chelsea?"

"Sure."

"I'm considering Jon Allan Blue for the third season, but I worry he's becoming a little overexposed."

Overexposed. Like Blue is a young Hollywood starlet who shows potential but has bad management.

She's seen this happen with other crimes. Suddenly, it's in the zeitgeist. Suddenly, it's everywhere. Detective fucking Frye and his goddamn book kicking it off. That stupid TV show trailer following. Blue's upcoming execution feeding the fire.

"If I were to do a season about Blue, I'd want to find stories people haven't heard," Rachel says. "So, what haven't I heard? What was your friend's story? And why would my show's listeners be interested in it?"

It's odd conceptualizing how to pitch Abby's short life. What makes someone's life captivating enough for attention?

Maybe sensing her inability to answer the question, Rachel rephrases it: "Who was she to you?"

I loved her, she broke my fucking heart, he killed her, and she's haunted me ever since, Chelsea wants to say. But she doesn't. She can't.

Instead, some platitudes come out of her mouth about friendship, and by the time she finishes talking, she's almost as bored as Rachel clearly is.

"I'll think about it," Rachel says, but it's obvious from her tone that the answer is no.

After she sets her phone down, Chelsea stares at a large painting of a very Aryan-looking Mary she bought at Goodwill and hung to hide some of the living room wall's cracked plaster. Mary's pale hand touches her chest, the immaculate heart rimmed in fire, her veil matching the blue of her eyes.

More than anything, Chelsea wants Abby remembered as something more than just a name in an article about Jon Allan Blue. But she doesn't know how to wrestle with the story of her relationship with Abby. Every time, it's a mindfuck. Every time, she can't figure out if the things she omits obscure a truth or highlight it.

When Chelsea was twenty, she tried therapy. He was a student in the university's psychology PhD program. For the first two sessions, they talked about her drinking and drug use, which had steadily increased in the weeks and months after Abby's disappearance. They met in an old classroom. He'd put a couple area rugs over the industrial tile and written inspirational messages on the chalkboard. *What if it all works out okay? Today can be different.* He kept the harsh overhead fluorescents off, but the two table lamps didn't provide enough light, and every time, Chelsea squinted at him in the dim room.

During the third session, after he asked when her drug use started, she told him about Abby. At first, she told him what she told everyone—Abby was her best friend, and it was indescribable to lose someone like that so abruptly. She explained that sometimes, even two years later, it was hard to believe Abby was actually gone. She had been so vibrant, so distinct. It felt impossible she could really be absent from this earth. Sometimes, late at night, she'd talk to her, asking, *Can you hear me?* What she was really asking was *Where do people go when they die? Where did* you *go?*

And then, when there were about ten minutes left in their session, in a breathless rush, she said all the things she never said.

When she was done, the young therapist stared at her for a long time. Finally, he spoke about survivor's guilt and complex grief. And then, after staring into one of the room's dark corners for a moment, he said, "In college, people experiment with their sexuality all the time. It's very common. It's nothing for you to be worried about, and it's not anything you need to define your identity around."

"She never wanted people to know," Chelsea said. "I think she realized being with me wasn't what she wanted."

It seemed important to tell him that. To say aloud the thing she most feared was true.

"She was probably just experimenting too," he said, nodding. "It's fine to hold on to the friendship you shared and let the rest go."

Chelsea followed that man's advice. It made sense to compartmentalize that part of their relationship. And as time passed, it began to feel very *If a tree falls in a forest…*

If two best friends have sex but never tell anyone and then suddenly you're the only person left alive who knows, did it really even happen? As the years went on, in many ways, it felt like it hadn't. Abby never wanted anyone to know. Maybe for her, it had been a phase, an experiment. Nothing that mattered in any real way.

Except Chelsea still remembers how she felt when Abby walked into a room—like there were bubbles popping in her chest. She remembers how she'd actually get weak in the knees when they kissed, even though she thought it was something that only happened in the romance novels her mother read.

In the twelve years since Abby, she has dated a couple men and fallen in love with one. But nothing, in all those years, has ever felt anywhere close to what she felt with Abby. She tells herself this is just because she was her first love. Of course, she'd have heightened feelings for her. Her feelings for Daniel are quieter simply because it's an adult relationship that isn't tinged with tragedy. Sometimes she believes this. Other times, she's not so sure.

ABBY

SEPTEMBER 2003

You're distracted during your next acting class as you sit on the hardwood floor next to Bree and the other students while Jay paces in front of everyone, talking about authenticity and vulnerability.

Ever since your conversation with Chelsea when she asked you to tell people about your relationship, she's been distant. You can't entirely blame her, but how can she be so sure about everything? Isn't it normal to think women's bodies are more beautiful than men's? Almost every time you go to a bar, you see two girls kissing. So how is what you and Chelsea do different? Are you both certain enough of what it means to blow up your lives?

"Abby?"

"Sorry," you tell Jay. "What did you say?"

"I asked if you'd ever done heartsharing."

You shake your head, and he explains "heartsharing" is a practice he first did during rehearsals for a community theater production of *Grease* in Des Moines.

"It was *invaluable*," he says.

You and your classmates will sit in a circle. One by one,

students will take turns sitting inside the circle, answering questions posed from those surrounding them.

"No question is off limits," Jay says. "Each question must be answered honestly."

"So, this is like half of Truth or Dare?" you ask.

"This is about cultivating honesty, Abby," he says, his tone even. "The best acting comes from honesty."

Jay explains that heartsharing only ends after ten minutes or when someone starts to cry, whichever comes first.

A snub-nosed girl named Ashley volunteers to go right away, scooting into the middle of the circle. There's an awkward pause as people look to Jay, uncertain of what to do next.

Ashley went to high school in a small town with your RA. One afternoon, you and she were eating in the cafeteria, and she saw you wave at Ashley. After Ashley passed by, your RA told you Ashley was infamous at their high school. As a freshman, she apparently got drunk at a party and blew a bunch of guys in a hot tub.

"The guys passed her around," your RA said when she relayed the story. For some reason, you've never been able to get that phrasing out of your head. *Passed her around.* Like she was a bag of chips.

You're not a prude—you're certainly no virgin—but there's something distasteful about letting yourself become a spectacle like she did. If you want to blow a bunch of guys in the same night, okay, but have some self-respect. Don't let yourself become a story—a cautionary tale people keep repeating.

Jay gestures for people to ask questions. They're innocuous at first—hometown (Weaver, Iowa), favorite hobbies (eating cheese, watching reality TV). It's clear she's delighted to have Jay's full attention. You can't blame her. You love attention, too. For senior superlatives, you won "Most Likely to Become Famous" and were nominated for "Biggest Flirt."

Then Jay asks what the worst thing that ever happened to her was. She hunches her shoulders, eyes lowering as she picks at the fraying hem of her jean skirt. A lot of people in class, you included, are in sweatpants, but Ashley dresses more carefully. And something about that, for reasons you can't understand, breaks your heart.

Then she's talking: about a party at a friend's house when she was fourteen, the smell of Hawaiian Punch and Everclear. She pauses for a few seconds, and Jay prompts her. "What happened next?"

He keeps prodding her like that, murmuring those words, every time she pauses from sharing the details: the chlorine from the hot tub burning her eyes; her gagging under the water; someone holding her tightly even when she tried to thrash free.

It isn't just Ashley's words that uncork something in you—it's something under the words. There's something so devastatingly sad and completely matter of fact in the way she tells this story.

"What happened next?"

Jay's expression is hawk-like as he keeps urging her along, making you even more upset. Why should he be allowed access to something so personal? But of course, it isn't just that. It's shame—thick and hot at the back of your throat. You judged Ashley like a total asshole.

Soon her ten minutes are over. Jay gives her his hand to help her rise from the center of the circle and go back to her seat among the rest of you.

"As actors we have to fully feel the most intense emotions from our lives," he says. "It's our bank. The stock we'll pull from on stage. It gives us the power to create from."

Everyone around you nods dutifully, eyes wide. You shift your weight, biting your lip. You can understand his point, but something about his eagerness, his urgency as he pressed Ashley, unnerved you.

"We have time for one more today," he says. His eyes roam over the group. *Not me*, you think. *Please.* But his gaze has already landed. He points at you, before crooking his finger toward the center of the circle.

Instead of scooting on your butt like Ashley did, you stand and walk into the circle, hesitating before you sit. It's awkward because, no matter what, you'll have your back to someone. You face Jay, his blue eyes boring into yours, and play with your brace-let. It was a gift from your mother for your sixteenth birthday. Although it's pretty, the thick links of the chain and the sterling silver charm are heavy against the skin of your wrist.

Bree sits next to Jay, and she flashes a supportive smile. You take a deep breath, but somehow it makes you more nervous. You know you can lie—make up some bullshit answers to whatever questions people ask. But, as you sit cross-legged with your class-mates appraising you, you know lying would make this an unfair fight. You want to answer honestly. You want to show you can look at your own tough shit and it won't break you.

With Ashley's heartshare, Jay let the other students ask the ini-tial questions. This time, though, he launches right in.

"Tell us about a time you were ashamed."

It comes to you immediately. A hot and sticky summer when you were seven or eight. You and another neighbor girl, Tori, used to play soap opera, taking off your cutoffs and dingy sneak-ers and climbing into bed naked. Warm skin against warm skin,

Tori smelling of soap, sweat, and grass, her square face framed by blond bobbed hair. Her knees always scabbed from falling off her bike.

You were kids, and it hadn't meant anything, but one afternoon your mother walked into the room as Tori took off her shorts.

You were already sitting naked on the bed, waiting for the moment when she would crush herself against you and say, "Baby, you're beautiful," like the actors on *Days of Our Lives*. Sometimes, she would put her fingers inside you—what Tori's older brother called third base—and it felt strange but exciting, like traveling someplace completely new.

Your mother paused in the doorway, her face all the scarier because it was expressionless.

"Put your clothes on, both of you," she said. "Then, Tori, you get out of our house."

Tori's lip trembled as she pulled her shorts up her skinny legs. When your father returned, your mother made you tell him what happened. He set his car keys on the counter, the lines in his forehead pronounced as he watched your face.

You could only get out the words, "Tori and I," before you began to sob and couldn't continue. You were so ashamed you dropped to the kitchen floor, your thin arms wrapped around your grass-stained knees, your head tucked against the warmth of your body. You pretended you were one of the pill bugs you and Tori used to poke until they curled into tiny, hard balls. You refused to move from that position until hours later, after your parents went to the den to watch TV. Once the kitchen was dark, you rose from the floor, your neck and arms sore, and got into bed. You and your parents never talked about it again.

Jay stares at you intently with his off-brand kind of handsome. No. You won't go there. You can't give him this. Instead, you tell him about being a freshman in high school. About being picked to be "the lamb."

Every year, a group of senior guys would pick a freshman girl and spend the day saying horrible—usually sexual—things to her until she finally cried. In past years, the lambs cried by third period, but you refused to. When Lee Chambers told you he wanted to titty fuck you and cum on your chin, you acted like you hadn't heard him. No matter what they said, you didn't cry.

At the end of the day, the guys offered to share a flask with you in the parking lot, but you ignored them.

"You were so cool about everything," one boy said, as if this had been some fun game you were all in on. "You're, like, Queen of the Lambs."

The guys pushed through the school's front doors into the August heat. You went into the musty, puke-green bathroom off the gym hallway. Safely locked in a stall, you cried until your stomach ached.

When you're done telling the story, your classmates look at Jay to see what he'll make of it.

He steeples his fingers under his chin and surveys you. "I don't think this is actually a memory where you were ashamed. I think it's an upsetting memory for you, but I don't think you're being totally vulnerable with us."

"This is what came to mind first," you say, although, of course, that's a lie.

"Fine," Jay says, sounding both disappointed and resigned. "Tell us each of the insults you remember from that day."

"I was a whore or a slut. They shouted all the things they wanted to do to me."

"Like what?"

"I mean, they weren't all that creative. It was all about sticking things in different holes."

"Do you think you're a slut?" Jay asks. He enunciates the word, the "t" at the end hard, so spittle flecks the air.

You've slept with six guys. In your senior yearbook, if you look at the four couples nominated for "Best Couple," you slept with three of those guys while they were dating the smiling girls they posed with in the glossy yearbook spread. Some people would call you a slut. Some people have. But you've never thought of yourself that way. You're just looking for something.

"Maybe," you say.

"Yes or no?" he says.

"I don't know."

"Are you purposely holding back from us, or do *you* not even know who you are?"

He's staring at you with that unblinking gaze, but there's a dismissiveness in his expression you haven't seen before, one edge of his mouth curled in disdain. Your face feels hot.

"What do you most want to hide right now?" he asks, leaning forward. "What do you *most* not want to talk about in this circle?"

Of course, it's Chelsea. How hard it is to stop thinking about her. How confusing it is.

"I don't know," you tell Jay.

"Why are you holding back?" he asks. Tears prick your eyes.

When you were ten, your mom got a bad haircut. It was much shorter than she wanted, almost like a bowl cut. You remember her standing next to you in the bathroom, surveying her hair.

"I look like a *dyke*," she said. You'll never forget how she said that word. She spit it out like Jay spit out the word *slut*. You hadn't known what it meant, but you knew it was bad.

"What are you holding back?" Jay asks again as tears stream down your face.

There was a girl in your high school who came out as gay. Jenny. You sat together in comparative lit, and you liked her so much. She made you mixtapes full of Hole and Bikini Kill while you made her ones with Britney Spears and P!nk on them, and that made her laugh. One day, during spirit week, you showed up wearing black fishnets. She told you that you looked sexy, and it was like someone lit a candle in your chest.

"If I could, I'd dress this way every day," you told her.

"Why can't you?" she asked.

Then, one class, without thinking, you called something "gay." It was just a thing everyone said. Another word for stupid. But Jenny's face was like a hand closing into a fist. There were no more mixtapes after that.

"Why are you holding back?" Jay asks again.

"I don't know," you say. You're openly crying now, your face hot, tears dripping down your chin.

This thing with Chelsea. You know there's something wrong with it, because it's normal to kiss girls and touch girls in front of guys for attention. But you and she do it secretly. You do it just for the two of you. That's how you know this is something you're going to have to reckon with.

You know you'll lose her if you don't tell people about your relationship. You can feel her pulling away. She always felt like a steady presence in your life, but now you see how fragile everything between you is. How easily it could be crushed. But you cannot imagine telling your mother. You cannot imagine standing in front of her and totally destroying the daughter she wants you to be.

The tears keep coming, and you don't bother wiping them away. You let them run down your face. Jay scoots forward and taps your sternum with his knuckle.

"This," he says, "is power. Whatever you're thinking about right now, whatever you don't want to share with us, it's the source of your power as a creator."

He scoots back from you and gives you a nod and a pleased little smile that makes you want to light him on fire. He gestures for you to leave the circle.

After class, as you grab your backpack, Jay says, "Vulnerability and honesty are a practice. It gets easier as you continue doing it."

You nod, but you want to know how willing he is to practice what he preaches. "What are you most ashamed of?"

"My father was a drunk," he says without hesitation. "He used to throw my mom around."

"I'm sorry," you say, slinging your backpack over your shoulder. You picture an ornate, gothic church inside Jay. One built, stone by stone, from the pain his father caused. Now he escapes there still, lighting candles and praying inside it, stewarding it and keeping it in pristine shape.

When you get back to your dorm after class, you feel both embarrassed and ashamed. You're ashamed Ashley could tell such a horrific story and be so vulnerable, and you couldn't even talk about Chelsea. You're embarrassed because Jay knew you were holding back. How did he know?

The dorm room phone rings, but when you answer, no one says anything. You twist the cord around your finger, annoyed, saying hello again. That's when the breathing starts.

It's a man panting, giving the heavy, strained breathing of someone exercising or jacking off. He blows static into the phone at certain moments when his breath hits the mouthpiece directly. You slam the receiver onto the cradle.

In high school, upperclassmen prank called you a lot, especially after being "the lamb." You know guys do creepy stuff like this or worse. When you, Bree, and Chelsea were sixteen, an old guy in the mall's food court pulled his dick out under his table and masturbated while staring at the three of you.

Still, it's only been a couple days since you saw that missing girl's face on the cover of the newspaper, so you lock your dorm room door and close the blinds. A few minutes later, the phone rings again, but you don't pick up. The answering machine message you and Chelsea recorded together switches on: *Hi, this is Abby. And Chelsea [laughter]. We're not here right now...*

The person hangs up.

Dinner that night in Burge cafeteria, or "Urge" as it reads now that vandals stole the "B," is a minefield. You fill a plate at the salad bar. From an article in *Cosmo,* you learned not to put the dressing on the salad. Instead, you should have it in a separate container and then dip the prongs of your fork into it before piercing each bite. Fewer calories.

Meanwhile, Bree, with her perfect metabolism, piles her plate high with greasy delights.

You stare at the curve of her breasts contrasted with the flatness of her stomach. If her shirt rode up a little more, it would reveal her belly button piercing. You and Bree got them together a few months ago, and when you watched her on the piercing table, you felt the same disappointment in your own body you feel now—your saggier breasts, the roll of fat around your belly.

Still, her more beautiful body never seems to get her anywhere. Unlike you, with your years of childhood ballet lessons and perfect posture, Bree's shoulders slope forward. When she talks, there's always a hesitation. Like she's looking for permission to speak.

"Bree is pretty, but she carries herself like she's not," Chelsea said once. "And that attracts a certain kind of guy. And not good ones."

Chelsea's pronouncement was true up until the beginning of college. After a streak of horrible boyfriends, Bree's dating someone who's actually nice.

Al sits next to Bree, eating a thick slice of pizza, the grease glistening on his fingers. Whereas Bree's other boyfriends were burnouts or somebody's creepy older brother who shouldn't have been dating a minor, Al's an art major who was valedictorian at his tiny high school.

He murmurs something to Bree that makes her laugh. She bumps him with her shoulder. Although her other boyfriends immediately picked up on her insecurities and learned how to use them to their advantage, you've never seen him be anything but kind to her. You've watched them in the lobby of the theater building, Al dropping by between his art classes, their heads bent together as she showed him photos she'd taken, his face cracked open in a big smile as he complimented her work.

Sometimes you feel the tiniest pang of jealousy watching them. It's not that you're attracted to him, but he's exactly the kind of boy someone's mom wants them to bring home. You can picture him sitting at your dining room table, your mom beaming, your dad actually present for once, talking with Al about the Hawkeyes' offensive line.

Bree swallows a mouthful of curly fries and asks if anyone saw the article in the campus paper about the body found in the woods outside Des Moines.

"It was that girl," Bree says. "The redhead who went missing. They found her head smashed in just like that girl from Sioux City."

"Stop," Chelsea says. "We're trying to eat here."

"Her hair was auburn," you say, and everyone looks at you. "You said red," you clarify.

Chelsea, who has heard you complain over the years about being called a redhead, rolls her eyes. "Not this again."

You open your mouth to try to explain—that poor smiling girl is dead and the least you all can do is get the color of her hair right—but Bree asks how you felt about your heartshare.

"Don't you think it's inappropriate for a teacher to expect us all to be honest and vulnerable about the darkest things in our lives?" you ask, stabbing a sad-looking piece of iceberg lettuce with your fork. "Isn't that weird?"

Chelsea swallows a bite of lasagna. "Don't get mad at your teacher because you're bad at being honest and vulnerable."

The two of you exchange a long look.

"That isn't fair," you say. She shrugs and continues eating.

"He sounds kind of weird," Al says. He meets your eyes, and you feel grateful someone gets it. He holds your gaze a little longer than expected, and you feel the satisfaction you always do when you get male attention. It's like wearing a skirt you look really good in that might be a size too small. Does it matter if it pinches a little?

Chelsea's quiet the rest of dinner. As you're walking back to the dorm, you ask her what's wrong.

"Do you have a crush on Al?" she asks.

"Of course not," you say. "He's dating Bree."

You pass a group of girls in high heels and miniskirts heading to the bars. Their perfumes mingle in a sweet cloud you can still smell even after they're several yards away.

"When the two of you are together, sometimes there's this dynamic you have that makes me jealous."

You're impressed how baldly Chelsea can admit to jealousy. You're constantly ashamed of your own and try to pretend it doesn't exist.

Instead of trying to convince Chelsea she has nothing to worry about, after a quick glance around to confirm no one's watching, you lean forward and kiss her.

The two of you kissed for the first time late fall your senior year of high school. You drove into the country in Chelsea's Honda Civic to watch a total lunar eclipse. Bree was probably somewhere with one of her terrible boyfriends.

It had been 30 degrees—winter hovering in the air—and you shivered while sitting on the hood of Chelsea's car, harvested cornfields covered in snow spanning both sides of you. While you watched the moon go bloodred, Chelsea put her arm around you. Eventually, you turned toward her, looking intently, as if you could see the eclipse in her face. Then you leaned forward and kissed her while the moon fell into shadow.

VARIETY MAGAZINE

"TV REVIEW: *MURDER IN THE MIDWEST*"

Serial killers are having a moment. With a boom in true crime shows, Midwestern murderer Jon Allan Blue is the latest to receive the small-screen treatment. While Blue hasn't had the notoriety of some killers—think Jeffrey Dahmer, John Wayne Gacy, or BTK—his upcoming execution and clean-cut good looks make him a compelling figure.

Following Blue's murders in the early aughts through his trial and sentencing, *Murder in the Midwest* is a twelve-episode limited series starring Disney alum Ryan Worth as the soon-to-be-executed serial killer. Worth's performance is startlingly good—showing range far beyond his heartthrob past. His boy-next-door handsomeness and obvious charisma make his portrayal of Blue even more chilling, contrasting the killer's life as a student and devoted boyfriend with the spree of horrific murders he committed across Nebraska, Iowa, and Kentucky.

Oscar nominee David Trader as Detective Doug Frye brings gravitas to the series, portraying an Iowa City detective trying to solve the murders of two college coeds bludgeoned in a sorority house. Much of the show's material comes from Frye's memoir of the investigation, *The Midwest Mangler: My Search for Jon Allan Blue*. By the time Frye can pin the murders on Blue, the killer has already fled the state, and much of the series follows various Midwestern police and FBI's quest to track Blue down.

The series's cinematography plays up Blue's hunting ground, with long, moody shots of cornfields, rusting farm machinery, and dilapidated barns, creating a tense and atmospheric show that keeps viewers on edge.

Blue, who was sentenced to death in Kentucky for the murder of twelve-year-old Erika Finch, is scheduled to be executed next month.

BREE

OCTOBER 2015

For the rest of her walk home, Frye's words thrum inside Bree. *It's about Abby. It's about Abby.*

Is this the news she's waited twelve years for? Is this the missing piece finally falling into place? She always thought it was what she wanted, the only thing she wanted, but now that she's faced with the possibility, she's scared. She wishes she had someone who could sit with her while she calls Frye back, someone's reassuring presence next to her.

It isn't that she doesn't have friends, she tells herself. She has friends. Well, she has people she's friendly with. She has some women from grad school she can email if she's having trouble with teaching or wants to commiserate about not winning a prize. But she sometimes sees in movies and on TV women who have close friends—people they can call whenever they need reassurance. She remembers what that was like.

She dials Frye's number. The phone rings and rings. It goes to voicemail—Frye saying his name and requesting she leave a message. The sound of his voice brings it back. She thought she loved him. Maybe she had. Who could untangle it—the trauma and the grief and the fact that he was the man who was supposed to solve it all?

"God dammit," she says, throwing her phone across the room, where it slides across the rental's beige carpeting, coming to rest in front of her bookshelf.

Frye does not call Bree back that night or the next morning. That afternoon in her intro to photography class, she keeps checking her phone. The classroom is dim while her students stare at the screen: a close-up of a woman's face, eyes closed, dark hair tied back, ears sticking out, a line of pale skin visible from her center part. Her full lips stay expressionless as blood pours from her scalp.

Bree is showing them clips of Ana Mendieta's work. A dozen years ago, Bree sat in a classroom like this the semester after Abby's death and learned how Mendieta, a graduate student at Iowa in the '70s, became obsessed with the rape and murder of a girl on campus, Sarah Ann Ottens. Bree's always careful to say Ottens's name when she teaches about Mendieta. She never leaves Ottens nameless or omits her existence entirely. It was that murder, Sarah Ann Ottens's bloody, battered body found in her dorm room in Rienow Hall, that spurred Mendieta to make some of Bree's favorite pieces of art.

The screen shows a different clip now, filmed with a Super 8 camera in downtown Iowa City. Mendieta smeared blood and entrails, bought from a local butcher, across her apartment's doorstep before filming people's reactions. They walk by, looking down at the blood and guts, occasionally pausing for a moment, perplexed. But no one stops to knock on the door where the bloody trail leads. They crane their necks to look at the carnage, but no one is willing to do anything about it.

The piece Bree most wants to show her students fills the screen now. It's called "Rape Scene." Mendieta invited fellow art students and her professor to her apartment. Before they arrived, Mendieta pulled down her pants, rubbed pig's blood on her naked thighs, bent over her kitchen table, and tied herself up. When everyone arrived, they found the door unlocked, Mendieta's apartment ransacked, her bloody body in the kitchen.

Bree wonders how long it took for Mendieta's classmates and teacher to realize they were witnessing performance art. How long had their hearts thudded before they finally, as it was reported, pulled up chairs so they could gather around and dissect Mendieta's artistic choices?

Bree turns the lights back on. Her students stare at her. A few have their usual bored expressions, but many look confused, disgusted, or even angry. She tilts her head. "Where should we begin?"

Alayna sits up straight, brow furrowed, her bleached-blond hair gathered in a messy topknot.

"I hated it, but I think that was the point?"

"Go on," Bree says, nodding.

"That last piece?" Alayna says.

"'Rape Scene'?"

Alayna nods. "You know how when you watch a scary movie, the violence is almost…attractive? It's stylized. That shot of her bent over isn't stylized at all. It's ugly. It's horrible. It takes the glamour away from that kind of violence, and I think that's the point?"

Zach sits next to Alayna, close enough their shoulders brush. Last night, Bree told him they had to stop seeing each other. She was determined not to do what Frye did and ghost. However, mid-breakup speech, she started to understand why ghosting might have been the superior option. He looked like a kicked puppy and kept saying, "I thought things were going really well. You don't like spending time with me?"

It appears his hurt has calcified quickly into anger. He juts his chin out and meets Bree's eyes. "That wasn't art. That was sick."

"Go on," Bree says. She keeps her tone even, but she puts a hand over her abdomen. She found herself doing it last night too, an embarrassing gesture she apparently does without thinking when she talks to Zach now.

"It isn't art to invite people over to your house and then stage it, so they walk in on you like…" Zach gestures to the now-blank screen. "That's shitty. That's selfish. And then, she supposedly does this because of some murdered girl. But it seems like it's not about that girl at all. It's just an excuse for her to be gross. I mean, how is the dead girl helped by this chick pouring pig's blood on herself or smearing it across the sidewalk?"

"Sarah Ann Ottens," Bree says.

"What?" Zach asks.

"You keep calling her the dead girl, but her name was Sarah Ann Ottens."

"Whatever," Zach says.

"Not *whatever*," Bree says. "You're making an argument that Mendieta didn't really care about her, but you can't give her the dignity of a name."

"There are some people who want an excuse to be fucked up,"

Zach says. "How much of this is really about patriarchy and violence against women, and how much of it is that she wanted to
take photos of herself naked and get attention?"

"If you'd like to talk about patriarchy, let's talk about patriarchy," Bree says, taking a few steps toward Zach. "Does anyone
know how Mendieta died?"

Of course, Alayna raises her hand. "She fell out a window."

"That's what some people say," Bree says. "Other people say
she was pushed. Her husband was an artist, too. Right before she
died, people in their apartment building heard them arguing."

"Maybe she killed herself?" another of Bree's male students
suggests.

"Her friends said that was unlikely, because she had a terrible
fear of heights," Bree says. "They said she wasn't depressed and
that her work was finally being noticed. She was becoming more
famous than her husband. When the police came, her husband
had scratch marks all over his nose and arms."

Bree glances at Zach and finds him scrolling on his phone.

"Put that away," she tells him. Alayna's eyes widen a little at her
sharp tone, unused to Bree scolding any of them. Bree can't stand
the smug smile on Zach's face as he looks up at her.

"I was just reading something interesting about her," he says.
"She slept with one of her art professors at Iowa."

Mendieta and a professor at Iowa, Hans Breder, had a ten-year
romantic relationship and collaborated on a lot of art together.
Bree turns her back to the class, so they can't see her expression.

"Gross," Alayna says.

When Bree turns around, she's collected herself enough to
give them instructions for their next project, but the whole time

she speaks, she's aware of Zach's hard expression as he watches her. *You deserve this,* she reminds herself. After she dismisses them to work on their projects, Alayna's and Zach's heads tilt toward each other as they whisper and smile.

When Bree gets home after class, her phone vibrates, and she sees the number with the Iowa City area code—Frye's number.

"Bree?" he says.

She works hard to keep her voice even. "What do you want, Frye?"

"Well, hello to you, too, after almost a decade," he says, sounding a little hurt.

"Sorry," Bree says. "Actually, I'm not. I'm sure your wife would prefer we kept whatever this is brief."

A long pause. Is he wincing like he used to when she'd see him on a difficult phone call? "Bree..."

"I enjoyed your book," Bree says. "It left out some things, but I doubt the whole 'sleeping with the murder victim's teenage friend' would have played well with your white knight persona."

"Bree, are you sitting down?"

"Fuck you, Frye," she says. "Get on with it." But she does sit down. She sits down on her couch and leans forward, so the phone presses against her ear and her head is between her knees.

"They found her body," he says.

Don't cry, she tells herself, in the same second the tears leak from her eyes.

"Where?" she says.

"There's some farmland down the Herbert Hoover Highway.

It had been abandoned for a while, but then it was sold to a big agribusiness a few months ago. When someone from the company did a walk-through, they found her."

She pictures it. Acres of land, one of those parcels you see from the highway and marvel at how lonely it looks. Only the barn's skeleton still standing, the farmhouse's roof sagging in the middle, a rusted grain silo off the dirt road, and farther in, a wooded area.

Some employee for the agribusiness walking through the site, making notes of what they'll clear before they can expand factory farming. When he first sees her skull, he thinks it's a large, smooth rock. It isn't until he's standing right in front of her that he sees the eye sockets. The light through the trees illuminates her open jaw, the slope of her occipital bone.

Did he wonder what series of horrible events had befallen her to end up there? Did he wonder who she had been?

Over the years, Bree told herself the pain would stop when she had answers. *Okay*, she tells herself. *Here is the end of the story. There is nothing more that can hurt you.* But she doesn't feel comforted. She doesn't feel like the sharp edges inside her have been softened by this knowledge.

"Is there any reason she'd go there?" Frye asks. "Is there anyone she knew who owned property or liked to spend time out there?"

"No one I know," Bree says. "Who owned the place?"

"A man named Marshall T. Williams. We haven't been able to find a connection between him and Abby, although it's possible someone just knew the place was abandoned and dumped her there."

That phrasing—*dumped her there*—makes Bree's stomach lurch. "When did you find her?"

Frye lets out a breath. "These things move more slowly than we'd like…"

"When, Frye?"

"We found her last January," he says. "Look, the main reason I'm calling is because there's going to be a press conference soon, and I wanted you to hear it from me first. You deserve that."

It takes her a moment to understand what's bothering her. "If you've known for nine months, why are you only announcing it now?"

"There was DNA testing," he says. "We had to find the rest of her remains and search the scene…"

"You're sure you didn't hold off announcing all this to correspond with the release of the TV show, so you could sell more books?"

There's a beat of silence. She pictures him clenching his fist and punching his upper thigh like he used to when he was frustrated. But when he finally speaks, he sounds more tired than angry.

"That's not fair."

"How did she die?"

"We're withholding that," he says. "We need to keep some information to ourselves while we investigate."

"Please," Bree says.

He's quiet for a moment. Then he sighs. "The forensics point to a head injury. There's a skull fracture."

Bree's staring at her bare toes on the carpet. Everything seems like she's seeing it in a fun house mirror—familiar but distorted.

"Do you think it was Blue?"

"Give us time," Frye says.

"He'll be dead in twenty-one days."

"We'll get you answers."

"Like you got us answers twelve years ago?"

"Bree."

"I have to go," she says and ends the call.

CHELSEA
OCTOBER 2015

It's late afternoon, and Daniel is at the shop working on a custom order for a rich couple—built-in bookshelves made from some type of luxury wood Chelsea has never heard of. Her week has not gotten better since the disappointing conversation with Rachel Morgan. Since then, she had a tense meeting about the budget, a parishioner scolded her for using gender neutral pronouns for God in a sermon, and Elly hasn't returned to church since Chelsea saw her in the sanctuary. She also hasn't replied to any of Chelsea's texts or DMs.

On top of all that, the hot water in their house went out, so she's been using water heated in a tea kettle to wash her hair. Their plumber, Carl, a gray-haired man who always gives them gossip about the former owners of their house, is in the basement right now, trying to figure out the problem. Every now and then, she hears him swearing and the ding of metal hitting metal.

Curling up on the couch, Chelsea decides to put on a mindless cooking show to relax. She turns on the TV and selects one of the streaming services she and Daniel subscribe to.

As soon as the landing page comes up, she sees it. The TV

show with Ryan Worth as Jon Allan Blue. Its thumbnail is black
and white, a still of a cornfield in winter. Across it, in bold, red
lettering are the words "Murder in the Midwest."

It is, inexplicably, a 98 percent match.

She stares at the screen. Why does it say "Continue Watching"?
And why would a show like this be a 98 percent match? She and
Daniel only watch cooking competitions and period dramas
about fussy British people.

That's when she notices the little icon in the top right corner
of the screen. It isn't a "C" for Chelsea, the account they always
use. Instead, it's a "D."

She selects the "Recently Watched" category and pages
through the results. They are almost exclusively true crime and
murder shows titled things like *Crime Scene Squad* and *Case Files:
Serial Killer Psychology.*

Why *the fuck* is Daniel watching this shit? And *when* is he
watching it?

She reaches for her phone to call him but stops herself, suddenly
wondering what other secret habits he has. She's not a snoop by
nature, so she almost doesn't know where to start, standing frozen
in the living room. Then she walks upstairs into their bedroom.

The dresser is her first stop, but in his drawers, she only finds
boxer briefs, balled socks, and neatly folded T-shirts. Loose
change, a Swiss Army knife, a small bottle of heartburn medication, and a snapshot of the two of them are the only things she
finds in his nightstand drawer. For a moment, she studies the
picture. It was the first time she met his family in Chattanooga.
Daniel and Chelsea smile next to his grandmother, a diminutive
woman who called her purse a "pocketbook."

"Daniel, get my pocketbook, so I can show Chelsea some pictures of you," she commanded.

When he was occupied, she said to Chelsea, "He must really like you. He's never brought a Mexican girl home before."

She didn't say it unkindly. In fact, she seemed to share it more so Chelsea might feel flattered in some weird racist way. In moments like that, Chelsea always felt stuck. To explain she wasn't Mexican felt like implying being Mexican was bad. But she also didn't want to pretend to be someone she wasn't, so she tried to explain.

"Navarro isn't Mexican. It's Spanish. From Spain. My grandparents were from Granada."

Daniel's grandmother patted her hand, a sympathetic expression on her face, as if Chelsea were a dumb but sweet thing who was speaking nonsense.

She places the photo back into the nightstand drawer and closes it. The closet in their bedroom is tiny, but she searches it anyway, finding nothing noteworthy except that he owns a sweatshirt from Bon Jovi's 1993 "Keeping the Faith" world tour.

There are two shoe boxes on the shelf above the closet rod. The first holds his dress shoes. However, the second is oddly light. When she opens it, it's empty except for a few dried flowers—yellow roses and cornflowers. She realizes it's the boutonniere from their wedding and places it carefully into her palm. She never knew he saved it.

This sentimental, sweet discovery shames her. Daniel has every right to watch crime shows if he wants. She's being ridiculous. Of course, he would know she wouldn't want to watch them, and it makes sense he'd create a separate profile so he wouldn't upset her.

After setting the second shoebox back on the shelf, she shuts the closet door and walks back to the stairs. Daniel refinished them as soon as they closed on the house, so the boards that were once cracked and discolored have all been repaired, sanded, and stained a uniform glossy walnut. The wood creaks under her as she shifts her weight, eyeing the slightly narrower set of stairs leading to the attic. It's the only place in the house Chelsea doesn't go, because it's creepy and unfinished. Their basement hasn't been finished either and makes her feel like she's in the opening of a horror movie, but she has to go down there to use the washer and dryer or scoop Pippa's litter. The attic holds only some items the previous owners left behind and a few boxes Chelsea and Daniel didn't unpack—the types of sentimental things you carry from place to place, unwilling to throw them out but knowing there's no real use for them.

If Daniel wanted to hide anything, the attic would be the perfect place. *Stop*, she tells herself. *You've had a hard week and you're being paranoid.*

Pippa stands on the stairs below and meows as Chelsea walks up the narrower stairs leading to the attic. Inside, the dust-coated Palladian window doesn't provide very much light, because it's overcast outside. There's no electricity running into the attic, so Chelsea waits a moment for her eyes to adjust. Once she can make out the wooden beams overhead and the exposed brick walls, she steps onto the brittle-looking floorboards, careful to skip any that look particularly rotted or unsound.

Light rain taps against the roof as she walks past sheet-covered pieces of furniture that look like oddly shaped ghosts. She sneezes once from the dust and rubs her itching nose. Once she reaches the dozen or so cardboard boxes, she crouches, reading the descriptions written on their sides in magic marker—*C: seminary stuff, D: high school, extra wedding prints*... She almost skips over the smaller box toward the back that says *Tax stuff*, until she realizes it's in Daniel's handwriting and Chelsea's the one who does their taxes every year. When she pulls it out from the pile, it isn't taped shut like some of the others. Instead, the flaps have just been folded shut.

Once she opens it, she takes the items out one by one, each perplexing her further. By the time she's finished, her hands are shaking.

What the fuck could Daniel want with this stuff? she wonders.

A voice from downstairs calls her name. It's Carl, the plumber.

"Just a minute," she yells, putting everything back in the box and hurrying downstairs. She finds Carl in the living room. When he sees her, he shakes his head sadly.

"You couldn't fix it?"

"No," he says. "You're going to need a new water heater."

They talk about models, costs, and how soon he could have a new one installed, but all Chelsea can think about is that box in her attic.

Before Carl leaves, he looks at something over her shoulder and points. She realizes he's gesturing to the TV screen. The series page for *Murder in the Midwest* is still visible.

"I've heard that's really good," he says.

———————

That evening, Chelsea stands in the sacristy before Wednesday Eucharist, about to ring the bell and walk into the Mary Chapel.

All she can think about is Daniel. When he came home from the carpentry shop before she left for the church, she didn't say anything to him—not about the stuff he'd been watching on TV and not about the box tucked away in the attic.

What could she say? Really, how would the facilitators at the "intimate conversation" retreat they've booked suggest she broach this? Something like: *Hey, I noticed you've been watching a lot of true crime, including the series about the man who killed my friend. I also realized you've been keeping a lot of creepy shit in a box in the attic labeled "tax stuff." Do you have the capacity right now for us to dialogue about that?*

Truly, why the fuck would Daniel want or need a map of Iowa City with little red dots inked on the sorority house, the cemetery, and their dorm? Why would Daniel have a copy of Abby's original missing person report? And if he keeps things like that in their attic, what kinds of stuff must he be hiding at the carpentry shop?

Chelsea has been married to this man for two years. She dated him for four, and now she's replaying everything. Does he want her to open up because he's a concerned husband who wants access to his wife's inner life? Or has there been another reason all along?

As she rings the bell and strides out into the sanctuary, she sees someone new in one of the chapel's chairs. It's a blond woman in leggings and a sweatshirt with the logo for a tiny college forty-five minutes north. It isn't until she zeros in on the woman's profile— long straight nose, full lower lip, slight underbite—she realizes it's Bree. Lines run from her nostrils to the edges of her mouth, and she stopped bleaching her hair, letting it return to its natural dirty blond. Despite that, she looks very much like the girl Chelsea knew.

Chelsea passes her on the way to the altar, and she almost reaches out to touch her, almost puts her hand on the solidity of her shoulder. Almost says, *It's you.*

Wearing the intricately embroidered vestments in front of Bree feels absurd. She tries not to stare at her, tries to focus on kissing the altar, crossing herself, and saying, "Blessed be God: Father, Son, and Holy Spirit."

As she starts the service, it's impossible not to feel Bree watching her. Everything she does, she sees through her eyes. *Why should anyone listen to you?* she imagines Bree wondering. It feels like the person she's worked so hard to become is nothing but smoke and mirrors in front of her.

She glances at Bree during Prayers of the People and sees her watching, expressionless. Her face looks puffier than Chelsea remembers from social media posts, eyes bloodshot and dark circles pronounced. For the first time, Chelsea has the reaction she realizes she should have had from the beginning—concern. Is Bree okay? Is she here because she needs spiritual guidance? How bad must things be for Bree to have come to Chelsea?

During the Eucharist, Bree stays seated, watching as the rest of the parishioners receive the body and blood.

When the service is over, Chelsea talks to her parishioners. She checks on Anita Martin, asking how her hip is doing. She talks with Aaron McKelvey to see how his aging father is holding up in the nursing home they recently put him in. Bree sits quietly, hands folded in her lap. At one point, while Chelsea is talking about the upcoming Thanksgiving Day soup kitchen shifts with three parishioners, she watches Bree approach the statue of Mary with its stand of flickering devotional candles.

Years before Chelsea was hired at the church, a woman offered to pay for a statue of "Our Lord, being held by His Mother." It had been a shrewd way to get a Mary statue. Yes, Mary was holding the infant Jesus, but He was small and not the focus. Instead, Mary stood tall, Jesus in one arm, her other arm palm up, as if she was saying everything was going to be okay.

Bree lights one of the devotional candles, closes her eyes briefly. What is she thinking? When everyone filters out—even Norm Milam, who Chelsea always has to be firm with or he'll stay for hours telling stories about the church's history—Chelsea sits down next to Bree.

"Well, this is a surprise."

"Chels," Bree says, turning to face her. Her expression coupled with the use of Chelsea's old nickname makes the hair on Chelsea's arms rise. Although she doesn't know exactly what Bree is about to say, she knows her life will be delineated into before and after. She raises her hand to stop Bree. She wants to stay in the before for a moment longer.

Dear God, she prays. *Help me.*

She doesn't feel God's comfort. She doesn't feel God at all, but she nods at Bree anyway.

Bree's quick rather than gentle. Chelsea can picture all of it. Did they drive past that land on the highway sometime in those twelve years? Had Chelsea been close without even knowing it? Only the farmland visible from the highway, the woods with their thick underbrush hidden from the road, the bones below. Chelsea doesn't hide her tears, doesn't wipe them away.

You took her from me, she thinks. *You left her in those woods.*

She isn't addressing Jon Allan Blue.

God let Abby's body lie in those woods for a dozen years, that body Chelsea loved disposed of like garbage. Above the altar, the giant crucifix hangs. Jesus, bloody and hurting. No matter where she goes, she can't escape broken bodies. The things people will do to one another.

She knows God never promised anyone a life without pain. But why? Why shouldn't God have promised that? God was God. God was all-powerful. All the theological interpretations and close readings of Scripture feel dull and toothless compared to the sound of Chelsea's blood in her ears, the thumping of her heart, as that lava-like rage she's been trying to tamp down for years erupts.

She lurches forward, grabs the bottom of the altar cloth, and pulls hard. The large brass candlesticks and the heavy brass cross tumble, the cross landing on its side with a clatter while the candlesticks fall onto the floor. One of the candles has broken in half, the candlestick rolling back and forth before finally coming to rest.

———————

Afterward, Chelsea's grateful her routine tasks ground her and give her an excuse not to look at Bree as she shuts off the lights and returns stray hymnals and copies of the Book of Common Prayer to the book racks on the back of pews. Still not looking at her, Chelsea walks through the sanctuary toward the doors, but she feels Bree following, standing there while Chelsea locks the front door and sets the security alarm.

Finally, she can't put it off any longer. They're outside on the church's front steps and Chelsea looks up to see Bree watching her. Her expression is not what Chelsea would have expected, considering how unfair Chelsea was to her all those years ago. Bree bites her lip, looking like she used to when they were teenagers and one of her asshole boyfriends stood her up.

"Well," Bree says. "Goodbye for another twelve years."

The awkward little laugh she gives makes Chelsea's heart ache. *I'm sorry,* she wants to say. *I'm sorry for all the ways I blamed you when you were already blaming yourself.*

Chelsea's phone vibrates, and she holds it up to Bree. "I'm sorry. It might be a parishioner."

"It's fine," Bree says. "I should start the drive back anyway."

As they walk around the side of the building toward the parking lot, Chelsea sees the number isn't a parishioner's—it's Rachel Morgan's.

"Have you already heard?" Rachel asks. Chelsea hesitates, and the voice on the phone clarifies. "About Abby?"

"I have. How did *you* hear?"

Rachel talks fast and sounds a little out of breath—like she's hurrying to get somewhere. "I have good sources. Look, this changes things. I'm going to cover Blue for the next season, and I want to talk with you about Abby."

Chelsea looks at Bree and gestures for her to wait. They stand at the edge of the parking lot while Rachel says she's been reading about Abby's case, and she hates the way she was always overshadowed by what happened at the sorority house.

"I'd like to bring her back into focus."

Her tune is so different from their last conversation that Chelsea wants to laugh. She wants to tell Rachel to fuck off. To say, *How much of a goddamn vulture are you that you needed her bones to be found for her to matter?* But she knows the most important thing is making sure Abby isn't forgotten. She failed Abby in so many other ways. She can't fuck this up.

"That's wonderful," she says into the phone.

Soon, Rachel says, her assistant will email Chelsea about the logistics. She offers to send some of the questions she'll be asking, so Chelsea can feel prepared.

"There's one other thing I wanted to talk to you about," Rachel says. "I'd really like to interview Bree Hadley, too. I'd like to have both of you there—the last two people to see Abby..."

Alive is the final word in that sentence, which Rachel leaves unspoken.

Chelsea looks at Bree, who's standing next to her staring up at the cloudy sky. "I'm not sure if she'll be interested or not."

There's a pause. Then Rachel says, "Part of why my show is so good is because I don't leave any stone unturned. If I try to do a story, and I can't get the full picture, or it isn't going to resonate with viewers, then I cut it loose. If having Abby's story out there matters to you, then it's in your interest to help me get Bree Hadley on board."

Bree leans against her Honda, which has a dent in the driver's side door.

"Let me talk to her," Chelsea says.

ABBY
OCTOBER 2003

In your next acting class, Jay draws out more people's pain—a guy whose father died from pancreatic cancer and a girl with an alcoholic mom. As much as it unnerves you, you have to admit there's an art to Jay's probing. He's as precise as a surgeon as he cuts through the extraneous details of someone's life to find the throbbing center where their pain lives.

As you swipe your key card to enter your dorm, you're relieved to be away from his urgent expression and your classmates' tears. Bree is at an art class, so you and Chelsea should have privacy. Despite not agreeing to tell people about your relationship, you and she seem to have come to an understanding, your normal dynamic relaxing back into place. You hope there's enough time to fool around before she has to leave for her political science class.

But when you reach your floor, the door's open and Chelsea's mom sits on the futon. She's short like her daughter, and her feet barely touch the ground. Chelsea stands by the dresser, holding a piece of paper.

"Jeff," she reads aloud. As you walk toward her, you see there's a phone number below the name.

Mrs. Navarro greets you before turning back to her daughter. "Do you remember him?" She pushes her straight, dark hair behind her ears. "You did Vacation Bible School together as kids. Mrs. Henson's son. He's studying engineering and would love to take you to dinner."

Mrs. Navarro's a nurse whose main hobbies seem to be reading thick paperbacks with shirtless men on the covers and chairing various meetings at her church.

"Are you setting me up with a guy?" Chelsea asks, her thick eyebrows raised.

"He was at the church potluck last weekend. I had him write down his number for you. If you had gone, you could have met him in person, but since you were busy studying…"

Of course, Chelsea hadn't been studying. Bree was working, so you and she drove to Lake MacBride. It was in the low sixties, too cold to go in the water, but you held hands and ran in anyway until it reached your hips. You wrapped your arms, goose bumpy and slick from the water, around her as you both shivered.

"Don't let go," she told you, resting her head on your shoulder.

Chelsea surveys her mother, her upper lip raised in disgust. "I don't want to go on a date with some rando from your church."

"*Our* church," Mrs. Navarro corrects.

"*Mom*," Chelsea says, folding the piece of paper and placing it on her dresser. You notice she doesn't throw it away.

Mrs. Navarro stays a little longer. She asks about your classes. She reminds the two of you to be careful walking around at night.

"Those poor girls," she says, shaking her head. "You look out for each other."

"We will," you say.

When she leaves, she hugs you both goodbye. You wonder if she'd still be eager to embrace you if she knew her daughter's head was between your legs last night.

Right before Chelsea says her final goodbye and shuts the door, she promises her mother she'll be at mass Sunday. You went with her once and had so many questions—what was the incense for? How long did it take her to learn all the choreography, the bowing and the crossing oneself and the rote responses?

"Did you seriously just call it choreography?" Chelsea had said, laughing the deep belly laugh she gave when she was truly amused.

The question you wanted to ask, but hadn't felt like you should, was what did she think when she knelt on the threadbare kneeler? What went through her mind when her clasped hands rested on the top of the pew in front of her, head bowed, eyes closed?

Once Mrs. Navarro shuts the door behind her, you turn to Chelsea. "Are you going to let her fix you up with that guy?"

In high school, after you started fooling around, you both still had boyfriends. You'd go to dances and take guys as dates. You always loved and hated those nights—you, Chelsea, and Bree dressed up, posing in your parents' living room in front of the fireplace for photos. Chelsea's dark hair coiled in an intricate updo, her usually bare face powdered and painted with the makeup Bree put on her, the gleaming skin of her shoulders set off by some glitter gel you'd applied. She'd look so beautiful, but it would be some stupid dude who smelled like Abercrombie cologne who was holding her hand, putting his arm around her slim waist. And you'd be standing a few feet away, held by some other dude who you knew would want to fuck you in his car after the dance. And you would, and it would be fine, especially if you were on top, especially if you could get him to last long enough, but it always left you wanting something.

"I don't know," Chelsea says. Her expression is a little amused, and she has the maddening calm of someone with the upper hand. "I mean, it's not like I can go on a date with *you*, is it?"

"I don't want you to go on a date with him."

Chelsea tilts her head. "I don't really think you're in a position to tell me what I can or can't do."

You picture Chelsea on a date with this *Jeff*. You see them at the Italian place downtown, eating bruschetta and plates of pasta. What would they talk about? Would he make her laugh like you can? Of course, you can see why he'd want her—her sarcasm, her strong opinions contrasted with those delicate features. How would he make his move? You picture a big hand reaching across the table to cover hers.

"We can tell people," you say, your heart beating faster.

Chelsea smiles, tilting her head. "For real?"

You feel a little light-headed and take a deep breath. "Yes."

Chelsea embraces you so fast you almost lose your balance until she puts a steadying arm around your waist. Later, lying in her lofted bed, she presses for details. When will you tell Bree? And how? Although Chelsea has been the one pushing for this, even she admits it's hard to know the best way to do it. You pull away from her and lie on your back, staring at the ceiling tiles.

You're thinking about the heartshares today. More people who were brave enough to talk honestly about the hardest things in their lives. Why are you such a fucking coward? Why does the idea of disappointing your mother, of not being the girl she wants you to be, scare you so much?

"What?" Chelsea asks, noticing your expression.

"I need to tell my mom first," you say.

She props herself on her elbow, the sheet falling to reveal part of one almond-colored nipple. "No one jumps in the deep end before they've spent time in the wading pool."

You understand what she means. Bree is the safer person to tell first. Although she might be hurt you've kept this from her, she'll almost certainly be supportive. But telling your mom would be an opportunity to redo your heartshare. You could prove to yourself that you can be brave, too. You can be honest and vulnerable and stare straight at the thing that scares you most.

"I need to do it," you tell Chelsea. "It's important to me."

She gives you a look like you're the most exasperating person in the world. Then it dissolves into something tender.

"Okay," she says, wrapping her arms around you, spooning you. The warmth of her chest feels good against your back.

You usually don't spend the whole night in Chelsea's bed. The twin is too small for either of you to get a good night's sleep. But after you have sex, you always lie together for a while, holding each other. You'll spoon her for a while, until she says, "Let me big spoon," and then you'll switch.

Tonight, you're spooning her, your face in her hair, breathing in her familiar smell—vanilla body spray, the familiar tang of her dried sweat—and you fall asleep together in her bed, your forehead resting on the warm skin of her back.

―――――

The next day, you and Chelsea are getting ready when the phone rings. She's running late for class, but she sets down her hairbrush and answers.

"Yeah, just a second," she says, before handing the receiver to you, kissing you on the cheek, and grabbing her backpack.

You say hello, the phone cradled between your chin and your shoulder while you slip on your UGGs. There's a beat of silence as Chelsea shuts the door behind her. Then the heavy breathing starts, making the hair on your arms rise.

You hang up and stare out the window at the empty courtyard below, thinking about what Chelsea said before she handed you the phone. *Yeah, just a second.*

Whoever it was asked for you. You hoped the calls were random, someone arbitrarily pulling a number from the campus directory. It's creepier to know someone has targeted you specifically, and that they know your name.

Fuck this asshole, you think, picking up the phone and dialing *69. What you told Jay and the class during your heartshare was true. There are any number of people from your high school who thought you were a slut. There are any number of guys who might want to call and pant into the phone, but that doesn't mean you're going to let them get away with it.

But when you call the number *69 gives you, the woman who answers tells you it's a pay phone inside a bar downtown. You explain to her what's been happening, and she tells you the guy who had been using the phone just left.

"What did he look like?" you ask.

"Average height. White guy. He was wearing a hoodie."

That afternoon at the mall, you stand with your mother in a dressing room as she holds a pair of low-rise jeans for you to try.

You briefly consider telling her about the creepy phone calls, but you know exactly what your mother would say if you told her. *It's what happens to girls.*

She'd say it after a heavy sigh with a tone like, *Why are you surprised?* And then she'd share some even more horrific thing that happened to her as a girl. Something her father or brother did to her. Something that would worm into your brain and keep you awake at night.

You mother hands you the pair of low-rise jeans. As you perform an awkward shimmy, trying to pull them over your hips and black thong, she looks away. They're the size you've always worn, but it takes extra effort to zip and button them. A little pudge hangs over the side. A muffin top, you've heard it called. You and your mother stare at your reflection in the mirror. Without saying anything, you take them off and hand them to her to put back on the hanger.

"It's the Freshman Fifteen," she says. "You should go on the Atkins diet. Stop eating carbs."

You and your mother wait for Bree outside the dressing rooms. When she emerges, she's empty-handed.

"Nothing worked?" your mother asks, raising a perfectly waxed eyebrow.

"No," Bree says.

"Look at you," your mother says, gesturing to Bree's tight stomach. "I can't believe that."

Bree looks down, worrying a spot on the department store's green carpet with the toe of her high-heeled boot. "There was a dress I liked, but it's way too expensive."

"Let me see it," your mother says.

Bree hesitates for a second then disappears into the dressing room. When she returns, she's holding a skimpy, strapless Lycra dress in powder blue. You can imagine just how good it looks on her. Your mother takes it, flips over the tag, then lays it across her arm with the shapeless sweaters she's buying you. ("Some looser clothes will look best until you're back to your regular size.")

"Oh no, Mrs. Hartmann," Bree says, her cheeks already turning pink. "You don't have to do that."

"I'm happy to," she says as the three of you walk toward the juniors checkout counter. The saleswoman scans the items, as your mother pulls out her American Express card. By the cosmetics counters, big posters of Elizabeth Hurley hang advertising some perfume. She's beautiful and has the perfect body, and Hugh Grant *still* hired a hooker for a blow job.

Once you leave the department store, your mother's ready for a glass of wine. Chelsea's nickname for her is Mrs. White Zin, and your mother immediately orders a glass once you're seated in a booth at Bennigan's.

"How did you do on your French quiz?" your mother asks as the server walks away.

Not great, would be the honest answer. You always got As in French in high school, but now you're realizing that was probably more because Mrs. Connor was in the same book club as your mom and liked to spend boozy nights at your house drinking cosmos and talking about anything other than the novel they were supposed to have read.

In your college French class, your teacher, a grad student from Chartres, constantly critiques your pronunciation. On the first day, he even corrected you when you said *bonjour*, wearing this dismissive look like he was embarrassed for you.

"Good," you tell her. You'll make sure to pull your grade up before the semester's over.

"Have you given any more thought to adding a double major?"

"I was thinking journalism," you say. "Theater would be a good double major with broadcast journalism."

"You could be a news anchor," your mother says, the delight clear in the pitch of her voice. "That's perfect."

Truthfully, you have no interest in journalism, but you've learned pleasing your mother often feels the same as pleasing yourself. It's hard to distinguish between the two sometimes, so you bask in her pleasure as she chats with you and Bree about the local news anchors she watches each night and how she's sure you'd be better than them.

When you were younger, your mother told you stories about her father on nights when she had too many glasses of wine. Afterward, you'd walk her to bed, get her tissues to wipe her eyes, and leave a glass of water on the nightstand, all the while trying not to replay her stories in your mind. Her father climbing into her bed at night. The puppies she cared for that he let die in the snow.

Although it hurts to feel like you're constantly failing her with every pound you gain, every B+ you earn, your attempts at perfection seem like a small price to pay compared to what she went through. More than that, they seem like something she's owed. If you can make her happy, why shouldn't you after everything she's gone through? It's why telling her about you and Chelsea seems so impossible.

It isn't that your mother is completely against gay people. She isn't religious, and your dad has a surgical tech who's gay and lives with his partner. Your mom has always been friendly to them. Still, you've always had the feeling that being gay is like being chubby or becoming a garbage person—something your mother would consider fine for *other people* but not for you.

You decide to test the waters. "Amanda Tucker came out," you say, watching her face.

Your mother never cared for Amanda's mother; the two of them were both strong voices on the PTA. Meanwhile, you and Amanda were often rivals for solos in choir.

"*Really?*" Bree says. "I never would have expected that."

You feel a brief flash of guilt at the potentially awkward interaction Bree and Amanda might have the next time Amanda's home from Northwestern, but you've got to stay focused—what's going to be your mother's reaction?

Her face is expressionless as she sips her wine, taking in the information. Then she shrugs. It's the most miraculous movement, the rise and fall of her bony shoulders, because you think, *Oh, my God. She doesn't even care!*

Then she sets down her glass and smirks. From the twist of her lips, you know whatever she's about to say will hurt.

"She'll never give her mother grandchildren."

"People adopt," you say. "Or do in vitro."

Your mother shrugs again, but the movement no longer seems miraculous. She stares at you like you're the naivest person she's ever met.

"It will be harder for her. *Everything* will be harder for her. And I can't imagine as a mother how much that would hurt to watch."

Your mother swallows and looks out the window.

EXCERPT FROM
BLOODY-MINDED: A TRUE CRIME PODCAST EPISODE 23 TRANSCRIPT:

"LIVE FROM THE WARNER THEATRE IN WASHINGTON, DC"

KATE MADALINKSY, COHOST: Okay, so on Halloween 2003, Abigail Hartmann goes missing. No one has ever tied her officially to Blue, but consider this: she's the age of the girls he's killing and she disappears only a few weeks before Blue kills two other girls in her town and then flees to Kentucky.

AUDREY CORIN, COHOST: Not suspicious at all.

MADALINKSY: The night she goes missing, she was hanging out with her friends in a graveyard.

CORIN (laughing): As you do.

MADALINKSY: She and her friends get into some kind of fight. Hartmann leaves on her own, and she's never seen alive again.

CORIN: See, that's the thing. Ladies, what the fuck? Make sure your friends get home okay. Friends don't let friends get murdered.

MADALINKSY (laughing): That's good. We should get that cross-stitched on something.

CORIN: So, what happens?

MADALINKSY: They never find Hartmann's body. A couple weeks later, Blue breaks into the Alpha Psi Theta sorority house and bludgeons these three poor women. He kills two of them and disfigures another.

CORIN: Jesus. How did he get into the house?

MADALINKSY: You're going to love this.

CORIN: Can I guess?

MADALINKSY: Please do.

CORIN: They didn't lock the door.

MADALINKSY: Close. There was a back door that automatically locked, but someone forgot to pull it closed all the way.

CORIN: How many times do I say it? Ladies, check your doors. Check your windows. Don't trust creepy fucking dudes who say they need help loading a couch into their van because of the cast on their arm.

MADALINKSY: Walk your friends home at night.

CORIN: That's exactly right.

MADALINKSY: Okay, so what happens to Blue when he gets to Kentucky—we'll talk about that in a moment, but first let's hear from one of our sponsors.

CORIN: How many times have you woken up overheated on hot summer nights? If you want deep sleep with perfect temperature regulation, look no further than Thimble & Fields' All-Foam Cooling Sleep Mattress. Try it free for thirty nights using the code "Murder30" at checkout.

BREE

Inside Chelsea's creaky Victorian house, Bree feels like she's getting a weird behind-the-scenes tour. Here are things Bree has seen on social media: gorgeous hardwoods and beautiful religious icons hanging from the walls; the little office nook with floor-to-ceiling bookcases.

But there are things the social media posts leave out: cracked plaster walls, rooms that haven't been renovated and sit empty, Chelsea picking her right thumb's cuticle until it bleeds. She and Bree sit on the couch together in the living room. Chelsea's hands rest in her lap against the dark cloth of her priest's garb. She says nothing, staring into space. Bree doesn't know for certain, but she can imagine Chelsea's thoughts.

Over the years, Bree tormented herself with potential scenarios. Jon Allan Blue's hand on Abby's arm, his fingers digging into her flesh, pulling her into the shadows. Or that same hand over her mouth, a blade at her neck, her eyes wide and panicked as she screamed into his palm. She pictured Abby's body suffering all manner of abuse. Now that she knows the real pain she experienced, her skull cracking like the plaster on Chelsea's walls, she finds no comfort.

When Chelsea excuses herself to the bathroom, Bree snoops around her office nook. There's a to-do list written on the back of an envelope in Chelsea's exceptionally tiny print. *Write sermon* has been crossed off. *Add $ to joint account* has not.

There are sticky notes affixed to the top of Chelsea's closed laptop. Names that mean nothing to Bree because she's not part of Chelsea's life anymore. *Email Melissa. Check w/ Louise & altar guild.*

A framed four-by-six-inch snapshot sits in the corner. It's angled so it doesn't face the rest of the room but would be visible when Chelsea sits in her desk chair. Bree's teenage self smiles, clad in black fishnets, garters, and a corset. Abby's in a white bra and half-slip that Mrs. Hartmann would have forbidden her to wear if she had known. Chelsea's hair is teased out in her maid's costume. They were seventeen years old and went to see *The Rocky Horror Picture Show* at the historic theater downtown.

Why did Chelsea choose this out of all possible pictures? Teenage Chelsea leans against the base of a light pole, her head resting against the black metal as she smiles like Mona Lisa. Bree poses next to her, upper arms pulled close to her body to push her cleavage up even more. Her teenage self's smile is wide and devastatingly open. There could be a sign on her forehead that says *Please pay attention to me.*

Then there's Abby. She stands a little off to the side. Bree remembers seeing this photo when it first got developed, but back then she was more focused on how her own tits looked. Now she studies Abby's expression. Abby stares at Chelsea, not smiling, wearing a look of bewilderment, as if she can't quite believe what she's seeing. Something about the expression nags at Bree, like a word caught on the tip of her tongue, but the toilet flushes and she retreats to the couch.

Chelsea reenters the room, still picking the skin around her right thumb. When they were friends, she did this occasionally when stressed—the days before exams or the moment before the doorbell rang for dates to pick them up for school dances. Now tiny scabs dot the base of her thumb, and a penny-sized circle of smooth, pink scar tissue shines in the lamp light. Chelsea notices Bree looking and sits on her right hand as she settles back on the couch.

"Thank you for telling me in person," she says, her tone somewhat formal, the way Bree imagines she might address people at her church during a budget meeting. "You could have emailed me or just let me hear about it online, and I know how weird it is to hear about stuff relating to her that way."

"The same kind of weird it was for me when you went to visit Jon Allan Blue, and I had to read about it online? Weird like that?"

Chelsea recoils as if Bree slapped her. For a moment, a nasty sort of pleasure grips Bree's chest. Almost immediately, though, she's distracted by something else—the urge to take a photo.

It's not like with other shots lately. She doesn't just see the technical merits in it: Chelsea's bowed head and her dark hair falling out of its bun, little wisps free at the base of her neck and by her ears. A large painting of the Madonna behind her, head similarly bowed, both looking dignified in their suffering. A crack in the plaster zigzagging from the painting's edge across the wall. More than it being a good shot, Bree feels hunger to freeze the moment, the same warmth behind her breastbone that made her pick up a camera in the first place.

She only has the camera on her phone, but it's been so long since she felt this way, she doesn't want to lose it.

"Can I take a picture of you?" she asks. She doesn't wait for Chelsea's answer, so she takes two shots reflecting the initial image she found so captivating and a few more showing Chelsea's expressions cycling through bafflement and anger.

"You insult me and then you want to take pictures of me?" Chelsea demands.

Before Bree can respond, the front door opens and Daniel appears. It's strange to see him in person after scrutinizing him online for so long. It feels like those '90s sitcoms they used to watch as kids when a series regular appears for the first time in an episode. There should be applause from the audience, an acknowledgment everyone has been waiting for this moment, ready for the character to say their catchphrase.

When he introduces himself, shaking her hand with a strong grip, his eyes widen when she says her name and he realizes who she is. He's shorter than Bree expected, but he smells pleasantly of sawdust.

Once again, it's a behind-the-scenes tour of Chelsea's social media life. Here's the handsome husband who immediately brings Bree a can of fizzy water and sets a bowl of pretzels on the coffee table he made himself from reclaimed barn wood. But look, too, at the awkwardness between Daniel and Chelsea, the way she leans back from his welcome-home kiss. How he touches her like someone might pet a half-feral cat.

Daniel sets more food in front of Bree and Chelsea. Hummus and tortilla chips. A little bowl of olives. He vibrates with energy, like one of those tiny dogs that shake constantly from excitement.

His hair is short on one side, almost buzzed, the other side long. He calls Chelsea "pea," which Bree knows from social media is an endearment shortened from "sweet pea." He tells Bree he bought the bowl holding the olives on their trip to Jerusalem. Bree doesn't tell him she already knows—that because of Chelsea's robust social media presence, she even knows the provenance of this bowl.

"I didn't know you were coming over, or I would have cooked something," he says, his voice lilting with southern vowels.

Bree waits for Chelsea to tell him about Abby's body, to explain the reason for Bree's presence, but she says nothing. Daniel stands in the kitchen doorway, clearly unsure if he should join them or give them space.

"*Infamous* is doing its next season about Jon Allan Blue," Chelsea says. She's staring at the Turkish rug on the floor, so it's hard to know if she's addressing Bree or Daniel or both. "I'm going to do it. Be interviewed."

"You think this time you'll get the cover of *Christianity Today* instead of just a feature article?" Bree says.

"Hey, that's not fair," Daniel says. He walks halfway to the couch, his eyes ablaze, nostrils flaring. Bree feels both heartened by his defense of his wife and annoyed he's getting in the middle of them.

"Daniel," Chelsea says, sounding like someone scolding a dog that jumped on a guest with muddy paws. She turns to Bree. "Rachel Morgan really wants to interview you."

"I don't give a fuck what Rachel Morgan wants," Bree says. Still, Abby's inclusion is unusual. Usually, it's just her descriptor: *the eighteen-year-old University of Iowa student.* Just another dead girl—not even worthy of a name.

There was never any hard evidence linking her disappearance to him, even if people suspected it. By the time the sorority house murders happened, something so shocking and unimaginable, Abby's disappearance was old news, as easily ignored as the faded missing person posters Bree and Chelsea put up around town.

When they were younger, Bree had hoped increased media coverage about Abby might get them answers. But talking about Abby never led to anything good.

"It's a bad idea," Bree says. "Don't you remember the Linda Joy interview?"

"Of course I do," Chelsea says. She shakes her head, clearly not wanting to linger on that horrific experience. "And if you remember, that was your idea."

Daniel clears his throat. "I think Bree's right. You should be focused on moving on. Not being pulled back into all of this again."

When he says the phrase *all of this*, he gestures toward Bree, as if she is the living embodiment of their whole sorry story. Maybe to Chelsea she is, but it still hurts.

"They're including her," Chelsea says. "That's what we've always wanted. For her not to be forgotten."

"That's what you wanted," Bree says. "What I wanted was just to know what happened."

"Maybe Rachel Morgan can find out," Chelsea says, leaning forward. "She's a good investigator."

They sit in silence for a while, the old house creaking in the wind, a tree limb tapping the living room window. Daniel still hovers awkwardly, having retreated toward the kitchen, halfway in the room, halfway out.

Chelsea fetches her laptop, setting it on the coffee table in front of Bree. Unlike Bree's laptop screen, which is caked with dust and smeared with her greasy fingerprints, Chelsea's glows a pristine white, open to a list of questions. "Rachel emailed me some of the questions she's planning on asking. Maybe if you read through them it would help you decide?"

No, Bree wants to say, but she can't ignore the plea in Chelsea's voice, so she reads the first one aloud: "Who would Abby be today, if she had lived?"

Sometimes, at night, Bree plays a game where she stares at the ceiling and thinks about all the ways she's squandering the life she has been given, all the ways Abby would have done more had she been the one spared. Maybe she would be a famous actress. Or a news anchor. Bree lost hours picturing what Abby's adult life might look like. Once, she even ran her photo through a website that aged people. The result was a little cartoony, the lines from Abby's nostrils to the outside of her mouth too deep (Abby would have gotten Botox), her crow's feet exaggerated, but Bree stared at the image for a long time anyway. *Who would you have been?* And, of course, in that question, another waited, like those Russian nesting dolls: *Who would I have been?*

"If she were alive, Abby would probably have kids by now," Bree says.

She is, of course, thinking about her own pregnancy. She pictures Abby with two toddlers. Abby giving Bree advice about pregnancy and motherhood in her typical way—a little patronizing, a little bossy, but so obviously grounded in love you couldn't get annoyed. She pictures Abby as someone she could call when worried or scared during pregnancy. Someone she could turn to for support.

Bree would say to her right now, *I want this, but I know I've already really fucked it up. I don't know what to do.*

Abby would grab ahold of Bree's hands like she always did when she gave a pep talk she especially wanted her to take to heart. *If this is what you want, this is what you should do.*

This imaginary version of Abby, this grown-up version of her, comforts Bree in a real way, and she wants Chelsea to inhabit the fantasy with her just for a moment.

But Chelsea's voice is flat. "She wouldn't have kids."

The disagreement doesn't just feel like a disagreement about who Abby was, although that's upsetting enough. It feels like a condemnation of Bree's vision of an Abby who would tell her she can do this. She can be a mother.

"She always said she didn't want to be an older parent—like her mom and dad," Bree says.

"She didn't even want kids."

Bree has not missed this. Chelsea's voice is so certain, even though she's so fucking wrong.

"She picked out their names—Carrie and Henry," Bree says.

"I picked out names back then, and I definitely don't want kids."

"Fine," Bree says, staring out the bay window at the night sky. She can see an almost-full moon shining through the tree limbs.

It's such a small thing, but it hurts. When someone is dead, they can't set the record straight. They can't interject and say, *Actually, this is who I was. This is what I wanted.* The living are left to assert their version of the dead as the real one. Not for the first time, Bree remembers she and Chelsea grieve two different people, two different Abbys. If Bree lets Chelsea be the only person Rachel

Morgan interviews on *Infamous*, it will be Chelsea's version of Abby who's cemented into public record.

Bree reads through the rest of Rachel Morgan's questions. They're mostly expected, but some of them show a level of depth: *How did it feel for Abby's case to always take a backseat to the sorority house murders? What is your personal relationship to true crime after being so intimately involved with a case like this? Do you find it exploitative?*

Daniel disappears into the kitchen, and the faucet runs. Bree points to one of Rachel's questions—*Why do you think Abby's body was the only one not found?*—and murmurs, "Why didn't you tell him?"

"I will," Chelsea says. "But I want to sit with it for a while on my own."

This answer both breaks Bree's heart and makes her want to take another picture of Chelsea—face in profile, jaw set in determination, priest collar contrasting with the black fabric of her dress and the dingy taupe of the walls. Bree spent so many years thinking having a husband meant Chelsea was not alone with her grief in the way Bree has been. She suddenly sees the wrongness of that assumption and aches for Chelsea.

"Can I take your picture again?" she asks. Again, she takes a couple shots before Chelsea gives a nod of assent. Instead of looking angry, this time Chelsea looks bemused as Bree puts her phone away.

"Why do you keep wanting to take my picture? I'm sure you have better models than me."

"I can't explain it," Bree says. "It would be like you explaining what the presence of God feels like. It just *is*, and I have to honor it."

Something about this answer clearly pleases Chelsea, and she nods.

Bree has read through Rachel's questions. She told Chelsea what she came here to tell her. There's no reason for her to stay any longer, so she grabs her purse and lets Chelsea walk her to the door. Standing there, they're suddenly shy with one another. Chelsea writes something on a slip of paper and hands it to her.

"My phone number," she says. "In case you change your mind about the podcast."

Then Chelsea puts her arms around Bree. It isn't a casual hug, something one-armed or loose. Chelsea grips the fabric of Bree's coat, holding her tightly. Bree responds in kind, her arms around Chelsea's tiny waist. She allows herself a moment of familiarity, resting her cheek on the top of Chelsea's head like she used to.

As Bree walks into the night, she expects to feel relief. She did what she needed to do and told Chelsea. It's done. She should be able to drive home and handle her shit—figure out what she's going to do about this pregnancy, get her personal and professional life in order. But walking away from Chelsea, her chest aches with something like homesickness.

CHELSEA
OCTOBER 2015

Chelsea watches Bree's headlights turn on. Since the last time Chelsea saw her, Bree straightened her teeth. Chelsea never thought much either way about those crooked front teeth, one twisting over the other like tangled tree roots, but she finds herself missing them now.

She leaves the front window to find Daniel standing in the living room, watching her.

"Should we talk?" he asks.

She's still upset and confused about what she found in the attic. When she's this angry at someone, she can barely speak. *You're like a hedgehog when you're mad,* Abby complained once. *You just curl up and it's all spikes.*

"Do you really think doing this podcast is a good idea?" he asks, sitting on the couch.

She has no idea if she'll once again be left regretting this foray into true crime, but she's not going to tell him that.

"I'm afraid it won't help you move on," he says.

"I'd think you'd love for me to do it," she says, walking toward him. "Since you're such a fan of true crime stuff."

He swallows. "What are you talking about?"

"I came home yesterday, and the Jon Allan Blue series was half-watched."

"I can explain—"

"—and then I found that box in the attic."

"You went through my things?" he asks, standing up.

"No, you don't get to deflect," she says. "Explain to me why you have a bunch of shit about Abby's case in a box up there."

He looks down at the floorboards, a shock of his sandy hair falling in front of his face.

"A map. Her missing person report. Daniel, why the fuck do you have all that? *I* don't even have that."

"Well, maybe you *should*," he says, and she's taken aback by the frustration in his voice as he stares at her.

"What the fuck does that mean?"

He takes a deep breath. Then he sits back down on the couch, gesturing for her to sit next to him. She shakes her head, and he exhales slowly through his mouth.

"Have you ever heard of the website Gumshoe Nation?"

She shakes her head.

"Before I met you, I went on there a lot. It's one of those forums where people look at cold cases and go through evidence and create theories about what happened. We'd run down whatever leads we didn't think the police considered."

Daniel has never once talked about true crime with her. She feels like there's a stranger sitting on her couch. "This was like a hobby to you?"

"Kind of," he says. "I'd think about the cases and the theories while I'd work in the carpentry shop. It was like a puzzle. Something useful I could put my mind to while I worked."

"They were real people. Not a puzzle or a game for you to play detective with."

"We got a lot of messages from victims' loved ones," he says. "They appreciated how we kept attention on cases law enforcement had given up on. I think you of all people should understand that."

Daniel doesn't get it. That's what Bree wants. Bree wants a bunch of people puzzling out what happened to Abby, tying her definitively to Blue, and confirming exactly what happened in the last moments of her life. What Chelsea wants is simply for Abby to be remembered as more than the worst thing that happened to her.

"So what?" Chelsea says, crossing her arms. "You approached me that day in the church while you were redoing the woodwork, because you knew I had a murdered friend? This was all part of your hobby?"

Daniel looks horrified. "Oh my God. No. I had never heard of Abby before I met you, and I had no idea you lost someone like that. Once I did, I never talked about the website, because I knew you'd think it was weird."

"You still haven't answered my question," Chelsea says. "Why do you have that stuff in the attic?"

Daniel scratches the back of head. When he looks at her, his mouth quirks up on one side in a sad and apologetic way. She suddenly understands.

"You thought you'd try to solve her case."

"I think I hoped if I could figure out what happened, you could finally move on."

The laugh Chelsea gives is bitter. "Wow. How much ego does

it take to think you and your little keyboard detectives can do what real law enforcement wasn't able to do for over a decade?"

"You were the one who always said you thought the detective on her case fucked up."

This is true, but she can't let him have it. She can't let him have any of this. How long has Abby's missing person report sat up there without her knowing?

"How did you picture it going?" she asks. "I really want to know. Did you think, once you solved it, you'd tell me right away? Or did you think you'd wait for a special occasion? Like Valentine's, maybe?"

"Chelsea."

"No, really," she says. "How did you think this would go? You thought you'd say, 'Oh, I solved it. Okay, now you can stop hurting. Now—poof! It's magic—you can finally move on.'"

When Daniel speaks, his voice is soft. "You don't want to move on."

"What?"

"You don't. I don't know what it is about this, but there's something you won't let go of."

"Fuck you," she says, walking to the staircase. She wants to put as much distance as she can between them.

"Chelsea…"

When she's standing on the third stair, she stops and peers over the banister at him. He looks exhausted, but she's too full of rage to have any pity.

"How many cases did you solve?"

"What?" he asks.

"How many cases did you and your website friends solve?"

He's quiet for a moment. Then: "Well, none, but we—"

She walks up the stairs without waiting to hear the rest.

Daniel comes into the bathroom that night while she's brushing her teeth. When he speaks, he doesn't look at her, instead staring down at the cracked bathroom tile while she brushes her teeth.

"Why was Bree here tonight?"

She spits out a mouthful of toothpaste. She isn't ready to talk to him about Abby's body being found. Even the thought of saying the words feels impossible.

"She was here about the podcast," she says and then rinses her mouth out.

"You're sure there wasn't another reason she was here?"

"What are you talking about?" she asks.

"Maybe you should sit down."

He waits until she's sitting on the closed toilet. Daniel stands in front of her in his boxer briefs. The way he breaks the news is slower than how Bree did it. It's gentle, but if she were hearing it for the first time, it would be excruciating.

He can't come out and say it, so he dances around it, until finally he's able to say, "Honey, they found Abby's body. It was on the news."

What she said to Bree earlier was true. She had planned to tell Daniel, but she wanted some time to hold on to the news alone first. Now she's run out of time, and she realizes if she tells him the truth—that she already knew—he'll be wounded she just lied to his face. He'll see it as more proof of how she's always shutting him out, unable to handle this grief in a normal way. Maybe he'd be right.

She nods, working to keep her facial expression appropriate for someone learning something like this for the first time. Daniel, for all his earnestness, isn't dumb. He studies her for a moment before saying, "You already knew. That's the real reason Bree was here tonight."

Chelsea doesn't say anything, and Daniel shakes his head. "When were you going to tell me? You can't be mad I keep things from you," he says, gesturing to the attic. "And then keep stuff from me."

"I was going to tell you soon," Chelsea says.

But she sees by his expression he isn't convinced.

The Friday before Halloween, Chelsea drives across Iowa to record the podcast. Cows graze in already-harvested cornfields, their bodies black specks against the gold landscape and gray sky. She passes a red barn on the outskirts of a withered cornfield. Combines demolish the stalks, cornfield-dust clouding the air. A billboard advertises a steak house where customers pay by the pound. A quartet of silver grain silos loom in the distance.

By the time she exits I-80, the sun is a bloody smear on the horizon. Driving through campus, she passes the fraternity and sorority buildings flanking the Iowa River. Fallen leaves scuttle down the street in the wind.

When she talked to Rachel's assistant yesterday, who was calling to confirm she had received her itinerary, Chelsea asked why Rachel didn't just record people over the phone or through Skype. When the woman answered, it was like Chelsea had asked why you couldn't just put Big Mac sauce on Kobe beef.

"That might be fine for *some* podcasts," the assistant said. "But Rachel's work is really informed by the space where these stories happened."

Chelsea hasn't lived in Iowa City since the winter after her first and only semester of law school. The river was frozen solid when she drove her packed-up car out of town. Since then, she's visited a few times: to help her parents move to a fancy retirement community in Florida, to attend the occasional diocesan event, or to get drinks with friends who still live in the area. She doesn't like returning. She lived in this city for twenty-two years. There are so many memories layered onto it, a million past versions of herself walking the streets like a parade of ghosts.

Today, groups of costumed students walk toward house parties and the bars downtown. A boy in a Donald Trump mask. A girl dressed like "Sexy Pizza Rat"—fishnets, silvery lingerie, a tail and mouse ears, plastic toy pizzas stuck to her thighs. Mario and Luigi chase after a clearly drunk sexy nurse.

Chelsea thinks of that night, her and Abby and Bree getting ready in their dorm room. Chelsea's Going Out Mix CD cranked up as loud as the RA would allow, the room filled with hairspray and the Black Eyed Peas and the smell of Abby's Clinique Happy. Normally, they'd have been debating something stupid: Was Jessica Simpson really as dumb as she acted? Who was more annoying on *The O.C.*: Marissa or Summer? But that night something was already wrong. Chelsea was angry at Abby, the fight brewing.

In her hotel room, Chelsea finds a note from Rachel, encouraging her to settle in and save her receipts for anything she has for dinner or breakfast. The show will reimburse her. She should meet Rachel in the lobby at 9:00 a.m. tomorrow. Rachel's hand-writing is small and precise. There's something endearing about the handwritten note when her assistant already emailed Chelsea this information.

Chelsea smells the tiny bottles of shampoos and lotion, throws the germy, oversized throw pillows on the floor. She sits on the edge of the king-sized bed and stares at the hotel art hanging on the wall across from her—a color photo of a John Deere harvester reaping corn, its signature green standing out from the golden stalks. It's 8:00 p.m., and she isn't sure what to do to fill the hours before bed.

Students in Halloween costumes congregate in front of the bars. A boy with a Jason mask calls out to a girl dressed like Dorothy from *The Wizard of Oz*. Chelsea sees the Methodist Church's sandstone tower and the brown shingles of the United Church of Christ's gothic spire. In those last months before she dropped out of law school, Chelsea went to church every Sunday. She was usually hungover from the night before, and sometimes she got high in the church parking lot before she walked in. But she still showed up. The Methodist church with its huge stained-glass rose window and large pipe organ playing "Come Thou Fount of Every Blessing." The United Church of Christ with its fellowship hour afterward where old hippie ladies would ply Chelsea with vegan desserts and ask her about her classes. The Quaker services in the historic meeting house that smelled like old wood and fresh coffee, Chelsea's back aching from trying not to fidget during the hour of silent worship.

She tried not to investigate her need to attend these services, because there seemed to be something sad and pitiable at its core.

A reasonable person would have become an atheist after what happened to Abby. A reasonable person would accept that God clearly didn't answer people's prayers. And yet, there was Chelsea, eating part of an edible in her car before going to sing "Holy, Holy, Holy" with the Presbyterians.

One Sunday after the Eucharist, the female pastor at the Episcopal Church approached Chelsea, inviting her to her office. They drank strong coffee and talked about the liturgy. Finally, Chelsea asked a question she had been mulling over as she flitted from church to church—how could this woman believe in God when so many horrible things happened all the time?

"I believe the story of Jesus is true, because I've seen it again and again," the woman said. "Something must die for something else to live."

Abby had died, but Chelsea hadn't let anything else live. For the first time, Chelsea asked herself what she wanted to grow in Abby's wake. Within three years, she was in seminary.

She texts Daniel to tell him she arrived safely. Their text conversation is like their in-person conversations lately—strained, awkward, quick.

I love you, she texts him. She types it, not so much because she feels it, but because she wants to feel it. It's like a prayer.

The three dots appear at the bottom of the conversation, showing he's typing. Then they disappear.

ABBY

The Old Capitol's gold dome shines in the honeyed, late-afternoon sun as you and Chelsea sit on the grass in between classes. In the week since you went to the mall with your mom, you haven't gotten any closer to figuring out how you might tell her about you and Chelsea. Thankfully, Chelsea hasn't pushed you.

On the sidewalk, a small crowd has gathered around Brother Dave. Some people are yelling, while a guy in an Iowa hoodie tries to grab today's cardboard sign, which says *You Deserve Hell.*

"He just wants a reaction," Chelsea says. "Why can't people see that?"

The dude in the Iowa hoodie, unable to take the sign from Brother Dave, consoles himself by flicking him off and screaming, "Fuck you," in his face.

"Some real pastor should go out and debate him," Chelsea says. "You can't be about Jesus but only talk about hate."

"It bothers you."

"Doesn't it bother you?"

"I think most religious people are hypocrites or weirdos."

"They don't have to be," she says.

Chelsea's family is very Catholic. A framed photo from her First Communion sits on top of their piano in the living room. Young Chelsea in a sleeveless white dress, pleated skirt fanned out, legs crossed demurely at the ankles, revealing the frills of her white ankle socks.

You always loved the photo, studying it each time you were at Chelsea's house, because it seemed like access to a version of Chelsea you rarely saw—earnest where Chelsea was cynical, smiling where Chelsea was scowling, ladylike where Chelsea was more of a tomboy.

As Brother Dave yells about homosexuals deserving hell, you realize people would expect Chelsea to be the one more resistant to telling people about your relationship. She's the one who has the religious family. She's the one whose faith says being gay is a sin. But when you've asked her about this, she's always seemed unbothered.

"The church isn't right about everything," she told you once, shrugging.

You smile at her. She's wearing sunglasses, a white puffy coat, and jeans. Her face is as impassive as ever, and her legs are stretched out as she leans back on her elbows. You put your palm on her hand before she pulls it away and looks across the Pentacrest's lawn.

"It's been over a week, and you still haven't told your mom."

"I know," you say. "Things have just been stressful lately."

"With the prank calls?"

You nod. A few days ago, you told Chelsea about them. They happen around the same time every Tuesday and Thursday.

You've stopped answering the phone around that time, but it hasn't stopped the person from calling, the phone ringing until the answering machine picks up. Then they call back and do it again.

The last time you did *69, you paid the extra nickel to be connected. It rang for a while before a girl answered.

"Did someone here just call me?" you asked.

"This is a pay phone," she said. "So maybe."

"Which pay phone?"

The girl sounded distracted, like she was moving her face away from the receiver and you had to ask her to repeat herself. "The pay phone near the food court in Old Capitol Mall."

"Did you see who just used it?"

"A guy," the girl said.

"What did he look like?"

"I only really saw his back."

"Well, was he tall? Short? Younger? Older?"

"In between?" the girl said. "Look, I've got to make a call, okay?"

And then you heard the dial tone. Chelsea told you to tell the RA, but you can't help but feel more embarrassed than creeped out, imagining all the kids from your high school who would say, "Well, she was kind of slutty. It's no surprise someone's prank calling her like that."

Over the yelling of the crowd surrounding Brother Dave, Chelsea says, "You didn't tell me about those calls until after you agreed we could go public."

"So?"

She fiddles with her watch's band. "They never happen when I'm in the dorm room." She stares at you, but it's impossible to gauge her expression because of her sunglasses. She sighs. "I'm just wondering if maybe you're regretting agreeing to tell people, and this is an excuse you made up."

"You're accusing me of lying?"

"No," she says and then lies back, so she's flat on the ground, her hair sprawled across the grass. "I don't know. Maybe. I just wondered if you felt like you needed an excuse."

That she would suspect you of making this up hurts, but it hurts more that she's picked up on something real—your reluctance to tell people. Like Jay, she's seen straight through to the coward you are at heart.

"I'm not lying about those calls, Chelsea," you say, your voice rough even though you're trying hard to control it. "To be fair, I don't see you running out to tell your parents about us."

"I'd do it this second if I knew it would be worth it," she says, reaching into her backpack for her chunky Nokia cell phone. "But I'm not going to when there's a good chance you'd leave me high and dry."

You sit in silence for a few minutes. Finally, when you can keep your voice even, you say, "I'm going to see my mom this weekend. I'll do it then."

Chelsea doesn't respond. On the sidewalk, Brother Dave yells, "The end is near."

The next morning you're waiting in the lecture hall for your intro psychology class to begin when you hear it—that heavy breathing. You turn toward the sound to see a tall, skinny guy in gray sweatpants and a Bears sweatshirt staring at you, breathing with his mouth open. There are two empty seats between you and him. Your staring doesn't seem to make him self-conscious. Instead, he just stares back, still making that horrible noise as he breathes through his mouth.

You face forward in your seat, but his breathing continues, and then you can't help it—you have to turn back to him and ask, "Have you been calling me?"

"Calling you what?"

His voice is strange—more nasally and higher pitched than you expected. He looks genuinely confused, and you start to second-guess yourself. Didn't the voice of the guy who called you seem a little deeper in the moments he moaned a little? Is this just some socially awkward guy with sinus issues who happened to sit by you? Are you becoming totally fucking paranoid?

He's still staring at you.

You shake your head and turn away from him. "Never mind."

Your mother is too busy for a long lunch where you might ply her with wine, but she has time for a late morning walk Saturday. As the weekend nears, you become more and more of a mess—dropping your full tray in the cafeteria, so your salad and dressing and glass of Diet Coke coat the dingy tile; forgetting your room key; snapping at Chelsea when she makes the tiniest noise while she studies for an exam after you've gone to bed.

When Saturday morning arrives, Chelsea seems nervous, too. It's like *she's* your mother getting you ready for your first day of school—asking: *Do you need a scarf? Is that coat warm enough? Should I be nearby waiting for you if things go badly?*

When you're finally with your mother, it's almost a relief just to be away from Chelsea's endless questions. The two of you meet for a walk in the cemetery, which is something you did a lot when you were younger. Your parents lived in an apartment nearby when you were a toddler, and your father was still in his oral surgery residency. There are a bunch of photos of you in frilly dresses walking around the tombstones, occasionally the Black Angel looming in the background. You always thought that someday, when you were a famous actress, the first line of your autobiography would be *I learned to walk in a graveyard*.

However, it seems less and less likely you'll ever be an actress of any kind, much less a famous one. As you and your mother sit on a bench, you tell her about your acting class. Thankfully, heartsharing has ended, and you're staging scenes for the midterm showcase. You're in one from *The Uninvited*, playing Wendy, a glamourous actress who comes to a haunted seaside estate.

"Is Wendy the lead?" your mother asks.

"It's just a scene," you say. "Everyone has a pretty equal number of lines."

You know this because you counted them.

"What part did Bree get?" your mother asks.

You can't help but sigh because you know where this is going. "She's in a different scene."

"What scene?"

"It's from *The Seagull*...by Chekhov."

"I know who it's by," your mother says. "That sounds like a better scene."

"Well, it's not," you say, although this is patently false. It's easy to see from the cast lists that Jay divided them into two groups by perceived skill. The sub-par performers, like you, are in the scene from *The Uninvited*. The better students, like Bree, all have their own short monologues and two-person scenes.

You watched Bree rehearse in the theater yesterday, standing center stage, head bowed, hair shining under the spotlight. "Do you remember how you shot a seagull once?" she said. "A man chanced to pass that way and destroyed it out of idleness."

"You'll just have to work harder," your mother says, watching fallen leaves blow across the gravestones. "Speaking of that, I have Atkins diet stuff in the car. Low-carb cereal. Low-carb energy bars. They even make low-carb ice cream, but the mini fridge in your dorm doesn't have a freezer, does it?"

You shake your head, feeling suddenly exhausted. Maybe telling her about you and Chelsea will be a good thing, because you're already not living up to who she wants you to be. Better to tear down the whole facade and say, *Here, this is me. I'm a not-very-good actress who eats carbs and is in love with a girl.*

Your mom has been drinking coffee spiked with Bailey's out of a thermos, and she takes another sip. You watch her profile as she swallows, the delicate nose, strong chin, and high cheekbones. She sets the thermos down between you and stares across the cemetery. The day is cool but sunny, and the leaves are bright reds and oranges. Fall is your mother's favorite season, and she sighs.

"What a beautiful day."

This is it. This is the moment to do it. There won't be a better one. You've practiced the beginning of your speech over and over in the single-occupancy bathroom on the first floor of your dorm.

Mom, I need to tell you something, and I know it might be hard to hear. But I want to be honest with you, and I want to be close to you.

You face her, and she looks back at you.

"I need to tell you something," she says. "It's about your dad."

As you watch her swallow, you assume she'll say they're getting a divorce. The best thing about no longer living at home is that you don't have to watch them interact very much. When you were younger, their fights were yelling matches that could go on for hours, until someone stormed out of the house. As awful as those were, the cold silence that fell over the house as the years passed was somehow worse.

"What about Dad?"

She hesitates for a few seconds, the wind pulling her hair. Finally, she says, "He was in your room, looking for an extra extension cord, and he found a picture. A picture of you and Chelsea. It must have fallen behind your desk."

You swallow. It didn't fall behind your desk. You hid it there, thinking it was a place no one would ever look. You never should have left it at your parents' house. You can see the snapshot, taken with a disposable camera: you and Chelsea kissing with your eyes closed, both of your faces a little blurry because you were too close to the lens.

Your father has always been a workaholic who feels more like a polite acquaintance than a parent. To picture him holding something so personal, such a candid image of you, is surreal.

Tell her, you think. *This is it. All you have to do is say it.*

Your mother puts her sunglasses up like a headband and studies you, her eyes roaming your face. "It was a photo of you two kissing. Your father got upset because he thought it meant something.

But I told him, you three were always putting on plays and filming home movies, and Bree was always directing you in her little photography projects. So, I explained it to him. I explained it didn't mean anything."

In her eyes, you see how much she wants you to agree with her. You see all the hours she spent waiting in the car for you at dance lessons or choir rehearsals. You see the silly games she used to make up to entertain you on rainy days—hiding candy somewhere in the house and telling you if you were getting warmer or colder. She'd do it for hours as you scoured the house, delighted.

There are so many opportunities she didn't get, because of her childhood, that she made sure to give you. Isn't it ultimately selfish to hurt her simply because you *think* you might like women? Shouldn't you wait until you're completely certain? Who is Chelsea to force you to do this?

Please, your mother's eyes are saying.

"It didn't mean anything," you say, giving a little laugh, careful to make it sound light and unbothered. "I think it was from some photography project Bree was doing. I had honestly forgotten about it."

Your mother smiles, relief etched across her face. "That's what I told your dad!"

A crow jumps in front of a gravestone and caws, scaring a couple sparrows away.

"Do you need help memorizing your lines for the showcase?" your mother asks.

Your mouth is dry and it's hard to speak, but you nod and pull out your copy of *The Uninvited* from your bag. The script opens on your lap to the page with your first line, highlighted in yellow: *Ghosts hate mirrors. They're terrified by their own reflection.*

Chelsea's waiting for you when you get back to the dorm that afternoon. As soon as you walk through the door, she puts her arms around you.

"Did you tell her?" she asks, her voice muffled in your hair. You breathe in her smell—the vanilla perfume from the Body Shop she's used exclusively since middle school, but under that, the smell of her, the tang of her skin and hair. It's gross, but you love the smell of her hair a couple days unwashed, sharp but still a little sweet. Chelsea Concentrate, you've called it before, and she laughed, rolling her eyes.

You prepare yourself to disappoint her, squaring your shoulders, clenching your jaw, but do you have to? You're an actress, after all. Why shouldn't you use the skills from this impractical major to buy yourself some time?

"I told her."

"What did she say?" Chelsea leans back to study your face.

Although you still think Jay is a weirdo, you pull from the place right behind your breastbone where every little bit of your shame lives. When you start to cry, it doesn't feel like you're faking it. It feels cathartic.

Chelsea leads you to the futon and sits down with you. She pets your hair and hands you tissues. She kisses the top of your head, your earlobes, the tip of your nose, your fingertips.

"I'm so proud of you," she says.

ENTERTAINMENT WEEKLY

"FIVE QUESTIONS WITH PODCASTING
PHENOM RACHEL MORGAN"

Without a doubt, the media sensation of 2012 wasn't a TV show or movie. It was the true crime podcast *Infamous*, which followed host Rachel Morgan's deep dive into the 2002 murder of Mandy Williams. Morgan interviewed Williams's friends and family, as well as the man convicted of her murder—husband Bill Williams. The result was a complicated and intriguing portrayal of a case that had previously boiled down to "the husband did it."

Infamous's second season centered on the 2000 murder of Joshua Petersen, a junior at Penn State, and concerns surrounding the conviction of Petersen's roommate, Michael Gutierrez. Since the season aired, evidence Morgan uncovered about racial profiling led to a new appeal filed for Gutierrez, and fans are eagerly awaiting the show's third season.

Morgan herself is as interesting as the subjects she reports on. When you meet her, the first thing you notice is the scar running up her right lip and cheek. You might expect her to favor her left side to hide it, but she doesn't. Although she's coy about what caused the scar, many fans believe it's evidence Morgan has had her own run-in with violent crime. Whatever its origin, the maiming caused her to quit her career as a dancer with the Boston Ballet in her early twenties and go back to school to study journalism. After a stint as an assistant at the *New Yorker*, she struck out on her own to achieve podcasting glory.

We caught up with Morgan to ask her about her overnight success, her interviewing secrets, and what we can expect from season three.

Entertainment Weekly: What has it been like to go from unknown to someone with one of the most popular podcasts of all time?

Rachel Morgan: It's surreal. My background was in newspapers, and then I got a job as a fact-checker and assistant at the *New Yorker*, so I was used to doing work that not a lot of people read or work that strengthened other people's writing. Being the face of something is a strange and sometimes unsettling experience.

EW: Something a lot of people have talked about is your ability to get people to share such personal, emotional stories. It's especially impressive, because these are often people who have been interviewed a lot and never divulged these stories. What is it about you that draws things out of people?

RM [laughing]: I can't divulge all my secrets, but I do think a big part of it is showing empathy. By the time I'm interviewing these people, I've read almost everything that exists about the case and the people involved. The victim feels like a real person, and I think that care and attention come across to the people I'm speaking to.

EW: People are eagerly awaiting *Infamous's* third season. What can we expect?

RM: Rather than one murder, like season one and two, the third season tackles a series of murders. Right now, I'm in the early stages, getting interviews lined up.

EW: Is it harder or easier to get people to agree to participate this time around?

RM: It's a mixed bag. Some people are more eager because they know me and know what I'm about. Some people are more hesitant, I think, because they know the level of attention the show will receive.

EW: What drew you to true crime in the first place?

RM: Crime stories show the best and worst of humanity. There's nothing more compelling than that.

BREE

OCTOBER 2015

When Bree returns from visiting Chelsea, she reads article after article about Rachel Morgan. Although she knows she's right to distrust true crime, she can't deny that Rachel is a skilled investigator. If Rachel Morgan can uncover something that gets Jon Allan Blue to admit what he did to Abby before he dies, how can Bree not agree to participate?

She wonders what Rachel Morgan's aim is in including Abby in her season about Jon Allan Blue. Does she want to definitively tie Blue to Abby's disappearance? Is she hoping diving into Abby's less well-known case could shed light on all Blue's murders? Is Rachel going to be one of those soft-voiced podcast hosts who spend hours digging into every conceivable detail of the case, only to reach the end of the season and give their listeners the podcast equivalent of a shrug? Like, *Sorry, after all these interviews and all this obsessive research, all I can tell you is we'll never know.*

Bree knows she needs to modulate her expectations. Rachel's interest in interviewing them does not mean she'll uncover anything. Rachel is not going to be some savior who swoops in and gives her the answers she's waited twelve years for. Still, Bree can't help but want to pick her brain.

The afternoon she leaves for Iowa City is six days before Jon Allan Blue's execution. Bree puts an auto-reply on her work email and saves some student portfolios to her laptop to grade during her trip to Iowa City to record the podcast. She's also dusted off her camera, checked the battery, and put in a blank memory card.

Being around Chelsea seems to have reset something in Bree creatively. She's been editing the photos she took of her. They're not as good as she'd like, because they were just taken on her phone, but for the first time in a long time, she's eager to take photos again.

There's a knock, and Alayna appears in the doorway. Bree gestures for her to come into her office, but as soon as she does, Bree knows something's wrong. From the way Alayna's standing, shoulders back, chin tilted, eyes narrowed, she knows immediately Zach has told her.

"He's your *student*," Alayna says.

Bree rises from behind her desk, but she can't find her voice and glances above Alayna's head and through the doorway to see if anyone is coming down the hall.

Alayna gives a laugh, and it's so bitter it makes the hair on Bree's arms rise. She studies one of Francesca Woodman's photos Bree hung on her wall. It's one Woodman took in a room with ripped wallpaper. Woodman's naked body stands against the wall. She's holding strips of the wallpaper over herself in a way that makes it look like she's disappearing into the wall, only her ankles and pale belly exposed.

Alayna's expression is so disgusted; Bree has to look away.

"I'm not coming to your class anymore," Alayna says. "But you're still going to give me an A."

When Bree doesn't respond, Alayna says, "Okay?"

"Okay," Bree says, but she's so ashamed she still can't meet Alayna's eyes.

———————

As Bree starts the drive to Iowa City, the sun sets over the cornfields. She passes the skeleton of an abandoned barn, and as three hawks fly low over the golden stalks, she wonders if this was the type of place Abby's body was found. It occurs to her she'd rather think about Abby than what Alayna just said to her. What does it mean when your past trauma feels like a safer place to rest than the concerns of your real life?

It means you're really fucked up, she thinks.

Once she arrives in Iowa City, she feels claustrophobic in her hotel room, with its white walls and white bedspread, so she goes downstairs to the bar. When the bartender approaches, she surprises herself by ordering a club soda. It's the first time she admits it to herself: *You want to keep it.*

There's a thrill at the thought, at the truth of it, but that feeling turns quickly to shame when she thinks about Alayna's face as she stood in Bree's office. How could someone who has fucked up this badly be fit to become someone's mother?

The bar has filled with white women in their early thirties who order giant glasses of wine. It isn't until Bree notices the Greek letters on two of the women's shirts that she understands—it's the women from Alpha Psi Theta, laughing and smiling. They're relieved, Bree assumes, to be done recording their part of the podcast.

Maybe when it airs they'll listen to it while they run dutifully on the elliptical, sweat beading their brows, or as they slice an apple for their kid's lunch, the knife heavy in their hands. Maybe they'll listen while they walk the dog, and as the sky grows dark, they'll feel the familiar panic tighten their chests. They'll look over their shoulders as they make their way home. At night in bed, while their partners snore softly, they'll stare at the ceiling and remember what it was like the night he broke into the sorority house, the exact pitch their friend wailed while her face was smashed with a fireplace poker. The exact texture of their other friend's walls, speckled with her blood and skull fragments.

He killed two women that night and disfigured another.

Bree rests her hands on the smooth surface of the bar. How many women did he hurt? And yet, Chelsea was happy to sit with him. To pray with him. To offer him forgiveness that wasn't hers to give.

"Bree, is it?" a voice asks.

A woman sits on the bar stool next to her. Bree turns her head before looking straight ahead again. She doesn't want to seem like she's staring.

"I'm Jessica," the woman says, although of course Bree knows. Everyone knows.

While Jessica orders another chardonnay, Bree studies her. The news articles said she had over a dozen surgeries on her face. Her heavy foundation can't hide all the scarring or the way her nose remains a little off-kilter. It looks almost like the whole left half of her face is made of wax. The skin of her left eye is scarred and puckered at the corner. He shattered her nose and broke three of her ribs.

"You're Abby Hartmann's friend, right?" Jessica asks.

Bree nods. "How did you know?"

Jessica's smile is eerie—maybe because her jaw doesn't hang quite right or maybe it's the expression someone wears when they survived a nightmare and are still breathing.

"The Linda Joy interview," she says. "I didn't see it at the time because I was in the hospital. But I saw it online later."

During Linda Joy's almost 24/7 coverage of the Alpha Psi Theta murders, Bree was able to convince the show's producers to have her and Chelsea on. Bree thought more coverage of Abby's disappearance might prevent her from being forgotten in the wake of the more gruesome murders.

When Bree is in a particularly self-recriminating mood, she'll pull up the interview on YouTube. She watches the version titled "Linda Joy Interviews Missing Girl's Friends: Heated Exchange!" Sometimes, she watches it muted, looking for the exact moment when the interview goes sideways and it's clear Bree and Chelsea are the ones being grilled. She'll watch Joy's eyebrows raise, the way her blond bob shakes as she gets more and more animated, demanding to know why Bree and Chelsea allowed their friend to wander off on her own at night.

Chelsea, a high school debate state champion, had come to the interview high, wearing a wrinkled button-down and a perpetually mystified expression, staying mute for almost the entirety of the interview.

In the clip, Bree's expression changes, from sad to confused to angry. The more attacked she feels, the more she gestures with her hands. She wishes there had been someone in her life back then who could have told her, *Don't wear such a low-cut top. Don't wear such heavy eye makeup. Take out the metal stud in your tongue. No one should judge you for these things, but they will. You don't want to look like what you are—a white trash girl on the defensive.*

"They're interviewing us for the podcast tomorrow," Bree says. Jessica nods. She points to all the women sipping their drinks. "It's a strange little club we've got here."

Jessica is The Final Girl. Bree first heard the term in a film class she took her senior year of college.

"The Final Girl is the one who lives to see the end of the horror movie," her professor said. "She's Jamie Lee Curtis in Halloween. *She's Neve Campbell in* Scream. *She's the one left to tell the story."*

Bree thought of Jessica immediately. It was painful—the idea that only one got to live. Because, of course, Abby was not *The Final Girl.* She was just *A Girl.*

"It may sound strange," Jessica says, swirling the wine in her glass, "but Abby's story always really got me."

"It did?" Bree asks, surprised. Although there shouldn't be a hierarchy of victims, there is. Abby's story doesn't have the terror and carnage of "The Sorority House Slaughter" or even the pathos of twelve-year-old Erika Finch, who Blue lured away from her middle school and whose body was later found in a hog shed.

"Yeah," Jessica says. "There are just so many unanswered questions. As horrible as some of the other murders were, at least their families had a body to bury all those years ago."

Bree nods. Once, Frye had started crying after they had sex. He told Bree Mrs. Hartmann had come to him earlier that day, got on her knees in the middle of the police station, and literally begged, "Please, just give me one bone to bury."

"Was finding the body a comfort for her family?" Jessica asks.

"Well, Mrs. Hartmann…" Bree trails off, and Jessica winces.

"I'm sorry," she says. "I forgot about what happened to her."

"I'm not in touch with her father anymore," Bree says.

During the Linda Joy interview Bree had felt so attacked she blurted out something she and Chelsea had only told Frye at that point. She said Abby had slept with her boyfriend and that was why they had let her leave that night. She still remembers Linda Joy's expression. Her nose wrinkled, her upper lip raised to expose her teeth, as if she smelled something foul. "Are you saying she deserved to die, because she slept with your boyfriend?"

Bree tried desperately to explain. In the clip on YouTube, you could see her eyes widen, see her shake her head. "No," she said. "That's not what I'm saying at all. I'm just trying to explain why we let her go on her own."

But the damage was done. Briefly, the media did give Abby more attention, but not the kind they hoped for. People started reporting on Abby's "promiscuity," asking if that was part of the reason she was targeted. It was ugly, it was sad, and Bree was the one who started it. After that, the Hartmanns stopped returning their calls.

A week ago, Bree had seen Mr. Hartmann on the news talking about the private family memorial service they would have for Abby's remains. Mr. Hartmann had been a non-entity when they were growing up, always busy at work or drinking scotch in the upstairs den. Bree remembered him as stoic and intimidating, so it was strange to see him gray and slightly stooped, like a photo of himself that had been left too long in the sun.

The interview with Linda Joy hadn't just severed Bree's relationship with the Hartmanns. It had also been the final note in the slow death of her friendship with Chelsea. In some ways, the saddest part was how mutual it had been. Bree didn't call Chelsea after that day, and Chelsea didn't call Bree. By the time Blue was being marched into a jail cell in Kentucky in handcuffs, Chelsea and Bree didn't even nod when they passed one another on campus.

"It's hard to believe they'll actually kill Blue this time," Jessica says.

His case has gone through what seems to Bree like a million appeals. Then, in 2010, a Kentucky judge ordered a stay of all executions because of concerns about the drugs used in lethal injections. It was only in the past year the stay was lifted, partly because of pressure from the governor to move forward with Blue's execution. Bree's not a legal expert, but it seems this time is actually it.

"You don't feel like your friend feels?" Jessica asks. "You know, praying with him? Focusing on forgiveness?"

Bree meets Jessica's pointed stare. Her heavy, orangey foundation makes her blue eyes pop. She feels a pang picturing Jessica in front of the mirror every morning, trying so hard to cover what Blue did to her.

"I don't," she says. "Save your forgiveness for someone who deserves it. Not him."

"You have to hand it to her," Jessica says, after draining her glass. "I mean, I've never been on *Jezebel*, and I've got all this going for me."

She gestures to the left half of her face, her expression mocking.

Bree smiles politely and sets down some cash as a tip for her club soda, but she thinks *No one wants to see you.*

It's a horrible thing to think, but she knows it's true. People prefer the photos of the dead girls, frozen in their teenage beauty. There's something more appealing about the pure, clean loss in those pictures. Look at their promise. Look at their sparkle. Look at the women these girls will never become.

CHELSEA
OCTOBER 2015

When Chelsea enters the hotel lobby in the morning, Bree's talking to a woman in skinny jeans and calf-high boots. At first, Chelsea assumes it's Rachel, who they're supposed to meet. As she gets closer, though, the woman's scarred face comes into view.

Jessica McCabe. The only surviving Blue victim.

Chelsea and Abby walked past Alpha Psi Theta's massive Tudor early in the fall semester, chocolate-colored timber framing beige stucco. "AΨΘ" in gold on a plaque over the front door, shining in the early evening sun. It was initiation, and the sorority girls all wore white dresses and pearls, holding lit taper candles, as they walked single file, some of them unsteady in their heels like foals walking for the first time.

"Run!" Chelsea yelled to them. "It's not too late. You can still escape!"

Chelsea hadn't even been all that anti-sorority. She just wanted to make Abby laugh, and she had while the girls craned their necks toward them, pursing glossy lips.

Had Jessica been one of those girls? Reddish hair cascading down her back, her face unmarred?

Although Jessica looks at Chelsea, she speaks to Bree. "When they kill him, let's get a drink to celebrate."

"I'd like that," Bree says.

Chelsea works hard to smile. *Chelsea can't help that she has a bitch face,* Abby had said once when she was very drunk. After a stunned silence, they all burst out laughing, even Chelsea because it was true.

"You're Chelsea Navarro," Jessica says.

Chelsea's careful not to let her eyes linger on Jessica's scarring. She remembers that early morning after the murders, squad car after squad car speeding down Washington Street toward the sorority house. Chelsea has seen photos from that morning. Pictures of the sorority girls wrapped in blankets, embracing each other, police officers in the background.

She tries to look Jessica steady in the eyes. Chelsea sticks out her hand for her to shake. She doesn't take it.

"You sat and prayed with the man who did this," Jessica says, gesturing to her face. "You told him you forgave him."

That's not at all what happened when Chelsea met with Blue, but it's too late to tell the true story now, so she clears her throat.

"I forgave him for the ways he hurt me," she says. "I, obviously, can't forgive him for the pain he caused you. That's not my place."

"But you don't think he should die, do you?"

The various hotel sounds distract Chelsea. The bank of elevators ding to sound their arrival, their doors opening and slamming shut, people drag rolling suitcases with squeaky wheels as the front desk clerk checks people in and out with a chipper voice. Some man in a University of Iowa sweatshirt fills his whole water bottle from the complimentary cucumber water dispenser. She's aware of Bree watching her.

"I don't think the murder of another person will fix what we all lost," she tells Jessica.

She tries to speak confidently, but despite everything she has said publicly, in her heart, all she wants is for Blue to die. All she wants is to watch him look scared and small as they strap him to a table and jam needles into his veins.

Jessica's face contorts as she gives a bitter laugh. "I lost my physical health, my mental health, my sense of safety. I'm in physical pain *all the time*. You lost a friend. Someone we don't even know if Jon Allan Blue actually killed. Of course, you can forgive him. You'd feel differently if you were in my place."

Chelsea's overcome with an urge to slap Jessica. *How dare you minimize my loss*, she wants to say as she looks down, studying the hotel's tile floor. When she glances up, Jessica's hands are shaking. The man with the water bottle and a woman in the check-in line stare. They look at Chelsea with expressions that say, *What have you done to make this poor woman so upset?*

"Can I pray with you?" Chelsea asks.

"Fuck you," Jessica says. She grips her suitcase handle and exits the lobby through the automatic sliding doors. Her limp makes her left leg drag a little.

Arms crossed, black skinny jeans clinging to her slim legs, chunky Doc Martens on her feet, Bree holds a large camera. The strap of a well-worn leather bag cuts across her black velvet blazer. Despite the acting classes, she always had a terrible poker face. She's almost smiling.

"I'm guessing you share her sentiments?" Chelsea asks, gesturing to where Jessica disappeared through the sliding doors.

"You can't blame her," Bree says, shrugging.

A woman in her early thirties with brown hair and cat-eye glasses approaches them. She's not tall. She only has a few inches on Chelsea, who barely clears five one, but she has an undeniable physical presence. A swagger that makes it hard for Chelsea to take her eyes off her.

"Bree? Chelsea?" she says. "I'm Rachel."

Her oval face has high cheekbones and narrow, close-set eyes. That scar cuts across her full upper lip and pronounced Cupid's bow and up across her cheek toward her ear. She isn't pretty—not truly—but this, oddly, makes her more compelling. If she were classically beautiful, it might be easy to assign her appeal to mere prettiness. Instead, Chelsea stares at her for a long time, trying to figure out what it is that makes her unable to look away.

While they shake hands, Rachel holds Chelsea's eyes a little longer than expected. Her grip is strong, and a smile cuts across her face, her teeth white and straight.

"How was your night last night?" Rachel asks.

"Fine," Bree says.

With this woman's eyes watching her, Chelsea can barely string words together. "Cool," she finally stammers. "It was cool."

Cool? What is she even saying?

Rachel thanks them for coming, for being willing to be so vulnerable with her and her listeners. She's different than she was on the phone—the hurried, businesslike persona evaporated. In its place, Rachel's warmth makes Chelsea feel relaxed and almost excited.

But as Rachel gestures for them to follow her to the parking lot, it's like whatever spell she's put her under weakens. Chelsea's reminded of what she and Bree are actually about to do. They exchange a look. The hesitation on Bree's face matches the pit forming in Chelsea's stomach. Bree grabs Chelsea's hand. For a moment, her hand goes limp in Bree's before Chelsea disentangles it and they walk to Rachel's rental car.

————————

The GPS from Rachel's phone chirps directions as they drive through downtown toward the cemetery, even though Chelsea could tell the way blindfolded. She sits in the passenger seat as Rachel drives, staring out the window at the beautiful, sunny Saturday in the middle of football season. Iowa fans mill around downtown bars, their gold and black clothes and unsteady gaits familiar from Chelsea's own football Saturdays on campus.

Over the GPS's robotic voice, Bree speaks from the back seat, her voice so nakedly full of hope, it raises a lump in Chelsea's throat: "So in researching everything, do you have any theories about what happened to Abby that night?"

Rachel glances at Bree in the rearview mirror. When she answers, her tone shows more gentleness than Chelsea would have expected based on their phone calls.

"I don't know, Bree. On the one hand, it seems unlikely two people were wandering around Iowa City murdering teenage girls with red hair."

"Auburn," Bree and Chelsea say in unison, and Rachel glances at Chelsea and then Bree before continuing.

"Okay, auburn. On the other hand, people hurt girls all the time. I think the strangest part is the lack of evidence. Was he especially careful when he took Abby? Did he plan it for a long time and that's why he left nothing behind? Some people believe he was in what psychologists call an 'organized' phase when he was killing in Nebraska and his first Iowa murders. Then, by the time he did the sorority house, he had moved into a 'disorganized' phase, leaving a lot of evidence behind and becoming less careful as he moved on to Kentucky."

There's a story about Blue staying in a hotel room in Des Moines and removing every fingerprint and bit of his DNA before he left, even wiping down things like lightbulbs and using a screwdriver to open the drains and remove his hair from inside them. Chelsea always wondered if that was an urban legend, another story designed to mythologize him as an evil genius.

A woman in her early fifties with coiffed blond hair and wearing an Iowa sweatshirt over a turtleneck staggers down Iowa Avenue, her bespectacled husband trying and failing to help her stand upright.

Someone got Iowa City-ed, Chelsea thinks. It's what they used to say—she, Abby, and Bree. Iowa used to be one of the top party schools, and it was common to walk around downtown Sunday morning and see vomit and broken glass and bloody footprints decorating the pavement. How many times had Chelsea woken up with her own puke crusted around her? There was always that momentary panic and cataloging: *How did I get home? Where's my wallet?*

Rachel gestures to the drunk woman, whose husband has now propped her up and is walking her toward the Old Capitol. "That poor woman is really lit."

"This town will do that to you," Bree says.

"Did Abby drink a lot?" Rachel asks.

Bree and Chelsea both hesitate. Despite Rachel's casual tone, Chelsea knows how quickly things can get spun a certain way.

Bree says, "She drank like any college student." At the same time, Chelsea says, "None of us really drank that much."

"Huh," Rachel says. "Abby's dad said she drank starting in high school."

"You talked to Abby's dad?" Chelsea asks.

At Rachel's nod, Chelsea frowns. Of course she would. But for some reason it feels intolerable Rachel is allowed access to someone who so cleanly cut off contact with Chelsea.

As they pass Phillips Hall, a modernist building with a grid of recessed windows, Brother Dave stands in one of his favorite spots, holding a cardboard sign. It's one of his most inflammatory: *God Hates Homos.* He must be in his late thirties now, his brown hair a little thinner, his face more lined, but he's still wearing the same self-satisfied expression, shouting at the people walking past.

"Holy shit," Bree says. "He's still at it. Want to pull over and talk theology with him, Chelsea?"

"No, thank you."

A little while after they turn onto Dodge Street, the cemetery's granite monuments appear. The last place they saw Abby.

This is the world's most morbid tour, and Chelsea has the almost hysterical urge to laugh. It dies as Rachel parks, and they step onto the asphalt path leading farther into the cemetery.

Rachel carries a bag with all her recording equipment, and it thumps against her hip while they walk. The wind rattles the dead leaves across the sea of graves. Even though Chelsea knows it's coming, her breath still catches when they round the bend and the Black Angel appears.

"Oh," Rachel says, putting a hand to her mouth.

Chelsea remembers when she first saw it as a kid. It made the hair on her arms rise, all nine feet looming in the distance above the tombstones. Unlike the wings of most statues of angels, the Black Angel's wings aren't lifted, and she isn't looking heavenward. Instead, one wing droops at her side, and she uses the other to shield her bowed head, the effect both sinister and mournful.

"What's it made of?" Rachel asks.

"It's bronze. It oxidized over the years, which gives it that greenish-black color."

Growing up, they heard all kinds of superstitions about it. Any girl who kissed the statue would die in six months. If a virgin kissed it, it would revert to its original bronze color. Every Halloween, the angel supposedly turned a shade darker. A pregnant woman would miscarry if she touched it.

After Abby's disappearance, the ground under the statue became a makeshift shrine—full of devotional candles, bouquets of daisies, single long-stemmed roses, Mylar balloons flying high in the wind over the tombstones. A month later, after Alpha Psi Theta, the balloons deflated, and the flowers wilted.

Today, there are only a few sparse, old offerings: a bedraggled teddy bear, a deflated balloon puddled across the dying grass next to an artificial rose with mud caked on its fraying petals, and, at the statue's base, a photo of Abby. Someone has done a makeshift lamination job on the picture—covering it in strips of clear tape to protect it from the weather. Bleached from the sun, only her white teeth and the roundness of her face are discernible.

Rachel bends over, opening her bag of recording equipment. When she stands, her glasses have slipped down her nose a little,

and she's holding a microphone that looks like a black corn dog—
the foot-long ones Bree always bought at the Iowa State Fair.

"Can you tell me about that night?" she asks.

Somehow, they have already started recording, Chelsea realizes. Although Rachel's face is a mask of concern, a deep wrinkle
between her nose and eyebrows, her head tilted, Chelsea feels
unnerved by how quickly things are moving. She isn't sure what
she expected. Maybe a sound test? Maybe Rachel to ask if they
were ready? She doesn't think she's ready.

Rachel's expression says that she knows just how much she's
asking of them. That recognition allows Chelsea to speak, and the
lights on the tiny black box connected to the microphone pulse in
time to Chelsea's voice.

"We were at a party a few blocks away," she says. "And Abby
wanted to walk here to see the Black Angel on Halloween."

Rachel steps closer, the angel looming behind her. Chelsea's
already exhausted. She didn't expect standing here after all these
years would fill her with such emotion, but it feels like in some
primal way she has never left this cemetery, that every day a part
of her has been right here, rooted to this spot.

Sometimes, it's hard to parse what she remembers and what
became a mythology she built about that night. But some details
stay sharp. It was a clear night before the snow started, the tem-
peratures dropping into the thirties, too cold for Abby's and Bree's
skimpy costumes and Chelsea's thin sheet. Despite the cold,
they didn't wear coats. They never did back then. Partly, it was
vanity. They wanted everyone to see their bare arms and legs and
cleavage. But part of it was logistical—once you were drunk, you
didn't want to keep track of a coat. The sidewalks were slick with

clumps of wet, frosted leaves, and Abby and Bree kept slipping in their high heels, eventually linking arms to steady each other, the goose bumpy flesh of their upper arms pressed together, as Chelsea trudged behind them in her ghost costume.

The air smelled of burning leaves, the moon a sickle above them. It was hard not to see everything as an omen, in retrospect. Everything a sign they should have paid attention to but didn't.

Rachel asks why they were fighting that night, and Bree says, "Abby slept with my boyfriend."

Although Chelsea wants Abby to be characterized through Rachel's podcast, for her to be more than just another dead girl, she also feels protective of Abby's memory. It's hard to balance the two desires, and she says quickly, "It was a misunderstanding."

Annoyance quirks Bree's lips, but she doesn't contradict Chelsea. Instead, she holds her camera up and snaps photos of the Black Angel.

Rachel asks if there was a lot of competition between Bree and Abby. Bree lets her camera hang from the strap around her neck and opens her mouth to answer. Before she can, Chelsea says, "No, mostly we all really supported each other."

Bree shakes her head, staring at Chelsea, but Rachel is adjusting a setting on her audio equipment and doesn't seem to notice. Then Rachel asks *the* question and Bree freezes.

"I know this might be hard to talk about, Bree, but I have to ask. You knew Jon Allan Blue. Did you ever suspect anything?"

Chelsea's initial reaction is a smug satisfaction. It's the angry eighteen-year-old girl inside her who's happy to have someone else to blame. Someone to point to and say, *Look, you failed her even worse than I did.*

That angry girl's voice quiets, and Chelsea's satisfaction dissolves as she sees Bree's anguished expression. The self-blame on Bree's face is so familiar, it brings a lump to Chelsea's throat, and she has to look away.

Chelsea studies the statue's broken fingers. A few years ago, she looked up the statue online. City historians said it was built for a Czech woman's dead son. They said the angel wasn't supposed to look scary. It was supposed to be a tribute, a monument to a mother's grief. Despite all the superstitions, the true story boiled down to this: a woman, many years ago, had loved someone. That person had died, and to grieve, the woman had built something no one understood.

"I knew him," Bree says. "Or I thought I knew him."

"Tell us about him," Rachel says.

ABBY

OCTOBER 2003

It's been two days since you met with your mother in the cemetery, and Chelsea has barely stopped touching you when you're alone. She traces a line down your shin with the tip of her toe under the sheets.

"I'm not sure how I'm going to tell them," she says of her parents. "I didn't actually get as far as planning it out. I didn't believe you'd ever tell your mom."

Her eyes are bright, and you've never seen her smile this much. The guilt is almost suffocating as you lie back against her pillow.

"Why did it matter so much to you?" you ask.

"I needed to know it was real on your end."

She rests her head on your chest, draping an arm across your stomach. As her breathing deepens into sleep, you listen to the sounds of the building—doors opening and closing, the clunking of pipes, and the radiator's hissing.

You have to make sure Chelsea and your mother don't see each other. Chelsea plans to talk to her own parents next week, so then you'll need to keep her parents from your mother, too. And after she tells her parents, she'll want to share things with Bree, and then…

As you shake your head, Chelsea shifts slightly in her sleep. You're overthinking it. You're just buying yourself a few weeks. Soon you really will tell your mother, and this small span of time won't matter.

———————

Later that week, you and Bree peek through the gap in the curtain to watch the audience take their seats before the midterm showcase. You've always loved the sound of an audience talking in a theater before curtain, the anticipation building as all those people's eyes are about to be on you, and you'll be able to control exactly what they see.

It's a free performance in one of the campus's smaller theaters, but other professors have offered extra credit for their students to attend, so it's almost a full house. Chelsea has a night class, so she won't be able to come. This disappointed you at first, but after you put yourself in such a tenuous situation with Chelsea and your mother, it's for the best.

Bree points out Al, sitting in the fourth row with some of the art students.

Scanning for your mother, your eyes stop on someone in the front row. It's the mouth-breathing boy from your psychology class. You open your mouth to tell Bree about him, but she's pointing somewhere else.

"There's your mom. And Chelsea."

Sure enough, toward the fourth row's right aisle, Chelsea and your mother sit next to one another. They aren't talking, both studying the programs Jay printed.

It's like there's a bird trapped in your chest, and each flap of its wings makes you feel more like panicking. What has Chelsea said to your mom? What has your mom said to Chelsea?

"I guess she skipped her class so she could come," Bree says. "That's so sweet."

You nod, mouth dry. The panic stays with you as the curtain rises and your classmates begin your scene. As you step onstage, the crinoline under your blue satin dress scratches your legs. You realize you've forgotten to put the powder compact in the black satin evening clutch you're holding. You need the compact so you can open it, see a terrible vision behind you, drop it dramatically, and say your lines. Without the compact, you're fucked.

Your heart flutters as you stand center stage, but you try to keep your shit together. Despite the bright stage lights, you see Jay in the front row, watching impassively, fingers steepled.

Jimmy Markle, a theater major who can never stop staring at Bree's boobs, says his lines as you deal tarot cards to the other party guests with shaking hands. Your eyes dart around, looking for something to use instead of the compact.

On the table, shining under the stage lights, sit wine glasses filled with grape juice. When the time comes for your dramatic moment, you grab the glass closest to you and hold it as if you can see something behind you reflected in it. Then, when you gasp, you drop it. Shards and grape juice cover the stage floor. The other actors give you startled looks but recover quickly.

You say your lines, and Jimmy Markle bends over, attempting with a cloth napkin to clean up the mess you made. Crouching to help him pick up the glass, you only succeed in slicing your index finger open. Your character is supposed to be led off stage anyway, but Ashley has to wrap your bleeding finger in one of the cloth napkins before doing so.

Once the scene is over, you stand in the wings, blood soaking through the bandage the stage manager gave you. You watch Chelsea and your mother's faces. They're both completely expressionless, so it's impossible to tell what they've said to one another.

You stay in the wings to watch Bree's monologue. She's so good it makes something inside you ache. Her vulnerability in life, what you have always pitied, creates something fierce and brave on stage, something hard to look away from.

After the performance, students' families and friends greet them in the lobby. People clutch bouquets or hold Mylar balloons that say, *Congratulations* or *You're a Star!*

Chelsea and your mother stand by the floor-to-ceiling windows near the theater's front entrance, a study in contrasts. Chelsea: short, wearing jeans, Converse, and a puffy white coat, her olive skin scrubbed of makeup. Your mother: tall, wearing heels and a long, black wool coat, her fair skin appearing even paler because of the slash of wine-colored lipstick. As you and Bree approach, your mother nods at something Chelsea says.

There's a moment where both their faces are unreadable, and your stomach lurches, but then Chelsea smiles. She holds two red roses, giving one to you and one to Bree.

"I thought you couldn't come?" Bree says, hugging her.

"I asked my TA if I could come to class late."

Your mother cradles the yellow roses she always brings to your performances. She gives them to you, but her brow creases.

"Was that supposed to happen? With the blood?"

"Not exactly," you say, holding the flowers in one hand so you can show her your bandaged palm.

She nods and turns to Bree. "Your monologue was wonderful. Your teacher must really see something in you to give you such a big part."

"You *both* were really good," Chelsea says quickly.

Bree smiles. She's so happy, she's flashing her crooked teeth without a second thought. The urge to deflate her, like taking a pin to a balloon, is too strong. "You mixed up a couple of your lines. But I don't think anyone noticed."

Bree would normally wilt at a comment like this, neck lowering, shoulders lifted to her chin. But tonight, she holds your gaze.

"Well, I guess Jay gave me so many lines it was hard to keep them all straight. I know he only gave you a few, but you recited those perfectly."

Chelsea looks between you. "I should get to my night class. Abby, will you walk me out?"

The two of you walk past a few clusters of students and their loved ones before reaching the theater doors.

"Bree is being such a bitch," you say, even though you know you started it.

"Oh, don't worry about that," Chelsea says, waving her hand. "Abby, your mom was so normal about everything. It's like...like it doesn't bother her at all. She didn't even mention it."

You nod, swallowing, as the two of you step outside. The cold air cuts through your thin dress.

It hurt when Chelsea accused you of lying about the prank phone calls, but she was right to suspect you. She stands here, breath fogging in front of her, happier than you've ever seen her, all because of your lie. She kisses you on the cheek and walks away, coat zipped up to her chin.

You have the urge to run after her and tell her everything. You call out her name, and she turns back. She raises her eyebrows, waiting.

"Be careful," you say finally. "Walking alone."

There haven't been any more disappearances since that girl from Des Moines, but you still don't like her out at night alone.

She holds up her key chain. "Pepper spray. My dad got it for me."

She walks into the night, white coat against the dark sky, and you watch until she disappears around the corner.

Back in the lobby, your mother talks to Al, who has his arm around Bree. He's wearing a baby-blue button-down and holding a leather jacket over the arm that isn't gripping Bree's waist. She cradles a bouquet of gerbera daisies like a baby. After they excuse themselves to talk to their art friends, your eyes follow them through the crowd. Everything's so easy for Bree, you think. She dates who she wants and no one cares.

When you look back at your mother, she's watching you. She nods toward Bree and Al. "Don't worry. You'll find someone, too, eventually."

Before you can respond, her arms wrap around you in a good-bye hug. You breathe in her scent of White Diamonds and hair spray.

"You looked so beautiful up there," she murmurs, kissing the top of your hair. A lump forms in your throat. How have you fucked everything up this badly? How have you created a situation where no matter what you're going to hurt someone you love?

"Are you crying?" she asks as she releases you.

Wiping your eyes, you shake your head and hold up your bandaged hand. "It just hurts a little."

The green room smells like hair spray, pancake makeup, and sweat. Most of your classmates have finished changing their clothes and filter out. Bree has taken off the dress she wore for her monologue and changed into a skin-tight, hot-pink shirt and low-riding jeans. As she and Al say their goodbyes to you, Jay enters. The three of them stop and talk for a few moments.

You focus on your own reflection in the mirror, using a baby wipe to remove the heavy base, blush, lipstick, and eye makeup. As you peel off your false eyelashes, Jay says something about Bree's talent. You try not to listen. The three of them say their goodbyes, and then the green room is empty except for you and Jay.

He sits on a stool next to you. "It can't be easy to be in your friend's shadow."

"What?"

"Bree," he says. "She's so talented."

You want to clarify for him—*no, Bree has always been in my shadow.*

In middle school you shepherded her from unpopular, white trash loner to nearly the highest rung of the school's social ladder. When Raquel Thomlinson had said at the end of seventh-grade biology that Bree would give them lice because she lived in a trailer park, you said, "Don't make fun of Bree."

Because your own social standing was so strong, that was all it took. Just a simple statement, a long look at Raquel. Raquel was smart enough—and her own popularity precarious enough—that she never said a bad word about Bree again.

"It's not like that," you tell Jay. Although weren't you just feeling jealous of her back in the lobby?

"Good," he says. "It's great you can have that attitude."

It's like you've dropped into some horrible alternate universe. But you're self-aware enough to know arguing further with Jay would make you look like even more of a pathetic loser. Instead you say, "I'm sorry I forgot to grab the compact."

"The wine glass was inspired. That's how you think on your feet."

"I thought you were going to be mad at me."

With the mirror across the room reflected in the mirror in front of you, it appears as though there are an infinite number of Jays looking mesmerized by an infinite number of raw-faced Abbys.

He tilts his head. "It was beautiful. The blood on the stage floor. The blood on your skin under the stage lights."

His gaze is piercing. You have to look away. After a moment, he says, "Bree is with her boyfriend, but who are you going to celebrate with?"

You carefully study your hair in the mirror, taking the bobby pins out of your chignon. "I'm just going home."

"We can celebrate together, if you'd like," he says, leaning toward you. He plucks a bobby pin out of your hair, his fingers grazing your scalp. When he's done, he holds the pin out to you. Meeting his eyes in the mirror as you take it, you swallow and shake your head.

"I should go home."

"Suit yourself," he says, still holding your gaze.

———————

By the time Chelsea returns from her night class, you're already in bed. You've been waiting up, so you could tell her what happened with Jay. As soon as she steps through the door, though, you know something's wrong. Her hands shake as she unzips her coat.

She gives a rueful laugh when you ask her what happened.

"It's stupid. I got freaked out walking home. I kept thinking about those girls and…"

"It's not stupid," you say.

While she gets ready for bed, the two of you make a plan. From now on, you'll each wait at the other's night classes and walk home together. Once Chelsea's in her lofted bed and you've turned off the light, she asks how your hand is doing.

In the dark, your palms stings. You've gone through several bandages, but it finally stopped bleeding. You tell her it's okay.

A few moments later, when you say her name, her voice is thin, as she says, "Uh-huh," and you can tell she's about to fall asleep. You decide to wait until the next morning to tell her what happened with Jay, but that means you spend most of the night thinking about it.

By the time you're sitting with Chelsea and Bree at breakfast the next morning in the dining hall, you're exhausted and your eyelids feel like sandpaper. You sip from a mug of burned-tasting coffee while Chelsea holds the ketchup bottle over her hash browns and Bree dips sausage links into maple syrup.

"Something weird happened last night after the show," you say.

When you finish telling the story, you wait for them to say what a disgusting creep Jay is. He hit on you, for God's sake. But after you finish speaking, there's silence.

"What did he say exactly?" Chelsea asks after a moment.

You tell them again. Bree and Chelsea meet each other's eyes, and you don't like their expressions.

"Maybe he just felt bad for you," Bree says. "You cut your hand. Then you're all alone after the performance."

"It wasn't pity," you tell them, but isn't that exactly what someone pitiful would say? You shake your head. "No, it was really weird, and I need to tell someone. Maybe the chair of the theater department? Bree, would you come with me? You could tell them how he's been in class. How weird the heartsharing stuff is."

Bree studies the sausage links on her plate, biting her lip. When she looks up, you see her answer.

"You won't," you say.

"I'm sorry. I just don't feel like he's done anything that bad. And—" she breaks off, looking away.

"And what?"

She takes a deep breath. "Abby, how much of this is just you having a hard time not being the favorite?"

You stand so abruptly your chair tips over and people at neighboring tables turn to stare. You zip your coat and grab your backpack.

"Wait, Abby," Chelsea says, but you keep walking.

The chair of the theater department moves an Uta Hagen book so you can sit down. His gray beard doesn't match his jet-black hair.

According to his bio on the school's website, he used to teach at the Actors Studio.

He walks around his desk, which is strewn with papers and scripts, to sit across from you. "Your email said you wanted to talk through some concerns about your class."

You nod.

"Remind me who your instructor is."

"Jay."

"Jay...?" He looks at his computer screen, scrolling with his mouse. He glances back at you. "What's his last name?"

It takes a second, because he's just *Jay* to you. You haven't seen his full name since memorizing your course schedule at the beginning of the year.

"Blue," you say. "Like the color."

The chair consults his screen again, scrolling. "Here he is. Blue, Jon Allan. Okay. This is Acting I?"

You nod, and he asks you to tell him what happened. Under his gaze, it all sounds flimsy. You find yourself saying, "He asked me to celebrate with him after our performance. He asks us to share things about ourselves, and people cry."

The more you talk, the more this man's expression moves from worried to bored to impatient. His stubby fingers tap against his desk, flustering you. By the time you're done, you feel so stupid, you're close to tears.

"Well, keep me updated," he says, his tone even. "If something happens."

REDDIT.COM/R /COLDCASEMURDERS

"[UNRESOLVED] ABBY HARTMANN—MURDERED 2003—POSSIBLE JON ALLAN BLUE VICTIM"

u/swiftschnauzer: Abby Hartmann was eighteen years old in 2003 when she disappeared in Iowa City. This was only two weeks before Jon Allan Blue murdered two women in the Alpha Psi Theta sorority house. Hartmann's body was never found. When Blue was arrested in Kentucky, he was interrogated about Hartmann's murder but didn't confess to it (or any murders).

Originally, his live-in girlfriend in Iowa City said he couldn't have harmed Hartmann because he was with her all night. After Blue was arrested in Kentucky, his girlfriend (ex-girlfriend by then) admitted to investigators that Blue asked her to lie and give him an alibi for the night Hartmann went missing. In fact Blue wasn't home for most of the night.

u/oakforest: I wonder if Blue will ever admit to any of the murders? They only got him on Erika Finch's because of DNA evidence. I think they could have convicted him in the Alpha Psi Theta murders, too, but I understand why Kentucky doesn't want to agree to extradition.

u/pizzarat234: Anyone feel like this doesn't sound like Blue? I get that the timing and location make you think it has to be, but all of Blue's other victims' bodies were found fairly quickly

u/murderjunkie44: Not true. Investigators didn't find the remains of Lisa Dauscher from Lexington for nearly a year.

u/pizzarat234: There's a big difference between a year and almost twelve years

u/hollygolightly777: Wtf was up with JAB's gf? Your bf wants you to lie to investigators during a murder investigation? RED FLAG

u/murderjunkie44: His girlfriend, Maria Donahue, was struggling with alcoholism at the time. She's talked in interviews about Blue's psychological abuse and manipulation. I feel sorry for her.

u/oakforest: I feel sorrier for the Hartmann family who never got answers because she decided to lie back then

u/pizzarat234: Has anyone watched that Blue TV series with Ryan Worth. It's pretty good

u/murderjunkie44: Oh shit. They finally found Hartmann's body. Linking to a news article below.

BREE

When Bree endured new faculty orientation at a tiny school in Indiana, the facilitator asked them to go around and share the worst teacher they ever had and what it taught them. Bree was hungover that morning and flooded with impostor syndrome, sitting with these other new professors who had gone to fancier schools and had better CVs. People shared stories of teachers who had graded unfairly, hadn't provided helpful feedback, or hadn't created inclusive classrooms. They talked about how these experiences led them to craft thorough grading rubrics, provide ample constructive feedback, and make sure everyone felt safe in their classrooms.

When it was Bree's turn, she said, "Well, one of my professors was a serial killer, and it taught me not to murder anyone."

There had been a shocked silence after she spoke, before the facilitator, a no-nonsense woman from the School of Education, rolled her eyes. "Very funny, Bree. But what's something a professor really did that you learned from?"

Bree quickly made up a story about a teacher who didn't grade students' work in a timely manner and said it was why she was careful to return assignments within two weeks.

"That's great," the facilitator said, nodding. "Timely grading is so important."

Ever since he fled Iowa City, when Bree sees him in the news, she thinks of him by the name everyone else uses: *Jon Allan Blue.* That three-name combo, popularly used with serial killers and assassins. It was an attempt to compartmentalize the person she knew, her teacher, from the man who did such horrific things. It was an attempt to forget Abby's expression, angry but determined, that morning when she asked Bree to report Blue's behavior. The morning Bree made a choice that would haunt the rest of her life.

Now, standing here with Rachel and Chelsea, she thinks about the name she knew him by: *Jay.* It's a reminder he's both—the teacher who encouraged her and the man who caused so much pain. It's a reminder she's both—the girl who lost her best friend and the girl who is partially responsible for that loss. How different would all their lives be if she had believed Abby? Chelsea hadn't either, of course, but that was different. Chelsea hadn't known Jay. Bree had. What did it say that she could look at him and see only her eccentric but well-meaning acting teacher? What else hadn't she seen?

Rachel asks Bree to describe him, but she feels the real questions pulsing underneath—*How could you have sat in the same room with this man and not have known what he was? When your friend told you he made her uncomfortable, didn't you help her?*

Bree's eyes roam across the cemetery, searching for an escape. Why did she agree to this? Why did she think she could stand this? She opens her mouth several times, attempting to answer, but can't speak.

She has never stood under the Black Angel during the day. She's never seen the angel's bowed face this clearly. She always thought its eyes were closed, but now she sees they're open, staring at a point on the ground.

This is when she'd normally take a shot, sleep with the wrong person, smoke enough weed to knock herself senseless, or bury herself in grading—anything to avoid sitting with the guilt that has walked alongside her for a dozen years. She has never fully looked at it, never let herself feel it in her body. When she does, it's like a wave, rising from her diaphragm all the way up until her throat tightens and she starts to cry.

Rachel takes a step toward her. "Why are you crying, Bree?"

"Why do you *think* she's crying?" Chelsea says. "You're asking her to talk about something really painful."

Chelsea takes Bree's hand, which surprises Bree. She squeezes Chelsea's hand once, but then Chelsea lets go.

"Do you need a minute?" Rachel asks, tilting her head to an angle that says, *Look how compassionate I am.* She lets the little wrinkle between her eyebrows convey worry and sympathy. But during the interview, Bree has noticed the moments between her sympathetic expressions, brief seconds you can see her hunger, her need to wrench things out of people.

There, Bree thinks, watching Rachel's teeth graze her lower lip, eyes briefly narrowing as she leans forward.

Bree snaps a photo of Rachel, suddenly feeling calmer, because maybe she didn't see Jay for what he was, but at least she sees Rachel for what she is. Despite her artistic pretensions, deep down she's no different from the people rubbernecking on the highway at the twisted metal of a wreck.

Somehow Bree's able to answer Rachel's questions about Jon Allan Blue, and they continue the interview. For every question, Rachel has a bunch of follow-up questions: *How so? When exactly was this? And what were you thinking?*

Still, it isn't what Bree hoped for. There's no new information revealed about that night. There's no feeling of closeness with Chelsea and no catharsis in telling what she remembers, partly because of how determined Chelsea seems to paint everything with a rosier gloss.

At certain moments, Chelsea looks to Bree for confirmation, this expression like, *That's right, isn't it?* It extinguishes Bree's annoyance into sadness. Maybe Chelsea isn't even lying—she's convinced herself this more palatable story is true. That's even more disturbing to Bree. She wraps her camera's strap around her finger tight enough to cut off circulation and takes photos of the Black Angel as Chelsea tells a pretty story about three best friends who never did anything wrong, who never failed each other.

As soon as they arrive back from the cemetery, Bree excuses herself. She should have expected this kind of anticlimax. By now, she's familiar with her greediness for moments to attempt closure. Moments to lay down her grief. Memorial services. Every anniversary of the loss. It's easy to trick yourself that these things will free or heal you, allowing you to shed your grieving self like a snake's skin. That's never how it worked for her, though, and the letdown was always a whole new grief.

A half hour later, she sits at the hotel bar waiting for Frye. He texted her while she was at the cemetery, asking if they could meet. It's easy to tell herself she's meeting with him to get information about the investigation. It's what she told herself all those years ago when they first started spending time together, but already her chest feels tight as she waits.

To distract herself, she looks through the photos she took at the Black Angel. There are a few good shots of Chelsea. One especially pleases her: Chelsea's head bowed like the Angel's, the sun haloing around her like she's the Madonna from some Byzantine painting.

A few photos show the items left around the base of the statue, but Bree isn't impressed with their composition. However, a bright spot in one makes her pause. Zooming in, she sees it's coming from something next to the bedraggled teddy bear. It looks like a sun glare from something reflective.

The next photo has the bear in it, but it's shot from a slightly different angle. Bree's able to see the item and not just the light it reflects. It looks like a silver piece of jewelry. After zooming all the way in, she realizes what it is.

Sitting at the base of the Black Angel is a silver heart bracelet with the letters "AMH" engraved on the front. It's tarnished but otherwise looks identical to the one Abby always wore, the one Bree felt jangle against her bare arm as she and Abby steadied each other that chilly Halloween night.

Bree's so engrossed in the photo she startles when someone says, "Hey, kiddo."

Frye stands next to her, dressed in a navy button-down and jeans, wearing that lopsided grin of his. It looks more wistful than it did all those years ago. She rises to meet him, catching a whiff of chlorine from the hotel pool down the corridor. There's an awkward moment where neither can figure out how to greet each other. He still smells the same—Old Spice and cigarettes. Finally, he gives her a peck on the cheek and they sit down.

"I'll order you a beer," he says, glancing at the water in front of her before signaling to the bartender.

"I'm not drinking."

"Are you going Twelve Step on me?" he asks, raising an eyebrow. His tone is light, but she sees the worry in the lines between his brows.

She knows if she tells him, it'll change things. If she says, "I'm pregnant," he won't have sex with her tonight. Although huge swaths of her know she should take that off the table, she can't, and she hates herself for it.

"I'm doing a cleanse," she says in a self-mocking tone.

When the bartender takes his order, Frye asks for a beer and says, "A club soda for the lady. Her body is a temple."

The photo of the bracelet is still up on the display of Bree's camera. As the bartender sets down their drinks, Bree asks, "When they found Abby's body, did they give her personal effects to her dad?"

Frye sips the beer, eyes narrowed in a way that means he's trying to figure out how to phrase something.

"Her body wasn't…" He stops and tilts his head, trying again. "She wasn't—"

"You can just say it," Bree says, bracing herself.

"They found her skull first," Frye says, leaning toward her so he can lower his voice and not alarm the couple near Bree's age sitting to their right, watching a college football game on the flat-screen above the bar. Every now and then, the woman rests her head on the man's shoulder and he kisses her crown of curly hair.

"Animals must have carried some of her bones away over the years, because they were scattered. Eventually, they were able to put together almost a complete skeleton. The team who did the exhumation searched a wide perimeter, but they didn't find many items of Abby's."

"Did they find her bracelet?"

Frye shakes his head. "Why are you asking?"

She shows him the bracelet on her camera's display. As he leans in to study it, his knees touch hers under the bar.

"How do you know it's her bracelet?" he asks, leaning back.

"So, someone bought an identical bracelet, had it engraved with her initials, and then put it the last place anyone saw her alive?"

"It's possible her dad might have done that. Some ritual for closure?"

"Okay," Bree says. "Ask him."

Frye studies her and takes another sip of his beer. She can see him puzzling through scenarios. "Let's say you're right, and we determine it's her bracelet. Why is that significant?"

"She was wearing it the last time we saw her alive. I've gone to that statue over the years, and I've never seen that bracelet there. That means someone saw Abby that night and got her bracelet. And that person put it on the statue sometime between the last time I was there—between maybe 2008 or 2009 and today."

"And that person couldn't have been Blue because he was locked up during that time," Frye says, finishing the thought for her.

"You see?" Bree says.

But Frye's expression is almost a little pitying. "I know how much you want answers, sweetheart, but there are a lot of reasons that bracelet might have ended up there. Maybe someone found it that night—"

"And knew enough to put it at the last place she was seen but didn't know enough to contact the police? Does that make sense?"

He takes a sip of his beer. "I'm wondering if it was Maria Donahue."

"Blue's ex-girlfriend?"

"Picture it," Frye says. "It's 2008 or 2009. Blue's been convicted. You're Maria. Maybe you're moving, and you find a box with some of Blue's stuff. You realize what the bracelet is, and it breaks your heart, so you leave it at the angel."

"You don't call the FBI? You don't realize you have evidence that links him to an unsolved murder? Evidence that would give people closure?" She knows her voice is rising, but she can't seem to stop herself.

Frye puts his hand over hers. "No, kiddo, you don't go to law enforcement, because you feel so guilty about everything that happened. You can't face it. You leave the bracelet at the angel, and you push everything way, way down inside you."

He finishes his drink in a long gulp with a faraway expression on his face. She wonders what he's pushed down over the years. Of course, she knows what she's pushed down. She thinks of Chelsea taking her hand in the cemetery, and she swallows.

"I guess that makes sense," she says. Her voice sounds small and breakable.

"I'm sorry," he says. "I know you thought you'd found something big. And I'll send someone over to get the bracelet and do forensics on it. I just don't want you to get your hopes up."

She nods. "How's the investigation going?"

"Blue is about as helpful as you'd imagine," Frye says, signaling to the bartender for another beer.

"He's not telling you anything?"

"Didn't you hear?" Frye says. "Of course he didn't kill Abby. He didn't kill any of those girls. He's innocent as a choir boy."

"What happens next?"

Frye waves a hand like he's shooing away a fly. "It's been a cluster-fuck. We couldn't negotiate with any real offers because Kentucky was never going to agree to extradition. I want to see that son of a bitch croak more than anyone, but we couldn't even pretend taking the death penalty off the table was an option. He doesn't want to talk to us since we can't do anything for him. I wonder if that's going to change now that we're just a week out from the execution."

"You think he'll change his mind?"

Frye nods. "It happens sometimes. The killer gets scared, and they'll do anything to delay the execution a few weeks. I could see him agreeing to tell people what he knows if he could buy himself a little time."

He glances at her. "You know, he'd be happy to talk to you."

She thinks of the letters piled up in her office. "I know. I can't talk to him, though. I couldn't stand it."

"That's probably for the best. Too many cooks in the kitchen. Too many sad fucks talking to the psycho." Frye smiles at her. "You look good, sweetheart."

"How's your wife?" Bree says with faux brightness, fluttering her lashes.

He drinks deeply from his beer and sets the half-empty glass on the bar with more force than necessary. "Soon-to-be ex-wife. And she's good. She's fighting me for alimony and custody of our kid."

"I'm sorry," Bree says and immediately regrets it. Why is she apologizing for him experiencing consequences? But Frye gives her the smile he always wore when he considered something she said to be especially sweet. He clears his throat.

"I wanted to ask a favor. I'm in kind of a sticky situation."

"With your wife?"

"With internal affairs and the community review board," he says, pinching the bridge of his nose. "It's a bunch of horseshit. This woman is saying I detained her unnecessarily when I brought her in to question her about a robbery. Saying I denied her counsel."

Bree shifts her weight on the bar stool. "What does that have to do with me?"

"This pain-in-the-ass community review board is wanting to make out like this is"—he uses the index and middle fingers on both his hands to put the words in quotes—"*a pattern of behavior.* They're dredging up a lot of old stuff."

"What kind of stuff?"

Frye waves his hand. "Just bullshit. I only bring it up because I know how high-profile the podcast is, and this would be a really bad time for anything about you and me to come out."

Bree remembers the first time they had sex. Right before he kissed her, he had put his index finger under her chin, tilting her face up to meet his eyes. "No one can know about this."

"Okay," she had said.

"I mean it," he'd said. "No one. Can I trust you?"

"You can trust me."

"Why are you even still working?" Bree asks. "Don't you have all that book and Ryan Worth TV-deal money to coast on?"

"I'm going to lose half of that, thanks to my soon-to-be ex-wife and her shitheel lawyer. And I'll be damned if I'm going to lose my pension because of some assholes on a community review board."

"I didn't say anything about us in the podcast interview," Bree says. "I'm not going to say anything. To anyone."

He smiles. She knows this smile. Closed mouthed, crooked, a little higher on the right, eyebrows raised as if he can't believe his luck. Whenever he used to smile at her like this, she always felt so safe and cared for. As pitiful as it is, there's still something in her that's eager to please him after all these years. It's like reaching out and touching a younger version of herself, the one who lived to hear him say, *Good girl.*

He pats her hand and leaves his resting over hers. They're staring at each other.

"Do you have a room here?" he asks.

Her mouth opens to say yes, but something stops her. She's thinking of Chelsea taking her hand today in the cemetery. She doesn't want to do anything else she needs to be forgiven for.

"I have to drive back early tomorrow. I should pack."

"Of course," he says.

As they say goodbye, he reaches forward and puts a strand of her hair behind her ear. The gesture is so familiar she doesn't even stop him.

CHELSEA
OCTOBER 2015

Back in her hotel room after the interview, Chelsea feels drained as she studies her face in the bathroom mirror. Would she feel less empty right now if she had talked more honestly about herself and Abby?

It was cruel of Rachel to make them go back to the cemetery. Now Chelsea can't stop replaying the last moment she shared with Abby. Her voice caught on the words "Go away. We don't want you here." Almost as if her very mouth knew the lie, knew the opposite was true.

Don't leave me. All I want is you.

She fishes into her toiletries bag for the orange bottle of Klonopin, crushing one between her molars so it will hit her system faster. As she swallows, someone knocks at her door.

It's Rachel. "Can I buy you dinner?" she asks.

Too numb and exhausted to make a polite refusal, Chelsea follows her to the elevator and across the first floor to the hotel restaurant. Rachel orders a bottle of cabernet without asking. Other than the dregs of Eucharist wine from the shared goblet during the service, Chelsea hasn't had a real drink since a glass of champagne to celebrate her ordination. Her church hosts weekly AA meetings, but she isn't in recovery. She just remembers what she was like those years after Abby was first gone. No matter what, she would have been a walking wound. Alcohol made her a weeping wound, coating everyone and everything with the fluid of her loss.

But when the server opens the bottle and pours the wine into two big-bellied glasses, Chelsea takes hers and brings it to her lips without hesitation. She deserves this after the day she's had.

She eats a $20 hamburger she can barely taste. Rachel spears some kind of pasta with her fork. After small talk about restaurants in the Midwest, Rachel asks Chelsea about her time in seminary.

"It breaks you down, so you can be built back up piece by piece," Chelsea says, wiping the burger grease from her lips with the back of her hand. It's what she always says, and often it's enough to stop people from asking further questions.

But Rachel leans forward. "What was your most memorable moment from seminary?"

Her tone is the same as during their interview this afternoon. It's curious but not too curious—not invasive or voyeuristic. It's warm and has this vibe that says you won't be judged whatever the answer.

Chelsea wants to respond, but she reminds herself it's literally Rachel's job to seem interested in what people say. She shrugs.

"What are you thinking, Chelsea?" Rachel asks. This afternoon she called Chelsea and Bree by their names a lot. Chelsea likes hearing her name in Rachel's mouth—the way she lingers on the last syllable.

"I think I'm just tired," Chelsea says. They eat in silence. She studies Rachel's face. Her scar emphasizes the plumpness of her lips, drawing Chelsea's eyes up to her thick lashes.

"How did you get your scar?"

Under normal circumstances, she would never ask something so personal, but the wine makes her whole chest tingle, and she figures Rachel owes her for everything she's been asked to relive today.

Perhaps because she understands why Chelsea's asking, Rachel's lips quirk. "It's not a nice story."

"Yes, because talking about my murdered friend has been so nice."

As they stare at one another, something tightens in Chelsea's chest. Rachel runs her tongue across her bottom lip.

"How about this," she says. "Come back to my room and have a drink, and I'll tell you the story."

Rachel's room smells like her perfume, notes of vanilla and something earthy, like carrots pulled out of the dirt in early spring. Everything is neat—her closed laptop on the desk with a composition notebook beside it, a capped pen placed on the black-and-white marbled cover. On her nightstand, there's an orange prescription bottle of something, a glass of water, and a turquoise vibrator.

When Rachel sees Chelsea looking at it, she smiles and shrugs, deeply unembarrassed, before setting down her bag and fiddling with her phone for a couple seconds. There's a bottle of Johnnie Walker next to the coffee maker, and eventually Rachel pours three fingers into two of the hotel's glasses.

They sit next to one another on Rachel's king-sized bed, sipping their drinks. For a few moments, the only sounds are the TV in the next room and a door slamming down the hall.

"It was my dog," Rachel says eventually.

"What was?"

She gestures to her face. "He was a rescue, and I knew he had problems, but I thought I could…you know…save him. He could be such a sweet boy." She stares at the pristine white comforter. "I think I spooked him. I got too close to his face. Anyway, the blood and pain were bad. Thirty-six stitches. But the worst part was having to put him down. There's something heartbreaking in accepting something's so damaged it can't ever be fixed."

"I'm sorry," Chelsea says, but she's oddly deflated. She had pictured something else—maybe a mugger with a knife? Then she's ashamed of her disappointment.

Chelsea judges the women she sees online who are super fans of podcasts like Rachel's. They post photos of themselves wearing sweatshirts that say *Serial Killer Documentaries & Chill*, and cross-stitch lines from their favorite true crime podcasts. But Chelsea isn't any better. Just like them, she's sitting here wanting a salacious story—some man jumping out of the shadows with a knife.

"It changed me for the better," Rachel says. "Before that, I was"—she puts her hands in a V under her chin and bats her lashes—"the perfect daughter and ballerina. My mom's first words after seeing me in the ER were, 'Not your pretty face!' You know when you have a new car and you're afraid to get it dented and are really uptight when you drive? Then you get a couple door dings and you relax a little? It was like that."

"Are you comparing your face to a dented car door?"

Rachel smiles. "Yes, Chelsea, that's exactly what I'm doing."

"Would you have felt the same freedom if you'd ended up looking like Jessica McCabe?"

Rachel tilts her head, considering. "That's a good question. I'm not unaware that my scar is minor as disfigurements go if that's what you're getting at. I know I'm still attractive, but I was no longer the perfect girl."

Rachel laughs, looking at her drink. "It probably sounds dumb to you."

"No," Chelsea says. "I think I get it. Abby tried to be the perfect girl to her mom. She would have been a lot happier if something could have freed her up like that."

"Tell me something about Abby," Rachel says. "Off the record. Something no one knows."

"Off the record?"

Rachel nods, sipping her scotch. Chelsea's loose from the pill she took earlier and the drinks, but that isn't the full reason she says what she does. Really, she's not so different from her parishioners when they schedule confession. She wants to say the whole truth to someone, laying down this thing that presses on her day after day, and then never speak about it again.

"Abby and I weren't just friends."

"Oh?" Rachel's eyebrows rise. She keeps her expression casual but leans forward, showing the same eagerness from the cemetery. Chelsea doesn't care. She just wants this weight off her chest.

"The first time we kissed was in a cornfield during an eclipse."

"Very Iowan," Rachel says, smiling. "You never told anyone? Not even Bree?"

"I wanted to tell people," Chelsea says. "I pushed her to. It's something I feel guilty about now because that wasn't my place. Her mom wouldn't have handled it well."

"If you always wanted to tell, then why didn't you tell anyone after she was gone?"

"I thought I was respecting her wishes by not telling anyone," she says. Even with the Klonopin in her system, Chelsea's heart pounds so hard it almost hurts.

Rachel tilts her head thoughtfully. Like in the interview, she keeps asking Chelsea questions: *Then what happened? In what way? How? What happened next? How did that make you feel?*

She's so thorough, she's even able to get Chelsea to talk about her first visit to see Blue. How she hadn't gone to pray with him, even though that's what she told the reporters.

"Then why did you go?" Rachel asks.

Chelsea hadn't completely known at first why she felt so drawn to speak to him. But by the time Blue was sitting across from her, a glass partition between them, she realized: she wanted to know Abby's last words. It was the thinnest, most pitiful hope—the possibility she might finally know if what was between her and Abby was real.

"What did you think?" Rachel asks. "That in her final moments she had said something about you? And that he was going to tell you?"

Rachel doesn't ask the question meanly, although Chelsea would understand if she did. Instead, her tone is gentle but a little pitying. Chelsea should be pitied. She should be judged. The answers Bree wants aren't selfish. She probably wants to know that Abby didn't suffer for long. Of course, Chelsea would like to know that, too. She has prayed for that to be true for over a decade. But, more than anything, Chelsea's needy, sad heart has wanted to know if Abby loved her, and she has been willing to overturn even a rock as heavy as Jon Allan Blue to see if the answer was there.

Of course, it was incredibly unlikely Abby said anything that would give Chelsea that answer. And Blue wasn't interested in telling anyone anything about his crimes. He was still maintaining his innocence. The whole thing had been pointless. Right after he sat down, he said, "You have really nice eyebrows." He seemed so sincere, so earnestly appreciative, that she reflexively said, "Thank you."

Most of their meeting was like that—awkward, stilted, completely ignoring the elephant in the room. Like two people making polite small talk while a house burns down around them.

What she was most surprised at, given how much the media played up his charm and good looks, was the nose picking. Even handcuffed, he could not stop picking his nose, flicking boogers onto the floor or against the glass partition between them. He liked to use big words that didn't fit in conversation. *Equanimity. Vicissitude. Pernicious.* He said *amendable* when he meant *amenable.*

At the end, once her adrenaline began to crash and she realized how pitiful the desire that led her there was, she started to cry. The guard came to check on her. He gave her such a tender, understanding look she cried even harder. Blue watched this through the glass partition impassively, like he was viewing a not-very-interesting TV show.

Finally, he said, "You're in a lot of pain. Let's pray together."

And he had led *her* in the Lord's Prayer.

When she left, he said, "I'm sorry about your friend. I hope you can find peace."

Once she's told Rachel everything, she feels relieved and emptied. Cold despite the alcohol in her system. Rachel sets her scotch on the nightstand and excuses herself to the bathroom.

The pill bottle next to Rachel's glass shines in the lamplight. Chelsea's loose-limbed from the Klonopin, and it comes back to her easily—the instinct to take what she wants. She remembers swallowing expired Vicodin in front of Bree in those endless days after Abby was gone.

"They're for pain," Chelsea said. "I'm in pain."

"You think I'm not in pain?" Bree asked.

To be honest, Chelsea hadn't given a shit how she was feeling.

The fan is still running in the bathroom, and Chelsea picks up the pill bottle. Xanax. Her movements are quick and fluid, unscrewing the bottle, fishing out a pill, putting it on her tongue, and replacing the bottle in the exact spot she left it, careful even to leave the label facing the same direction it had before.

When Rachel settles back on the bed, she brushes Chelsea's clerical collar with her index finger. "Do people treat you weird when you wear it?"

"Sometimes they just become really open and want to talk with me about all their baggage and fears about God," Chelsea says.

Rachel sips from her glass. "That sounds exhausting."

"I like it," Chelsea says. "It makes me feel useful."

A less flattering interpretation is that it makes her feel in control, the person whose job it is to listen and advise rather than to deal with their own messy inner life.

"Do you always wear it?" Rachel asks. She's sitting so close Chelsea feels her breath on her cheek.

"If I'm representing the church."

"The interview today was you representing the church?"

"I'm a priest speaking publicly about something, so, in a way, yes," she says.

"Are you representing the church right now?" Rachel asks, meeting Chelsea's eyes.

Her heart beats faster. "No, I guess not."

"How do you get it on and off? Can I?" Rachel asks, reaching her hands toward the collar.

"Okay," Chelsea says. She takes Rachel's right hand, guiding it toward the back of her collar. "There's a clip here." She places Rachel's fingers on it. "Can you feel it?"

"I think so."

"Just pull the little arms out, and it'll release the collar," Chelsea says. Rachel's fingers move deftly in the space between her neck and the collar, and then the collar springs open.

"Good," Chelsea says, guiding Rachel's hand again. "Now, there's another clip at the front."

Rachel's fingers brush against Chelsea's neck, warm and gentle against her jugular. A moment later, Rachel stares at the collar in her hands, appearing pleased.

"I did it."

She hands Chelsea the collar, and they look at each other. One second, they're sitting apart, and the next the space between them is gone, Rachel's lips on Chelsea's. Her hands tangle in Rachel's hair, trying to hold her close, trying not to let her go. Rachel's hands move under Chelsea's top, onto her stomach, up under her bra, until her thumb is brushing Chelsea's nipple. Chelsea moans into Rachel's open mouth. She bites Rachel's lower lip and runs her right palm down the side of her body, resting against her hip. It's like drinking water after running five miles in the summer heat. Chelsea's embarrassed of her own need, her own want.

But as Rachel's hands find their way to the button of Chelsea's black slacks, Chelsea stills and then pulls away.

"What's wrong?" Rachel asks, putting a hand on Chelsea's shoulder as Chelsea sits up.

She wishes she were stopping Rachel because of the reasons she should—she has a husband. A priest, of all people, shouldn't cheat on their spouse. But that isn't it.

She's stopping her, because she's only ever been with one other girl, and they spent today walking around the last place anyone saw her alive. She's afraid she might cry while they fuck. She's afraid it has been so long since she made a woman come that she won't know what she's doing anymore.

She says, "I can't do this." And adds: "I'm married." Because that's easier than saying *My whole sexuality was formed by a girl who has been dead for almost as long as she was alive. I don't even know how to begin to unpack that, and I'm not letting that ghost out tonight.*

Rachel tilts her head, about to say something. Chelsea's so embarrassed she feels like she might actually die, so she mutters apologies, grabs her clerical collar, and hurries to the hotel room door.

ABBY

OCTOBER 2003

Fineberg, the rabbi who teaches your religion class, lectures about prayer—why it matters and why it doesn't. Rain taps against the large lecture hall's windowpanes as the short, thin man paces on the stage.

This is your only evening class, and you're still exhausted from not sleeping last night. You can't stop picturing the theater department chair's bored expression as he watched you speak this morning. Are Chelsea and Bree right? Have you overreacted? He definitely thought so.

You try to focus on Fineberg's lecture, which is easier than it is with some professors. He swears and cracks jokes, lecturing in black jeans and a black leather jacket, even though he must be in his fifties.

Tonight, he tells you about a group of Polish Jews who survived the concentration camps. When they returned to their town, they were back among the very people who turned them in. Eventually, those people, their neighbors, gathered together with boards and other makeshift weapons and beat that group of Jewish people—mothers and fathers and children—to death.

"When someone tells you God intervened in a sporting game," Fineberg says. "I want you to think about these people. People who survived a nightmare, returned home, and then were beaten to death by their own neighbors. When someone thanks God for helping their team win the Super Bowl, I want you to think about those people, and how they must have prayed at the end for someone to save them."

The hall is quiet as Fineberg leaves, except for the rain and the squeaking springs in the auditorium seats.

As you walk home, tree branches move in the wind, the streetlights casting an eerie, orange glow over everything. You can't stop thinking about what Fineberg said. You picture the group of Polish Jews. They must have been emaciated by the time they returned to their hometown, exhausted and sick. How could people do that to one another? How are you supposed to believe in a God who allows people to do something that like?

The rain comes down harder, and you raise your hood. You walk onto the Cleary Walkway, a wide, paved pedestrian path through the heart of campus. Because you're from Iowa City, you grew up knowing about the murdered woman the walkway was named for.

In the early '90s, a graduate student shot six people, including T. Anne Cleary, an administrator. You usually don't think too much about the shooting or who the walkway was named after. However, tonight, after Fineberg's lecture, you have the uncomfortable thought that tragedy is a constant rather than an exception.

When you unlock your dorm room, you're surprised to find it dark and empty. As soon as you turn the light on and grab a towel, you remember the plan you and Chelsea made to walk each other home after your night classes. With everything that happened today, you completely forgot.

By the time she arrives, you're sitting in your lofted bed in dry flannel pajamas. Chelsea says nothing as she unzips her windbreaker and kicks off her sneakers. Her hair is soaked.

"I set out a towel for you," you say, pointing to her desk.

"Okay," she says, not looking at you.

She dries her hair and steps out of her wet clothes. Once she's wearing a pair of yoga pants and a sweatshirt, she sits on the futon and surveys you.

"So, you were pissed about what happened this morning with Bree not backing you up about Jay, so you stand me up in the rain?"

"No," you say, shaking your head. "I just forgot we were going to meet. It was a long day."

Chelsea nods, but she doesn't seem convinced. "Should we talk about the Jay stuff?"

"Please," you say, exhausted. "Let's just forget about it."

She climbs into her lofted bed and turns out the light. After a few minutes, though, you can tell by her breathing that she isn't asleep. You tell her about Fineberg's lecture. You speak into the darkness and ask her why she thinks God allows people to do evil.

For a moment, you don't think she's going to answer. Maybe she's fallen asleep after all. Then she says, "I don't think God allows it. I think people have free will."

"But why does God allow free will, then? Why did God create evil?"

"I don't know that evil is separate from humanity," Chelsea

says. "To have the ability to do evil…that's part of being human. Evil is a human problem—not a God problem."

"But why make humans that way in the first place," you press.

"He's God. If God's all-powerful, then God set up the terms of the game. And I think they're shitty."

"You know when you're using the microwave, and your dog is sort of staring up at you like, 'What the fuck is happening?' I think humans are the dog, and God is the person using the microwave. Like, we're not ever going to understand. It's beyond our capability."

"That seems really convenient. Any time we question this set-up, we're just met with, 'Well, God must know something we don't.'"

"What's the other possibility?" she asks.

"There is no God, and we are, all of us, alone."

"I can't believe that," Chelsea says. "I choose to have faith."

You haven't thought about it a lot until this class, but now you can't stop thinking about it. You hear Chelsea's breathing slow and deepen while you lie in the dark with your eyes open.

You think about Brother Dave telling people they're going to hell. You think about Jay, asking everyone to relive their pain. You think about your own cowardice and deceit. You think about those boys who took Ashley into that hot tub. You think about whoever is out there murdering girls in your state.

At what point is it okay to say the simplest answer is the most realistic one? There is no one watching. There is no one who cares. And what people do is ultimately up to them. No one is coming to save you.

EXCERPT FROM
PEOPLE MAGAZINE:

"THE ALL-AMERICAN KILLER: JON ALLAN BLUE"

A Nebraska farm boy. Devoted son. Dutiful uncle. An aspiring actor who held starring roles in his high school's productions of *The Sound of Music* and *Godspell.*

"The most beautiful tenor I've ever heard," says his former choir teacher, Lisa Marshall, of Denton, Neb. "I remember Jay Blue as just a real sweet boy."

But today that "real sweet boy" sits on death row after being convicted of the grisly murder of a 12-year-old girl (and suspected of killing at least seven other young women). Although his execution is set for one week from today, Blue has continued to maintain his innocence. And many of the people who knew him growing up say he seemed like the furthest thing from a killer.

"He was well behaved," says second-grade teacher Roxanne Leader. "A quiet little boy who never caused me any trouble."

Blue was a cub scout who did chores on the farm and developed a strong work ethic, which helped him work his way through a theater degree at the University of Nebraska before trying his luck on the audition circuit in LA. After landing a pilot that was never picked up, he came back to the Midwest. After a brief stint back home in Denton, Blue enrolled in the University of Iowa's MFA in Acting program.

As part of the stipulation for his graduate student stipend, Blue was responsible for teaching an undergraduate acting course.

"He was kind of intense," says one of Blue's former students, Ashley Lindsey. "But I never thought he would be capable of something like this. I mean, who thinks anyone they meet in their daily life is capable of that?"

Much has been made by psychologists about the resemblance between Blue's alleged victims and his mother. Anna Blue, who died after a heart attack in 2005, was red-haired and voluptuous with a round, youthful face. Although Blue has not talked much about his mother publicly, he has discussed witnessing his father's physical abuse of her growing up.

Celebrity psychologist Dr. Dave Mackinaw says Blue's unstable home life was the perfect environment for his homicidal urges to flourish.

"He watches his mom get beaten up as a kid by his primary male caregiver," Dr. Dave says. "It makes total sense he has a primal desire to replicate that abuse on women who look similar once he's an adult."

One week before Blue moved to Iowa City, a 19-year-old girl went missing from Lincoln. Then, during the same period Blue traveled to Iowa City, a 17-year-old girl went missing from Sioux City and a 17-year-old girl disappeared from Des Moines.

One person who did suspect Jon Allan Blue from the beginning is Iowa City Police Detective Doug Frye. Frye, whose memoir of his time on the case has been made into a TV series starring actor

Ryan Worth, says he suspected Blue after an 18-year-old student of Blue's disappeared.

"There was no evidence, though," Frye says. "None. And at the time, we thought Blue had an alibi."

Blue's alibi, Maria Donahue, his girlfriend at the time, later admitted she lied to police, saying the 27-year-old graduate student was home with her when in actuality his whereabouts were unaccounted for.

Once two other girls were killed in the infamous Alpha Psi Theta sorority house murders, one of whom Blue was directing in a student production, Frye tried to arrest Blue, but he had already fled to Kentucky where he would go on to murder a 22-year-old woman and 12-year-old girl.

When asked about the people from Blue's youth who are unable to match the boy they knew with the man he became, Frye gives a dark chuckle. "If we could all predict who will become serial murderers based on how they act in the school choir, my job would be a lot easier. But people are a hell of a lot more complicated than that. I'm sure Jay Blue was a real sweetheart to his second-grade teacher, but don't for one second think that means he wasn't capable of some truly brutal behavior toward young women later in life."

Frye's own behavior during the investigation has been the subject of some scrutiny as of late. *Cedar Rapids Gazette* reporter Danielle Lopez wrote an article and a viral Twitter thread questioning some of the facts presented in Frye's memoir, namely his claims about his involvement in Blue's apprehension in Kentucky and some of the details about the investigation in Iowa City.

"His book makes it sound like he single-handedly apprehended

Blue and suspected him from the beginning," Lopez says. "But the facts paint a different picture. Actually, mistakes in the Iowa investigation allowed Blue to kill again and get away. It's why *Murder in the Midwest* is so troubling to me. This is the narrative of the Jon Allan Blue case most people will remember, and it's factually inaccurate."

When asked about Lopez's claims and an internal investigation the Iowa City Police Department and the city's internal review board are conducting against Frye, he provided no comment.

BREE
OCTOBER 2015

Bree remembers being eighteen years old, standing in the checkout line at the grocery store, UV Blue vodka on the conveyor belt next to her. It was three days after Abby's disappearance. Chelsea had lost her fake ID and begged Bree to get her some booze. She really needed to take the edge off.

This wasn't the first time Bree bought alcohol with her shitty fake, but every time she felt nervous. Her heart dropped to her toes when Detective Frye stepped in the checkout line behind her. He knew she was Abby's friend, so he must have known she wasn't twenty-one. On one hand, she was worried. On the other, that worry belonged to an old life. Abby was missing. Who gave a fuck if she got in trouble for buying booze underage?

Frye pointed at the UV Blue. "Is that drinkable?"

"It tastes like blue raspberry," Bree said.

"Huh."

The cashier narrowed her eyes at the fake ID. "Honey," she said, glancing at Frye, "there's no way I can accept this."

In the parking lot, Bree checked the cell phone her dad bought her. Since Abby's disappearance, he had been on a self-defense and safety jag, and the phone was part of it. There were two voice-mails from Al. Bree had been steadily ignoring his calls.

She heard footsteps behind her and whirled around, ready to pull out the pepper spray her father gave her, but it was Detective Frye, holding a plastic bag.

"Here," he said, handing it to her. "You're going through a lot, kiddo. I'm not going to begrudge you your gross vodka."

Their fingers touched when she took the bag from him. "You want to go someplace and talk?" he asked.

They sat in his Ford Explorer in a nearby park, passing the bottle of UV Blue back and forth. "We won't get in trouble for open container?" she asked, before taking the first sip.

He smiled like she was the cutest thing he had ever seen, before shaking his head. "Not if you're with me."

By the time the bottle was a quarter empty, she was telling him about Al and Abby, how much it hurt her.

"That little shit," Frye said. "Imagine anyone thinking they could do better than you."

He wasn't classically handsome, with his long nose and receding hairline, but he had a sense of humor, even with such a dark job. He talked like he expected people to listen. Bree wanted that for herself. It never occurred to her she could have it any other way than by fucking some man who possessed it.

It was different than with Al. Frye didn't give a fuck about her photography. He listened with barely veiled impatience when she talked about the things she learned in her art classes, but she was so scared during that time. She told him how worried she was about someone following her—about whoever had taken Abby coming for her.

He would always say, "I'd never let anything happen to you," and she believed him.

They never talked about his wife, but she was there as an implication. When he said Bree's skin was so smooth, so perfect, it implied his wife's wasn't. When he told her how sweet she was, how good-hearted, it told her his wife wasn't. Coming out on top in comparisons with other women was a new and intoxicating experience.

It should have occurred to her that while he was fucking her— in his parked car and shitty motel rooms and even in his wife's bed while she was taking their newborn to the pediatrician—it was time he *wasn't* working on Abby's case. But it didn't.

Things changed once the sorority murders happened. Suddenly, news vans were everywhere and the FBI was in town. Frye couldn't sneak away to be with her. Jon Allan Blue was the main suspect right away because he had made Abby uncomfortable and had directed one of the sorority house victims in a student production. But by then, he had already skipped town.

She would never be completely sure what made Frye stop returning her phone calls. Maybe she was too needy. Maybe he was tired of her constant questions about Abby's case when all he wanted to focus on was the sorority house murders. Maybe he realized that if he was going to become a shiny, media darling, Bree was a liability. Maybe he looked in the mirror one day and asked himself what a fortysomething guy with a newborn and a wife was doing fucking a teenager.

Whatever it was, he quit her cold turkey, and all the Abby grief she had been able to push away in the haze of their romance came back multiplied by ten. Suddenly, she was grieving both Abby and

Frye. What was worse, she knew she deserved the pain. The other woman deserved hurt when the man went back to his wife and child. The girl who hadn't believed her friend when it mattered deserved all the guilt and shame the world could muster.

———————

After saying goodbye to Frye at the hotel bar, Bree takes the elevator to her floor, trying not to think about Karissa Martin, the seventeen-year-old Jon Allan Blue murdered in Des Moines. She and her parents were staying in a Holiday Inn, and she left the lobby to grab a magazine from her room. A month later, police found her body in the woods.

Despite what Frye said, Bree still hopes the bracelet in the cemetery means something. She's come here for answers, after all, and this is the only thing she's found. She doesn't want to go back to her real life and all her failures empty-handed.

On Bree's floor, two teenage girls in Iowa shirts, obviously drunk, struggle with their room key. One tries again and again, inserting the card, then jiggling the door handle with no success. She growls in frustration, before her friend says, "Let me try." But the same thing happens to her.

They stand there for a moment, staring at the door, and then the first girl says, "Wait, I don't think this is our room."

The other girl fishes around her big purse and pulls out the little cardboard sleeve their key came in. "This is 307. We're in 407."

They collapse into laughter, resting their hands on their tanned thighs, heads thrown back. Finally, they link arms and walk to the elevator together.

Bree wonders if she'll feel this seamless mix of envy and pity for the rest of her life when she looks at young girls. What would she feel looking at her own daughter? Could she stand it?

Her phone vibrates and there's a message from Zach: *She told me she wouldn't tell.*

Bree stares at the screen, brow furrowed. Who is he talking about? Another message arrives: *I'll figure it out. I'll make sure you don't get into trouble.*

Does he mean Alayna? Who did she tell?

A door to her right opens, and Chelsea staggers into the hall. Her dark bun is falling apart, strands of long, dark hair hanging loose around the sides of her face and the nape of her neck. She holds her priest collar in her hands. Her eyes widen when she sees Bree.

"I had a question for Rachel," she says, her words slow and thick. Is she slurring?

They stare at each other. Chelsea fastens the collar around her neck with unsteady hands. When she's finished, she doesn't say anything.

"Do you want to talk about it?" Bree asks.

Chelsea shakes her head, expressionless as a robot, but this is not the first time Bree has witnessed a fucked-up Chelsea in dissociating mode.

"Will you take a walk with me?" Bree asks. "There's something I want to check."

Although the day was sunny and crisp, now the outside air feels damp, the sky dark. Next to her, Chelsea stares straight ahead as she walks. What the fuck just happened in Rachel's hotel room? Bree wishes they were close enough she could ask. She wishes they were close enough she could share how badly she's screwed up with Zach. Because what the hell did his texts mean? Who did he tell, and what kind of trouble might she be facing?

Bree's practiced at not thinking about things she doesn't want to dwell on. To avoid thinking about it further, she tells Chelsea about the photo of Abby's bracelet she unwittingly took earlier.

They pass groups of students in Halloween costumes on their way to the bars or house parties.

"Frye didn't think it meant much," Bree explains.

"Fuck Frye," Chelsea says.

Bree tries to keep her face expressionless. Chelsea never liked him. She always seemed to think there was something more he should have been doing to find Abby in the two weeks between Abby's disappearance and the sorority house murders.

Bree has the same complaints, but sometimes she wonders if she's being unfair. It wasn't like he didn't do anything during those two weeks. He talked with the obvious suspects—Abby's dad, Al, and Jon Allan Blue. All three had alibis, although Jon Allan Blue's girlfriend would recant hers. Because of the lack of physical evidence or leads, Frye wondered if Abby ran away or killed herself. They checked bus station surveillance footage and dragged the Iowa River.

Because her physical description matched the description of the other girls who had gone missing, he looped in law enforcement covering the other missing girls' cases. Although none of them had a physical description of the suspect, by that point, the Lincoln Police Department did have a DNA sample.

Abby's dad and Al voluntarily came to the police station to be swabbed and have their samples compared to the one from the "Midwest Killer" as people were calling him then. Jon Allan Blue—via his lawyer—refused. A day later, the sorority murders happened. By the time police were driving to the Alpha Psi Theta house, Jon Allan Blue was on his way to Kentucky.

A guy dressed like a tampon—white pants, white shirt, a white string affixed to his forehead with Scotch tape—sees Chelsea's priest collar and yells, "Forgive me, hot lady, for I have sinned!" Chelsea ignores him.

"What if there are cameras in the cemetery?" Bree asks. "They might have caught whoever put the bracelet there. There's also a caretaker who lives in that house near the entrance. We could ask them where they keep the footage."

Chelsea's silent. When she speaks, she slurs just a little, but her gaze as she meets Bree's is steady.

"You want answers, because you think it will make you feel less guilty for not seeing what a monster Jon Allan Blue was. But no matter what, this will always hurt."

What do we owe the dead? Bree wonders. Maybe Abby would want them to move on and let this go. To have her body buried and all the questions along with it. Is Bree's desire to know what happened really for Abby, or is there something more selfish at its core?

"Don't you want answers?" Bree asks.

"Not the ones you want."

"What does that mean?"

Chelsea shakes her head. "It doesn't matter. I'll go with you to the cemetery."

A few minutes later, Chelsea gestures to a group of college girls in lingerie and various animal ears. "We were their age once."

"Both an eternity ago and a second ago," Bree says. "My students look at me like I'm ancient, because I can tell them about a time before Facebook."

"TheFacebook.com, thank you."

"'In the olden days, kids, we printed directions on paper from a site called MapQuest.'"

"We had cell phones. You couldn't google anything on them, but you could play a cool snake game," Chelsea says.

There's music playing, probably from a house party. Bree can't make out the song, but she can feel the bass. Chelsea's wearing a long, black wool coat over her priest garb, and she buttons it as the wind picks up. A group of students cross the street in front of them, and a guy yells out a window, "Hey, where are you going?"

"Fuck off," someone yells back.

"Did you hear?" Bree says. "The high school named the soccer field the Abigail Hartmann Field."

Bree had seen a video of the dedication online. Abby's mother was still alive then, and she held a ridiculous pair of oversized gold scissors for the ribbon cutting. When it was time for the big moment, she struggled with those large, dumb scissors, unable to get them to cut, and finally she ripped the ribbon in two with her bare hands.

"It's ridiculous," Chelsea says. "She didn't even play soccer."

"I know, but the new theater was named after that kid with the brain tumor."

"He was in my English class freshman year," Chelsea says. "After his surgery, part of his head was shaved, and you could see the stitches where they cracked him open. He was honestly kind of an asshole."

"Well, if you're dying of cancer..." Bree says.

"No, even before. He called Michelle Milne a cunt once. Not something they mentioned at his memorial."

"People die, and then it's like they were never people in the first place. They become saints. Abby wasn't a saint."

"I know," Chelsea says.

"Do you?" Bree shakes her head. "The way you talk about her, it's like you forgot all the parts of her that were hard. But those were the parts that made her Abby."

"Forgive me for not wanting to speak ill of the dead."

"When you don't talk about all of her, it's like you erase who she really was. It's no different than all those shows that don't include her at all."

Chelsea doesn't respond. They walk the rest of the way to the cemetery in silence. By the time they arrive, it's dark. The streetlamp over the caretaker's limestone house coats everything in a sickly yellow light.

"Should we just knock?" Bree asks, but Chelsea is already walking up to the house's front door. There's movement inside before she even knocks.

Bree expected the caretaker to be some old, gray-haired man. Instead, a tall, skinny guy close to their age wearing a sweatshirt and sweatpants flings the door open. He's pale with a piggish nose and dark circles under his eyes.

"If you're here for some Halloween prank, you can fuck off." His voice is nasal and high-pitched, and he breathes through his mouth as he surveys them.

"We're not," Bree says.

He nods and clears his throat. "You wouldn't believe what these kids try to pull every Halloween. It's chaos."

"We just wanted to know if there are any cameras in the cemetery," Chelsea says.

His eyes narrow as a few fat raindrops fall on Bree's head. "Why do you ask?"

When Bree's done explaining, the guy nods. "You just missed the police. I'll tell you what I told them: when the hard drive is full, the computer rewrites the old footage, which usually happens about every ninety days or so. I gave them what we have, so if there's anything in there, they'll find it."

Bree's surprised the police moved so fast, but at least Frye was true to his word. Chelsea thanks the guy, but Bree feels more desperate. "Do you remember anything? Anyone weird around the statue in the last few years?"

The rain falls more steadily, soaking Bree's hair and the top of her pants. The man gestures for them to come inside.

The house smells faintly of body odor and mildew. The living room is dark, but there's a light on in the kitchen, and they follow the man toward it as rain lashes the windows. The kitchen looks like it hasn't been remodeled since the 1960s. On the Formica table, half a sandwich sits on a paper plate. Otherwise, everything is relatively neat. Bree notes he uses generic dishwashing soap and that the calendar affixed to the side of the fridge has kittens on it and hasn't been changed since August.

They all sit at the table, and he resumes eating his sandwich. The paper plate sits on a maroon place mat covered in crumbs and salt and pepper. For a moment, he doesn't say anything to them or even acknowledge their presence. Chelsea and Bree make eye contact, but then he speaks.

"You ever been to the website Haunted USA?" he asks, chewing with his mouth open. His calcified teeth mash what looks like ham and cheddar.

"No," Chelsea says.

"It's got listings of the most haunted places for people to check out in each state. Even before your friend went missing, the Black Angel was a big one for Iowa. Then, after she disappeared, it became even bigger. So, when you ask me, 'Have you seen any weird people?' well, fuck yeah. There have been ghost hunters. Mediums doing seances. That statue sees a lot of traffic, so there are a lot of people who could have left that bracelet there."

Another dead end. Bree is so tired of this. The hope and then the anticlimax, over and over.

"Is that a Halloween costume?" the man asks, pointing to Chelsea's clerical collar, which is peeking out from her coat.

"No, I'm an Episcopal priest," Chelsea says.

"Oh," he says. "Well, I'm sorry I was swearing earlier."

"That's okay," she says.

"I knew your friend," he says.

"What?" Bree asks. "You knew Abby?"

He nods, chewing another mouthful of his sandwich into beige goo. "She was in one of my classes freshman year. I recognized her picture on the news."

Bree and Chelsea make eye contact but don't say anything.

"She was really pretty, wasn't she?" It's phrased as a question, but he says it like a statement.

"She was," Chelsea says softly.

He eats his sandwich, and they listen to the rain against the windows and the hum of the refrigerator. Bree has to look away from his open-mouth chewing, that meat and cheese mashed up with his saliva, as a wave of nausea hits her. She wonders if it's the pregnancy causing it or just the smell of the house and his messy eating. She looks up at the ceiling light, but she can see the silhouette of dead bugs—moths maybe—lying inside it.

"Are you okay?" Chelsea asks.

"I'm not feeling well."

Outside, the rain comes down harder than ever. It's at least a fifteen-minute walk back to the hotel.

"I have some umbrellas," the man says, gesturing vaguely. "Somewhere around here."

His chair screeches against the linoleum, and he opens a door next to the fridge, which must lead to his basement. Bree tries to breathe through the nausea, but the smell of the body odor and mildew is too much. The man's footfalls fade as he disappears downstairs while she runs to the kitchen sink and vomits.

A second later, there's a hand holding her hair away from her face and another patting her back. How many times has Chelsea done this for her over the years? How many times has she done this for Chelsea?

After there's nothing left to vomit and the dry heaves have started, she rinses her mouth out from the tap, trying not to study the kitchen sink too closely, with its film of brown grime and old particles of food stuck to the sides like barnacles.

"Are you okay?" Chelsea asks.

There's so much concern on Chelsea's face that the words tumble out. "I'm pregnant."

Chelsea blinks. She opens her mouth, but before she can respond, the man's voice calls out: "I got a few umbrellas and rain ponchos, too, if you want to come down here and see what you want to take."

The two of them study one another, each clearly weighing the same thing, the thing women are constantly weighing—*how likely am I to be sexually assaulted or killed if I do this thing?*

"That's okay," Chelsea calls down to him. "Two umbrellas are good enough."

"I've got a bunch of umbrellas. I'm not sure which ones you want."

"Just grab the two biggest ones. The sturdiest."

"Sure thing," he calls up.

"I'm not going in this dude's creepy basement," Chelsea murmurs and Bree smiles.

As his footsteps on the stairs grow louder, Bree notices a pile of mail on the counter. One unopened letter catches her eye. A white envelope, the address written in familiar handwriting. At the bottom right corner, someone has stamped in red *Mailed from a state correctional institution.*

The return address is J. A. Blue, Kentucky State Penitentiary.

CHELSEA

OCTOBER 2015

When the girls were in seventh grade, it snowed on Halloween. To fight the biting wind, they grudgingly wore coats over their costumes. Abby wore bell bottoms and tie-dye as a hippie. Bree wore a poodle skirt she sewed herself. She didn't have the money for saddle shoes, so she drew on her white sneakers with a black permanent marker to mimic the look. Chelsea dressed as a witch, although her witch's hat kept flying away in the wind, across the dead grass of people's lawns.

At one house, a middle-aged woman surveyed them. Her mouth was a straight line as she held out her bowl of candy. After they each took a couple small Tootsie Rolls and said thank you, she said, "You don't think you girls are a little old to be doing this?" Without waiting for a response, she shut the door.

The three of them hadn't spoken as they walked to the house next door, but the mood had changed. At this next house, there were no pumpkins or decorations on the front porch. When they said, "Trick or treat," the thirtysomething-year-old man who opened the door said, "Trick."

They stood there in silence for a moment, deeply thrown by

this change in the normal routine. Finally, Chelsea said, "We don't know any tricks, sir."

He wore a gray sweatsuit, and his belly shook as he laughed. "Okay, then," he said. "Come in out of the cold, and I'll find some candy for you."

Despite every stranger-danger thing the three of them had been taught, politeness and a desire not to offend took over, and they stood in his entryway.

When he came back, he didn't have any candy, just a fruit bowl. Bree took an overripe banana, and Chelsea and Abby both took apples.

"Want to see something scary?" he asked. "It's in the basement."

"That's okay," Abby said. "We should get going."

"It'll just be a moment," he said. "You can wait here."

The three of them looked at each other, but still, they waited. When he returned, he had an overturned glass jar over his hand. Under it was a very large spider.

"Who wants to hold it?" he asked.

"We should get going," Abby said again. And yet, they didn't open the unlocked door and leave. Why? Why hadn't they left?

Both Chelsea and Bree knew how afraid Abby was of spiders. Bree reached out and let the man set the spider on her palm. After it crawled onto the sleeve of her coat and up her arm, the man pinched it between his fingers, dropped it to the ground, and stepped on it, making a crunching sound as the rubber sole of his suede house shoe pressed it against the linoleum. His gaze didn't move from Bree's face the whole time he did it.

And then they did leave. Chelsea pushed Bree toward the

door, and Abby pulled it open. They didn't stop running until they were back at Abby's house.

Chelsea thinks of that Halloween now that she and Bree sit in the lobby of Chelsea's old dorm, shivering in cold, wet clothes. They're both still out of breath from running from the cemetery caretaker's house. After sprinting in the pouring rain for several minutes, they got on the first bus they saw, which deposited them in front of the building where Chelsea and Abby last held each other. *God is masterful*, a friend in seminary used to say about these kinds of painful synchronicities.

Through the big front window, the wind and rain shake the tree limbs. Bree has the letter from the prison on her lap. It's rain-splattered but not completely soaked. Chelsea grabs it to study while Bree fiddles with her camera, presumably checking if the rain damaged it.

"Oh fuck," a blond girl says, coming into the lobby. "Look what Thomas posted," she says to her friend. They lean together, their faces lit in the blue glow of the blond's phone screen, their jaws slack as they stare.

The blond's companion, a girl with tight coils of black hair, shakes her head. "It's like, bro, I'm bi," she says. "I mean…I've got options."

"Damn right, you do," the blond says, and their flip-flops slap against the lobby's tile as they set off down the hall, voices rising and falling, the blond gesturing with her hands as they round the corner out of view.

Chelsea wants to run after the dark-haired girl and say, *When I was your age, I was afraid to tell anyone I wanted to fuck girls.*

She knows this is akin to all the times her mother used to say, "Well, back in my day…" Hearing those stories always felt like a not-very-urgent history lesson, something she was supposed to absorb yet couldn't summon any passion to care about. And now, she knows how her mother felt.

It's not that she wants life to be as hard for these girls as it was for her. Of course not. She just wants them to understand what it was like when she was younger. She wants them to be grateful. But why? Why should they be grateful things are closer to how they always should have been?

"Stealing mail is a federal offense," Chelsea says, gesturing to the letter.

"If Blue is writing to him, then he could have been the one who put that bracelet there. Maybe Blue told him where to find it."

"Maybe," Chelsea says. She holds up the letter. "Should we open it?"

Bree shakes her head. "I'm going to give it to Detective Frye."

"Smile," Bree says, holding up her camera and taking a selfie. They must look like drowned rats.

Chelsea has never liked Detective Frye. She didn't like him when they were teenagers and he was looking at Bree like she was a piece of meat (*I think that old detective guy wants to fuck you,* she told Bree once, and Bree laughed the comment away, even though Chelsea could see she was pleased by the attention).

In the years since, she hasn't appreciated the way he's leaned into the Blue media circus. "What good is Frye going to do?"

"He's the reason her body was found."

"He's the reason her body *wasn't found* for *twelve years,* Bree."

Bree holds up her phone. "I'm texting him now."

"You're *texting him*?"

Bree sets her phone on her lap, her camera between them on the dorm lobby's couch. "He gave me his number when he called me about her body being found."

Something occurs to Chelsea that she's never questioned before. "Why did he just call you when her body was found? Why wouldn't he call us both?"

Bree shrugs, but Chelsea knows that face—that faux-innocent purse of the lips and widening of eyes.

"Do you want to go up to your old room?" Bree asks, gesturing toward the elevator. She's clearly changing the subject.

"Absolutely not," Chelsea says. She doesn't want to see other girls' possessions in that space. Give her Abby's twee Audrey Hepburn poster and her Harry Potter pillowcase. Give her the chipped paint and shitty pine furniture.

"Imagine if we could tell the girls we were then we'd be back here today, but this is what would be happening," Bree says. "They'd be like, what are you talking about?"

"Well, first thing, they'd be like, what the fuck is a podcast?"

They laugh so hard a girl passing through the lobby gives them an alarmed look. This makes them laugh even harder, until they're wiping their eyes.

The letter from the prison is still in Chelsea's hands, and she taps it against her arm. The Klonopin and Xanax in her system have left her empty and loose.

Bree's phone lights up on her lap with a text notification, and Chelsea grabs it as soon as she sees the sender is Frye and his first words are *Sweet girl.*

"Don't," Bree says, trying to pull her phone back from Chelsea. Chelsea lets her because she's already read the whole thing.

Sweet girl, you're looking at a five-year sentence for stealing some-one's mail :) Where do you want to meet?

Bree clutches the phone to her chest.

"When did you start fucking him?" Chelsea gestures to Bree's stomach. "Is he the father?"

"No," Bree says. "I'm not fucking him."

"But you did. You have."

"Chelsea," she says, but it's all over her face.

"You were fucking him back then." Chelsea lets out a humor-less laugh. "Of course you were."

She fucked the piece of shit who failed their friend? A married man with a kid? He'd promised he'd find out what happened to Abby. He'd promised Mrs. Hartmann. How much of what hap-pened to Mrs. Hartmann could have been prevented if Frye had just done his goddamn job?

"I wanted to get answers," Bree says, her voice small.

"By fucking the detective who was supposed to figure out what happened to her?"

"You don't understand," Bree says. "I felt like if I found answers, at least I would have done right by her in some way. You don't know what it was like to live with that kind of guilt over the years. Knowing I failed her."

For Bree to sit here and imply Chelsea hasn't been haunted by guilt about Abby, that Abby hasn't been the ghost hovering over everything she's done for the last twelve years, is too much. When she speaks, her voice is low and it takes effort to get each word out.

"Don't ever speak to me like our losses were the same. You were *her pet*, her *little project*. She was my—"

Love. My love.

Chelsea swallows. "She was my best friend, and I was hers. You were just a girl she felt sorry for."

Chelsea can tell from Bree's face that the blow landed. She blinks rapidly. Then she stands up and walks away.

"Bree," Chelsea says, but she's already opened the door to go back into the rain alone.

———

Abby and Bree had been assigned to work on a school project in seventh grade. A few weeks later, Abby started inviting her to hang out when Chelsea was around. Chelsea didn't like this wide-eyed blond girl edging in on her friendship with Abby and excluded her whenever possible.

At Abby's thirteenth birthday party, Chelsea was forced to be around her. As an adult, Chelsea has wondered what that was like for Bree. Had she been intimidated? All the houses on the street Chelsea and Abby lived on were bigger than the run-down part of town Bree lived in, and Chelsea and Abby's neighborhood had its own private pool.

They sat in Abby's parents' finished basement and played a game where you had to hum a song and get your partner to guess it. Amped on Twizzlers and Mtn Dew, Chelsea was guessing while Bree, her assigned partner, kept humming something incomprehensible. Finally, when the round was over, the last grain of sand slipping through the little plastic hourglass, Bree told Chelsea what the song was.

"It was 'Feed the Birds' from *Mary Poppins*," Bree said.

"I know that song," Chelsea said. "What you were humming sounded nothing like that song. Are you tone deaf?"

Chelsea made her tone as cool and dismissive as possible. The other girls laughed.

As an adult, Chelsea wondered if Bree already felt defensive around them—girls who had moms who French-braided their hair, who washed their sleeping bags so they didn't smell like mildew, who helped them buy and wrap a gift for Abby with pretty paper and shiny ribbon.

That night, like so many nights, Chelsea couldn't sleep. She started crying in her sunflower-patterned sleeping bag somewhere around 3:00 a.m. All the other girls were fast asleep, and Abby was snoring.

"What's wrong?" a voice whispered.

Chelsea looked over to see Bree sitting up in her sleeping bag.

"I can't sleep," Chelsea said, wiping her tears.

"But why are you crying?"

Chelsea sat up. "Have you ever been stuck awake when everyone else is asleep? It's the loneliest feeling in the world."

"Well, I'm wide awake," Bree said, even though she looked exhausted. "What should we do?"

They painted each other's toenails and talked about who was their favorite Spice Girl and what happened with Monica Lewinsky and Bill Clinton. Chelsea hadn't known what oral sex was, but everyone was talking about the president and the intern. She thought oral sex must be a very intense form of French kissing. A blow job, she had figured, involved blowing on a guy's penis. It wasn't until Missy Russell explained everything during group work in social studies that Chelsea understood. Missy could be trusted about those things—she had given Rob Preston a hand job behind the Family Video.

"I feel bad for her," Bree said of Monica Lewinsky. "She must be lonely."

It was the empathy for this public figure who had mostly been treated as a joke that made Chelsea want to be Bree's friend. When the sun came up that morning, bathing the basement in thin, gray light, Chelsea finally fell asleep. But from then on, Chelsea always invited Bree to hang out too, if she was with Abby. From then on, they were a trio.

The rain stops as Chelsea walks back to the hotel. When she passes the redbrick Congregationalist church, its gothic spire piercing the cloudy sky, she normally prays. *But why?* she wonders now. God doesn't listen. Or, if God does, the outcome never changes.

She used to tell her confirmation students prayer was meant not to change the world but to change your own heart, and she believed that. She believed, down to her marrow, God had made her go through hell so she could help other people.

She served each week at the Eucharist, standing on the altar with the deacon and the priests, swinging a thurible, letting the stream of incense float around the church. She stared at the sun reflecting the colors and patterns from the stained glass onto the church's brick walls, watching how the light made the incense's smoke look thick in the air. She believed God was right there with her.

Now she can't find that belief anymore. It's like she's a balloon someone blew up but didn't tie closed. Look at her fly all around the room deflating until she lands at someone's feet, completely empty.

When she gets into the hotel elevator, she doesn't press the number for her floor, she presses the number for Rachel's. While she stands in the empty elevator, she notices a text from Daniel, saying he's thinking of her and hopes the day went okay. *Call if you can,* he says.

She tells herself she's just going to Rachel's room to implement damage control. She needs to apologize to this woman, plead grief, plead insanity, and do whatever she can to make sure Rachel isn't going to tell anyone about their kiss.

Rachel answers the door in a black bralette and panties. Chelsea tries very hard not to let her gaze linger on her legs or cleavage. She has two tattoos—one on the inside of her left elbow and one on her upper right thigh. They're both black shapes, but Chelsea can't decipher them without obviously staring, so she looks away.

Rachel smirks as Chelsea meets her eyes. "Hello, again."

"Can we talk?" Chelsea asks.

Rachel opens the door, and Chelsea steps back into the smell of Rachel's perfume, the physical reality of her and all her possessions—a pile of dirty clothes puddled in front of the desk, her discarded gold rings and necklaces on the nightstand next to the bottle of Xanax. The turquoise vibrator has been stowed away somewhere, Chelsea notes, and she has a brief thrill picturing Rachel using it after Chelsea left, thinking of her. It's that thrill—the warmth of it pooling in her stomach—that makes her realize how dangerous it is for her to be in this room.

How many times has she sat in her office with parishioners and talked about overcoming temptation? If she were her own parishioner, she would say, *You know you can't be alone with her. You know that's a bad idea. Call on God to help you make choices you can live with.*

Chelsea could never understand why so many parishioners would nod in her office, vowing they would make better choices, then come to confess the same mistakes a few weeks later. It seemed embarrassing that people would betray a loved one's trust for something as base as lust. But now, as Rachel sits in the middle of the unmade bed, throwing the covers over herself and surveying Chelsea, she understands perfectly.

Chelsea perches on the edge of the bed. She feels Rachel's proximity and can't stop looking at her lips as they kiss the rim of her water glass.

"I'm sorry about what happened earlier," Chelsea says finally.

"Why?" Rachel says. "I'm not."

"I'm married," Chelsea says. "I'm a priest. It shouldn't have happened."

"If you're scared I'm going to tell my listeners you're some adulterous monster, I'm not going to do that," Rachel says, crossing her arms over her chest. "So, if that's why you're here, you can rest easy."

"Okay," Chelsea says, but she doesn't move to leave.

"Why are you here, Chelsea?"

"I don't know," she says, studying her own hands.

Rachel gets up and pours herself two fingers of Scotch neat. She holds the bottle up to Chelsea, and Chelsea shakes her head. After settling back under the covers and taking a few sips,

Rachel says, "Growing up as a ballet dancer meant a certain kind of pressure. There was a version of me my parents wanted, and I didn't always live up to that.

"When you want so much to be what people want you to be—or even what you think they want you to be—you can start to lie to yourself. At first, they're little lies—you like wearing the frilly white Easter dress, you like holding hands with that cute boy at summer camp—but the little lies can make the bigger lies easier to swallow until you know what the fake version of you wants better than you know what the real you wants."

Rachel gets up to add ice to her glass. When she comes back, she sits next to Chelsea. Her posture is perfectly straight. Chelsea's eyes are drawn to the swell of her breasts in that bralette, but she forces herself to look away. Why, though? Why is she making herself look away? At what point did she convince herself that she couldn't trust her own desires?

All those years ago, she pushed Abby so hard to stop projecting an image and be who she really was. Then Abby died and somehow Chelsea had picked up the same mantle. Why? Had she done it as a form of punishment? Some weird way to stay close to Abby even after she was gone?

Rachel doesn't say anything when Chelsea turns to face her, but there's a ghost of a smile on her lips. Chelsea does what she's thought about doing since she walked back into this room: she follows Rachel's scar with her lips, kissing a line down her cheek. When their lips meet, Rachel pulls Chelsea to her.

ABBY

OCTOBER 2003

The first class after the midterm showcase, Jay has everyone go back to heartsharing. It might be your imagination, but you think you see some annoyance or resignation on some of your classmates' faces as everyone scoots into a circle. Maybe you're not the only one sick of Jay's favorite exercise.

Bree has never had a turn, so Jay gestures for her to go into the center of the circle. She sits cross-legged, her low-riding jeans slung down to reveal the whale tail of her hot-pink thong. Things have been awkward between the two of you since she refused to go to the department chair about Jay.

Neither of you has said anything directly about the incident, but she's quieter than usual. She has always believed she needs you more than you need her, but in the days after the midterm showcase, you've realized it filled something in you to have her constantly watching you as a guide for how to be in the world.

You shift your weight so your ass won't fall asleep against the studio's hardwood floor. The light shines through the row of high windows on the back brick wall, and Bree presses the edge of a patch of sunlight with her index finger, as if she can pin it to the floor. She rests her chin in the palm of her hand, regarding Jay with a worried expression that makes her big blue eyes look even larger.

"Let's begin," Jay says. Now that the weather has turned cooler, he's switched from his uniform of pastel-colored polos to sweater vests in earth tones over collared shirts. At least he's wearing boots instead of sandals, so you're spared looking at the disturbingly long nail on his left big toe. He's still wearing the silver ring he always has on—the two theater masks, one laughing and one crying.

Your classmates watch Jay, but they don't pay attention to the things you notice. The pleased nod he gives when one of your classmates finally breaks down crying in the circle, his teeth bared in a thin smile. How he picks his nose, casually, as if it isn't completely disgusting.

You wonder if the chair of the theater department ever said anything to him about your complaint. Considering how dismissive he was, you doubt it. You don't think he wrote down a single thing you said.

Jay looks at Bree. "Tell us the worst thing that ever happened to you."

Before she even opens her mouth, you know what her answer will be.

"My mom died in a drunk driving accident when I was little," Bree says. "She was the drunk driver."

Jay's eyebrows raise, and he inclines his head. Now he's interested.

Bree's spine straightens like a plant angling toward the sun. "I guess I've always wondered if she drove drunk a lot, or if it was one bad decision."

"What do other people say about your mother?"

"That she was a drunk—white trash." Bree studies her chipped nail polish. It's hot pink like her thong. "People say she cheated on my dad."

When you asked your mother about Bree's mom, she said, "That woman used to mow the lawn in a string bikini." She said it like that one detail told you everything you needed to know.

While Jay regards Bree with steepled fingers resting under his chin, the other students ask questions—how old was Bree when she lost her virginity? Fifteen. How many guys has she slept with? Four.

"When was the last time you were jealous?" Jay asks.

When Bree speaks, it's so softly Jay leans forward to hear her better.

"I'm always jealous."

You wonder how Jay knew to ask, but he has a weird sense about what will draw people out, allowing him to eat their pain and taste each distinct flavor.

"Always?"

"I'm jealous of girls who grew up with more money than I did. I'm jealous of girls who have moms who are still alive. I'm jealous of girls who are prettier. Smarter. More creative. I'm always jealous."

"Describe the most recent time you were really jealous," Jay says. "In detail."

Bree rakes her lower lip with her teeth.

"People who grow up with money carry themselves differently than people who don't," she says, looking at Jay. "They project this self-confidence, and people respond to it. One of my friends is like that. She carries herself like people should watch her, so they do. When we were on a choir trip in high school in New York, grown men were handing her their business cards."

You remember. A man in a pinstripe suit had yelled, "You are beautiful" on Wall Street, his voice faintly accented, so it sounded like "bee-you-tee-full."

Chelsea's stupid high school boyfriend, *Nolan*, had been with them. Every time he draped his arm possessively over her shoulder, you wanted to punch him in the back of the skull.

All right, you thought. *I'm glad men want me.* If this was how it was, then better they worship you than ignore you. If you had so little power in every other way, you'd be a fool not to relish the power you did have.

"My boyfriend's really sweet," Bree says. "He's the first guy I've dated who's ever actually been nice to me." She puts a hand over her face for a moment. Then she looks at Jay. "That sounds really pathetic, doesn't it?"

Jay's face is expressionless. "Go on."

Bree swallows. "He looks at the pictures I take for my photography class, and he tells me I'm talented."

Bree doesn't talk for a while. She clicks the metal stud in her tongue against the bottom of her front teeth, staring at the floor.

"He's one of the best things in my life," she says. "But sometimes, I catch my friend trying to..."

"What?" Jay asks. The urgency in his voice makes goose bumps rise on your arms.

"It's not *flirting* exactly," Bree says. "But it's like it bothers her that he chose me. I see her trying to win him over, get him to pay attention to her."

"Why does that upset you so much?" he asks.

"She has everything," Bree says. "The grades, a perfect Audrey Hepburn face, two parents who pay for her college. She got a BMW convertible on her sixteenth birthday."

It was used, you want to say, before realizing this thought is more indictment than defense.

"It's like the few good things I do get…she can barely stand," Bree says, and now she's looking at you. "She has everything, but she wants the little I have too. I can tell."

You open your mouth to protest, but isn't she right? Haven't you carefully cataloged every single thing she has—Al, the praise from Jay, her perfect body—and begrudged her all of it?

Bree doesn't take her eyes off you, so you force yourself not to blink like during the staring contests you used to have when you were younger.

"Okay," Jay says. "That's been ten minutes."

Bree doesn't move right away. You both keep staring at each other, and you wonder who will look away first.

The day after Bree's heartshare, you sit in a converted classroom with the overhead lights off, a couple desk lamps illuminating the room. The woman in the chair across from you says her name is Maria, and she's a student in the graduate counseling program. She studies you with a placid expression and asks why you've come today.

She's kind of mousy looking, with limp brown hair the color of weak chocolate milk and an unremarkable face, but she has kind eyes. You explain you've never been to a therapist, but you feel overwhelmed.

"With schoolwork?" she asks.

"No," you say, but then you think of Jay. "Kind of. Overwhelmed by a lot of things."

She watches you with those kind eyes, and once you start talking, you can't stop. You tell her about Chelsea and your mom. You tell her how your teacher makes you uncomfortable, but your friends and the department chair don't believe you. You tell her how Bree sees you—how her heartshare cut you so deeply because you worry she's right. You are spoiled and petty and jealous.

Maria stares at you, her eyes deep pools of worry. "It sounds like you're feeling overwhelmed and not supported."

She hands you a tissue while you cry. "Let's talk more about this teacher."

It takes a while to explain it all, because you start from the beginning with that first heartshare. You tell her everything, all the way to what happened after the midterm showcase.

This time, you get the reaction you wanted from Chelsea and Bree. With every anecdote you tell, her eyes widen. By the time you finish, she's very still, and her mouth gapes open. "What's the name of your acting teacher?"

"Jay Blue," you tell her.

She nods slowly. There's a long pause as she sits there staring into space. Finally, you ask her if something's wrong.

After a deep breath, she smiles, her placid demeanor clicking back into place. She talks with you for the rest of the session about breathing techniques and how stress can affect people's perceptions of things. Her tone is even, and she's perfectly pleasant, but you know something has changed in the room. You can feel it.

The same way you can feel there's something off about Jay, even if the other students can't.

In your session's final minutes, she encourages you to visit student health. "College is a stressful time. A doctor could talk with you about medication options."

It's only when you get up to leave that you see the small, gold-framed photo on the table where she keeps the tissue box. In the picture, Maria and Jay wear flannel and stand in an apple orchard. She stares up at him, smiling, while he holds an apple toward the camera.

You look from the photo to Maria, who holds your eyes for a moment.

"Abby," she says. There's something in her expression that makes you think, despite the photo, she might actually believe what you told her about him.

"Yes?" you say.

Then she looks away, clearing her throat. "Please shut the door on your way out."

TWITTER TRENDING TOPIC RESULTS: "JON ALLAN BLUE"

Marky Marc Marc @markymarc8941　　　　　**3d**

Jon Allan Blue really wasn't as smart as everyone makes out. Females just gotta be smarter and more careful when they're dealing with men they don't know

Infamous @infamous　　　　　**1d**

Our third season is in production! Infamous S:3 will cover the Jon Allan Blue murders, bringing you the stories you haven't heard about the Midwestern serial killer and his victims. Coming Dec. 15.

Kelsey Martinez @kelseymartinez7491　　　　　**1d**

Stoked about @infamous doing their 3rd season about Blue!

Nzx @nzx_twy2　　　　　**1d**

y'all on this bird site would listen to jon allan blue talk about his crimes & then say "plz don't kink shame him"

Alisha Morris @iamalishamorris   10hr

ok jon allan blue is kinda hot

Phantom Mentos @phantommentos879   3hr

I was always anti death penalty but jon allan blue makes
me rethink that

Ryan Worth @therealryanworth   2hr

Playing Jon Allan Blue was the challenge of a
lifetime. Thrilled MURDER IN THE MIDWEST was
the No. 2 streaming show in the US today #blessed
#methodacting #murderinthemidwest #jonallanblue
#actor #grateful

Astrological Momma @astromomma   1hr

Some people say no one could have predicted Jon Allan
Blue's crimes. His astrological chart says differently.
Listen to our latest podcast to hear how his murders
were written in the stars from the beginning #astrology
#truecrime

BREE

When Bree was twelve and her father worked the night shift, she would call the local radio station when the cute twentysomething DJ, White Hot Jason Schott, was on. She pretended to be older than she was, and it didn't take long before he asked her what she was wearing. She played along because she knew that was what was expected of her. But really, she was lonely, scared to be home alone at night, while the girls she was friends with from elementary school had long since fallen asleep in their pretty homes in nice subdivisions with parents who were both home, too. Eventually, she preferred lying in the dark staring at her lava lamp to listening to White Hot Jason Schott talk about how hard his dick was.

A few months later, in seventh-grade social studies, she and Abby were assigned to work together on a project. Bree can't remember the assignment guidelines, only that she and Abby made a diorama of an Iowan landscape. They sat in Abby's bedroom for hours, laboring over it. Bree had never put too much effort into schoolwork, and her dad never expected her to. But Abby wanted everything to be perfect. She sat cross-legged on her floor, patiently folding green craft paper into origami corn-stalks, the tip of her tongue sticking out the side of her mouth, while Bree painted cardboard grain silos.

Abby's parents seemed nice. Her mother brought them Fig Newtons on a wooden tray, and her father let Bree stay for dinner if they worked late ("Do we need to let your dad know?" he'd ask, and Bree would always shake her head). But on their third day working together, Abby's parents' yelling drowned out the Spice Girls CD the girls were listening to.

Abby didn't even look up from the toy John Deere tractor she was gluing to the base of the diorama. "They do this."

Bree didn't comment on the yelling. Instead, she handed Abby a bag of cotton balls. "Want to help me make clouds?"

Abby smiled at Bree, this grateful smile that made Bree feel more useful than she had in a long time.

That evening when she was leaving, after Abby's mom slammed the front door, got into her car, and sped into the night, Bree told Abby her dad worked nights, and sometimes it was lonely being there in the empty house.

"You can call me," Abby said. "I'll always be here."

The rain lets up as Bree walks through downtown back to the hotel after leaving Chelsea behind at the dorm. Brother Dave still stands on the corner, holding his sign, the cardboard soft and bloated from the rain.

In grad school, one of Bree's male classmates ranked the women in the program based on fuckability. Bree heard about it later. She also heard what the guy said specifically about her: *I would have ranked her higher, but you can tell when a girl doesn't respect herself and it's a turnoff.*

She thinks about all the men who didn't respect her. They all knew she was the kind of girl they could press their advantage on. The kind of girl who would keep their shitty behavior secret. Was that what Abby had seen in her? Was that why she pitied her enough to befriend her?

Bree's still holding the damp envelope from the cemetery caretaker's house, Jon Allan Blue's handwriting across the sender and return addresses. Over the years, Bree has tried self-help and therapy and insipid affirmations said to herself in the mirror. Maybe trying to find out what happened to Abby that night is just another excuse. Just another thing Bree can use to say, *Once this happens, then I'll be okay.* Maybe, no matter what they learn, Bree will still be that lonely girl in a dark house.

A few blocks from the hotel, she becomes so light-headed she has to sit down on a rain-slick bench outside the psychology building. She's only eaten crackers today and couldn't even keep that down. After decades of ignoring her body, it's strange it's asserting itself now. Her pregnancy doesn't allow her to ignore it. For years, she's thought about her body in terms of what it can get her—men, attention—but now she has to consider what her body needs from her.

She eats a slice of pizza at a place she never went to with Abby or Chelsea. It's nice to step inside a place that isn't haunted. Her phone vibrates as she's leaving, and she wipes her greasy fingers on a napkin. Once she steps outside, she realizes it's Marianne calling.

After seeing Chelsea leave Rachel's hotel room and everything that happened at the cemetery caretaker's house, Bree forgot Zach's concerned texts.

Her stomach drops as she answers.

"Well, this is awkward," Marianne says, giving a tight laugh before taking a deep breath. "I ran into Alayna Edmonds today, and she made some troubling claims about you and Zach Sawyer that would violate the faculty/student dating policy and raise a whole host of ethical concerns…"

She trails off, as if it should be clear that the list of ethical lapses of Bree sleeping with Zach would be too numerous to list. Of course, she's right. Bree hasn't really let herself feel the full weight of the shame until now, and it sits in her stomach like a heavy stone.

"Marianne—" she says.

But she's already speaking again. "—That's why it was a relief when Zach emailed me and confirmed Alayna was just spreading rumors."

"Rumors," Bree says.

"Yes. Zach explained that he broke up with Alayna, and she knew he had a crush on you and was jealous and hurt, and"—Marianne chuckles humorlessly—"things really snowballed from there."

"Oh," Bree says. Neither of them says anything for a moment. It seems impossible Bree is going to escape this unscathed. "Is that the end of it then?"

"What Alayna did goes against the school's honor code," Marianne says. "The Honor Council will decide how she should be punished. I'm guessing it'll be minor—just a few hours of community service."

"I don't want her punished," Bree says.

"That's very sweet of you, but I would be livid. Rumors like this can destroy people. We can't have students thinking they can spread lies. It's harmful for everyone."

Bree nods, even though Marianne can't see her. She can't stand the idea of Alayna being punished for telling the truth. But what more can she do?

After ending the call, Bree feels sick, but it's impossible to know if it's from the pizza and her perpetually sour stomach or the guilt of what she's done to Alayna. Downtown is busy, full of laughing and shouting college students in costumes.

Bree's phone vibrates, and she's grateful to see it's Frye. Anything to take her away from sitting with her own shame. They make plans to meet, so she can give him the letter she found at the caretaker's house.

"The hotel bar?" he asks. "I'll buy you a drink. A seltzer," he amends.

"Meet me at my hotel room," she says and gives Frye the room number.

When Frye arrives, he kisses Bree on the cheek and shucks off his long, black wool coat.

He holds a manila envelope, which he hands to her.

"You're bringing me something, so I brought you something too," he says as she gives him the letter from the caretaker's house, and they sit on the edge of her unmade bed.

"I thought I was going to serve five years in prison for mail theft," Bree says.

"If it's anything significant, I'll do a little sleight of hand to make sure it appears it was acquired through only the most legal and ethical channels. Don't worry."

She's a little taken aback by how cavalier he is about this, especially with the community review board's investigation, but she supposes she can't really complain since she was the one who committed the crime. He puts his thumb under a gap in the side of the seal and tears it open, leaving the envelope jagged.

"Let's see what Johnny Boy has to say to his friend the graveyard man," Frye says as he pulls out pages that appear to be ripped from a yellow legal pad. He squints then holds the letter farther away from himself before finally handing it to Bree.

"Can you read it?" he asks. "I should have brought my cheaters, but I didn't."

Jon Allan Blue writes in neat Palmer script with a blue ink pen.

Dear Kelvin, the letter begins. *I'm writing in response to your letter from late July. I apologize for the delay, but as you might understand, I receive a large volume of correspondence and my replies are not always as prompt as I'd like.*

Bree glances at Frye and sees he's rolling his eyes to the hotel ceiling. "He acts like he's a fucking Beatle answering fan mail."

Bree reads on: *Your letter outlined the many ways your community was affected by the crimes that occurred in 2003. While you have my sympathy, you must understand that I was not the cause of the— as you call them—"disgusting acts." I am simply a decent man who has been falsely accused and convicted.*

He signed it *Peace, Jon Allan Blue*

"Well," Frye says, taking the letter from her and balling it up. "There goes your theory about the caretaker being some nefarious accessory."

Frye attempts to throw the balled-up letter into the wastepaper basket across the room but misses. Bree punches the bed with her fist.

"Easy there," Frye says. "I've still got people looking into the bracelet, and investigators are questioning Blue. I have every confidence you'll get something more definitive about what happened to Abby before that fucking psycho croaks."

But that's not entirely what's bothering her. The cemetery caretaker—Kelvin—hadn't known Abby well. She had just been a pretty girl in one of his college classes many years ago. And still, he was moved to confront Jon Allan Blue about what he'd done. If even Kelvin was moved to do that, then what did it say that Bree was unwilling to?

She waves the manila envelope Frye brought her. "What's this?"

He runs his tongue over his bottom lip. His gun, in its holster, peaks out from under his suit jacket. "It's Abby's forensics report. There's something in there that might interest you."

The envelope feels too light to answer so many questions. Bree's first thought, despite their fight, is *I want Chelsea.*

It was a joke between the three girls. One night in high school, Bree got too drunk, and Abby and Chelsea took turns holding her hair back and making sure she didn't fall and hit her head on the toilet. Whenever Chelsea was with her, she'd say, *I want Abby.* Whenever Abby was with her, she'd say, *I want Chelsea.*

She doesn't want to read the forensics report with Frye in the room, so she carries it to the desk and sets it down next to the little card with the hotel's Wi-Fi info. She's numb as she walks back to where Frye sits. They don't speak.

Chelsea was probably right. She probably was nothing but a pet to Abby—someone she felt sorry for. For twelve years, she's used Abby's death as an explanation for all her self-destructive, shitty behavior. What does it say she's this fucked up about the loss of a girl who maybe never even cared about her? Abby fucked her boyfriend, didn't she? Abby was competitive as hell with her, wasn't she?

"I'm afraid if I don't talk to Jon Allan Blue before the execution, I'll regret it."

Frye gives her a sad smile. "Maybe it's for the best if you don't, though. Do you know what Blue said to Jessica McCabe when she came to talk to him?"

Bree shakes her head. "I didn't even know she visited him."

"She did," Frye says. "A couple months ago. I think she needed to stand face-to-face with the monster under the bed."

Bree nods. She can understand that. Frye's quiet for a few moments. The toilet flushes in the room next door and the mini fridge cuts on, humming.

"I guess it was relatively uneventful," he says, before holding up a hand. "Or as uneventful as meeting the man who attacked you can be. But as she was leaving, he said—" He breaks off, shaking his head.

"What?"

"He said, 'Don't worry, you'll always be beautiful to me.'"

"Jesus," Bree says.

"He still likes his games."

Bree nods. She thinks about Jessica, what she carries every day. And yet, Blue gets a hot Disney star playing him in his docuseries. He's becoming a household name. What does Jessica get? The occasional quote in the newspaper on anniversaries of the murders? A Xanax prescription and a close relationship with a reconstructive plastic surgeon?

When Frye moves Bree's hair away to kiss the nape of her neck, she lets him. It doesn't feel good, but it feels right. This is what she deserves. This is who she is. She feels very little as he takes off his suit jacket and unclips his holster from his belt, setting it on the nightstand before unbuttoning his shirt.

It's hard not to compare everything to how it was when she was eighteen. Back then, he'd have her strip while he sat on the side of the bed. *Slowly,* he'd say, as she shimmied out of her jeans, trying to look sexy while keeping her balance. Once she was naked, he'd turn her around and slap her ass, hard, before bending her over the bed. *Good girl.*

He doesn't do any of those things tonight, though. He undresses her himself, kissing each of her shoulder blades and her stomach. She hates the intimacy of it. She wishes he would bend her over, pull her hair. Instead, he kisses her neck and gently rubs her clit until she fakes an orgasm. Once he's on top of her, he comes relatively quickly, crying out.

It starts as the generic groan most men make, but then it rises in pitch. He pulls out and rolls over to lie on his back—still making that horrible noise. He sucks in a deep breath and draws his knees to his chest.

"Are you okay?" she asks.

He doesn't say anything for a few seconds, his face scrunched, brow furrowed. Finally, when whatever it is seems to pass, he turns to look at her.

"I was prescribed some medication. One of the potential side effects the doctor mentioned was pain when you ejaculate."

"Oh," Bree says.

He quirks his lips. "Pretty cool, huh?"

"What's the medication for?"

"An infected prostate," he says. "Don't get old, kiddo. It's awful."

"I'll try to remember that."

He tries to cuddle her afterward, but she feels claustrophobic and retreats to the bathroom. She turns on the shower and stays there for a long time. She doesn't feel guilty for using such a passive-aggressive method to get him to leave. She learned it from him, after all.

When she exits the steaming bathroom wrapped in a scratchy hotel towel, he's still lying in bed but has put on his boxers and black socks. He looks ridiculous wearing them and nothing else.

He cranes his head to look at her. "Do you want to get a drink?"

She wants his back hair and Old Spice stink out of her bed.

"Remember?" she says. "I'm not drinking anymore."

"That's a shame," he says. "You were all of five foot five, but you could drink a grown man under the table."

She always judged Chelsea for how drunk and drugged up she was after Abby first disappeared, but it occurs to Bree that she spent a lot of time pretty fucked up, too. She just happened to be doing it with another person rather than alone. But that was the thing—Frye made everything seem so reasonable, so normal, with his confident, assured way of moving through the world.

"I used to drink so much with you I'd have to go to the bathroom and make myself throw up so I could keep drinking," she says, sitting on the edge of the bed. "Which in retrospect seems really weird, since you were working on my friend's case and shouldn't have been drinking in the first place."

Frye leans back against the pillows, lacing his hands together and putting them behind his head. "Go on, tell me what an asshole I am."

His expression—so dismissive and hard—makes her feel about three feet tall. Over the years, it's been easy to forget these moments with him.

"You promised Mrs. Hartmann you'd find her," she says. "You promised me. But you didn't. He took her to that farm. Or *someone* took her to that farm."

Abby's footprints in the snow leading out of the cemetery. Her bones in the woods twelve years later. That blank spot in between.

"I did find her."

"Twelve years later." She wills herself not to cry, but her eyes are already welling.

"How many years have you been a detective for, Bree?" His voice is soft, but she knows it won't stay that way. "How many missing persons cases have you worked?"

She doesn't answer him, and he sits up. When he speaks again, his voice is louder. "Answer the question."

"None," she says. "Obviously."

"Then I don't want to hear shit from you about what I should or shouldn't have been able to do. You think it's so easy? *Fuck*." He hits the nightstand with his fist, the phone rattling against its cradle. "You think it was all up to me? After Alpha Psi Theta, the FBI was here. They were running the show."

"That's not what your book says."

He rolls his eyes. "Well, the book wouldn't have sold many copies if it was about a detective who was bossed around by the FBI, would it?"

Bree sits on the edge of the bed, and goose bumps form on her arms from the hotel's overactive air conditioning.

When Frye speaks, there's a tremor in his voice, and he has to clear his throat several times before he can continue. Finally, he says, "When the DNA results came back for her remains, and we knew it was really her, the first person I thought of was Mrs. Hartmann." He stares at a spot across the room. "I know you think I'm some asshole who fucked you and ran and milked the Blue media train for all it was worth. And maybe I am, but I'm also just a detective who was doing his best. And so, I thought about Mrs. Hartmann when we found Abby. I thought about how she begged me just to find one bone to bury. We finally did, but she wasn't around to see it."

Last year, on the eleventh anniversary of Abby's disappearance, on a beautiful sunny afternoon, Abby's mother crushed a mixture of Valium, OxyContin, and Dilaudid before washing it down with a half-bottle of vodka. The rumor was that she took a prescription medication to prevent nausea. She lay on the comforter in Abby's bed. She had a boning knife next to her in case the pills didn't work. But they did.

Bree picks at the fraying edge of the hotel towel. "Why did you start things with me all those years ago?"

He sits up, his mouth twisting in a confused smile as he gestures at her. "Look at you. You're beautiful."

"No," she says. "I'm not fishing for compliments. I really want to know. Why start things with an eighteen-year-old?"

"Bree," he says, splaying his right palm out like he doesn't understand the question. But she sees the answer in his eyes. It's the same reason she slept with Zach. He did it because he wanted a distraction from his own issues. He did it because he could.

"I think you should go," she says.

"Bree," he says, reaching for her hand.

She pulls it away.

CHELSEA

OCTOBER 2015

Chelsea falls asleep curled against Rachel without needing Ambien. She sleeps so deeply she's disoriented when she wakes. The only light is the glow of Rachel's laptop. She's sitting up in bed next to Chelsea with headphones on. When she sees Chelsea's awake, she takes them off.

"I want to play you something," she says. "I'm going to tell you up front: I won't post the episode this way if you don't want me to. But I want you to consider it."

Rachel holds Chelsea's gaze until Chelsea nods. Then Rachel hits a key on her laptop. *Infamous*'s opening music starts, a mournful instrumental with deep bass. Then, suddenly, it's Chelsea's own voice coming out of the laptop's speakers. Chelsea almost doesn't recognize it. It's breathier and deeper than normal.

Abby and I weren't just friends. The first time we kissed was during an eclipse.

Rachel's voice cuts in on the recording: *This is Chelsea Navarro. On the night of October 31, 2003, her best friend, Abby Hartmann, disappeared in Iowa City, Iowa. You may have heard about Abby. You've certainly heard about Jon Allan Blue, the man Chelsea believes killed her. But one story you haven't heard is about the girl Abby loved, and the secret they kept from their friends and family, a secret Chelsea kept for over a dozen years. I'm Rachel Morgan. This is* Infamous.

Chelsea reaches out a hand. "Stop."

Her voice is still playing through the laptop: *People couldn't take their eyes off her. It was like a spotlight was trained on her wherever she went. It's what makes her getting overshadowed by him even shittier. She was never supposed to be a supporting character in anyone else's story.*

"Stop," Chelsea says again. She sits up, leaning over trying to find the key to silence the audio. She can't listen to this for one more second. There's something about the sound of her own voice talking about Abby that makes the hair on the back of her neck stand up.

Off the record, Rachel had said. Where had she hidden the recording equipment?

Chelsea jumps out of the bed and feels along the floor to find her underwear and bra. Rachel stops the episode. She watches Chelsea, who stands by the foot of the bed pulling her black pants on.

"What the fuck is wrong with you?" Chelsea says. "You told me that was off the record."

Rachel closes the laptop. She's infuriatingly calm. "It *was* off the record. I'm not going to release it this way if you don't want me to."

"I absolutely do not want you to."

Rachel turns on the bedside lamp, bathing the room in beige light.

"It's a beautiful story," she says. There's that raw emotion in her voice again. The raw emotion that tricked Chelsea into thinking Rachel was someone she could trust. Someone who would understand.

"It's not a story," she says. "It's my life."

"Chelsea," Rachel says, holding out her hands. Chelsea loved hearing her name in Rachel's mouth today, but she's only reminded now that saying a person's name is a tactic they teach in sales courses.

"It's a story a lot of people would respond to," Rachel says. "Think of all the women in our generation who had experiences like that with their friends and hid it."

Chelsea can't stand Rachel reducing what she and Abby were to one another to some generational cliché—closeted millennials. Were there a lot of women who had similar experiences? Everything about what happened with Abby had been so singular and traumatic. It was hard to consider it might be, in some ways, a very common story.

Chelsea sits down on the bed. "Abby never wanted people to know about us. She made that clear. I pushed her back then. I pushed her *hard*, and I shouldn't have. It was unfair."

Rachel takes the water glass from the nightstand and offers it to Chelsea. Chelsea shakes her head and Rachel brings her lips to the glass and swallows. Despite how angry she is, Chelsea still admires the movement of Rachel's long, graceful neck as she swallows.

Rachel surveys her, one eyebrow raised. "So, you're going to keep this secret for the rest of your life? Are you going to stay closeted for the rest of your life, too?"

"Don't be dramatic," Chelsea says. "I'm not *closeted.*"

"You're clearly attracted to women and no one in your life knows it," Rachel says. "What would you call it?"

"You don't actually care about my sexuality," Chelsea says. "You just think you've found a good story, and you're going to say anything you can to get me to agree to release it. Sorry, though—I'm not going to divulge my secrets so you can get a higher iTunes ranking."

"I don't want you to make a decision tonight," Rachel says. "I'll finish editing this version and then email you the full audio, so you can listen to it and decide. Just think about it, okay?"

Chelsea slams the door in response.

As she leaves Rachel's hotel room, she has a couple missed calls from Daniel. She's already picturing him in their bed at home, Pippa curled at the top of his pillow, as he sleeps peacefully with a trusting heart. A heart that would never believe Chelsea capable of what she has done. She has lived out one of the worst stereotypes of bisexuality—the cheater. She's a terrible cliché.

There's one person who won't judge her, even though Chelsea has done nothing but judge Bree in return. Why does she always hit the lowest blow with her? After all these years, even after seminary, there's a self-righteousness in Chelsea that turns cruel. Partly, it's that Bree thinks their losses are equal, but why shouldn't she? Chelsea can't choose to keep a secret and then blame the people around her for not knowing what she's really feeling.

When Bree answers her door, she's crying. Her face is shiny and puffy and mottled pink.

Chelsea puts her arms around her. "I'm sorry I was so mean back at the dorm."

"You weren't mean."

"Yes, I was."

They sit down on Bree's bed. "Well, I deserved it. I shouldn't have fucked Frye."

Earlier that night in the dorm lobby, it was easy for Chelsea to judge Bree's eighteen-year-old self. Chelsea only saw all the ways Bree was culpable. She saw her as a home-wrecker and a fool, a girl so insecure she'd fall for the slick words of a fortysomething man whose suits were always wrinkled and whose breath smelled like cigarettes and beef jerky. Someone charged with finding their friend.

But now that she's cooled off, Chelsea sees it differently. She can see how Frye would have strung Bree along, promising her he would find Abby, he would get her justice, he wouldn't forget her. He was a police detective. He probably made Bree feel safe. Frye used her fear to his advantage, targeting a terrified, insecure teenager and manipulating her into fucking him.

"We were still basically kids back then, Bree," Chelsea says. "Frye was an adult, and he should have known better."

But this just makes Bree cry harder. "It isn't just Frye. It's like I'm actually incapable of making good decisions. I fucked a student, Chelsea."

At this confession, Bree's whole body shakes with sobs. Chelsea puts a steadying hand on her back. On social media over the years, Chelsea's mostly seen Bree with older men, so picturing her with a student, some young college kid, is difficult. But the more she thinks about it, it makes sense. There's this feeling of unworthiness Bree has. If she's with an older man, she always has her youth as currency. If she's with a much younger guy, she always has her experience and worldliness to hold over him. When will she ever realize she's enough?

"I fucked Rachel," Chelsea says.

Bree's eyebrows raise, and she bites her lower lip. When she speaks, her voice is soft. "You're allowed to make mistakes, even if you're a priest."

"Not a mistake like this."

"You're allowed to be who you are even if that's inconvenient for some people," Bree says. "Even if it's inconvenient for you."

Chelsea wonders how Bree sees her. Does she think Chelsea is experiencing some late-in-life queer realization? The reality, she thinks, is much sadder. It's sadder to be a person who has stuffed everything down for over a decade. Until you're thirty, suddenly realizing you've never owned the sum of yourself.

She wants to tell Bree. She wants to tell her what she would have told her all those years ago if Abby had agreed to it. But telling Bree would be different than telling Rachel. Because Bree knew Abby. What if she tells Bree and Bree looks at her with pity? What if Bree knows that in Abby's heart it was just a phase? How sad would Chelsea be—the person who has kept something like this inside for so long, letting it get pent up and twisted—if it never really meant anything to Abby at all?

"Frye gave me Abby's forensics report," Bree says.

"Have you looked at it?"

"No," Bree says. "I think I was waiting for you."

She grabs a manila envelope and settles back in the bed, the envelope in front of them on the white comforter. Chelsea looks at her and Bree nods. Chelsea opens the envelope, and they lean their bowed heads over the document.

ABBY

OCTOBER 2003

The day after your counseling appointment, Al appears in your doorway, wearing jeans and a black hoodie, looking for Bree. You've been deep in thought, staring unseeing out the window at the yellowing grass in the courtyard, wondering if Maria will say anything to Jay about your session.

Al tells you he just finished taking an art history midterm in the building behind your dorm. You invite him in, even though Bree rarely stops by your dorm during this time, and lately she hasn't stopped by at all if Chelsea isn't there, too. Still, you're relieved that Al must not know anything about the friction between you two. He's acting completely normal.

He sits on the futon, pulling his textbook out of his canvas backpack, thumbing through it to find the painting he knows he misidentified.

"*Ophelia*," he says. "Damn it. It *was* John Everett Millais."

It's a Thursday near 11:00 a.m., so when the phone rings, you pick it up and immediately put your finger on the hook switch to hang up. Then you leave the receiver off the hook.

Al watches all this without comment until the off-hook tone's beeping begins. "Are you in a fight with someone?"

"I've been getting these prank calls," you say. "They usually stop by noon."

"Your phone doesn't have caller ID?"

You shake your head.

"Have you done *69?"

"Yeah, but it's always a different pay phone."

"Man," Al says. "That sucks."

You shrug, but it's nice to have someone take you at your word, not second-guessing you like Chelsea or Bree. You sit next to him on the futon, and it's oddly companionable as he pages through his textbook. You listen to doors opening and closing down the hall. You're still in the boxer shorts and T-shirt you slept in, but it doesn't feel awkward.

You can't help but think about how much easier things would be if this were your life. If you just wanted the things you were supposed to want.

The textbook is still in Al's lap, but he isn't looking at it. He's looking at your bare legs. You smile at him through your lashes in a way you know makes you look good. This is familiar. You know exactly how this works. You can pick something you want and get it. It's why you used to like solving for x in pre-Algebra. The clean clarity of the equation is comforting.

It isn't desire that makes you angle your body toward him. It's that image of how easy everything could be.

Afterward, you and Al sit on your lofted bed, naked. It's awkward. In the sinking maw of guilt, there's one thing you have: certainty. You can pretend to your mother that you're straight, but you can no longer pretend to yourself.

You're so deep in your head you don't notice the doorknob

turning until it's already started to crack open. You and Al try to pull a sheet over yourselves, but it doesn't help anything—you're still sitting in your bed, both of you clearly naked.

Chelsea stands there, staring at you both, her face unreadable. And then, suddenly, it's very readable. She's smiling in this horrible, self-mocking way, her lips twisted at the edges, her eyes filled with tears. She nods, as if you've said something she's taking in, very seriously. Then she turns and slams the door.

You have never dressed so fast. You run after her, barefooted, down the hall, and descend the first-floor stairs. You push the stairwell door open on the main floor and call to her, her name thick in your mouth.

She turns toward you, standing in front of the mailboxes. "What?" she says. "What do you think you can possibly say?"

"It wasn't..." You want to say it wasn't what it looked like, but of course it was. But it wasn't. You had to figure this out. You had to know. You know now. That's what you want to say. *I know now. I know it's you.*

"I had to know...I had to know if what was between us was real."

Chelsea surprises you by throwing her head back and laughing, a bitter, mocking noise. "Please explain how fucking Al made you understand the dynamics between us more clearly."

You lick your lips. Your mouth feels dry. It was all so clear in your head a moment ago, but now, under her stare, it feels harder to explain.

"You never actually told your mom about us, did you?" Chelsea asks.

"Chelsea," you say, your voice wavering so much it doesn't even sound like you.

"Of course you didn't."

You open your mouth. You feel certain if you can find the right words, you can help her understand. But she holds up her hand.

"Don't talk to me. I mean it."

"Chelsea."

"*Don't.*" Her voice is low and harsh, and she doesn't take her eyes off yours.

"You're a spoiled child who doesn't care who she hurts if she can get what she wants. I see that now. When we're together, the three of us, I'll be polite. I don't want to hurt Bree. She idolizes you, and I don't want her to know what a selfish bitch you are. But you and me? We're done."

Without waiting for your response, she turns and walks across the lobby and through the dorm's front doors.

LINDA JOY

"THE KILLER NEXT DOOR: JON ALLAN BLUE"

AIRED NOV. 1, 2015—19:00:00 ET

(BEGIN VIDEOTAPE)

LINDA JOY, HOST (voice-over): From cub scout to killer. Tonight, we're covering serial murderer Jon Allan Blue, whose execution date looms after slaughtering women across the Midwest. We'll talk to experts to find out what caused this bright, handsome young man to become such a monster and how you can keep your loved ones safe from people like him.

We're joined by Dr. Natalie Zhang, author of *True Blue: A Psychological Assessment of a Killer*. Dr. Zhang, thanks for being with us.

DR. NATALIE ZHANG, FORENSIC PSYCHIATRIST: Thank you, Linda. It's good to be here.

JOY: We also have Detective Doug Frye, lead detective on the Alpha Psi Theta sorority house murders. Doug, it's always a pleasure.

DOUG FRYE, BLUE DETECTIVE: Likewise, Linda.

JOY: Okay, I want to start with what I think my viewers most want to know. How do young women protect themselves from monsters like Jon Allan Blue?

FRYE: Well, there are the obvious things—don't drink too much, be aware of your surroundings, don't be out late alone at night...

ZHANG: If I might—

FRYE: But then you have the situations where the girls were just home in bed.

JOY: Right. That's what I find the scariest. These poor girls were sleeping and woke up with a monster in their bedrooms.

FRYE: Blue was good at taking the opportunities presented to him. An unlocked back door. A girl walking home alone. Whatever you can do to prevent those opportunities, you should. In Iowa City, we held a lot of self-defense courses for the girls in town. Every little bit helps.

ZHANG: Sure, but I want to reframe the question. Linda, you're asking what women can do. I'd rather pose the question, what can society do to prevent nurturing men like Blue? Education, parenting, the prison system, media, our culture. All of this would need to change.

FRYE: Well, while you're working on changing all that, I'm going to be teaching my daughter how to throw a punch and to keep her doors locked at night.

JOY: How much is bad parenting to blame for someone like Blue, Dr. Zhang?

ZHANG: There's usually both a genetic role and an

environmental role. Not all people with Jon Allan Blue's genetics would grow up to become a serial killer. And not all people who grew up with his home life would become one, either. But something about the combination—of genes and experience—created him.

JOY: Sick, sick stuff. Up next, we'll hear from *Cedar Rapids Gazette* Investigative Reporter Danielle Lopez, whose recent article and viral Twitter thread about Blue's murders is raising questions about *Murder in the Midwest*. All that and more when we return.

(COMMERCIAL BREAK)

(BEGIN VIDEO CLIP)

JON ALLAN BLUE, SERIAL KILLER: I'm just a normal guy.

(END VIDEO CLIP)

JOY: Jon Allan Blue. Evil genius or a guy who got lucky because of investigators' incompetence? Journalist Danielle Lopez says it's the latter. Danielle, thanks for joining us.

DANIELLE LOPEZ, REPORTER: I'm glad to be here, Linda.

JOY: Okay, so you've gotten a bit of attention recently, because you wrote an article, and then a viral Twitter thread, explaining how Blue should have been caught sooner. Tell us about that.

FRYE: Can I just say—

JOY: Doug, we'll give you a chance to respond afterward. Danielle, go on.

LOPEZ: Thank you, Linda. As my article in *The Gazette* explained, I received a tip from some amateur cold case investigators on the website Gumshoe Nation. Through FOIA requests and combing police reports, it's clear there were multiple sex workers in Iowa City, Des Moines, and the Cedar Rapids area who had complained to police about someone matching Jon Allan Blue's physical appearance.

FRYE: Look, when we have women like that coming in, we can't trust—

(Cross talk)

JOY: Doug, I don't want to have them cut your feed, but I will. Let Danielle finish.

LOPEZ: In Iowa City alone, there were two women who made complaints. One was in August of 2003 and the other was in September of 2003. These were sex workers who used Craigslist to find their customers and offer their services— this was back before Craigslist cracked down on that. Both women made incredibly similar reports. They described the man as almost six-foot, blond, blue eyes, late twenties.

FRYE: There are a lot of people who match that description.

LOPEZ: They both provided the same yahoo email address and said they had not agreed to rough sex. With both women, the assault was similar—choking, followed by punching. In one woman's case, he beat her with the motel's bedside lamp. She had a fractured occipital bone, a concussion, and needed seven stitches. In talking with this woman, though, she told me it seemed like the police weren't interested as soon as they heard she was a sex worker. She filed her original police report and never heard anything else.

FRYE: Am I allowed to respond now?

LOPEZ: Please.

JOY: Go ahead, Doug.

FRYE: First, let me just say it's a lot easier to go through all our records when you know what you're looking for. What seems obvious with the benefit of hindsight is not obvious when you're working these cases.

LOPEZ: But that's the point. It doesn't seem like you worked these cases.

FRYE: This is not going to sound politically correct or whatever, but the truth is that a lot of sex workers get hurt while they work. They're not dealing with great guys, so it's not uncommon for something like this to happen.

LOPEZ: So, your answer is to ignore those reports? Even when it's clear there's a serial murderer operating in the state who enjoys bludgeoning young women to death?

FRYE: Hey, I'm the one who walked into that sorority house and saw what that guy could do, okay? I will never, ever forget what those girls' bodies looked like. That will stay with me for the rest of my life.

LOPEZ: I'm not saying it won't. I'm saying there were leads you could have investigated that might have stopped him sooner.

FRYE: This was a guy who was killing the girl next door. Karissa Martin was going to be valedictorian, for Christ's sake. The Alpha Psi Theta girls were on the honor roll. We didn't think his victim pool was overlapping with—

LOPEZ:—with whores?

(long pause)

FRYE: That's not what I was going to say.

LOPEZ: Okay, let's take the accounts of the sex workers out of it. What about Abigail Hartmann?

FRYE: What about her?

LOPEZ: She was Jon Allan Blue's student, and she disappeared about two weeks before the sorority house murders.

FRYE: That's right.

LOPEZ: Okay. So why didn't you catch him then?

FRYE: I talk about it in my book—there was no CCTV footage, his ex-girlfriend—

LOPEZ: —gave him an alibi, yeah. Except I've talked with Maria Donahue. She says after she gave the false alibi, she came into the station to meet with you and told you Jon Allan Blue scared her sometimes, but—

FRYE: She was drunk! She showed up stinking of bourbon. I'm supposed to believe what she's saying when she's in that state?

LOPEZ: It's interesting. None of that is in your book.

FRYE: Look, if you think—

JOY: I'm sorry, Doug; we have to break for commercial. Up next, we'll hear more from reporter Danielle Lopez and Detective Doug Frye. Then we'll have a word from fan favorite Dr. Dave about his theory of why Jon Allan Blue became a killer. Hint: it has to do with Blue's relationship with his mother. All that and more, after the break.

(COMMERCIAL BREAK)

BREE
OCTOBER 2015

In the vigils held after Abby's disappearance, people would play "Angel" by Sarah McLachlan—a song Abby never cared for when she was alive. Years later, they started using that song in those ASPCA commercials. All of it became bound up for Bree— the fear and uncertainty in the weeks following Abby's disappearance and the expressions on those shaking, underfed dogs' faces as they gazed up at the camera.

How many ways can you hurt a living thing? those PSAs seemed to be asking. So many ways, Bree knows. And yet, somehow it feels different seeing it laid out in such clear, clinical terms in the forensics report.

The author of the document believes the skull fracture was the cause of Abby's death but wrote it was impossible to know for certain. Still, they noted there was no other damage to the skeletal remains that would hint at a cause of death.

Bree spent years thinking she needed to know everything that happened to Abby. Now she knows. She knows her occipital bone was fractured. She knows they found all her remains except for some of the smaller bones on her right hand—the trapezoid, the scaphoid, the lunate. She knows her femurs, tibias, and ribs had teeth marks from animals, and they were found the farthest from her skull.

Chelsea puts her face in her hands, and Bree wonders which part got her. For Bree, it's a line in the forensics report about Abby's right fibula having been fractured at one point before healing. Bree remembers the summer sun beating down on them, the smell of the rubber seats of Abby's swing set and the grape bubble gum they chewed constantly when they were thirteen. Abby pumped her legs hard to get height and then jumped from the seat, arcing through the air, until she landed wrong on her right foot, crying out in pain.

Bree rubs small circles on Chelsea's back with her palm. After a moment, Chelsea looks up.

"You're going to be a good mom," she says. "You've got the comforting a sad-kid thing down."

Tears prick Bree's eyes, and she has to clear her throat. She doesn't want Chelsea to know how much that comment means.

"Should I turn the page?" Bree asks, and Chelsea nods.

The next page is a grid of photos. Yellowish bones lying on a metal surface. Bree's stomach lurches, and she hurries into the bathroom. The pizza comes up while the hotel bathroom's fan rattles. Once Bree has brushed her teeth and left the bathroom, she finds Chelsea sitting on the bed holding a bottle of water and a package of peanut butter and crackers. The forensics report has been put back into the manila envelope and sits on the nightstand.

"I got them from the vending machine," Chelsea says, handing the food and water to Bree.

She sips the water and nibbles on a cracker. If Chelsea weren't here, would she have taken care of herself in the same way? She doesn't think so. Punishing herself has become second nature, and if she's really going to have this baby, it has to stop.

Chelsea watches her as she eats another cracker and washes it down with a mouthful of water.

"This is the second time I've been pregnant," Bree says. "The first time was when I was eighteen."

By then, Frye hadn't been returning her calls for about a month. He was already doing the media circuit after Blue's arrest in Kentucky. When she was finally able to get him to talk to her, he sighed, long and loud over the phone.

"I'll get you some money," he told her. "And you can get it taken care of."

The phrasing, she understood, was deliberate. *You* can get it taken care of. Not *we*.

"How old was he back then?" Chelsea asks, after Bree shares this story.

"Forty-two."

"That rat fuck," Chelsea says.

"I knew I couldn't raise a baby on my own at eighteen," Bree says. "But I knew, even then, that I did want a kid someday, so I told myself, *Okay, the next time you're pregnant, you'll be stable and you'll be ready.* But twelve years later, here I am. Still knocked up by the wrong person. Still a fucking shit show."

Chelsea draws her knees to her chest and rests her cheek on them, watching Bree. "So what would help you not be a shit show?"

Bree grabs the letter from Blue to Kelvin, the cemetery care-taker, that Frye left crumpled near the wastepaper basket. She hands it to Chelsea, summarizing the content.

"I'm sorry," Chelsea says, looking up from the yellow paper. "I know you wanted something that was going to give you an answer."

"It's not even just that," Bree says. "Here was this guy who barely knew her, and he was still moved to confront Blue. You even went and confronted him. I've been a coward."

"Me going to see him wasn't brave," Chelsea says. "It was desperate."

Bree tells her how Frye described Jessica McCabe going to see Blue. "He said she thought she needed to face the monster under the bed."

"Is that what you need?" Chelsea asks.

Bree swallows. She has been trained as a photographer to look at the world, yet there is something in her unable to see things as they really are. Her gaze is suspect, flawed. Would sitting across from Jay help her reckon with that?

"What if I went with you?" Chelsea asks. "Do you think you could do it then?"

"You'd do that?" Bree asks, and Chelsea nods.

"Frye told me there was something in the forensics report I'd find interesting," Bree says. "What do you think he meant? Was there anything else after the photos?"

"Items found near her body," Chelsea says, reaching for the envelope and handing Bree one of the pages inside. "Other than her belly button ring, I didn't recognize anything else."

The page shows square thumbnail photos in a grid with text next to them describing each picture. The letter and the number for each one correspond to a map. It takes Bree a moment to realize the coordinates are where different items were found in relation to Abby's remains.

Most of the items are meaningless to her—it's possible some of these objects were there for decades before Abby's body was put into the ground. An old glass bottle. A Coca-Cola cap. An arrowhead. A rusted nail.

But, like Chelsea said, the thumbnail labeled "7N" makes Bree's stomach lurch. Abby's belly button ring.

Bree knew that ring. She had put it back in one night when Abby was too drunk to do it herself. She'd held Abby's hand when the piercer put the hollow needle to her navel. And there it is. Sitting on a white table, mud caked around the edges of the rhinestone, as it sits above a ruler, showing it's one inch tall and a half inch wide.

Bree skims the rest of the images. They don't seem important—coins and pop tabs and other detritus—but she stops when she reaches the last image. Someone, Frye maybe, has circled and drawn asterisks next to it.

As Bree studies it, her breath catches in her throat.

It's a silver ring—comedy and tragedy masks rendered without much detail. She can see it shining on Jay's hand all those years ago before it ended up in the same soil as Abby's body.

CHELSEA
NOVEMBER 2015

When Chelsea arrives home, she rests her head on the steering wheel for a few moments before going into the house. Inside, Daniel's cooking breakfast and singing some sort of made-up song to Pippa that sounds like, "Ms. Fluff, Ms. Fluff, why are you so pretty?"

He greets her with a hug and a kiss, but it feels a little forced. She knows he expects her to tell him about everything that happened in Iowa City, but she's emotionally exhausted. And she realizes part of why she hates sharing her feelings is that she doesn't always understand them herself, making them hard to articulate honestly.

You did it with Rachel, though, she thinks. *You were able to do it with a total fucking stranger.*

When they sit down to eat pancakes and eggs, she does her best to give him an honest, if not thorough, rundown of the past couple days. She told Abby's story as best as she can. Seeing Bree was good but complicated. She is very tired.

This seems enough to satisfy Daniel. The rest of the meal feels less forced as he talks about the renovations he did around the house while she was gone and updates her on some of the carpentry projects he's doing for his clients.

After breakfast, Chelsea rinses the plates and silverware while he loads everything into the dishwasher. As a bit of egg slides off a knife, Daniel brings up the couple's retreat.

"When are we supposed to leave for that again?" she asks.

"The day after tomorrow," Daniel says.

His expression is untroubled as he talks about the list of optional activities they can choose from.

"I'm not really sure if personality tests would be that helpful, but a couple's massage would be fun."

Chelsea swallows as she rinses a coffee mug. It's one Daniel purchased on his first trip to meet her family, and it says *Hogs and Kisses from Iowa*.

This morning, Bree texted to say Jon Allan Blue's defense attorney had confirmed Blue was willing to speak with them and the warden had signed off on the request. The execution is Wednesday, which means if they want to go, they have to leave tomorrow.

She's been rinsing the same mug for a while, and Daniel stares at her. "What's wrong?"

Turning off the water, she explains the timing. "I'm going to have to miss the retreat. But maybe we can reschedule?"

"It's nonrefundable. Chelsea, we've been planning this forever. Besides, you've already visited Blue, and it didn't help you. In fact, it seemed like it traumatized you more. Why would you go through that again?"

"Bree needs me," Chelsea says.

"You haven't talked with this woman in twelve years."

"This is it," she says. "After Wednesday, he'll be dead. If I can talk to him one more time, I should."

He shakes his head. "You're never going to let go of this, are you?"

She opens her mouth to contradict him but closes it as she actually lets the truth of his words sink in. No, she doesn't want to let go. What she wants is to be able to hold on, confident that she isn't holding on to a fiction she created. She wants to grieve what she lost without worrying she's grieving something that was never real in the first place.

Daniel is still watching her, leaning against the table. He made it himself from walnut, spending hours in his shop right before they were married, so he could give them this solid thing. He doesn't speak for a long time. When he does, he wears an expression she's never seen in the four years they've been together. It's tired and unmistakably sad.

"I think I've always been pretty understanding," he says. "I've accepted there's a lot I'll never really understand about how what happened affected you. But I think I see now…you're never going to let me in, are you?"

She grabs his hand. She wants to slow this down, to stop this. If he stops speaking, they can stay like they are. It isn't perfect, but it's safe. It's something she knows how to control.

He lets her take his hand, but he keeps talking. "This isn't working, Chelsea."

"I love you," she says.

"I love you, too," he says. "I really do, but this isn't right for either of us. This isn't a marriage. It's a place for you to hide."

The look he gives her is gentle but so knowing. She feels laid bare. Everything she thought she was hiding from him, everything she thought she could keep control of, she wasn't fooling anyone the whole time.

Bree and Chelsea leave for the Kentucky Penitentiary the next morning, taking Chelsea's Prius. In seminary, it was a joke with no punch line: *How many Priuses can fit in the parking lot of an Episcopal church?*

The drive is over ten hours. In some ways, it's like all the road trips they took over the years. Bree still eats cherry licorice pieces washed down with Dr. Pepper. She still rests her feet on the passenger seat dashboard when she isn't the one driving. Her voice is always a little sharp when she sings along with the radio.

But in more important ways it's nothing like it used to be. Abby isn't with them. There's a weariness to everything. It's impossible to escape for long where they're going and why. They'll meet with Blue the morning of his execution. From what Chelsea's been able to piece together on the news, he still hasn't said anything definitive admitting to his crimes, but he's starting to feel investigators out to see if his full confession could buy him more time.

At one point, as the radio loses signal and crackles with static, Bree searches for a different station. She lands on one playing the Talking Heads' "Psycho Killer," and they listen for a moment before they burst out laughing, laughing until tears roll down their cheeks. And then, Bree is crying.

"I'm sorry," she says. "It's hormones." Chelsea hands her a tissue from the pack she keeps in the center console and keeps driving.

Bree makes them stop several times at rest stops and gas sta-
tions, so she can throw up. She runs inside, and when she returns
her eyes are red and watery. As they're going down I–65, somewhere in Indiana, Bree gags.

"Pull over," she says.

Chelsea signals and stops on the interstate's shoulder, flipping
on her hazards. While they click, Bree opens the passenger door
and vomits. Chelsea's stomach lurches as semis zip past them,
shaking the car.

When Bree shuts her door, Chelsea hands her another tissue.

"Thanks," Bree says.

Chelsea pulls back onto the interstate. They pass a lonely
farmhouse.

"It's the size of a kidney bean," Bree says. "The baby."

Her expression is so open and worried and needy. It's very
much the Bree who Chelsea remembers, in need of love, in need
of reassurance.

"You don't think it's crazy?" she asks. "Me doing this alone?"

"You deserve to have the things you want, Bree."

"I don't even have anyone to be in the delivery room with me,"
she says. They pass harvested cornfields and corrugated-metal
sheds. Grain silos and gravel roads and broken fences.

"Then ask me," Chelsea says.

"You're scared of pregnancy. When we watched that childbirth
film in health class, you almost fainted."

These things are both true. Chelsea has gagged reading group
text threads with the women from seminary talking about vaginal
tearing during childbirth, but she shrugs.

"We'll hire you a doula, then."

The ditches are coated in last night's snow, but the golden brown of dead grass and corn stalks peak out across the farmland, a dull gray sky above them. They pass a billboard that says *Hell Is Real*. After Indianapolis, tall, almost-bare trees appear on either side of the highway, casting shadows across the road. Is this what the woods where Abby's body was found were like? Did he take her out there, forcing her to walk to her final resting place, or was she already dead by then?

Midway through the drive, Daniel calls, because that's the type of person he is. He's calling Chelsea to wish her well even though she has never let him in and even though when she returns from Kentucky she'll be moving out.

The sun sets over frostbitten fields, and Daniel tells her, "I think this is really brave."

She gives a harsh laugh. "I'm not brave at all."

"You are," he says. "You're doing a hard thing."

There's silence for a moment. She wants to apologize to him. He has only given her love and consideration, and what has she given him in return but heartache?

Somewhere near Louisville, Bree looks up from her phone. "Rachel emailed us. Our episode will drop next month."

Yesterday, Chelsea received an email from Rachel. It contained the version of the podcast episode she began playing in the hotel room with the subject line: *Can we talk?* Chelsea saved the file to her desktop but didn't listen to it or read the body of Rachel's email. She was too terrified.

Now that she's away from her, away from her probing questions and performed empathy, Chelsea understands she's not in love with Rachel. What she was attracted to was the intimacy Rachel so quickly and efficiently manufactured. Rachel did it for her job. She did it to get a good story. It was a manipulation, but it was one Chelsea was, at the time, grateful for because it allowed her to unburden herself. Now, looking at the situation with clear eyes, she doesn't feel the relief of sharing a secret. She only feels regret and fear of how her disclosure might be leveraged against her.

She thinks of Rachel's fingers on the back of her neck, undoing the clasp on her priest's collar, brushing the tiny hairs at her nape.

Bree says, "She sent us the audio file. Do you want to listen?"

Chelsea starts to say no, but Bree hooks her phone up to the aux cord. At first Chelsea's tense, worrying it will be the version Rachel played in the hotel room. However, after a few seconds it's clear Rachel kept her word. It's the sanitized version: Bree and Chelsea, the dead girl's friends. It humanizes Abby more than most media ever has, and Rachel frames her as the forgotten girl, the one overshadowed by Blue and his larger crimes. It's everything Chelsea wanted from the media all these years, but once they've played the whole thing, she wishes she hadn't listened to it. The story of a person's life can't be satisfying when you've built up so many evasions and half-truths.

Bree unplugs her phone from the aux cable. "She did a good job."

Chelsea makes a noncommittal noise. She's thinking about all the hard things she's avoided in her life. The conversations she should have had with Daniel. The conversations she should have had with parishioners. Every sexist statement she let slide. Every racist statement she ignored to keep the peace. She's not brave. She's a fraud. She's someone only concerned with appearances— that she appears to do and say the right things. Not that she's actually righteous in her heart.

There's a verse from the Gospel of Thomas that always stuck with Chelsea: *If you bring forth what is within you, what you bring forth will save you; if you do not bring forth what is within you, what you do not bring forth will destroy you.*

ABBY

OCTOBER 2003

You sit in lecture halls and listen to professors speak and take notes. You make small talk with your classmates. But you aren't actually there. At one point, you find yourself noting this with detached fascination. Look how you can be present without being present at all.

You hoped you could talk to Chelsea before Bree came over to get ready for the Halloween party you had all planned to go to, but by the time you return to the dorm after your last class, Bree's already standing in front of the mirror with her makeup spread across the dresser, her hourglass figure emphasized by her black Playboy bunny costume.

Chelsea doesn't look up when you come in. She's sitting on the futon, her poli-sci textbook open on her lap.

"What do you think?" Bree says, shaking her little white rabbit tail.

"You look gorgeous," you say, and she beams.

When you returned to the dorm room after your confrontation with Chelsea, you and Al promised one another you wouldn't tell Bree. Because in the end, what will telling her give her? Maybe you'll feel a little lighter, briefly, but it will hurt her. It'll hurt her terribly. She'll never forgive you. And for what? A misguided emphasis on honesty?

No, you tell yourself. *Don't.* What matters most is fixing things with Chelsea, and you can do that without coming clean to Bree.

You clear your throat. "I hurt Chelsea's feelings earlier today, and I'm really sorry."

Chelsea's head jerks up, but then she immediately goes back to staring at her book.

Bree's gaze goes from Chelsea to you. "What did you do?"

Chelsea snaps her book shut. "It doesn't matter. Let's get ready for the party."

She opens and shuts the medicine cabinet with more force than necessary, grabbing her toothpaste and violently brushing her teeth. When she spits, there's blood mixed with the tooth-paste foam.

Bree gives you a look, eyebrows raised, as if to say, *Best of luck with whatever this is.*

You're used to getting ready together—your perfumes and hairspray mixing, each of you grabbing makeup from one another's bags without asking. All three of you singing along to the going-out mixes Chelsea curates. But tonight, it's awkward. Bree tries to lighten the tension, telling some stories from her art classes, but they fall flat, and then the three of you finish getting ready in silence except for the Black Eyed Peas in the background.

You put on a short, pleated skirt to complete your Sexy Hermione costume, rubbing a shimmery lotion down your legs. Bree arranges her black bunny ears in the nest of her teased hair. Behind you both, Chelsea yanks the twin extra-long white sheet from her lofted bed. As you put on lip gloss, she grabs scissors from her desk and cuts two small holes in the cloth. Then she throws it over herself.

"I'm a ghost."

"What about your other costume?" you ask. A few weekends ago, Bree found a skin-tight cheetah-print dress for Chelsea at Goodwill, and you bought her a pair of cat ears from the mall.

"That's what you wanted me to wear," Chelsea says. "This is what I want to wear."

"You're not really going like that," you say.

"I am," Chelsea says through her ridiculous sheet. "Ghosts are usually invisible to people."

You've spent the time getting ready feeling intense self-loathing, but now your anger flares. This is exceptionally passive aggressive. Chelsea was on the debate team in high school. Once, in debate class, she made a male classmate cry. For her to feign this helplessness, this victimhood, is ridiculous.

"You're not invisible to me."

Chelsea doesn't respond. Bree smiles, tentatively. She reaches out and pats Chelsea's arm through the sheet. "Yes, you're very solid and present, Chels."

The three of you stand in silence for a moment, Chelsea unmoving in her white shroud.

"Will someone tell me what happened?" Bree says.

You want to. You want to desperately, because at least then Chelsea couldn't ignore it. But, of course, you can't without hurting Bree. So, you stand there in silence and eventually Chelsea says, "It's nothing."

As you walk to the party, the cold air hitting your bare legs and arms, you think about everything you ignored over the years. How much you loved the cartoon Catwoman from *Batman: The Animated Series*. The curving lines the cartoonists used to draw her figure. You loved Harley Quinn and Poison Ivy for the same reasons, but Catwoman was your favorite. You thought you wanted to *be* her, but that wasn't it. You wanted to be *with* her. You see that now.

In high school, you'd always try to get people to go to eat with you at Hooter's. After you turned eighteen, you'd sometimes buy copies of *Playboy*. You told yourself you were being a cool girl. It was the same thing you told yourself when you'd encourage your boyfriends to tell you when they thought a woman was sexy. You told yourself you were being a really understanding girlfriend when the two of you pointed out the curve of a woman's ass or the nip to her waist.

How did you allow yourself to ignore so much for so long? It was like there was a picture hanging in your room you never let yourself look at too closely, and written across it in bold, red lettering were the words *Abby, honey, you're gay*.

What do you do when you've ruined everything? How do you make things right?

As you walk up to the apartment complex where the party's being held, you tell yourself you'll find a way. You'll explain to Chelsea, and you'll explain to Bree. There won't be any hiding anymore. From either of them.

You feel the bass before you're even inside. It's a basement apartment across the street from a hardware store. Inside, it's humid

and beer-scented. Bree wanders off to find Al, and you and
Chelsea make a beeline for the keg. You hope after a drink she'll
listen to you.

She takes off her ghost sheet to chug a red Solo cup of beer in
the kitchen. The guys around the keg applaud.

"Drunk ghost!" one cheers.

"Drunk ghost, I like your style," another one says. She puts the
sheet back on, and one of the guys high fives her through the thin
fabric.

You grab her arm as she leaves the kitchen. "Can we please just
talk?"

Her voice is muffled through the sheet, but you understand
her perfectly. "I have nothing to say to you."

She wades into the crowd, and you turn back to the kitchen to
pour yourself a shot of vodka from a bottle on the counter.

When you enter one of the apartment's bedrooms, a guy holding a lighter and a bowl stares with wide eyes at Chelsea's ghost
costume.

Al sits in a chair in the corner with Bree on his lap. He laughs.
"Dude, it's just our friend Chelsea."

"Fuck," the other guy says. "I'm too stoned for your costume."
He lights the bowl, and the skunky smell wafts around the room.

Al is dressed like Hugh Hefner to match Bree's costume, his
smoking jacket gaping open to reveal his bare chest. Bree cracks
jokes loudly and angles her cleavage under his nose. It's sad. How
much of her life will be spent exhausting herself for men?

Al stares at you, and you give him a look that says, *Stop it*,
before excusing yourself to use the bathroom. The sink, toilet,
and tub are all avocado-colored. The whole bathroom is filthy,

dust bunnies in every corner, crusted toothpaste in the sink, pubic hairs lining the back of the toilet. You stare at yourself in the dirty mirror. You didn't eat much today, and the shot of vodka you took in the kitchen is going to your head. You feel like you might pass out. You weave through the sweaty bodies dancing in the living room and step out the front door. Seated on the front stoop, you take deep, bracing lungfuls of cold air.

The thin fabric of your skirt is no match for the cold concrete. Through the bedroom window, you can see where Bree and Al sit. Every now and then, Chelsea leans forward, and you see her profile. She's taken the stupid ghost sheet off, and her dark hair is mussed.

Watching her makes your chest ache. You almost don't notice when someone clears his throat and steps right in front of you.

"I thought that was you," he says.

It's Jay.

ETSY LISTING FROM THE SHOP *MURDERABILIA*:

"IT'S ALL OVER NOW, BABY BLUE" JON ALLAN BLUE EXECUTION TEE

1,034 SALES $25.99   IN-STOCK

Celebrate justice being served by buying one of these screen-printed, 100% cotton unisex tees designed to commemorate Jon Allan Blue's execution. Soft, comfy, and available in multiple colors. We also do child sizes!

BREE
NOVEMBER 2015

As they near the Kentucky border, Bree sees an email notification that Alayna withdrew from her class. Even though she was getting an A. Even though she has made it almost to the end of the semester. She won't get any tuition back, and she'll have to retake the class at some point since it's required for her major. If it didn't hurt so much, Bree would admire Alayna for it.

Yesterday, Bree passed Alayna in the hallway in the bowels of the art building. At first, Alayna stared straight ahead, ignoring Bree. Then, as they passed one another, she looked at her and said, "You didn't just fuck him. You fucked me."

Bree tried to keep walking, but Alayna grabbed her arm. "They're making me do community service, because Zach stuck by you and now I look like the liar. If I don't do all the hours of service by the end of the semester, I get expelled. But if I do all the hours of service, I won't have enough time to work and get tuition money, so guess what?" She threw her hands up in the air. "Either way, I'm fucked."

Alayna's expression stayed with Bree because it wasn't anger. It wasn't even disgust. It was an expression that said clearly, *You are nothing like the person I thought you were.*

Bree tells herself she's so close to answers. Tomorrow, she and Chelsea will meet with Jon Allan Blue. Tomorrow, she'll have the answers she's waited a dozen years for. Once what happened to Abby isn't hovering over her like a ghost, she'll be able to figure things out.

Bree and Chelsea underestimated the crowd Blue's execution would draw. There are no vacancies in any of the motels in Eddyville, and news vans clog the parking lots.

In the lobby of the Hampton Inn, while Chelsea checks if they can get rooms, Bree listens to a newspaper reporter interview a man in a gray sweatshirt with iron-on black lettering that reads *It's All Over Now Baby Blue.*

"Drove in from Nebraska today," the man says.

"What made you come all this way?" the reporter asks.

The man tells her he works with the father of one of Blue's early victims, Stacy McCloud, a seventeen-year-old from Lincoln. He's ready to see "justice served."

Chelsea appears a moment later, telling Bree this motel is full too. Finally, in Paducah, they find a vacancy. When they go to the Holiday Inn's front desk, Bree's surprised Chelsea wants to share a room. Although it would have been more than she can afford, Bree was prepared to pay for her own. But while they stand in front of the clerk, a woman who must be about their age with hair bleached platinum, Chelsea says, "Abby was the one who snored, so let's just share."

The clerk laughs, as she runs Chelsea's credit card. "I have one friend like that. We all hate sharing a room with her. Last time on a girl's weekend, I used ear plugs *and* put a pillow over my head, and it still didn't drown out her snoring."

The woman hums as she checks something on her computer screen. "Is this a girl's weekend? Do you have other friends coming? I can put you next to an empty room, so when they arrive you can have adjoining rooms."

Bree indulges in the fantasy. She and Chelsea checking in, Abby running late. Three thirty-year-old friends ready to catch up together for a weekend. Who knows why they'd pick Paducah, but maybe it's equidistant from where they all live. Bree tries to imagine what kinds of problems they'd have. The banal sort. Abby always getting the most attention, the most conversation time, until Bree gets so flustered she monologues for too long, annoying Chelsea. Chelsea's insomnia. Abby's snoring. Maybe there would be the old awkwardness of Chelsea and Abby picking restaurants that were too expensive, leaving Bree to order a water and a side salad until it clicked for Abby and she would shovel a bunch of her food on Bree's plate, saying how full she was and how helpful it would be if Bree could split some of it with her.

Bree feels pretty fucking sorry for herself when she comes back to the Holiday Inn lobby, the blond clerk watching them with a tilted head. *This isn't a girl's weekend,* she wants to tell her, just to watch the smile slide off her face. *We're here to see the man who murdered our friend.*

Chelsea clears her throat. "No, it's just us."

———

Once they're in the room, Bree responds to student emails on her phone while Chelsea does something on her laptop in her bed. What kind of emails does a priest send, Bree wonders?

After a while, the typing from Chelsea's bed has quieted, and the TV's volume is higher. Bree looks over, and Chelsea stares at the TV with an expression of delight, head leaning back against her pillow, jaw slack in an open-mouthed smile. On the screen, a mustachioed bus driver tells a group of four teenage girls to watch out for "the weirdos."

A girl with pale skin and dyed-black hair lowers her red-lensed sunglasses to address him. She's wearing all black. A silver rosary hangs from her neck.

"We are the weirdos, mister," she says before the bus doors shut.

"Oh, my God," Bree says. A VHS tape of *The Craft* was required viewing at any sleepover when they were in middle school. How many times had they performed their own stupid spells or done "Light as a Feather, Stiff as a Board," modeled off the girls in the movie, hoping that they, too, might be magical, might have some kind of power?

Chelsea looks over at Bree, still wearing that open-mouthed smile. "I haven't watched this in at least ten years."

By the time the girls in the movie are invoking the spirit, standing on a beach at night, arms raised as lightning flashes above them, Bree and Chelsea sit together on Chelsea's bed, a cheese pizza they had delivered between them, a pile of candy from the vending machine strewn across the comforter. If Bree doesn't use her peripheral vision, she might be thirteen again, pizza grease on her lips, the beginning of a sugar crash edging toward her.

Once the credits roll, Chelsea glances back at her laptop screen. When she looks up, her lips quirk in a smile. "Of course."

"What?" Bree asks.

"It was directed by a man and written by a man," she says. "Of course, they couldn't let the girls stay united against the world. They had to make them turn against each other."

She's smiling, but the expression fades as she watches Bree's face. Maybe she's thinking what Bree is thinking. She, Abby, and Bree managed to fuck things up in that department, and they couldn't blame that on a male director.

"If she hadn't…" Chelsea lays her palm out flat. "We would have all made up eventually."

Bree nods, but she isn't sure. The competition between her and Abby was getting worse and worse. Would Bree have forgiven her for what happened with Al? Or would they have all drifted out of each other's lives? She knows so many women who are no longer in touch with their close high school and middle school friends. Without Abby's murder, would they have been reduced to friends who sometimes got drinks during the winter holidays when everyone was back in town? Would Bree have attended Abby's wedding, not as someone in the bridal party, but just a guest who vaguely kept up with the bride on social media? It's a depressing thought, so she changes the subject.

"Why did you become a priest?" She heard the answer Chelsea tells everyone on social media. It situates Chelsea as a woman who experienced great tragedy, lost her faith for a time, but found her way back, ready to tell others the Good News. It's a nice story, but there's nothing of Chelsea at its core. It doesn't completely explain what drew the girl Bree knew to this singular occupation.

Chelsea has rolled onto her side, her left cheek on her pillow, facing Bree. Bree mirrors her body language, so her right cheek is on the other pillow. How many hours had they spent like this, talking late into the night?

Chelsea puts a hand to her face, rubbing her forehead, and Bree prepares herself for a stock, rehearsed response. But when Chelsea's hand drops from her face, she meets Bree's eyes, her expression almost sheepish.

"What?" Bree asks.

Chelsea shakes her head. "It's embarrassing."

"You've seen me piss my own pants. How much more embarrassing can it be?"

"Have you ever gotten obsessed with someone online?"

"Of course," Bree says.

"Like really obsessed, though. Like going through their whole profile to read seven years of past posts. That kind of obsessed."

"I do that with you," Bree says. For a moment, she regrets admitting it, but Chelsea's face registers surprise rather than alarm.

"Really?"

"Yeah," Bree says. "I think I missed you, but I didn't want to admit that." Before Chelsea can open her mouth to respond, Bree interrupts her. She doesn't want Chelsea to feel obligated to say she missed Bree, too.

"So, you becoming a priest."

"There was this woman I stumbled on online," Chelsea says. "She had a blog, and she wrote about going through the discernment process to become an Episcopal priest. I got obsessed with her. I read every post she'd ever written. I bought books she'd read. I tracked her down on other social media platforms and read all her posts there."

Bree realizes it's possible she has read books or tried recipes that Chelsea only tried because of this random woman, like some sad chain of lost women desperately trying to find something to make them feel better. The lost leading the lost through social media posts.

"What drew you to her?" Bree asks.

"She seemed so *certain*. I don't know if that makes sense," she says, looking to Bree.

Of course, it does. The illusion of certainty, of peace, was exactly what drew and repelled Bree from Chelsea's own social media posts.

"It was like she had found this real, true thing," Chelsea says. "I wanted that, too."

"Did you find it?" Bree asks.

"I thought so."

Bree waits for Chelsea to say more. After a few moments, when it's clear she isn't going to, Bree says, "I'm scared to see Jay. What was he like when you saw him?"

Chelsea stays quiet for a few moments. She swallows and says, "I didn't go to pray with him. I know that's what I told the reporters. I know that's what everyone thinks."

"Then why did you go?" Bree asks.

"I think I wanted answers from him."

"You wanted to know what he did to her?"

Chelsea shakes her head. "I wanted to know…" She opens her mouth then closes it, frowning. "We have to trust God and trust that whatever needs to be revealed will be revealed."

It's not only the religious stuff that bothers Bree. It's the fakeness. Chelsea was real for a few moments here before something shifted and she put her mask back on.

"There is no God," Bree says, rolling on her back. "There's

no one guiding us and helping us. We're all completely fucking alone."

"That's a really comforting worldview for your future child."

"I think it's better than giving them sweet little fictions that fall apart the moment something bad happens."

They both sit up. Chelsea pulls her laptop toward her. "I should answer more emails before I go to sleep," she says, clearly wanting Bree to fuck off and get back on her own bed. But before Bree moves, she notices a file on Chelsea's desktop. It's titled, *Infamous_Ep_3_Chelsea_Abby_Love_Story*.

"What's that?" Bree asks, pointing.

"It's nothing," Chelsea says, shutting her laptop, even though she just said she needed to answer email.

"Did Rachel send you a different version of our episode?"

"No," Chelsea says, her face expressionless as she tugs on the band of her watch and walks toward her suitcase.

"Then what is it?" Bree asks.

"It's just the version you played today," Chelsea says, voice smooth. She rifles through her suitcase, and then, holding a pair of striped, flannel pajamas, she gestures to the bathroom. "I'm going to take a shower."

Once the fan's on and the water's running, Bree opens Chelsea's laptop. It immediately asks for a password. *Fuck.* She shuts it and sits on her own bed. There's no reason someone would title the file for their episode "a love story." Unless? Did Chelsea talk with Rachel without Bree? Did she tell Rachel about her and Frye? Whatever it is, Chelsea's obviously worried about Bree hearing what's in that file.

The water's still running, and she gets up and sits on Chelsea's bed, opening the laptop again. She tries a couple different passwords. Abby's first name and the numbers of her birth date. Chelsea's cat's name. Chelsea's childhood dog's name. Daniel's name. Nothing works. The water shuts off, and Bree's about to close the laptop again, but then she remembers the printer in Chelsea and Abby's dorm room.

This was before the days of wireless printers, so only Chelsea's computer was hooked up to the printer. In case the other girls ever needed to use it, the password for Chelsea's computer was their birth dates in order. The muscle memory of it is still there, and Bree types the twelve digits (02–03 for Abby, 03–24 for Chelsea, and 07–30 for Bree) and hits enter. After a moment, Chelsea's desktop appears.

The water's off, but the fan's still going. Bree hears a hair dryer start and double-clicks on the file.

CHELSEA
NOVEMBER 2015

When Chelsea gets out of the shower, Bree's already under the covers with her light off. Chelsea pulls the stiff hotel sheets over herself and turns off the lamp next to her bed.

After the adrenaline spike from Bree asking about that file from Rachel, Chelsea can't sleep, so she scrolls through social media in the dark. There's a message from Elly. In the whirlwind of everything that's happened since Chelsea drove to Iowa City, she hasn't thought much about her, and she feels guilty.

Sorry I haven't been at church, she writes. *I'm ok I guess. My mom is still acting weird about everything. My gf says I should be proud I was true to myself, though, and I'm starting to believe her.*

Chelsea hearts the message and tells Elly she hopes she sees her in person soon, but after she sends her response she stares at Elly's message for a long time.

Once she puts her phone away, the slam of doors down the hall and the roar of the fan cutting on and off keeps her awake. She can tell Bree's awake, too, shifting in the other bed. But neither of them says anything, and they lie in the dark all night in silence.

The prison is about forty minutes from their hotel. The next morning, Bree scrolls on her phone in silence as Chelsea drives, farmland blurring by on either side of the highway. Bree's been quiet all morning, and Chelsea assumed it's just from the anxiety of being about to see Jon Allan Blue. But midway through their drive, Chelsea realizes Bree's staring at her.

"What?" Chelsea asks.

Bree's studying Chelsea as if she's seeing her for the first time.

"What?" she asks again.

Bree shakes her head and goes back to her phone as they turn onto the road leading to the prison. The Kentucky State Penitentiary sits on a piece of land jutting into the Cumberland River. People call it "The Castle on Cumberland," because it's an imposing fortress with buttresses and tall, arched windows. The previous time Chelsea visited Blue, it was summer, and the trees surrounding the limestone building were green and full, the air heavy with humidity and the smell of the brown river water. Today, the trees are bare. Although the sky is gray rather than blue, the razor wire lining the perimeter is the same, and so are the guards with guns in the towers, looking down on the grounds.

About twenty people gather in the field across from the prison, waiting for the execution. As Chelsea and Bree drive past, people in the small crowd sip coffee and play radios and battery-operated TVs tuned to *CNN* and *Headline News*. There's even a vendor selling commemorative T-shirts with a cartoon of Jon Allan Blue strapped to a gurney. It's the world's most morbid tailgate, Chelsea thinks.

They check in at the gate and pull into the visitor parking.

The steeply pitched green roof gleams in the late fall sunlight as Chelsea and Bree climb the tall stone steps to enter the prison doors.

The last time Chelsea visited, she was overwhelmed with rules and restrictions—the strict dress code for visitors, the list of what she could carry on herself, the multiple places she had to be searched and checked in. This time, though, on the day of Blue's execution, she and Bree are treated differently. They're led to the warden's office to check in. Then a short, round man with gray hair and a gray mustache in a sergeant's outfit appears to lead them farther into the prison.

As they walk, the man introduces himself as Sergeant Palanko, explaining he has the job of guarding Blue on his last day alive. Chelsea's disoriented and can't tell if this is the same area she visited Blue before. The day before yesterday, Blue was moved into a "death watch cell," so he can be monitored twenty-four hours a day. His visiting schedule and routine are different from those of the rest of the death row inmates these last days before execution. She knows they'll be visiting him again in one of the no-contact visiting rooms, glass between them.

There's a distinct smell to the prison Chelsea remembers from the last time—plaster, stone, metal, and a whiff of something unwashed mixed with some type of cheap industrial cleaning product.

Sergeant Palanko leads them down a narrow hallway and through a door into the no-contact visiting room. Like the last time, Chelsea takes her seat at a bolted-down chair in front of a glass partition. This time, though, Bree's next to her, looking pale and drawn. While they wait, Chelsea starts to pray, but it's like when you start to call a friend before remembering you're mad at them. Instead, she tries to take deep breaths, but the prison smell makes her queasy.

She hears the creak of a door and the rattling of chains. There's a flash of orange, and then Jon Allan Blue is sitting across from them. He smiles.

ABBY

OCTOBER 2003

W hat do you want?" you ask Jay as he sits down on the stoop next to you.

His lips quirk. "That's not a very enthusiastic greeting."

"You're really observant."

He's in jeans and a black wool coat rather than a Halloween costume. Pointing across the street to a sad-looking clapboard house, he says, "I live right over there. I was just coming home from campus."

You nod absently, wishing he would leave.

"Do you want to talk about it?"

"About what?"

"Whatever's upsetting you."

"You've had quite enough of my pain, thank you very much," you say, crossing your arms.

"Whatever it is, you can act your way out of it." He's not looking at you but instead watching a group of girls walk past on the sidewalk laughing together, their hair blowing in the wind.

"What do you mean?"

"Pretend you're not you. Pretend you're someone else.

Someone braver. Someone who gets what they want. How would they act? What would they do?"

"Is that how you move through the world?"

"Sometimes. There are moments when...when I can lose myself. It's like I'm on stage, but I'm in the real world. It's the same feeling—the loss of time, the control. You can give that to yourself. You don't just have to save it for the stage. You can have it whenever you want."

He's still not looking at you, but it's oddly helpful advice. What would the braver version of you do? What does she want? You've been so lost in your thoughts you didn't realize Jay's staring at you, his expression hungry. It makes you shiver.

"I'm cold," you say. "I should go inside."

"Do you want to come over to my house? I've got booze."

"That's okay. I'll see you in class Monday."

You start to walk toward the apartment complex's front door but turn around when he asks you to wait.

"Here," he says, handing you something. It's the ring he always wears—the silver theater masks. He must see the question on your face, because he answers it. "To remind you. You can pretend to be whoever you want to be. And eventually, it won't be pretending anymore. It'll just be who you are."

You tuck the ring into the tiny pocket on your skirt. It's a kind gesture, and you wonder if maybe Bree was right. Maybe you've read something sinister into what are just Jay's eccentricities.

"See you in class," he says. But he doesn't move. He stands there watching you as you open the door and go back into the apartment complex.

Chelsea's quiet under her ghost shroud as the three of you walk the block to the cemetery. Bree is an exuberant drunk and chatters about some drama going on at the party—a girl who slapped her boyfriend after he danced with another girl. You nod and try to follow along, but you can't focus. You keep stealing glances at Chelsea, but of course you can't read her face under that goddamned sheet.

When you round the bend in the cemetery, the Black Angel startles you, even though you've seen it so many times. It looms against the night sky, this dark figure, head lowered, wings aloft. In the past, Bree and Chelsea argued about it. Bree believed it was beautiful, while Chelsea believed it was terrifying. Tonight, you realize they're both right. It's terrifying and beautiful.

With every step you take, dread pools in your chest. You can't figure out what to say to make things right.

Bree snaps photos with her digital camera. You study the angel's missing fingers and the jagged parts lefts behind.

"People break them off," you say to Chelsea, trying to get her to look at you. "It's a shitty thing to do."

"It is shitty," Chelsea says. She has taken off her sheet and stares at you. "A really shitty thing to do."

You realize what's going to happen a second before it does. You look at Bree, and she smiles at you before putting the camera back to her eye and framing her shot.

"Chelsea," you say. "Please don't."

"Go ahead and tell Bree."

"Tell me what?" Bree asks, coming to stand by them. Snow is falling thick and fast, blanketing the top of the graves and the angel's head and hands. When did it start? How did you not notice?

"Tell Bree about you and Al."

Bree's long face tilts to the side, her mouth a little "O" that grows as it dawns on her.

"Tell her what I saw," Chelsea says. Her spit flies through the air from emphasizing the consonants of the sentence. Her face is flushed, her body shaking.

"Please," you say. This isn't going the way you planned. Now, however, staring at the two of them, these twinned expressions of rage and hurt reflecting back at you, you're uncertain why you thought this would go differently. But in the past, they've always deferred to you. They've always listened.

Bree waves her hand dismissively. "Stop. I don't want to hear it."

"Let me explain." You can't tell if the wetness on your face is the snow or your own tears.

"There's nothing to explain," Chelsea says, wiping her runny nose with her ghost sheet. "We understand perfectly."

You can't tell which is worse—the hardness on Chelsea's face or the complete woundedness on Bree's. You open your mouth to try to explain again, but Chelsea yells at you. "Go away. Nobody wants you here."

There's nothing to do but go. You walk down the blacktop path, the snow falling on your hair and the bare skin of your legs, until you're standing outside the gates of the cemetery crying. You have the urge to run back to Bree and Chelsea and try to explain yourself again, but you realize there's something you need to do first.

As you turn down Dodge Street, walking toward your parents' house, a silver car slows down next to you, the driver rolling down his window.

"You need a ride?" Brother Dave asks.

BREE
NOVEMBER 2015

Bree and Chelsea don't say anything as they stare at Jay's smiling face through the glass. He's still handsome, although the years behind bars have aged him. He looks older than forty, with the deep lines between his brows and across his forehead, his skin sallow against the orange jumpsuit, the gray in his sandy hair leaving it dull and lusterless. He licks his chapped lips before he speaks.

"How was your trip?" He speaks casually, as if they're seated together at a dinner party making polite conversation.

"It was fine," Chelsea says, her voice even.

For a moment, Bree thinks she won't be able to do this—she won't be able to endure being in this room with him.

"What about you, Bree?" he asks. "How was your trip?"

It takes her a second, but she's able to speak in a mostly steady voice. "It was fine."

Jay makes a pouty face, his lower lip sticking out. "Are you scared of me now, Bree? You're so quiet."

"No," she says, but she speaks too fast, giving herself away, and he smiles again. After a second of silence, he picks his nose.

It always seemed strange to her back when he was her teacher. He was handsome and charming, but he never hesitated to flick a booger across the dance studio floor during their classes. He smears one on the lower right part of the plexiglass partition.

There's something oddly deflating about it. Like if you believe these women were murdered by a force larger than nature, someone spectacular in their evilness, there can be glamour to the horror. But he's nothing special. He's incredibly common. No matter how you want to frame it, mythologize it, study it, he's just one man among many who hurt women for reasons probably not even they understand.

It reassures her, and she's able to speak. "We're here because we want to know what happened to Abby. They found her body."

He ignores Bree and looks to Chelsea. "What do you think happens when we die?"

Chelsea's voice is smooth. "I think when we die, we go to God."

"Do you think that's where Abby went?" There's a smile playing on his lips that seems mocking, but Chelsea's voice is even.

"I do. I think she's with God now."

"You're lying," he says.

His words, and the confidence with which he states them, seem to ruffle Chelsea for the first time. She opens her mouth like she's going to contradict him then takes a deep breath and folds her hands in her lap. Bree sees, though, that she's started picking the skin on her right thumb.

"We need to know if you were the one who took her that night," Chelsea says.

"I need a stay of execution from the governor," he says, leaning back, crossing his arms.

"I don't know the governor," Chelsea says. "There's no reason he'd listen to me."

"But you're a priest," he says. "He might listen to a clergy member."

Chelsea swallows as he holds her gaze. "Okay."

Blue stares at her for a second before he gestures like he's waving away a dog. "Go make the call. The warden has the governor's number. Bree and I can wait while you go."

The idea of waiting alone with him is abhorrent, but when Chelsea goes to Sergeant Palanko, who's standing in the corner of the room, he explains that if she leaves, she won't be able to come back.

"Sorry, Jay," Palanko says. "Them's the rules."

When Chelsea sits back down, she tells him she can make the call after they're done talking. She promises him he can trust her. Jay studies them, his hands steepled under his chin. "All right, but I want something else, too."

His tongue worries his bottom lip as he surveys them, satisfaction relaxing his face.

"There's an exercise I used to like to do," he says. "Do you remember heartsharing?"

Bree doesn't know what she expected him to ask for, but it wasn't this. Not him asking to play a theater class game.

"You want to ask me questions?" Bree says, blinking.

"No, I want to ask *her* questions," he says, gesturing to Chelsea.

Something about the smile on Jay's face makes Bree's stomach lurch. She's been angry with Chelsea since last night when she listened to the version of the podcast episode on Chelsea's laptop and learned what Chelsea and Abby had kept from her twelve years ago. However, Jay's expression makes her feel, suddenly, protective of Chelsea. She can see why he wants to crack her. Unlike Bree, who has been a stammering, flustered mess since he walked in, Chelsea has kept that calm, capable priest persona. Unflappable. Of course, he wants to break her. Hadn't Bree wanted the same thing? For Chelsea to show any bit of vulnerability?

There's a flash of trepidation on Chelsea's face, and then the mask is back on.

"Fine," she says to Blue. "How do we start?"

Jay smiles. "Bree and I will ask you questions. The only rule is that you have to answer honestly."

Chelsea nods once. Bree turns to Jay. "Why do you do this?"

Jay raises his index finger in a scolding gesture. "We're supposed to be asking Chelsea questions."

"Please," Bree says. "Why do you do this?"

"There's more than one way to splay someone open," he says. He licks his lips, turning to Chelsea. "Why are you here?"

"To get answers," Chelsea says.

"Answers about what?"

"Abby."

"What about Abby?"

Here, Chelsea hesitates, and Jay smiles, pleased, no doubt, to have found some area of resistance inside her.

"I want to know what happened to her that night."

"But what *specifically*?"

"If you hurt her," Chelsea says.

Jay tilts his head. "But there's something else you want to know, right?"

She swallows. "I want to know if she said anything about me."

"About you?"

"Before she died."

"Why?"

"I need to know…" Chelsea swallows roughly. "I want to know…"

She's still picking at the skin on her thumb, and it's streaked with blood.

"What do you want to know?" he prods.

From listening to the version of the podcast on Chelsea's laptop, Bree understands what Chelsea wants to know. Bree can see it: Chelsea is about to share this thing she's tried so hard to keep private.

All those years ago, they had both been right—Jay and Abby. Jay had been right that telling the truth, sharing vulnerability, was a power. But Abby had been right, too. She had been right that it wasn't something everyone deserved access to. And Jon Allan Blue does not deserve access to this from Chelsea.

"I want to know—"

Bree puts her hand on Chelsea's arm. "No," she says, softly, shaking her head.

Chelsea's eyes are watery when she turns to look at Bree, her expression questioning. Bree shakes her head again. She meets Blue's gaze.

"No," she tells him. "We're not doing this."

"If I don't get what I want, then you don't get what you want," he says.

Does he know what Chelsea is here for? Did Abby say something about her in her final moments? Or is he just bluffing?

"That's fine," Bree says. She means it. Over the years she thought she'd pay any price for answers, but that's no longer true. It's not worth Chelsea baring herself to this man.

All these years, she has been hoping closure will be given to her—after he was arrested, after his trial, after his sentencing, after Abby's body was found, after recording the podcast. At what point will she accept that no amount of answers will be enough? That whatever she's looking for can't be given to her? She has to give it to herself.

"Bree," Chelsea says, her expression asking quite clearly, *Are you sure?*

Bree swallows and nods. She gestures for Sergeant Palanko to let them out of the room. Right before he opens the door, she looks back at Jay. She wishes she had her camera. The man standing there in his orange jumpsuit, handcuffed, doesn't look scary. She sees him for exactly what he is—a small, frightened man who, in a few hours, will die.

CHELSEA
NOVEMBER 2015

Sergeant Palanko leads them to a small, windowless room where a few metal folding chairs have been arranged around a fraying area rug. Chelsea's crying so hard she has barely been able to see where she was walking, but Bree has kept a firm hand on her shoulder.

"This is the family and friends visiting area," Sergeant Palanko says. "You can stay here as long as you need."

He turns to go, but Bree's voice stops him. "Where are they? His family and friends?"

Palanko tilts his head and purses his lips, as if to say, *Are you really surprised?* But Chelsea is, actually. She would have thought he'd have hoodwinked a few people into spending time with him on his last day alive.

"Take as long as you need," Palanko repeats before closing the door.

"Did you know?" Chelsea asks Bree. "About Abby and me? You stopped me from saying it to him, like you knew."

"I listened to the file," Bree says. "The other version of the podcast episode that you saved onto your laptop."

It's hard to look at Bree. Chelsea feels like she's skinless.

When she's able to meet her eyes, Bree's expression is searching. "Chelsea, you could have told me. You didn't have to carry this alone for all those years."

Chelsea looks away from her. "She never wanted anyone to know about us, and it makes me doubt what it all meant to her. I'll never know what *I* meant to her."

Bree leans toward Chelsea, putting her hand over Chelsea's. "I know what you meant to her."

The tears come again, and Chelsea doesn't bother hiding them. When she's composed enough to speak, she explains to Bree about the two versions of the podcast, how Rachel recorded her secretly in the hotel room.

"That's fucked up," Bree says, but then she bites her lip. "But have you listened to the version about your and Abby's relationship all the way through?"

"No," Chelsea says. "I couldn't."

"You should," Bree says.

Chelsea nods, but Bree shakes her head. "No, I think you should *now*."

As Bree rises from her chair, Chelsea asks, "Why?"

"Please trust me. I'll wait for you outside."

Chelsea's baffled by Bree's urgency, but as she leaves, Chelsea scrolls through her email, tapping on the file Rachel sent her and letting it play through the speaker on her phone.

This time, it's easier to hear her own voice when she's talking about Abby. Yes, she can hear the pain in it, but at least it's something real. It's different from the carefully couched phrases she spoke in the other version.

About ten minutes in, Rachel interviews Abby's father. He

talks about Mrs. Hartmann's suicide, how devastating it was for him after everything else he'd lost. Although Chelsea remembers him as taciturn and absent, his voice is rough with emotion.

"It happened last year, on the eleventh anniversary of Abby's disappearance," Rachel says.

"Yes," Mr. Hartmann says. "Several years before, Abby had been declared dead in absentia. I think it was the final blow for us. That day felt like a confirmation we would never get answers, never find her body, never really know what happened."

"That must have been horrible," Rachel says. Chelsea can hear the obvious empathy in Rachel's voice. She can picture her concerned expression, the one that would make Mr. Hartmann feel heard and understood, just like Chelsea had.

"It wasn't just that," Mr. Hartmann says. "It wasn't just the lack of answers."

"What else was it?"

Mr. Hartmann is quiet for a while, and Rachel left that silence in the recording, building tension. Before he can speak, he has to clear his throat a few times.

"Not long before she died, my wife confided something to me she hadn't told anyone," Mr. Hartmann says. "She had seen Abby that night—the night she disappeared. Abby had come to the house to tell her something, and they fought, and that was the last time she saw her. She didn't tell me at the time, didn't tell the police, didn't tell anyone. She said it was so painful, and she felt so guilty. She tried to pretend it never happened. I think on the anniversary that year, she couldn't push down that guilt anymore."

"What did they fight about that night?" Rachel asks.

Mr. Hartmann takes a deep breath, and then he explains.

ABBY
OCTOBER 2003

B rother Dave stares at you. His windshield wipers squeak. "No," you tell him. "That's okay. I don't need a ride." You stride ahead before he can say anything else. For a few seconds his car follows, trailing you slowly, but then it accelerates and drives past.

Your parents' house is a half-hour walk from the cemetery, but it feels much longer with the cold and your uncomfortable high heels. When you arrive, you let yourself in the front door with your key. From the street, it looks like all the lights are out. But, sure enough, when you walk through the living room, you see lights on in the kitchen.

Your mother sits at the table, bent over a magazine. Her glass of white zin is almost empty. You clear your throat, and she jumps in her chair, her head popping up to stare at you.

"You scared me," she says, clutching the neck of her black silk robe. "What are you wearing?"

You had, quite honestly, forgotten about the Hermione costume, and you're momentarily embarrassed. But then you consider that you've shown up here near midnight, nose and eyes obviously red from crying, shivering from the cold, and the first thing your mother asks about is what you're wearing.

"I need to tell you something."

"Abby, what's going on?" your mother asks, half-rising from her chair.

If you wait one more second, you'll talk yourself out of it. "I lied to you," you say. "About the photo of me and Chelsea."

Your mother's nose wrinkles like your father's forgotten to take out the garbage. "Have you been drinking?"

"No," you say. "I mean, yes, but it's not about that. Mom, I'm trying to—I'm in love with Chelsea."

"Did Chelsea talk you into this?"

"No, Mom," you say. "I'm trying to tell you something about me. About who I am."

"You're eighteen," your mother says. "You don't know who you are yet."

"I know this."

"We'll see," she says. Of all the reactions you expected from her—tears, yelling—you hadn't expected this complete dismissiveness.

"You're not taking this seriously."

"*You're* the one not taking this seriously," she says. "Do you know how hard things will be for you?"

"It's harder if I hide this."

"Honey," she says, taking a step forward and reaching out toward you, "people go through phases. You're so young."

You see that look in her eyes again. She wants you to agree with her. You swallow, shaking your head.

"I need you to respect this."

"I can't," she says. "Because I know you, and this isn't you. I don't know who this is, but *it's not you.*"

She turns away from you, her back bent forward. You realize she's crying.

Instinctually, you take a step forward, reaching for her like you always do when she's had too much to drink and starts to cry.

What would a braver version of you do? Jay had asked.

Your arms are out to touch her, to comfort her, but you stop. Her feelings about this aren't your responsibility. You take off the bracelet she bought you for your sixteenth birthday, setting it on the table by her wine glass. If she can't respect this about you, then you aren't going to wear it anymore.

As you walk toward the front door, you start to cry, but it feels good. It feels like something inside you is alive. You think of Jay tapping your chest as you cried during heartsharing. *This*, he said, *is power.* Maybe he was right.

EXCERPT FROM *INFAMOUS* SEASON 3 EPISODE 3 TRANSCRIPT:

"IOWA CITY: PART I"

RACHEL MORGAN, HOST: When your wife finally told you this story—about the last time she saw Abby—how did she bring it up to you?

BILL HARTMANN, ABBY HARTMANN'S FATHER: There was an afternoon—this must have been two or three years ago—when I came home from a business trip earlier than expected and I found Helen with Abby's bracelet. She was holding it in her hands, just staring out the window.

MORGAN [NARRATION]: Abby's bracelet was one of those sterling silver bracelets with a heart charm on it. You or one of your friends may have had one if you were a teenage girl in the early aughts. Unlike my own bracelet, Abby's wasn't a cheap knockoff—it was the genuine article, made by Tiffany & Co. and presented to Abby by her parents as a sixteenth birthday gift. She never took it off.

HARTMANN: When I saw my wife holding it, I was confused, because we never found it with Abby's things, and Abby's friends said she was wearing it when they saw her the night she disappeared. When I asked my wife where she found the bracelet, she explained that it had never actually been lost. She kept it hidden all these years.

MORGAN: Just like the story of her fight with Abby.

HARTMANN: Yes. [Clears throat] Helen and I had our problems, and I think it would have been easy for me to blame her. To think, "If you had just been more accepting that night, our daughter would still be alive." But I've never seen a person more eaten alive by guilt than she was, and I just...she blamed herself so much. I couldn't blame her, too.

MORGAN: Did you tell law enforcement? That there was one more place Abby had been seen alive?

HARTMANN: My wife could barely tell me, let alone the police or FBI. And at that point, I was more worried about her mental health. We took the bracelet to the Black Angel, the last place Abby had been with Chelsea, and my wife told Abby she was sorry.

MORGAN [NARRATION]: Two days later, Helen Morgan committed suicide.

[Instrumental music]

MORGAN [NARRATION]: I've thought a lot about Abby and Chelsea since I learned their story. Part of what haunts me is that I was a queer girl near their age, and I remember the secret make-out sessions I shared with female friends—in an empty bedroom at a party, a bathroom stall at a bar, or a dark corner on the dance floor.

Those girls and I never spoke about the encounters

again, and it was clear they were moments they wanted to keep secret. I kept them secret, too, figuring if they were ashamed, there must be a good reason to be. Because of the shame, I didn't let myself think too much about those moments for years, inadvertently ignoring the bread-crumbs that would have helped me figure out my own sexuality much sooner.

There's a trope in queer film and literature where the character is punished after they come out. When I first learned Abby's story, that's what I thought of. Here is a girl who finally shares who she is and then is immediately punished by the world. But Jon Allan Blue is not the world. He's one man. And Abby was more than just the way her life ended.

[Instrumental music]

BREE
NOVEMBER 2015

Bree waits for Chelsea outside the prison. Across the yard and the tall chain-link fence, she watches the crowd, which has grown since they entered the prison a few hours ago. News trucks line the prison gates.

Bree pictures Chelsea inside, listening to the podcast episode. When Bree listened to it last night while Chelsea was in the bathroom, it had been like when she got contacts in middle school. Suddenly, the blue lines of the teacher's dry erase marker on the board were crisp. Suddenly, she could see each individual leaf rather than a blur. Every awkward silence when Bree walked into a room Abby and Chelsea were in, each time Chelsea hugged Abby longer than she hugged Bree, every long look Abby gave Chelsea—suddenly, Bree could see they hadn't been about Bree at all.

Bree always believed her friendship with Chelsea and Abby was complicated because it was a trio. With a trio, there's the relationship you're in and the one you're watching. She always thought about the relationship between Abby and Chelsea in terms of what it said about her individual relationships with each of them. Like with Jay, it was one more place where Bree had been unable to see things for what they were.

She grabs her phone and opens her photos, scrolling back to some of the old snapshots she scanned. The pictures aren't organized, and it's strange to see them out of order. Her in grad school, sitting on her front porch wearing falling-apart Converse and paint-splattered overalls, holding a bottle of beer. Her at nine standing next to one of her father's girlfriends, both wearing the same shade of red lipstick. Her at thirteen in Abby's basement, her and Chelsea lying on their stomachs on the white carpet reading a magazine, their heads so close they're almost touching.

Finally, she finds the one she wants—her, Abby, and Chelsea with their dates in Abby's parents' living room before homecoming their junior year of high school. The girls' hair twisted in intricate updos. All clad in strapless dresses—Bree's navy, Chelsea's a Creamsicle orange, and Abby's bright red.

The guys have their arms around the girls, and the girls hold out their wrists to model their corsages. All of them smile at the camera except Chelsea, who, out of the corner of her eye, is looking at Abby.

Sontag said a photograph was, by its nature, a violation. It allowed the photographer to see people the way they never saw themselves, giving them knowledge the subject couldn't possess. She called it a "soft murder."

It feels wrong that for all these years this photo has existed, laying bare something in Chelsea she could barely admit to herself. Bree stares at the photo. Chelsea's dark eyes search for Abby. Everyone else smiles at the camera.

A reporter in a navy suit is doing a live broadcast. Bree watches her through the chain-link fence.

"His victims were teenagers. They were just kids," the reporter says.

Chelsea was just a kid when she lost her first love in such a brutal way. Bree is reminded, though, she was a kid, too. For the first time, she believes that. Frye should have known better. And she knows both things are true about her and Zach as well. He was a kid. And she should have known better. Because of that, she'll face whatever the consequences are.

Bree pulls up her email and writes a message to Marianne. She has to take a deep breath before she hits Send, because she knows what will happen once she does, but it's the right thing to do.

The reporter in the navy suit gestures to the crowd, who have started singing, "Na Na Hey Hey Kiss Him Goodbye."

Bree watches the circus—the vendor with his T-shirts. The college students with their lawn chairs.

All these years, she has been waiting for something to happen to change her, but after sitting with Jay, she knows that transformative moment is never coming for her. It's up to her to choose something different.

CHELSEA
NOVEMBER 2015

Chelsea listens to the podcast episode all the way through, as Bree requested. She understands why Rachel wanted to publish it. Rachel has made it about Abby and Chelsea and Bree, the complexities of female friendship, the complications of Abby and Chelsea's romance, but it's about more than that. It's about how young women are treated in the media. How romance between two young women was handled in the early aughts. About the way the world can tell you who you are for so long that you start to believe it rather than yourself.

Tears prick Chelsea's eyes as the instrumental music plays while Rachel reads the credits. All these years, Chelsea has focused on what their relationship meant to Abby—the uncertainty, all the things she'd never know. But she never took the time to really think about what it meant to *her*.

She stares at her hands while the episode finishes. She's still wearing her wedding band, despite how she left things with Daniel. Chelsea chose the ring, an antique gold band from the '60s, for its solidity. *It makes me feel very definitively married*, she told Daniel when they bought it.

She wonders if she'll ever be able to let another romantic partner in to the degree she did with Abby. What will it take for her
to let herself be that intimate with someone again? What would it
take for her to believe it would be safe to?

———————

As it grows dark, the anti–death penalty activists light vigil candles and sing "Amazing Grace." They're quickly overpowered as
the rest of the crowd belts, "Bye, bye, Jon Blue, goodbye," to the
tune of "American Pie."

Bree and Chelsea stand in the crowd, not singing either song.
They didn't plan to stay for the execution, but both feel drawn to
see this to the end, despite the crowd and the cold.

Chelsea emailed Rachel, asking her to air the version of the
podcast that tells the full story. Rachel emailed her back, thanking
her and asking if they can see each other again. Chelsea hasn't
replied.

"So, we come to the end for Jon Allan Blue," says a TV reporter
doing a live shot nearby. "After a decade on death row and three
murder charges."

The hearse that will transport Blue's corpse post-execution
arrives, and as it passes, the crowd cheers and claps. A man next
to Chelsea makes a "yeehaw" noise she's only heard in cowboy
movies as a police escort follows the hearse, flashing red and blue
lights into the night.

At 8:23 p.m., a young female AP reporter in a black parka runs
out of the prison holding her reporter's notebook aloft. From
behind the tall chain-link fence, she waves it back and forth, signaling the execution is over.

The crowd's cheers swell around Bree and Chelsea. People clap and bang pots and pans. Someone behind them sets off Roman candles. A college-aged guy sitting on his friend's shoulders pops champagne, and it foams over, before both guys take turns chugging from the green bottle.

People launch more elaborate fireworks. Brilliant gold, red, and silver blooms light up the crowd's faces before trailing toward the ground like the limbs of a weeping willow. A second after they flash across the night sky, Chelsea hears the crack, feels the vibration in her chest, before they burst and fizzle into nothing.

Through it all, Bree and Chelsea stand together, gripping each other's hands. Through it all, they don't let go.

ABBY

You were able to walk to your parents' house fueled on adrenaline, but the thirty-minute trek back to your dorm stretches out before you, cold air biting your legs and arms. If only you had grabbed a coat from the hall closet at your parents', but it felt more important to storm out.

The long walk gives you time to think. A plan forms. Back at the dorm, you'll talk to Chelsea. You'll stand in front of her until she listens. You'll fight for her. You're going to fight for Bree, too. You can see their expressions—angry and hurt at first, then shifting into something like forgiveness. Chelsea will give that nod she gives, head bowed, looking up at you through her thick lashes. Bree's eyes will soften, and she'll purse her lips. You'll have to prove yourself to them both, but you can do that. You want the chance to do that.

You don't know if your mother will come around. Will your parents stop paying for your college? Will you need to get a job? Where would you live if your parents don't pay for your room and board?

You've lived in this neighborhood your whole life. You've

walked down these streets in every kind of weather at every time of day. Up ahead is the house where the botany professor lives, her yard full of different flowers and plants, each with its own plaque staked into the grass boasting the scientific names of the species. One street over is the gingerbread-looking house painted bright blues and pinks. Tonight, though, the street looks suddenly unfamiliar, as if you're seeing it through someone else's eyes.

Because you're so distracted, it takes a little while to notice the car following you. The streets in this residential part of town are mostly empty past midnight, but there's a red Toyota Tercel going under the speed limit, staying about ten yards behind you. You cut down an alley, and it follows.

The snow falls in front of the streetlamps. You have the urge to run, although that seems ridiculous. When the car pulls up next to you, the driver rolls down his window.

It's Jay.

He offers you a ride just like Brother Dave. Unlike with Brother Dave, you briefly consider taking him up on his offer. It's freezing, and your high heels are giving you blisters, but something tells you to say no.

"That's okay."

His car's exhaust makes the crisp air stink.

"I'll follow you and make sure you get home okay."

"You don't need to do that."

But he does. The car follows as you walk, its engine a low rumble beside you. You wish you had your cell phone with you, so you could call a cab, but it was too big to fit in your tiny skirt pocket. Instead, you walk in your uncomfortable shoes, shivering.

At the place where Ronan Street overlooks the train tracks,

your pace slows. Your feet have gone almost numb from the cold. When Jay pulls over, you hope it means he's ready to leave you alone, but he gets out of the car and walks toward you. Your stomach feels strange, like a fish is swimming inside it. His presence has been more awkward than frightening, but he starts walking next to you. You pick up your pace, looking around. It's Halloween. Someone else has got to be out here, right?

"You look like you've been crying," he says.

You don't say anything. Your heart is already beating fast even before he reaches out to touch your bare thigh. You slap his hand and run. But he's fast. He has your wrist in his hand and yanks you down to the concrete. Your knees hit it hard, but you barely have time to recover before he's grabbing you under the arms, pulling you toward his car. You get a good kick at his shins, and his grip loosens as you break free, running, your shoes kicked off, your bare feet slapping against the freezing, wet pavement.

Behind you, his breathing grows heavier as he tries to close the distance between you. That's when you recognize it—the same breathing you heard on the phone all those mornings the past few months.

Ahead, at the other side of the overpass, the outside lights of homes shine. You put the safety whistle from your key chain up to your lips. You know if you can run four or five more yards, someone might hear you. A little farther, and you'll be safe.

INFAMOUS SEASON THREE:
ITUNES RATINGS & REVIEWS

4.5/5   15,8012 RATINGS

MOST RECENT REVIEWS

miz_tavi_s

Jan. 3, 2016

Season 3 is the best yet. I dare you to get through the episode about Abby Hartmann and her friend who was in love with her without BAWLING. How does Rachel Morgan just keep hitting me in the feels?????

kategeyser32

Dec. 28, 2015

Best pod of all time. Rachel is a genius.

moonlightinginbuffalo12

Dec. 23, 2015

I didn't know much about Blue before this—other than what everybody knows. Now I'm just really glad the fucker is dead.

awilliams0498

Dec. 15, 2015

There's a lot to unpack in the third season—how Blue used his authority as a teacher to gain the trust of some of these women, whether Blue was really as much of a criminal mastermind as people have made out (or if he was just a vaguely charismatic white guy)—but I think what I loved most was the Abby Hartmann episode. It made me think about the friendships I had with friends that were more than just friendships, even though we never told anyone (or even really admitted it to ourselves). Chelsea's loss and how she kept that secret for so long just BROKE ME. One of the most moving podcast episodes I've listened to in a long time.

jethromarshall321

Dec. 20, 2015

Rachel's voice is annoying af

BREE
MARCH 2016

On a Friday afternoon in March, when the air smells like mud and melting snow, Bree sees Alayna and Zach leave the art building. Zach's cheeks flush from the cold, and his eyes narrow when he sees her. Bree looks away and starts her walk home. However, a few seconds later, Alayna catches up with her.

"Hadley," she says, a little out of breath. "Professor Storey told me what you did."

In the email Bree sent on Jay's execution day, Bree told Marianne everything—that Alayna shouldn't have to do community service, because she had only been telling the truth. Bree admitted to her affair with Zach and offered her resignation. Marianne accepted but generously allowed Bree to finish the academic year.

Bree's six months pregnant, and her lower back aches. Alayna worries her lower lip with her teeth, studying Bree from under her lashes. "I don't have to do community service anymore, so I can work enough to pay my bills."

"You shouldn't have been punished for telling the truth," Bree says.

"Still, not everyone would have done what you did."

They meet each other's eyes. The admiration Alayna used to look at Bree with is gone, but so, too, is the obvious disgust.

"Where will you go?" Alayna asks. "After the semester ends."

Because of Chelsea's connections with the church, Bree has already secured a job teaching photography at an Episcopal high school. She tells Alayna she'll be moving to Des Moines, and Alayna nods.

There's a lot Bree wants to say to her—her favorite student who she has so spectacularly failed. She'd like to give her a pep talk about her art, telling her to believe in herself, but she knows she's given away any authority or any reason her opinion should matter to the girl, so she lets her walk away.

Bree starts her own walk home, but then Zach catches up with her. Unlike Alayna's, his expression is hard. As she stares at him, it all comes tumbling out. All the things she wished Frye said to her all those years ago. She tells him, despite what it might feel like, he wasn't disposable to her. She did care about him. She tells him what she did was a violation of trust. She broke something important by being an authority figure and crossing the line. She wishes him only good things, and she's so sorry for whatever damage her actions caused him, whatever pain she brought into his life.

He stares at her for a second after this verbal diarrhea stops. Then his face contorts into the same expression Abby used to wear when looking at Jay in class, this completely dismissive disgust. He gestures to her stomach. His bare hands are blotched from the cold.

"Is it mine?"

She wonders if the baby will have his long nose and thick eyelashes. He's trying to look fierce, eyes narrowed, a wide-legged stance, but she sees the worry in his eyes. He's chewing the inside of his cheek like he used to in class when she called on him and he didn't know the answer.

"It was a sperm donor," she says.

She knows, with sudden clarity, this will be the lie she tells for the rest of her life. As much as she harped on Chelsea for making up neat stories rather than embracing the messy truth, sometimes a lie is the kindest thing you can give someone.

"It was something I wanted to do on my own," she tells him.

"Whatever," he says and walks back to where Alayna is waiting.

Bree watches them, Zach's black parka and Alayna's red pea coat against the gray sky. Then they turn the corner and walk out of sight.

A week later, the Iowa City Police Department releases a statement that Detective Doug Frye has been put on administrative leave pending a conduct hearing. Frye calls Bree the night the statement's released.

It's almost 10:00 p.m. when Bree's phone vibrates. As Frye's number flashes on her caller ID, Bree's lying in bed, a book about newborn sleeping methods resting on her belly. She wonders if he's calling to yell at her for cooperating with internal affairs' investigation or if he wants to apologize.

Then she pictures Zach's dismissive expression as he watched her speak. It occurs to her that what Frye wants is no longer her concern. She silences his call, blocks his number, and goes back to her book.

In the ob-gyn office's waiting room, Chelsea sits next to Bree while she flips through a parenting magazine. The articles are full of things she didn't even know to be worried about—allergy-proofing her house, car seats that seem safe but aren't, gut health for babies, the dangers of radon. In the exam room, after the tech rubs the cold ultrasound goo on Bree's stomach, she watches her child's gray silhouette.

"Wow," she says. "It looks like a baby."

Chelsea squeezes her hand. She knows she sounds dumb, but the tech must be used to it. She laughs, her perky brunette pony-tail bobbing. "Yep, it's for sure a baby."

Bree studies its little profile. The slope of its head. Although it's probably no different from any other baby, it's the most beautiful thing she's ever seen.

"Do you want to know the sex?" the tech asks. "Or, if you're doing a gender reveal I can put it in an envelope for you."

"You can go ahead tell me," Bree says.

After the tech tells her it's a girl, she mistakes Bree's tears for happiness, although Chelsea's expression, as she grips Bree's hand, is knowing.

The tech beams and says, "A daughter is such a gift."

CHELSEA
MARCH 2016

Chelsea's sleeping on an air mattress in what will one day be Bree's daughter's nursery. When she wakes each morning, the mattress, which has a slow leak, is usually deflated, and Chelsea stares up at the mobile she helped make for Bree's daughter, origami animals Bree folded from bright paper.

Each evening, Chelsea tries to earn her keep by making dinner, even though she's not very good at cooking. Bree will usually eat Chelsea's attempts with the polite encouragement of a teacher who stares at not-very-good photos all day, finding something to praise. But one night, after a bite that Bree spits into a napkin, they both burst out laughing.

"Absolutely not," Bree says, pushing the meal, a cheeseburger casserole, away from herself. "We're ordering pizza."

It doesn't always feel like one extended sleepover, though. Sometimes, she misses Daniel so much she goes into Bree's bathroom and cries. She misses weird things about him—the sound of his made-up songs in the kitchen, how they fit together when she'd be the little spoon, his knees tucked perfectly against the back of her knees, the length of him pressed against her back, his arms around her.

When she first met him, she could only identify the smells he carried home from work as wood shavings, but over time, she started to pick up the differences—the woodsy, resinous freshness of cedar, the whiskey smell of white oak, the VapoRub scent of camphor, the sweet crispness of pine.

She misses her church, too, even though the leave of absence was her idea. The Episcopal Church is liberal enough that a divorce is not career-ending for her. Still, she had meant her marriage vows, and what she did with Rachel made her wonder if she was fit to be anyone's spiritual adviser.

Her bishop, himself in his second marriage, had been kind, telling her, "It may feel like Good Friday for a while, but Easter Sunday will come again."

She misses the smell of the previous day's incense. The taste of the communion bread and wine. The liturgy that gave her a home when nothing else in her life felt right. This will be the first Easter she hasn't presided over a Eucharist in five years.

At night it sometimes occurs to Chelsea she has no idea what her life will look like in a year. In taking a break from both her marriage and her career, she has removed the two things that gave her life any kind of shape.

"You get to build whatever you want," Bree says when Chelsea voices this thought. "You get to make it yours. A Chelsea-shaped life."

"I don't know what it should look like."

"You will," Bree says. They're sitting at either end of the couch, their toes touching in the middle. Bree looks tired, but she smiles so brightly Chelsea can't help but believe her.

The therapist's office is like any therapist's office—a couch with a sagging middle. A Sigmund Freud action figure on the coffee table. Diplomas hang on the walls. She must be in her sixties with short brown hair streaked with gray. She wears a linen tunic and flowy black pants and surveys Chelsea with a placid expression.

Chelsea has tried, as much as she can, to tell her everything. About Abby, about what they kept from people. About Daniel and how she loved him but couldn't let him in. How she was completely unable to nurture that kind of intimacy in her marriage.

"One thing you haven't mentioned is God," the therapist says. "Which surprises me, given your occupation."

There's a small ceramic bowl of butterscotch candies. Chelsea leans forward and grabs one just so she'll have something to do with her hands, unwrapping the crinkling yellow plastic and popping the candy into her mouth. Her tongue is slick with the chemical sweetness. She's already tired of the sickly sweet taste in her mouth, and she crunches the candy between her molars to make it go away faster.

She tells the woman some of her difficulties with her faith, and the therapist nods, tilting her head in thought. "It seems like you're aching for a world without suffering."

Tears prick Chelsea's eyes, and she's not sure why. She grabs a tissue from the coffee table and wipes them away. "Stay with that feeling," the woman tells her. "Can you sit with it?"

Chelsea has swallowed the candy, but she can still taste it, the flavor turning slightly bitter in its aftertaste.

"We were so young," she says.

The woman nods, her expression sympathetic. "You and Abby?"

Chelsea nods. "For God to allow her to be…I don't know how to forgive that." Chelsea stares at her hands for a moment. It's strange to see her left hand without its wedding band.

"She was my first love," Chelsea says. "In some ways, I think she was my only love. I loved Daniel, but I didn't love him like that."

"Do you still pray?" the therapist asks.

Chelsea shakes her head. "I studied so many Christian apologetics about why God allowed suffering or bad things to happen to people. But ultimately, I think I feel like Abby felt when we were eighteen. Why did God set up the world this way? If God is all-powerful and all-knowing, then why? Why let people be hurt like this?"

"What if God isn't all-powerful? What if he's just all-knowing?"

Chelsea swallows. Something about that breaks her heart because she can empathize with that. She knows how it feels to be aware of things you're powerless to fix.

"I think I've lost my faith," she says. It feels surprisingly good to say it aloud.

"What if your conception of God is just changing? Becoming more complex?"

"Maybe."

She gives Chelsea an assignment—before their next session, she's supposed to sit in silence with God for an extended period and be open to whatever happens.

There are no Episcopal churches in Bree's small town, which is a relief. Being at an Episcopal church is like being at work, leaving Chelsea too focused on how she's coming across and who she needs to be. She understands this is probably part of the problem with her religious life.

One afternoon while Bree teaches, Chelsea walks to the Lutheran church in town. It's unlocked, but there's no one in the sanctuary.

Chelsea climbs the stairs to sit in the balcony. There are stained-glass windows on both sides, but the day has been partly cloudy, so the light coming through them is muted. Chelsea sits in a pew with her hands in her lap.

Well, she thinks. *I'm here. Now it's your move.*

She doesn't feel anything special or hear a booming voice. Instead, her mind wanders as she watches the light through the stained-glass windows move as the clouds shift, little orange and yellow shapes dancing across the balcony's hardwood floor. Daniel would know what kind of wood it was.

Shortly after the podcast episode dropped, he emailed her, telling her he had listened to it. He said he wished she had been willing to share all of that with him. She wishes she had been, too, but for the first time, she has the hope that someday, she might be able to do that with someone again.

The sun comes in through the stained-glass windows, and the pale orange and yellow light shines directly on Chelsea's face. For one moment, she feels it—the crystalline connection to something larger than herself. It's only a moment, just a moment, and then it's gone. But the memory of it is enough.

Bree's been sorting through the photos she's taken the past few months. Chelsea doesn't understand everything she does, but she sees her blow them up on her laptop screen, studying them pixel by pixel. One afternoon, she asks Chelsea if she'd like to look at a couple.

Chelsea sits next to her on the couch. She sees herself in black and white. Bree must have taken it back in October, because she's wearing her priest's collar, standing in front of the Black Angel, her head mirroring the angle of the angel's head, both bowing slightly left. There's a subtle halo of light around Chelsea's head. It reminds her of some of her favorite photos of the Madonna, that same gravitas, the same seamless mixture of serenity and seriousness playing across her features.

Tears prick her eyes. She wants so badly to believe she might still be holy and that she might still feel God working in her life.

"There's one more I want to show you," Bree says.

Bree has taken two photos and set them side-by-side. The one on the left is a snapshot from when they were in college—Abby, Bree, and Chelsea sitting on the couch in the lobby of their dorm. Abby in the center. Chelsea remembers them taking that photo. It was their first day of college, and Abby reached her arms out long with her disposable camera to get them all in the shot. They're smiling wide enough to show every tooth—even Bree, who was always so self-conscious about those crooked teeth.

The photo Bree placed next to it is the one they took back in October when they were waiting out the rain in that same dorm lobby twelve years later. Chelsea's eyes dart back and forth between the two photos. On the left, there's Abby, face frozen in a big smile. On the right, she's gone. Just like that.

The two women who remain in the photo on the right aren't smiling. They both tilt their heads as they survey the camera, as if they know all too well what can be lost in an instant. But the very presence of them, their two bodies next to each other, heads almost touching, is proof of what remains.

ABBY

AUGUST 2003

You, Chelsea, and Bree are sitting in the lobby of your dorm. You've just taken a photo of yourselves to commemorate your first day of classes. It's evening, and outside lightning bugs blink at one another.

As you walked around campus today, blisters forming on your heels, you kept wondering, *Who will I be here? Who will I become?*

Through the big picture window, Chelsea points at stars beginning to appear in the sky. "In astronomy, Mr. Kent said the light from the closest star to the sun still takes four years to reach us. He said when we're looking into the sky, we're really looking at the past."

"Mr. Kent could never stop staring at my boobs," Bree says. "So, I'm not super interested in what he has to say."

Chelsea and Bree start to argue—about space and the sky and whether Mr. Kent is a perv or not.

You're only half-listening. You're not interested in thinking about the past, about dead stars and old light. You feel a great pressure in your chest as you look out the window. It's excitement. You're thinking of how much of the world you haven't seen yet, how much is still ahead of you.

Chelsea tickles your palm with the tip of her middle finger and you shiver. You don't look at her; you keep staring out the window. You're going to have to figure things out with her, you know that, but not just yet. There's still time.

"I'm hungry," Bree says.

"You're always hungry," Chelsea says.

"She's the skinniest, and she eats the most," you say.

Chelsea and Bree argue about which cafeteria they should go to for dinner. You know Chelsea wants the soft serve they have at Hillcrest.

Outside, raindrops start falling, a few fat drops.

"Burge is closest," you pronounce.

By the time you're all standing on the sidewalk, the rain is coming down fast and hard. You run toward the cafeteria, and you don't need to glance over your shoulder. You know Bree and Chelsea are right behind you.

READING GROUP GUIDE

1. What does Bree think she deserves? Where did that belief start, and how does it shape her actions throughout the book?

2. Describe Chelsea's relationship with her faith. What effect does her priesthood have on her relationships? Does that change throughout the book?

3. True crime filmmakers and podcasters insist that they are trying to honor the victims of the crimes without glamorizing their perpetrators. Why, as in the case of the Ryan Worth show about Jon Allan Blue, does spectacle continuously win over those intentions?

4. What effect do Jay's probing exercises have on Abby during her acting class? How does the rivalry between Abby and Bree prevent them both from seeing Jay clearly?

5. When Abby mentions an acquaintance coming out to test her mother's reaction, her mom replies that it would hurt

her greatly to watch her child deal with the challenges of a homophobic society. How does this reaction shut Abby down? How can our fears for our children send mixed messages about their identities?

6. Bree notes that she and Chelsea mourn different versions of Abby. How do their versions of Abby shape how they want her to be remembered? Why do we feel like different people in different settings?

7. What stops Chelsea from sharing the truth about her relationship with Abby for so many years? What kind of privacy do we owe to the dead?

8. How would you characterize Detective Frye? Do you believe he's "just a detective who was doing his best," as he claims?

9. Chelsea's husband is hurt that she can't "let go" of the case around Abby. How would you feel knowing that your spouse would always be dedicated to something you didn't understand?

10. How should Abby be remembered? What do you think is next for Bree and Chelsea?

A CONVERSATION WITH THE AUTHOR

What was your inspiration for *Don't Forget the Girl*?

Years ago, I was researching Ted Bundy for another writing project, and I wanted to know more about one of his victims, Caryn Campbell. There was little I could find about her other than the basics. She was a twenty-three-year-old nurse. She had a family who loved her. Because of all the books and series about Ted Bundy, he was everywhere, and she was nowhere—just a name in a list of victims. Something about the injustice of that gnawed at me, and I wanted to write a book centered around a victim and her loved ones.

Abby is positioned oddly in the Jon Allan Blue investigation, assumed to be a victim but unconfirmed as such. Why did you decide to add that layer of ambiguity?

To me, it seemed like one more way Abby was overshadowed by Blue. She can't even be counted fully as one of his victims, and yet everything about what happened to her is tied to him. That tension was interesting to me, and it seemed like it would make the true crime spectacle around the case even more painful for her loved ones.

Throughout the book, we see a number of ways that our memorials for the dead strip them of their humanity, particularly by sanctifying them. Do you think we are capable of grieving people in a more complex way?

I hope so, but I also understand the pressure to protect and curate people's reputations in death. Bree criticizes Chelsea for doing this with Abby, but as the author, I found myself doing it, too. When I first started writing Abby, she was totally different from the character in the published novel. She was sweet and meek and never made any mistakes. Because I knew what was going to happen to her character, I was protecting her, sanctifying her. I had to let myself write a messier version of her, despite knowing what lay ahead.

When Abby takes her concerns about Jay to the head of the department, she finds it difficult to express the magnitude of her discomfort, and she's sure that nothing will be done. Without being alarmist, how can we take students' concerns more seriously even when they're vague?

I think a lot of people—especially women and other folks from marginalized groups—have had the experience of knowing something was off without being able to articulate it to someone who hasn't experienced it. I was reading something the other day that said what some people call gossip other people call a survival mechanism. Whisper networks often allow people to identify someone who doesn't feel safe or who is displaying red flag behavior.

Chelsea realizes she's been holding her loved ones to a double standard by hiding the truth of her relationship with Abby

but expecting them to know the depth of her grief. **Why is it so hard to be truthful with the people we need support from?**

I think it can be really hard to be vulnerable, even with the people we love. We fear judgment or that people's perceptions of us will change. This is especially hard for Chelsea, because she's worked so hard to create a facade that protects her from people really knowing her.

Bree's decision to clear Alayna's name is a sacrifice not often seen in fiction. Why was it important to you to have her own up to her actions?

By the end of the book, Bree realizes she's not going to magically turn into the type of person she wants to be. Instead, she has to start making different choices. Clearing Alayna's name and owning up to her mistakes is a huge step she makes in that direction. It also allows her some closure from Frye. By taking responsibility for what she did with Zach, she's able to do what Frye was never able to do in his relationship with her—take responsibility for abusing his power.

The interstitials from various true crime media contrast starkly with Bree's and Chelsea's personal stories. Even Rachel Morgan's approach, which aims for greater empathy, doesn't always sit right with them. Do you think true crime as a genre is inherently exploitative, or are there ways to approach it more ethically?

Writing this book really changed my relationship with true crime. While I was writing it, whenever I listened to a true crime podcast or watched a true crime series, I started to become conscious of how the victims were characterized (or in many cases, not characterized). While I think true crime will always have an ethical tension because it's a genre centered on real life suffering, I do think some media is more exploitative than others. I've appreciated shows that give victims or their loved ones a voice or those that focus more on characterizing the victims versus glamorizing the killers.

ACKNOWLEDGMENTS

To my agent, Rebecca Gradinger, who believed in me when this novel was just a rambling story collection. Her care and attention made this book. I was beyond lucky she found it a home with Shana Drehs, fellow Iowa native and wonderful editor. Thank you to the whole Sourcebooks family, especially Jessica Thelander, Anna Venckus, and Cristina Arreola, for their hard work and thoughtfulness.

Thank you to Carolina Beltran and Hilary Zaitz Michael at William Morris Endeavor for taking care of the book's film rights. Thanks also to Kelly Karczewski and everyone at Fletcher & Co.

Julie Henson, Natalie Lund, Kelsey Ronan, and Cassandra Sanborn read so many iterations of this novel and supported Abby, Bree, Chelsea, and me at our roughest. N read chapters as I wrote them, giving me momentum to finish that first draft. Kelsey held my hand through querying, going on submission, and throughout the publication process. J, what can I say? Thank you for being my boat, my home, my heart. Deep gratitude also to Lindsey Alexander, Tim Bascom, Bethany Leach, Katie McClendon, and Emily Skaja, who provided thoughtful feedback on my writing over the years and have been wonderful friends.

Bree's class about Ana Mendieta owes everything to two excellent articles I couldn't stop thinking about: Jenna Sauers's *Village Voice* piece "Portrait of the Artist, Ana Mendieta, Iowa City, 1973" and Sarah Weinman's *Guardian* article "In Death, an Artist and a Young Woman Meet." Descriptions of Alayna's photos are inspired by Lauren Greenfield's exhibition *Girl Culture*.

To Greg Bouljon, my eighth-grade language arts teacher, who told me I would be a writer someday. To Rodger Wilming, my high school English teacher. At the University of Iowa, thanks to Bonnie Rough, Meenakshi "Gigi" Durham, Steve Berry, Lyle Muller, and Leslie Jamison.

Purdue University's MFA program gave me time to study and write. Thank you to Porter Shreve, Bich Minh "Beth" Nguyen, Chinelo Okparanta, Sharon Solwitz, and Patricia Henley, as well as to my thesis committee: Roxane Gay, Brian Leung, and Don Platt. Carrie Frye's Book Beast course nurtured this novel when I was about to give up.

To my colleagues at the University of Indianapolis, especially Colleen Wynn, Liz Ziff, Lacey Davidson, Molly Martin, Jen Camden, Kevin McKelvey, and Barney Haney. An extra special thanks to my work wife, Leah Milne.

Dr. Beth Fineberg, you changed my life. Thanks also to Adrienne Golota and Dr. Benjamin May.

In writing a book about female friendship, I was blessed to have such long and deep ones to draw upon. Thank you to Molly Erickson, Traci Finch, Elspeth Petersen, Danielle Sparks, and Allison "AJ" Vickers.

My parents encouraged me to love books and art my whole life. Mom, thanks for reading to me growing up and all the visits to the library and Waldenbooks (RIP) when I was a kid. Dad, thank you for all the indie movies you brought home and for helping with that first short story in high school. Your love and belief in me made this book possible.

Finally, and most importantly: to Chad Martin, who spent countless hours listening to me untangle plot threads and character motivations and provided me with pep talks and episodes of *Love Island* when I needed cheering up. Chad, you believed in me when I couldn't believe in myself. I will never know why I was lucky enough to find you, but I will never stop being grateful.

ABOUT THE AUTHOR

© Josh Saltsman

Rebecca McKanna was born and raised in Iowa. Her stories have been anthologized in *The Best American Mystery Stories 2019* and recognized as distinguished in *The Best American Short Stories 2019*. She has been published in *Colorado Review*, *Michigan Quarterly Review*, *The Rumpus*, and *McSweeney's Internet Tendency*, among other publications. She is an assistant professor of English at the University of Indianapolis. *Don't Forget the Girl* is her first novel.